I0706071

THE COHORT

THE COHORT

by

Charles S. Oliviero

© 2024, Charles S. Oliviero

All rights reserved. No part of this publication may be reproduced, stored in a retrieval system, or transmitted in any form by any process—electronic, mechanical, photocopying, recording, or otherwise—without the prior written permission of the copyright owner. The scanning, uploading, and distribution of this book via the Internet or via any other means without permission of the copyright owner is illegal and punishable by law.

Library and Archives Canada Cataloguing in Publication
Oliviero, Charles S., author
The Cohort / Charles S. Oliviero

Issued in print and electronic formats.
ISBN: 978-1-990644-88-7(paperback)
ISBN: 978-1-990644-89-4 (ebook)

Editor: Jennifer McIntyre
Cover Design: Pablo Javier Herrera
Interior Design: Winston S. Prescott

Double Dagger Books Ltd.
Toronto, Ontario, Canada
www.doubledagger.ca

DEDICATION

I dedicate this work to the generations of men and women with whom I had the honour to serve alongside, during my tenure in the Canadian Armed Forces.

Cohort [**koh**-hawrt]. noun.

1. a group of soldiers or warriors, or
2. a group or company

From this day to the ending of the world,
But we in it shall be remembered —
We few, we happy few, we band of brothers;
For he to-day that sheds his blood with me
Shall be my brother; be he ne'er so vile,

Shakespeare's *Henry V*
St. Crispin's Day Speech

ACKNOWLEDGMENTS

This is my first novel, and to say it was a voyage of discovery would be an understatement. A whole team of friends and colleagues offered guidance, assistance, and encouragement. Most important among this group were two friends and regimental brothers: Matt Lennox and Phil Halton. Their advice, editing and encouragement were invaluable and without their input this novel would simply not have been written. I owe them a large debt.

Next, I need to thank my younger son, Morgan, whose Machiavellian alter ego not only helped create the villains, but wonderfully also breathed life into their perfidy. His combat tour in Afghanistan was an invaluable source.

Last but not least, I must thank those who volunteered to act as beta readers, led by my wife, and elder son for wading through sometimes tortured prose to unearth spelling errors, storyline inconsistencies, and plain bad writing. Thank you, Jane, Quinton, Gord, Eric, Steve, Kevin, Chris, Greg, Ian, Alan, and Jeff.

Last but certainly not least, my thanks to Jen McIntyre, whose editing skills put a lovely polish on the prose.

Prologue

April 2013

SAINT-PIERRE-ET-MIQUELON

The explosion shattered the early morning calm. The upper apartment was devastated, and the back wall disappeared entirely. Below, in the boulangerie, the gas lines feeding the bread ovens ignited. In seconds the building was engulfed in flames. Saint-Pierre's tiny fire brigade arrived on scene within minutes, but it was already too late.

The explosion was loud but small, barely large enough to ignite the bottles of accelerant placed nearby, but once lit, the building's wood and plaster construction became perfect fuel. The bakery's gas lines fed the voracious fire and soon all was lost. The firefighters could not extinguish the blaze, so they let it burn under control. Even in the pre-dawn twilight, it was obvious there was little left.

The sirens woke Skip, and he pulled the window curtain to one side. Something was wrong, really wrong. It looked like the bakery was on fire. He dressed hurriedly and knocked on Jules's door. Jules, already dressed, opened it immediately.

"Oui, Colonel."

"Time to go," said Skip.

"I heard the explosion."

"La boulangerie is on fire. We need to get to the ferry, now. The café there opens at 04:00. We can grab a bite before leaving. I'll see you at the van in ten."

"*D'accord*, Colonel."

Jules was already waiting in the van with the engine running when Skip arrived.

"Go," he repeated.

Every emergency vehicle on the island was in le Centreville. The road was closed due to the fire, so Jules slowed as he approached the on-duty policeman, who waved him through. Jules took a hard right at the detour that took them past what used to be the bakery.

"Colonel, Qassem's apartment is gone."

"It's too much of a coincidence," said Skip. "Just keep driving."

Jules noticed an edge in Skip's voice that he had not heard before.

In the dockside café, the two men sat quietly over their breakfast of coffee and croissants. Jules could feel the tension building in Skip. Jules had his back to a muted TV but could see Skip's attention was fixed on the screen.

"*Qu'est-ce que c'est*, Colonel?"

"The local news is showing footage of the fire."

There were several talking heads were in the foreground. Skip recognized Stefan, the owner of the café across from the bakery, where he and his men had waited. A picture of Skip appeared on the screen, and Stefan was saying something to a gendarme. Stefan pointed to Skip's picture on his phone as a disembodied voice came from the café ceiling.

Votre attention, s'il vous plaît. Your attention, please. Nous sommes prêts à commencer l'embarquement. We are ready to begin boarding.

"Jules, give me your phone."

"Colonel?"

Jules turned to look at the TV in time to see Skip's face on the screen.

"Give me your phone and get on the ferry — now."

"Non, Colonel. I will not leave you alone."

Skip raised his voice.

"Chief, get on the damn ferry! Do it now, and don't argue with me."

Skip's forceful change of tone startled Jules. He had never spoken to him this way.

"Harry will be waiting for you in Fortune. I'll see you in Montreal. Now get the hell away from here. I'll be fine."

Jules rose reluctantly to do as he was told. A nagging suspicion that had been plaguing Skip resurfaced as he watched Jules walk away. Someone had betrayed him and his men, but who? One thing he was sure of: all was not as it seemed.

A New Life

December 2011 – April 2012

Ottawa

Colonel Amadeo Ignazio Schiaparelli had had enough of idiotic policies, enough of the stupidity that surrounded him, of the vacuity, venality, and vanity of those he worked for. All his life he'd striven to be an ethical leader, to put service before self. The three years he had spent working in National Defence Headquarters as part of the so-called "Defence Team" had made a mockery of a career lived in the service of his nation, his regiment, and his soldiers. This morning, when he got out of bed and looked at his uniform, something felt different. He didn't want to put it on. He couldn't put it on.

It was a moment of bewilderment for Skip. These feelings had been welling up in him for some time, and when they erupted, he felt lost and disoriented. For over three decades he'd not merely been employed as an army officer. Skip *was* an army officer, and so he wasn't sure of what to do. After a moment, he called his personal assistant, Major Gagnon, at home.

"Bonjour, Georges. I apologize for the early call. I'm taking a personal day. Don't worry, I'll be in tomorrow."

Skip showered, shaved, and dressed. As was his habit, he inspected himself in the mirror before going out. He was proud of how well he'd aged. He had taken care of himself. His brown eyes were still sharp, and he was still fit. His dark hair was greying at the temples, but he could easily pass for a man a decade younger than his actual age. Skip left his condo and walked to the Sparks Street Mall near Canada's Parliament. A friend stopped him.

"Good morning, Skip. You're not in uniform. What's up?"

"Good morning, Bob. I'm taking the day to enjoy the weather before the snows come. Even staff weenies like us deserve a day off, right?"

"Too right, Skip. I'm sure I'll see you in the headquarters. Gotta run."

Bob had said it all in two words, thought Skip: "Gotta run."

The brisk weather helped lift his mood a bit. Most of the leaves had fallen, but those that were left hung onto their brilliant colours. A hearty breakfast in a ByWard Market café cleared his head, after which he strolled through the centre of the city. Ottawa was beautiful this time of year. Passing the National War Memorial, and the Tomb of the Unknown Soldier, Skip decided to visit the War Museum. He loved the museum, and by the day's end he had calmed down and felt whole again. He had also come to a decision.

The next morning, he was back in the office an hour early. His PA reported at the usual time.

"Bonjour, Colonel."

"Good morning, Georges. Was there anything important yesterday?"

"No, sir. It was quiet all day."

"Here," said Skip, "take this letter upstairs to Major General Truman for me, and please deliver it to him personally. I'm going to the fifth floor to do a bit of admin."

Skip handed him an envelope and left. He returned an hour later to find the general sitting in his office, scowling.

"What the hell is wrong with you?" said Truman.

"Good morning to you too, Frank."

"Frank? Have you had a stroke?"

"Sorry, Frank. Did you change your name while I was away yesterday?"

Skip sat down behind his desk. He could see the anger rising in Truman's face.

"I have no idea what you're on about, but drop the bullshit, Skip. You can't quit. You're not even forty-eight yet and we have plans for you. We have big plans."

"Well, Frank, you're wrong, because I just did. I was down at the Admin Unit, and my release is now being expedited. As far as plans go, I have my own."

The general stared at Skip in slack-jawed amazement.

"Give me strength," he sighed. "You're slated to be the EA to the commander of ISAF in Kabul in a few months. The mission may be winding up soon, but that's a plum job and I've been pushing your file for months. You know that."

Truman softened his tone. "Skip, I've known you for forever. What's going on?"

"I've just had enough, Frank. I'm done, and as for the plans that you guys may have for me, well, I couldn't care less. Short of arresting me and convening a court martial, I'll be out of here in about ten days, Afghan mission or no Afghan mission. Is there anything else I can do for you, *sir?*"

General Truman was again struggling to hold his temper in check. He rose.

"Screw you, Skip," he said.

"My sentiments exactly," said Skip.

The general spun on his heel and left. Major Gagnon stood silently at the door after the general had gone.

"Are you okay, sir?" he said at last.

"I'm fine, Georges. Thank you. Grab us some coffee and come back. I need to speak to you."

Georges went on his errand without speaking. He'd overheard the conversation between his colonel and the general, and he knew what was coming. In minutes he was back in the office. Georges handed over a coffee and stood facing Skip.

"Colonel, I know what you're going to tell me. All I can say is please don't. You're one of the good guys. Too many good ones are leaving, sir."

"Listen, Georges. The army doesn't need or want me. You and officers like you are the future, and you can make it better. I'm the past. The Cold War ended a long time ago, son."

He waved for Georges to take a seat, then spent twenty minutes telling him what a fine job he'd done as his PA. He promised to leave a strong evaluation report on his file, and said he'd make sure somebody watched over him in the short term. Rising from his chair, he offered his hand to the younger man and wished him well.

"Take the rest of the afternoon and prep all my active files for a quick departure. After you've done that, go home. I need some quiet."

The major hesitated momentarily.

"Yes, sir," he said softly.

During the next couple of weeks, Skip disengaged both mentally and emotionally. He refused to wait for a replacement to do a handover, and simply left. He released from the army without even saying good-bye. People were mystified at his abrupt departure, but Skip offered no excuses or explanations. He wrote a dozen or so letters to people whom he respected. He sent one to his Regimental Sergeant Major and to a previous commander with whom he still corresponded. His RSM was now the Army RSM and expressed regret at his leaving. He wrote a short note to his good friend Lieutenant-Colonel Harry Monahan, who was currently on exchange in the Persian Gulf with the American Army, as well as to a few select others. Most of the men he had learned from were either dead or long retired, and he justified his actions to himself by saying that the Canadian Army he'd loved so much no longer felt like home. It was time to head for the exit, and so, he did.

One phone call he received on his last morning in the office stood out in his mind.

"Hello."

"Good morning, sir. Is this Colonel Schiaparelli?"

"Yes. Who's this, please?"

"I'm sure you don't remember me. My name is Dixon, sir. I was a corporal in the regiment when you were the CO."

"Dixon. Yes, I do remember you, Corporal. You were a driver in 'B' Squadron. I seem to recall you being brought before me for disciplinary action, and I sent you to the Detention Barracks for a couple of weeks. Was that you?"

"Yes, sir, that was me. I wanted to call and ask you not to leave."

"I beg your pardon?"

"Colonel, I was guilty, and I deserved my punishment. But what I will always remember is you coming down to the regimental duty room to speak to me before they took me away. You cleared the room so we could speak privately, and you told me that I was a good man who had done a bad thing, but that didn't make me a bad soldier. You said that I would be welcomed back with open arms. Then you said something I'll never forget. You promised me that you would make sure that the duty staff checked in on my wife every day that I was away to make sure she was okay."

"Yes, Dixon, I remember that. You took it on the chin, as I recall."

"Colonel, you were as good as your word, and my wife and I have never forgotten."

There was a long pause on the line.

"You can't leave, sir."

"What are you doing now, Dixon?"

"Sir, I'm a sergeant and instructing tactics at the Armour School."

"Sergeant Dixon, I'm proud to have served with you," said Skip. "Thanks for the call. It means a lot to me."

"Take care, sir."

"You too, Sergeant."

The line went dead. Dixon's call was an emotional wrench, and Skip momentarily hesitated, wondering if he was making a mistake. He knew he would miss soldiers like Dixon, like his old Squadron Sergeant Major, and his Regimental Sergeant Major. But the die was cast, and he wanted a complete break from his old life. He needed to start a new one, a life that was different from the one he had known. He wasn't sure what he was going to do, but it didn't really matter. There was no rush.

On a whim, Skip packed some clothes and bought an open ticket to Rome.

ROME

"I beg your pardon, sir. Are you Colonel Schiaparelli?"

Skip looked up from the chair in which he was dozing in the watery sunshine at one of Rome's many cafés.

"Sorry, do I know you?"

"No, sir. Please allow me to introduce myself. I'm Lieutenant-Colonel William Jefferson Davis Donovan, or rather, I used to be. Nobody calls me that. Everybody calls me Bill or Wild Bill."

Skip faltered, seemingly unsure of what to do, then he rose from his chair. Bill had his hand extended, so Skip shook it as Bill continued.

"May I sit?"

"Prego."

The stranger's pronunciation of the military rank confirmed him as an American. Skip pointed to the empty chair across the table.

"Please sit and call me Skip."

"Before you ask, yes, I know who the real Wild Bill Donovan was. When I got to West Point as a Plebe, one of my Firsties, a muscle-bound Neanderthal, thought it would be funny to give me that nickname. I was one hundred and forty-five pounds dripping wet, even wearing all of my battle rattle, but the name stuck."

Bill looked for a response but didn't get one. "Why do they do that?" he asked.

"Why do they do what?"

"Why do they stand at the bar when there are so many tables available?"

Skip didn't answer immediately. He was sizing up this American intruder who was pretending to be intrigued by the well-dressed men and women coming and going, always standing at the bar, never sitting at the café's tables.

"The café has two sets of prices, one set for the tables, and one for the bar. The *commercianti* are only stopping to top up their caffeine levels with a quick shot, then they return to their offices or stores. A short stop at the bar costs only a few cents as opposed to a couple of euros to sit at a table."

Bill smiled at the Canadian. "My friend was right. You invariably have a ready explanation for the many little oddities all around us."

"What friend is that?"

"It's not important."

The conversation stalled, and Bill could see that Skip was not in the mood to talk to him.

"I was hoping to discuss a proposition I have, but it can wait. I'm sorry to have barged in on you. Will you be here tomorrow?"

"I'm here every afternoon at this time. What proposition?"

"It can wait. If you don't mind, I'll come back and see you tomorrow. Enjoy the day."

Bill got to his feet and walked away. Skip shrugged and returned to his coffee, which was now cold.

As promised, Bill appeared the next day as Skip was once again enjoying the afternoon sunshine. After introductory pleasantries, Bill proposed that Skip come to work for him, and Skip promptly refused out of hand.

"Why not?" said Bill.

"Because I'm simply not interested."

Bill had already spent the better part of thirty minutes trying to get closer to this unusual Canadian Army colonel. He'd flown halfway around the world to meet him, but it wasn't looking positive.

"Skip, this is right up your alley. You'll pick your own team. Money won't be an issue, and the only person you'll ever have to deal with is me."

"Money already isn't an issue. Right up my alley? Are you serious? I'm an ex-armoured cavalry officer with a PhD in geopolitical policy. Do you seriously think that leading a team of wild geese is right up my alley? Have you spent too long sitting in the sun at the Piazza della Repubblica? You do realize you need to wear a hat."

Bill was growing frustrated, but he really wanted this guy, so he held his irritation in check. He stirred his coffee, yet again.

"I've done my homework. I know everything I need to know about you. For what I need you to do, you're exactly the right guy. If I needed a snake-eating special ops guy, I could find one in a heartbeat, but that's not what I need. It's also not what I want." Bill was staring at Skip. "I want *you*."

"And that's part of my problem," said Skip. "You seem like a decent guy, but I don't know you. You say you've done your homework, which is great, but what does that mean?"

Bill continued to stare sullenly across the table for a moment longer.

"Fair enough. You don't know me but believe me when I say that I've done my homework. For now, all I really need is for you to agree to discuss this further. Can you at least give me that?"

"Bill," said Skip as he played with the foam in his coffee cup, "maybe you've got the wrong idea. I'm comfortable here. I feel at home. I'm not some tortured soul who quit the army because I needed to find myself. I have no deep, dark angst in my life. There aren't any gaping emotional wounds I need to salve. I'm quite comfortable in my own skin. I had a great army career. I enjoyed the hell out of it and now I'm enjoying sitting here, trying to improve my faulty Italian. That's it. It's quite simple, and I don't need a job."

"I don't believe you," said Bill. "Sorry."

Skip now looked annoyed.

"No offence, Skip," Bill said, "but from where I'm sitting, either you're lying to me or to yourself. Sure, I get that you're content, and I didn't mean to imply you weren't. All I'm saying is that based on what I know, I think you're like me. I think you need a higher purpose. Brushing up your Italian isn't going keep that big brain occupied for long. You led troops at all rank levels for thirty years. Now you're just going to sit in cafés and drink expresso?"

Skip cringed visibly.

"What? said Bill. "What did I say?"

"Nothing. Never mind."

"Colonel, I'm offering you a chance to serve again. I can give you the opportunity to do what you love, but without a uniform, and without all the bureaucracy."

There it was, thought Skip. He wants to recruit me for some kind of security work in some godforsaken part of the world. Momentarily, Skip wondered if that might be an interesting challenge.

"Give me another day to think it over," said Skip.

"What's to think over? You live here like an exile. You don't have family attachments. Sorry, but I don't get it."

"You don't need to get it. I need more time to consider your offer. *Basta*."

"That's what you said yesterday."

"And that's what I'm saying now, and to be honest, you're getting on my nerves."

Bill got to his feet quickly and raised his hands in mock surrender. "Okay, I'll stop pushing. Apologies, Skip. I didn't mean to offend you. I'll see you again here, tomorrow. Same time?"

"Sure," said Skip. "Same time."

Skip had another sip of his coffee and watched Bill stride down the Via della Conciliazione toward St. Peter's Square, thinking it had been another an odd conversation. He got the waiter's attention and signalled for the check. He handed the young man a wad of euros and walked off in the opposite direction, toward the Ponte Vittorio Emanuele II. Crossing the Tiber, he decided to wander toward Piazza Navona and another of his favourite haunts.

Skip was enjoying his walk, and before long, he realized that he hadn't eaten since breakfast. He stopped for a light lunch in a café that he frequented and sipped on his beer while his mind wandered. Businessmen strolled in and leaned on the bar while the barista nodded and made their espressi. Rome is beautiful, he thought. Why was this idiot American insistent on tearing him away from it? Who the hell was Bill Donovan, and why was he hard selling him on some black ops bullshit venture? And how did somebody he'd never heard of manage to track him down in a Roman café? Deep in thought, he watched the pigeons circling the belfry of Sant'Agnese in Agone, the church across the piazza. Obviously, this American had connections, he mused, but who had squealed on him?

"*Dottore? Dottore* Schiaparelli?"

Skip was now aware of a disembodied voice intruding on his reverie.

"Dottore. *Tutto bene?*"

"*Scusi?*"

"I was speaking with you, but you do not answer me. You are okay, Dottore? Do you need something?"

"Si, Claudio. I mean no. Sorry. I am fine. I was thinking."

"*Va bene,* Dottore. Excuse me."

Claudio shuffled back behind the bar, and Skip put a bunch of euro notes under the plate, rose from his chair, and waved at the waiter.

"Ciao, ciao, Claudio."

"*Buona giornata,* Dottore Schiaparelli."

It was a perfect day to stroll the back streets of the ancient city. Exiting the piazza to the south, Skip ambled slowly down the shaded Via della Cuccagna to where it spilled into the Piazza di San Pantaleo, where he turned east onto the Corso Vittorio Emanuele I. Eventually, he found himself at the massive Tomb of the Unknown Soldier. Skip loved to come here, and always stood quietly for several minutes to pay silent tribute to the fallen soldiers it honoured. Skip knew that something was wrong, but he had no idea what. All he knew was that his daily routine in Rome was like a salve on his soul. He turned to walk to his apartment.

"Good evening, Dottore Schiaparelli."

"*Buona sera,* Signora Lucia," said Skip to the porter in his building. "Your English improves every day, Signora."

"Thank you so much, Dottore," she said, blushing slightly.

The following day, he rose late. Like he did every morning, he went down to the corner bar for breakfast and la signora brought his meal without him asking. Afterwards, he wandered through the morning markets enjoying the sights, sounds, and smells of the markets. Housewives rose early to get the freshest produce and eggs. He recognized a few and tipped his hat. These last couple of months had been better than any spa treatments or therapy. He hadn't realized how angry he had become this last year. Leaving had been the right choice, but was he ready to go back to Canada? Did he want a new job? Why leave here?

A while later, Skip rounded the corner and saw Bill already sitting at an outside table at the café. Via della Conciliazione was filling up, and crowds were forming in St. Peter's Square. Bill stood as Skip approached.

"*Buon giorno,* Bill. Not leaning on the bar?"

"Hi, Skip. I can afford a table, and anyway, I'm American. Are we ready to talk turkey yet? I'm not pushing, honest, but I have to fly to Germany in an hour or so. If I need to come back next week, then I will. I'm only asking."

Bill had anticipated Skip's arrival, and the waiter brought two glasses of red wine and a large pizza margherita. He smiled when he recognized Skip.

"Buon giorno, Dottore."

"Buon giorno."

The waiter turned to Bill after placing the pizza and beer on the table. "Prego."

"When in Rome," said Bill, sipping his wine.

"Bill, I'm sorry if I've been difficult. It was because I wasn't sure before, but now I am. I'm ready to learn more, but I have a few questions."

"I'm sure you do."

"Why me? Why now? Why not one of your classmates from the Point? There must be dozens of guys like me around. What exactly is the job, and who exactly would I be working for?"

Bill nodded approvingly at the pizza and took another small sip of wine.

"First, no, there aren't dozens like you around. For now, let's say I've been looking for quite a while. When a mutual friend suggested you, I dug a little deeper —"

Skip interrupted. "A mutual friend?"

"Like I told you yesterday, it's not important. Regardless, you and I have a lot in common. I need a non-American. You have no family ties, and by all accounts, you're a stand-up guy." Bill indicated that Skip should help himself to pizza. "Bon appétit."

"*Buon appetito*," said Skip. They pulled the pizza apart and began to eat.

After a few moments, Skip interrupted the silence. "Bill, from what you've told me, it sounds intriguing. But…."

"But?"

"But you haven't answered my questions. If you're looking for what are euphemistically called security officers, you can forget it. I'm not like that," said Skip. "And I'm not interested in what movies call wet work." He paused to take a sip of wine. "I'm not looking to create a mercenary group, so if you have anything like that in mind, I'm out. My understanding is you need folks with some special skills. Check. And you need somebody to wrangle those guys. Check. You think I'm that guy. Roger so far?"

He put his glass on the table.

"Roger all of that," said Bill. "You are just confirming for me what my investigation told me."

"Come again? What do you think your investigation told you?"

"Basically, what you've just said. And how the hell does a guy named Amadeo become Skip, anyway?"

"Don't change the subject. What makes you think I want to get back into the sandbox, as you Americans like to call it? I'm a happy man. I had a good career, and I was good at it. I —"

Bill cut him off.

"Actually, you were great at it. You loved leading soldiers. Moreover, you were never particularly adept at playing nice with the stupid kids. You love precision and complex problems. You love to be challenged, but you hate the dull grinders who work as drones. Most importantly," explained Bill, pausing for effect, "you despise the thought of becoming one of them."

"Is that so?" said Skip.

"In a nutshell, I'm offering you all the stuff you loved without having to put up with the stupid kids. Unfortunately, like I said, I have to run. My ride is due any minute, but when we meet again, I'll lay it all out, chapter and verse, I promise."

A large sedan approached. Bill gulped some wine and pushed his chair back as the vehicle pulled up.

"Here's my ride."

A fit-looking young man stepped out and held open the rear door.

"Skip, I'm sorry to stiff you with the tab, but I'll make it up to you, I promise. This is Marine Gunnery Sergeant Owen McAlister. Gunny, this is Colonel Amadeo Schiaparelli."

McAlister stepped to where Skip was standing and offered his hand.

"It's a pleasure to meet you, Colonel."

"Same here."

"Skip, Gunny will be back to escort you back home. Does one week from today give you enough time? You know, to wind up whatever you've got going on? I can give you more time if you need it."

"One week's fine. Where will we meet?"

"Don't worry, Gunny will come to you."

"That's not what I meant."

"Colonel, I will be at your apartment at 11:00 hours next Wednesday, sir."

Gunny held the door for Bill. He closed it, then got into the front passenger seat as Bill lowered his window.

"Skip, I know this is a bit rushed, but I'll make it up to you, I promise."

"Bill, that's three. You know what they say about the three Airborne promises?"

"I do, actually, but I've gotta run," he said, and chuckled.

The window rose as the car eased out onto the cobblestoned street. Skip sat down again and finished the pizza and wine.

Skip spent the next week preparing. He settled with his landlady, rounding up his payment to ensure they parted on amicable terms. He also tucked an envelope with cash and a note under Signora Lucia's door. Next, he transferred most of his money back to his Canadian banks. He spent the rest of his free time wandering the city, and as he was dining late on Tuesday, his phone buzzed. "Caller ID Blocked." He was tempted to ignore it.

"*Pronto*," he said.

"Good evening, Skip. It's only me," said Bill. "I'm checking to make sure that Gunny won't be making a wasted trip."

"All's ready here."

At 10:50 the next morning the porter rang Skip to tell him he had a visitor. He told Signora Lucia to send him up. Skip stepped onto the landing to see Gunny climbing the stairs two at a time.

"Good morning, Colonel."

"Morning, Gunny."

"I did embassy duty in Panama, and that lady downstairs would have fit right in."

"Signora Lucia takes her job seriously. Please come in."

Skip led his guest into the flat.

"Wow," said Gunny.

"I'll be sorry to leave," admitted Skip. "I have two suitcases. I'll leave those two boxes for Signora Lucia to ship home to Ottawa."

"No need, Colonel. I'll put them on the plane and get them back to Canada for you. No sweat."

"Plane?"

"Yes, sir. If you'll carry the bags down, I'll grab the boxes, or I can make two trips."

"Grab the boxes," said Skip.

They went down to the street where the same sedan idled at the curb. Traffic was light, which for Rome was unusual. Clearly, they were headed to the airport.

"You have a plane waiting at Fiumicino International?"

"Aye, sir. We're parked over at flight services on the private side."

Skip settled into the leather seat and let his mind drift while the driver negotiated the lesser mortals at speeds Skip didn't care to contemplate.

Did he really want to live in Ottawa again? It was a beautiful city, with lots of culture but too many bureaucrats. It wasn't really his kind of place. A passing building reminded him of Place Bonaventure, adjacent to Montreal's Gare Centrale, the main rail station. He'd always loved Montreal, though he had only visited a half-dozen times. He knew it through Gaston, his roommate at the Royal Military College. To Skip, Montreal was a true Canadian city. Like Toronto, it was deeply multicultural, but that's where the similarities ended. Montreal had an individual flair, a unique heartbeat, and it had a soul, something absent in most large Canadian cities.

At the airport, Skip saw a Gulfstream G500 jet, painted a dark, flat grey with a discreet US flag on the tail and subdued USAF roundels on the wings. Gunny jumped out as the vehicle came to a halt and opened Skip's door.

"Sir, if you'd like to board, the driver and I'll stow your gear."

"Thanks, Gunny. Does it matter where I sit?"

"You and me are the only passengers, so please make yourself comfortable, sir. I'll tell the crew we're ready to shove off."

Skip had once been aboard Commander Canadian Forces Europe's private aircraft. That plane couldn't hold a candle to this Gulfstream. It was luxurious, with leather upholstery and woodgrain panelling. Skip picked a forward-facing seat and settled in. Within minutes the flight crew was aboard, and the ground crew was disconnecting the power cables. Gunny leaned over.

"Anything I can get you, sir, like maybe a coffee?"

"No thanks, Gunny. I'm fine. Where are we going?"

"Deutschland, sir."

FREIBURG IM BREISGAU

When Gunny woke him, Skip looked at his watch. It was almost 15:00. Skip was surprised that he'd dozed and equally surprised by how at home he felt, like when he was a commander prepping for an exercise. He looked out his window as the plane was making its final approach. The ground below was hauntingly familiar. It reminded Skip of his time with his regiment in the Black Forest, and he soon realized why. The plane landed about twenty-five kilometres from Freiburg, a medieval university town in the heart of the Schwarzwald. There were no other planes at the private airstrip, and waiting on the apron were a couple of Mercedes; a black Maybach, and a dark grey G-Class, both with darkened windows. When he stepped out of the aircraft, he saw Bill waiting for him at the bottom of the mobile stairway.

"Hey, Skip. How was your flight? Did Gunny take care of you?"

"Very comfortable, thanks, and Gunny's been most attentive. Your driver in Rome was interesting. The last time I saw driving like that I was in a chase car escorting a royal visit."

Skip reached the bottom step, and Bill pumped his hand in welcome. He gave Gunny a look that said, "Take care of things," and guided Skip over to the elegant Maybach. Skip looked around.

"Is something wrong?" said Bill.

"No, said Skip. "Just wondering about customs and immigration."

"We're still inside the Schengen Area. Anyway, I have an arrangement with the *Bundesgrenzschutz*."

"I'm impressed with the ride. I've read about these in novels, but never ridden in one. I guess if you can smuggle me out of Italy on a private Gulfstream, then a Maybach is only appropriate."

"I'm pleased you appreciate the effort, but there was no smuggling involved, just best business practices. Let's get to the house so you can freshen up. We can have a proper German *Kaffee und Kuchen*. We've got a lot to discuss, and we can do it in the proper Black Forest way, over coffee and cake."

Skip sat quietly in the luxury car and gazed out the tinted windows. Like on the plane before landing, he was surprised to realize he felt like he had come home.

"By the way," he said to Bill, "Gunny is an impressive guy, but he looks too young to be retired."

"That's because he isn't retired. When I introduced him as Marine Gunnery Sergeant McAlister, it was because he's still on active duty with the Corps. He was injured during training with Marine Force Recon. Some medic was going to release him but a family friend of mine brought him to my attention. I pulled some strings to move him across to Navy Intelligence."

"Weren't you US Army Intelligence?"

"That's a story for another day. Gunny lasted less than six months before he was bored. Release was once more on the horizon, so I took him into my organization on a semi-permanent loan. He's been perfect as my go-to guy."

The car passed through a large gate and onto a pea stone gravel courtyard. The house wasn't what Skip was expecting. He wouldn't have called it a house, it was a country manor in the classic German Fachwerk style, likely seventeenth century. To a North American it would look vaguely English Tudor, and it sat surrounded by pastures on what looked to be a sizable chunk of property.

"Lovely *Landhaus*," said Skip.

The car came to a halt. Skip eyed the massive oaken double doors.

"What is it, maybe seventeen hundred?"

"I'm impressed. The original building is from sixteen fifty-four. There's the date chiselled into the door lintel," said Bill, indicating the carving. "It's been restored a couple of times. Most of it survived the bombings you

Canadians launched around here in nineteen forty-four. It sits on about thirty acres. We bought it about ten years ago to use as our European offices, and as far as the locals are concerned, it belongs to a wealthy and eccentric American, which I guess is mostly true. Let's go inside. Like I said, we've got lots to discuss."

The building's interior didn't disappoint. Filled with heavy oak and leather furniture, it was tastefully opulent while remaining true to its heritage. The walls were covered with antlers and oil paintings of hunting scenes. A couple of boars' heads flanked the fireplace. Skip was not a hunter, but he was quite comfortable in this sort of setting.

"Bill, did you slaughter all these innocent critters by yourself, or did you have help in all this murder?"

"Not me. I don't hunt. Most of this stuff was here when we bought the place from a count who was descended from Duke Alexander of Württemberg. He drank and gambled away his inheritance, and eventually had to sell off this place to pay his debts. The family was well connected in its day, I guess."

"It was and still is. If I remember, the Württemberg family married into both the English and the Russian royal families."

"Is this what you studied at that boys' school on Lake Ontario while your classmates were learning to be killers?"

"Any thug can be a killer, Bill. It takes style and effort to be a gentleman."

Skip was comfortable enough now with Bill to continue.

"You realize that the Royal Military College is overlooked by a substantial fort we built just after we whipped your butts in the War of 1812. We rebuilt it later when you were deeply into expansionism. One of the many reasons we Canadians are not the same as you."

"American expansionism — a nasty business," admitted Bill. "I'm not sure we're quite over it yet."

Skip dropped down into a large burgundy leather chair. "You mentioned coffee and cakes?"

"I'll be right back," said Bill, and he headed for the kitchen. He returned a minute later with two distinctive porcelain mugs filled with black coffee. "Here you go. Cake is on the way. There's cream and sugar on the sideboard."

He handed a mug to Skip, then sat in a chair opposite him.

"Thanks," said Skip. "I take it as it comes. I jokingly call it combat coffee. This is all very pleasant. Nothing like strong German coffee, especially in a Hutschenreuther mug."

"I had a feeling you'd notice the mug," said Bill, as he sipped and looked at his guest. "You never answered my question."

"What question?"

"How did someone called Amadeo Ignazio end up being called Skip?"

"You weren't the only cadet to have a Neanderthal senior at college. When I got to RMC, I was assigned to No. 1 Squadron, in the Stone Frigate. Every other cadet in my squadron was WASP to the core, and having some proud 'eyetie' from Hogtown with two medieval given names and an unpronounceable last one wasn't going to wash."

"Hogtown?" said Bill.

"Toronto. Anyway, it was the perfect reason to give me a nickname. All those vowels in one place somehow caused white-bread Anglo-Saxon brains to cramp up, so Schiaparelli quickly became Skip."

Bill nodded as he sipped coffee.

"After a while I accepted it, especially considering some of the names our seniors gave a few of my classmates, most of which can no longer be used in mixed company. By the end of my first year, it was all anyone ever called me."

"Maybe I should call you Iggy."

"Maybe I should punch your lights out."

Skip finally tasted his coffee.

"You've dragged me a long way, Bill. Don't get me wrong, I'm enjoying all of this, but now, what I really need to know is why."

Gunny appeared with a tray containing slices of dark chocolate cake and placed it on a small table near the two men. He looked to Bill, who shook his head.

"We can eat and talk, if it's alright with you."

Skip nodded.

"Here goes ..."

Bill went to the very beginning, starting with his own recruitment. And over the course of the next hour or so, accompanied by several cups of coffee and slices of cake, he laid it all out for Skip.

"Starting even before 9/11, the US government got itself into trouble.

Using 'semi-legal' methods like rendition was problematic, even when it was allowed by US law. The international press, not to mention the UN International Court of Justice, considered such actions as crimes against humanity. To avoid further embarrassment, the National Security Agency recommended contracting out these dealings to put the government at arm's length from questionable operations. It was all about plausible deniability. Questions so far?"

Skip shook his head.

"The NSA created a 'wholly owned subsidiary' with a secret budget. Eventually they named it Eagle Investments. A secret presidential order made it legit, and an open-handed Congress keeps it well funded." Bill paused. "Very well-funded."

Skip looked up and nodded.

"We recruit primarily ex-military operators who already have the skills and security clearances. By arrangement, if Eagle isn't interfering with official government business, I can discretely use certain government facilities and equipment, like that Gulfstream, for example. But like the fictional Impossible Mission Force, the feds will surely disavow any bad or illegal behaviour, if my boys ever get caught."

"Has it ever happened?"

"Being disavowed? Not yet."

"You said boys. Just men in Eagle?

"For now."

"Go on," said Skip.

"Through family contacts, I was originally recruited to run Eagle's intelligence section. I was only twenty years into my career, but I didn't enjoy the work. There were too many knuckle-draggers."

Bill looked Skip in the eye to see if he would react. He did not.

"I did that for a couple of years," Bill continued, "and then I was made the CEO. More commonly, I'm called the director. I reorganized Eagle, starting by retiring those who didn't share my personal credo that thinking trumps violence. I detest unnecessary violence or cruelty, and always have. I was also bothered that some ops we were running were still too close to the edge of American law. It occurred to me that if Congress could fund Eagle, then Eagle could fund a subsidiary of its own, not as a mirror but as a supplementary force. I've always been partial to Canadians, so I opted to look north. Nobody liked it, but eventually the director of the NSA blessed my plan."

"You're partial to Canadians? Care to tell me why?"

"Isn't it obvious?"

"No."

Bill shrugged.

"Taking the reins was not all hearts and flowers. As an aside, one of the effects of my budget re-prioritization caused the Senate Intelligence Committee to quash a hi-tech drone project that was the darling of the air force intel community, which made me some enemies on the joint intel staff — in particular, a guy named Andy Anderson. It was his baby. Hard luck, and he probably still hates me, but you have to break eggs to make omelettes."

"I guess so, yeah," said Skip.

"Once I got permission to create my subsidiary, I began making calls. I'd maintained a lot of my old contacts in the CANUS and Five Eyes intel communities and I made discreet — and purely hypothetical — inquiries. In the end, the choice to lead a new team came down to a retired Canadian two-star, and to you."

"Who was the two-star?"

"It's immaterial, and it was no contest. The two-star was competent, but I've always avoided hiring retired generals. I've known dozens, and with rare exceptions, moving into the upper echelons changes them."

"How so?"

"Even discounting personality and ego, most have forgotten how to work. You can't hand these guys a blank sheet of paper and ask them to design an operation. They've been out of the trenches for too long, and most've gone stale. For my money, colonels are the best bet. They're experienced enough to have the senior leadership skills and recent enough to pitch in if required."

"Let's continue our conversation from Rome," said Skip. "Why me? What makes you think I'm your guy?"

"Because you are. After I decided you were my guy, I did a deep dive into your life. Everything I saw told me you were exactly whom I needed. You're a veritable Renaissance man, buddy. Driven to succeed but flexible when you need to be."

"Is that so?"

"You're a military academy graduate and parachute qualified. You commanded an armoured cav regiment. You've got a PhD, and you speak multiple languages. You've never seen combat, but it wasn't for lack of wanting to go, and by the time Canada had got itself into a shooting war in Afghanistan, you were already too high on the staff list. No doubt if you'd stayed in, you would have been sent on some kind of tour. One guy even called you a mailed fist in a velvet glove."

"In fact," said Skip, "I was slated to go to ISAF this year."

"I'd heard that but couldn't confirm it," said Bill. "You have no kids or siblings. And as far as I can tell, you're the only armoured cav guy to have been seconded to a foreign intelligence agency."

"You know about that?"

"Like I told you, I know a lot of folks in the game. The only thing I wasn't able to find out was why you never married. My investigator doesn't think you're gay, but quite frankly, I don't care."

"For the record, I'm straight. I came close to getting married once, but it didn't work out. Being an army wife is not for the faint of heart. Besides, the lady in question had her own professional ambitions, but I have no regrets."

"I tracked you for months," said Bill.

"Months? Really?"

"Skip, you drove me to distraction. I planned to bump into you 'accidentally' in Ottawa, but I was too late. By then you'd already pissed off half the senior leadership in the Canadian Army and walked away. I would have paid to have been a fly on the wall for that. Anyway, your move caught me off guard. Then life got busy for me and by the time I could make time to see you, you were already living in a garret in Rome, doing whatever. You do realize you seriously annoyed a lot of people with how you left."

"I know, and I couldn't care less. My friends understand, and those who don't mean nothing to me. And I wasn't living in a garret, wise-ass."

Bill smirked and stared into his mug before continuing.

"When I tracked you down in Rome, I immediately got the sense you and I could work together. I don't need another snake-eater. I need a thinker. More importantly, I need a leader, somebody I can trust. That's what my gut tells me, even if you did tell me to piss off."

"I did not. My recollection is I paid for lunch and politely declined. Then you began stalking me."

Bill gave Skip a searching look. "Maybe it just felt that way. Let's get down to it. Are you ready to give up la dolce vita to start up your own maple syrup version of Eagle? You can set it up any way you like. Pick your own team. I can give you twenty-four hours to think it over. Supper is planned for 19:00."

Skip pushed away the plate of half-eaten cake and sipped the now-cold coffee, gazing over the bone china mug at Bill in contemplative silence.

"I've already decided," he said.

"And?"

"I'm in, but what am I going do with the other twenty-three hours and fifty-nine minutes?"

"Excellent," said Bill. "Welcome aboard, Skip. Can you stay a few days? We need to hammer out a bunch of details."

"My time is now yours. I'm on the clock, and I have no place to be."

The hammering took a little longer than Bill had expected. Though there were no major issues, Skip surprised him, nevertheless. He hadn't planned on Skip being so detail oriented. The two men sketched out Skip's organization and how he might put it together. Bill explained how it would be financed. Skip gave Bill assurances he knew enough talent to have a small crew ready within ninety days of startup. That was important to Bill, but he didn't share why. To help speed up the process, Bill offered Skip some names, a couple of which Skip recognized but rejected. He also had construction crews ready to help build Skip's new facilities. Skip accepted the offer of crews but confirmed he would pick his own men.

"You know a couple of these guys," said Bill. "What's wrong with them?"

"I'll be blunt. I don't trust them."

"I understand completely," said Bill.

Otherwise, there had been virtually no negotiations. Whatever Skip asked for, Bill agreed to, and vice versa. Bill was pleased he would soon have someone he could count on to watch his back. In fact, if anything, Bill's investigator had sold Skip short. The more they talked, the more Bill was eager to work with his new Canadian friend.

"I hate to admit this," said Skip "but you were right. I thought I'd be happy to spend the next decade in Italy. This'll be a challenge, but the truth is I'm looking forward to getting back into harness."

On the final day, the two men decided to share a celebratory glass of single malt.

"Here's to you, Skip."

"Back at you."

They raised their glasses.

"You do know you're going to need a snake-eater for a deputy," said Bill. "I have some names …"

"Forget it. I have someone in mind already. I just have to see if he's interested."

"I know the feeling," said Bill, smiling.

Skip opened his mouth to say something and paused.

"There is one thing we glossed over. It's time to circle back. I didn't press it, but now I have to. You know where I'm going."

"The wet work," said Bill. "I get it Skip, and I know it's not you. I won't be giving you jobs involving intentional killing, or even what the CIA likes to call enhanced interrogation."

Bill topped up his glass.

"But you do realize your guys are going to have to carry weapons. It's a necessary part of the package."

"Sure, but weapons will be primarily for self-defence. If that leads to killing some bad guys, then so be it. I just want to be clear about what I told you in Rome. I'm not interested in hiring a crew of gunslingers. As for the rest, I'll take you at your word."

Skip sipped his scotch.

"Skip, since we're poking each other in the eye, I have to ask you something for my own edification. Why did a guy who obviously loves the army and being among soldiers work so hard to earn a PhD? Especially in such an obscure subject?"

Skip smiled over the rim of his cut crystal glass but didn't answer right away. Bill began to worry he had offended his new friend. After a few moments, Skip replied.

"First, the military significance of saddle blankets is not an obscure subject. Second, that's an odd question coming from an ex-US Army officer.

You guys practically invented the idea of senior officers with PhDs. I'll bet the US Army has more PhDs than Harvard. Finding high-performance soldiers who can shoot, go without sleep, and live in a muddy hole is not that difficult. It takes careful selection, rigorous training, and dedication, but that's the easy bit."

Skip lifted the glass but stopped without taking a drink.

"What every nation needs is leaders with insight, education, and judgment. Unfortunately, once I became one of those leaders, I realized my country was not really interested. It was enthralled with the former at the expense of the latter. SOF guys run the show now and they're shooters instead of thinkers. Once that conclusion finally seeped through my thick skull, it was time for me to leave."

Bill saw he had indeed inadvertently touched a nerve and regretted his question.

"I'm sorry, buddy. I didn't mean to open a wound, honestly."

"I'm fine," said Skip. "Anyway, now I get to play with bad boys like you." He yawned and looked at his watch. "It's time for me to hit the rack. I'm beat, and it's been a long few days. I'll see you at breakfast."

Skip put down the glass, rose, and left his scotch unfinished. He went up to his room, leaving Bill ruing the fact he had unwittingly upset his new comrade.

Morning came early. After another robust German breakfast and several cups of rich black coffee, Skip was ready to head home. The Maybach, with Bill in the rear seat, picked him up and drove to the airport, pulling right up to the stairs of the Gulfstream. Gunny was waiting and quick to step over. He opened the trunk to get Skip's bags and took them on board. Bill turned to Skip as the two men exited the limousine.

"Hey, Skip, have you ever seen the movie *Casablanca*?"

"Are you kidding? When I first saw it, I immediately crushed on Ingrid Bergman."

Bill laughed. "Well, in the immortal words of the closing scene, this could the beginning of a beautiful friendship." He paused for a moment. "I'm sorry about last night."

Skip gave Bill an easy smile. "No need to apologize."

They shook hands, and Skip climbed the stairs to the plane. Gunny met him at the top.

"Welcome back aboard, Colonel. Luggage and boxes stowed. Permission to cast off?"

"Thanks, Gunny. Let's get this crate off the ground. I have much I need to do, including some gentle arm-twisting to attend to."

"Aye, Colonel."

Skip moved to a seat, grabbed a pillow and a blanket, and got comfortable. He was suddenly fatigued. He had worked hard not to show it, but the last couple of days had taken a mental toll. It was a little like delayed grieving, he reflected. In discussing military operations with Bill, many memories had been dredged up. Skip was forced to admit that he felt the absence of fellowship and camaraderie that he had known all of his adult life, and it surprised him to realize just how much.

Closing his eyes, Skip began scripting how he would approach one of his oldest friends and ask him to be his deputy. The jet's engines screamed to life as a memory came flooding back.

Harry was at Skip's office door. Skip had been expecting him. Harry saluted smartly and stepped in. He was on in-routine to the National Defence HQ. As a post-command lieutenant-colonel, Harry had to punch his staff ticket, just as Skip had done several years previously. They hadn't seen each other since Harry had given up command of his battalion. That was a night to remember — or forget. Skip had never seen Harry so drunk or disconsolate as that night; Harry had seen his life as a soldier coming to an end, and the thought of becoming a staff officer in NDHQ, or any headquarters, just added insult to injury.

"Morning, Harry." Skip pointed to a chair. "Coffee?"

"No thanks, Colonel. I can't stay. I'm on out-routine."

"You mean in-routine," said Skip.

"No, sir. Colonel Wilmot yanked my leash two days ago. I guess General Romanov has been getting heat from the Chief about me. Jason — I mean Colonel Wilmot —is sending me to the US mission in the Gulf as an LO. He's tired of the general chewing his ass about me. I guess he figures, 'outta sight,

outta mind.' It's a six-month rotation, but I'll move up here when I get back. I thought I should come to say good-bye."

"You're not supposed to be so delighted about this, Harry. Your regiment is punishing you."

"I know. Isn't it great?" said Harry, looking like he'd won the lottery.

Skip stood so he could hug his friend. "You are a dickhead. You do know that don't you?"

Harry grinned.

"I only have one question," said Skip. "Can I come with you?"

"I promise to send SITREPs from the Gulf," said Harry.

"Don't be surprised if I'm not here when you get back," said Skip.

"Sure," said Harry. "We both know you're a lifer, Colonel, just like me. I'll see you in six."

Building the Cohort

May – August 2012

Ottawa

The Gulfstream jet touched down at Macdonald-Cartier International at midday, but Skip's body clock told him otherwise. It had been a long flight, and even though he had stretched out and slept for most of it, he wasn't rested. He never felt rested when he flew. There was an SUV with diplomatic plates waiting on the apron. He looked over at Gunny.

"Let me guess. Donovan has a friend."

"You got it in one, Colonel. He'll take you home, sir."

"Thanks, Gunny. I look forward to working with you soon."

"Aye, sir, same here."

They shook hands.

The driver loaded Skip's belongings and drove him across to Canada Customs. The young woman inside was friendly, efficient, and pleasant. Skip wondered idly if she had been briefed by someone before his arrival. The driver stood by his vehicle waiting.

"That was unusually pleasant for Canada Customs," mused Skip aloud as he approached the vehicle.

"Sir, I have your address and know where it is. Please sit in the back and relax. We should be there in twenty minutes."

Once on the move, it took about thirty seconds for Skip to drift off to sleep. Again, the memories returned unbidden.

Harry Monahan was babbling. Standing at attention in front of Skip's desk, he was on the verge of losing his self-control and was wilting under the colonel's intense glare. He had blotted his copybook at a NATO conference in Halifax, Nova Scotia, two days before and was now in Skip's office being chastised. It wasn't going well. That he had known Colonel Skip since they had both been junior officers was of no help. Harry finally fell silent and fixed his gaze down at the desk.

"Sorry, Colonel," he said.

Skip's famous flares of temper came on unexpectedly, but they also went out like birthday candles on a cake. He took a moment to regain his composure.

"Harry, a lieutenant-colonel preparing to give up command doesn't need to have his name mentioned at the minister's morning briefing, and certainly not like yours was this morning. Luckily for you, I was there to answer questions on foreign training assistance, and when your name came, up I interrupted the briefer. The Chief gave me a withering look, but I assured the minister that I knew you, and I promised him I would speak to you and clear this up. That's why Georges grabbed you at the airport. Here's the plan:"

"Colonel, if I could —"

"Shut the hell up! I say again, here's the plan: Do not talk about the conference, with anybody. I mean it. Act like it never happened. I'll go down to the career shop tomorrow morning and speak to your regimental colonel. It was Jason's bright idea to send a hard ass like you to a conference full of sensitive bloody snowflakes. Now he can clean it up. Are you hearing me?"

"Yes, Colonel. Thank you, sir," Harry said, looking wilted. "Colonel Skip?"

"Yes, Harry."

"I'm really sorry. I didn't mean to offend all those people."

"I know," said Skip. "I know. It's your famous interpersonal flair. Didn't Lower Canada College teach you anything? Harry, you have a boatload of skills, more than most actually, but sensitivity isn't one of them. I guess that's why you'll be saddled with two sets of alimony payments for several more years. Or is it three sets now, I forget?"

"Very funny, sir."

"That's settled. Now you and I can have supper. You'll catch the morning train back to London. I already told Georges to book it and call your adjutant. I'm sure they both had a good laugh at your expense. Put on your forage cap and let's get out of here before the Chief's EA comes down here and drags both of us

Skip awoke in the back seat with a shudder. The driver was already
unloading the boxes from the trunk, and the noise had woken him.

"Colonel, I can carry these up if you wouldn't mind grabbing the two
suitcases."

"No need, son. I've got it."

"No, sir, I've got my orders."

"Follow me, then."

Once the driver was gone, Skip walked around his condo opening
windows. Normally it felt good to be back from a long absence, but not
this time. Oddly, it no longer felt like home.

Skip had a hot shower and a quick nap. Then, he sat at his desk and
began to plot out how he was going to create his new organization. He
wanted to keep it small. Bill's seed money was generous, and Skip needed
to put together a plan; he needed to consider structure, recruiting, training,
facilities, administration, and much more. He went to the liquor cabinet
and poured out a glass of bourbon. Scotch was for enjoyment; bourbon
was for thinking.

The following morning, he called his realtor.

"Heather, it's Skip Schiaparelli. I need to sell my condo."

"Sure, Skip. I'd love to help you with that."

They had a short discussion, and she connected him with an affiliated
realtor in Quebec. The following morning, he boarded the first train to

Montreal. The realtor was waiting for him at the Gare Centrale, where they grabbed a quick coffee and began the search for a condo. It only took him two hours. The third place they inspected was perfect, and Skip offered the asking price. When he phoned Ottawa the following day, there were already two offers on his place, both at his asking price. He told his realtor to accept the one that could close quicker. Within the month, Ottawa was in his rear-view mirror. Skip was officially a resident of La Belle Province.

Montreal

Skip's new condo was in the heart of Montreal, where he didn't know a soul. It was an ideal place to start a new life, but his wide circle of friends had grown concerned at his abrupt departure. Predictably, Gaston 'Bishop' Levesque, his oldest and dearest friend, found him immediately, but Skip put him off. Gaston, who was deeply embedded in the world of national security, and had witnessed his share of trauma, took no offence. Quietly, he put the word out that Amadeo needed time to be alone. The Bishop told everyone that he would keep an eye on Skip. Their friend had left the army because it was dead to him, and he would need to grieve on his own time and in his own way. He arranged for a terse message to be sent to Harry in the Gulf, assuring him that he would watch over Skip.

For his part, Skip worked hard at establishing his new life. He spent entire days lost in thought. Occasionally, he would pull all-nighters, something he hadn't done since being a student at the army staff college. After several weeks of avoiding everyone, the condo's concierge buzzed him one afternoon.

"Monsieur, you have a visitor."

Skip rudely told the concierge to tell his visitor to go piss off.

"Oui, Monsieur."

Five minutes later, there was a rap at Skip's door. Annoyed that he was being interrupted, Skip shouted, "Go away."

Harry, recently returned from the Gulf, had no such intention. He knocked again. Standing in front of the apartment door, he listened to his friend cursing him from inside. He could kick the door in. No, that would be unseemly and beneath the dignity of a war veteran and a senior officer in the Royal Canadian Regiment. He knocked a third time, this time louder and longer.

"For pity's sake, go away," growled Skip as he opened the door.

It swung open, and Harry stared at Skip standing in his housecoat with at least a week's worth of stubble on his face. The apartment was dark and the air stale. Skip squinted painfully at the sunlight streaming in through the large windows in the corridor.

"You, sir, are a shower of shite," said Harry. "I'm here to sort you out, Colonel."

Harry pushed his way past his friend and walked into the condo. He noticed a half-empty bottle of bourbon sitting on the coffee table. The TV showed muted talking heads from CBC. He turned off the TV, walked over to the balcony, and pulled open the drapes. Harry slid open the door to let some fresh air into the apartment, then turned on Skip.

"Get your ass into the shower, and shave. Do it now."

Skip began to raise his hand in a feeble objection, but Harry halted him.

"Do it now, I said."

Skip frowned, shrugged, and wordlessly walked to the bedroom, shedding clothes as he went. Harry heard the shower running and shook his head in dismay. He'd got a message from Skip's college roommate, but it was almost in code. Jason Wilmot had described how Skip had basically told everybody to go screw themselves and disappeared. Harry had no idea Skip had taken his departure from the army so badly. He had asked for a quick leave of absence to go to Rome, but his general had denied his request. Harry had saluted and left the general's office, muttering and angry. This was not what soldiering was about. Comrades came first. The tight-assed bastard didn't seem to understand that.

A few minutes later, Skip padded barefoot out of his bedroom, freshly shaved, in clean chinos and a golf shirt. He had a towel over his neck.

"You are supposed to be in the desert," Skip barked. "What in God's name are you doing here? You can't just barge into a man's home and start ordering him around, even if you are a light colonel in *the* RCR."

Skip always put emphasis on "the" in the regimental title because he knew it annoyed his friend.

"Well, what do you know? I was going to ask you the same question. Montreal? Really? I got short-toured. There's something about a board of inquiry. This is my redeployment and decompression leave. I'm decompressing. Can't you tell?"

"No, I can't."

"I'm here for a mini-reunion at Lower Canada College," said Harry.

"LCC is closed for two weeks."

"I meant to say McGill. My mistake. It's a mini-reunion of my McGill class."

"You hated McGill almost as much as they hated you, which is why you only stayed a year. I'll bet you can't name even one of your granola-crunching, sandal-wearing, anti-military classmates."

Harry stood silently for a moment, pondering the situation.

"Listen up, you grumpy bastard. Go put on a pair of your expensive Italian loafers and let's move. You may not know this, but gentlemen do not dine in fine restaurants unless they are wearing shoes. And hurry up. I'm hungry, I'm still jet lagged, and I missed my afternoon nap. Make tracks, Colonel."

Skip did what he was told, muttering that he refused to wear socks, again because he knew how much it annoyed his friend's sense of gentlemanly propriety.

The late afternoon sun was fading behind Montreal's skyscrapers. Harry hoped the walk down to the Fairmont Hôtel Reine Elizabeth II would be helpful for his friend. Skip needed to get out into the world again. Besides, the hotel's famous restaurant, Rosélys, did a superb prime rib. Add a couple of bottles of decent wine, and maybe he could put the colonel back onto his feet. At least it would be a start.

"Where are we going?"

"The Fairmont."

"Why?"

"I already told you — I want to visit McGill, and the Fairmont's on the way."

"No, it's not."

"Shut the hell up and keep walking, soldier."

Over supper, Harry expressed concern at the state in which he had found his friend. He said something about mourning the death of his army career.

"Mourning?" said Skip, laughing. "The army?"

"What's so funny? Yes, mourning your past life."

"No, Harry. I know how it looks, but you have it wrong, buddy. I'm not mourning. I'm so deep into a new project I simply lost track of time. I'm touched that you were worried enough to do an intervention, and as always, I'm glad to see you, my friend. Thank you for coming to save me," he said, chuckling.

"You are one son of a bitch, Colonel. Here I was thinking you were crawling into a bottle because you pissed off everybody in NDHQ. Instead, you've been working on cold fusion. Well, forgive me for trying to repay a friend. How often did you drop everything and come to my rescue? Two divorces, that time I nearly punched out that idiot general, then —"

Skip cut him off with a gentle raise of his hand.

"Hey, I'm sorry. Forgive me, old friend. Seriously, I'm pleased you're here."

Harry stayed for a couple of days, and by the time he booked his first-class train back to Ottawa, he was satisfied that Skip was fine. Better than that, he seemed reinvigorated somehow. Skip wouldn't say much about his new project, but he promised Harry that he would explain it all very soon. Harry convinced Skip to reach out and apologize to those whom he had shunned; a lot of people were worried about him. They needed to hear that he was okay.

In the Via 1 Panorama Lounge at the train station, they gave each other what Harry always referred to as an 'eyetie' man hug, and Harry took the escalator down to his train.

Skip headed the other way, up the escalator into the Fairmont. He already missed his anal-retentive friend, though he'd see him again soon. But first, he had to put all the pieces of his complex puzzle together.

The concierge greeted Skip as he entered the lobby.

"Bonjour, monsieur. May I help you?"

Skip deliberated before replying. It was too early to go home.

"Do you still have payphones?"

"Certainly, sir. Over in the corner."

He walked through the expansive lobby to the phones, picked up the receiver of the closest one, inserted a quarter into the slot, and dialled a number he knew well.

"Oui, bon soir."

"Is this the Ecclesiastic Escort Service? I'm new in Montreal, and I'm lonely."

"You are a pig, mon frère. Shame on you."

"How did you know it was me? Are you in town?"

"A lucky guess, and yes, I am here."

"Gaston, I'm calling to apologize. I was wondering if you were free for an evening drink. I'll buy."

"No apology necessary, and since you are willing to pay me a drink, I am available. Even intelligence officers need to take an occasional Saturday off. Where are you?"

The two men met at a quiet brasserie that Gaston suggested, where they could talk in private. Over the course of several hours, Skip apologized at least twice, asking for forgiveness for behaving so badly. His old roommate assured him all was well.

"It does not matter," he said. "All is forgiven, mon cher. Everyone is entitled to grieve in his own manner."

"Thanks, but I'm not grieving."

"Bon, I believe you. What is next for my favourite soldier?"

"Seriously, I'm not grieving, Gaston. I do miss the army, but the truth is I was missing it for over a year before I left. No, mon ami, I am up to my neck in a new project that I can't talk about yet, but I'm excited about it."

Gaston made a strange face, so Skip changed the subject.

"What are you up to these days, Gaston?"

"Moi? Nothing new. Spying on innocents, stealing secrets, helping to bring down foreign governments. Only the usual things, mon vieux."

"Is this your way of telling me to mind my own business?"

"Skip, I am relieved to hear I was mistaken about you. I know that you can become morose when you are bored," said Gaston as he sipped his Campari and soda.

"You aren't going to answer my question, are you?" said Skip.

"Non, mon cher Skip. I am not."

"Fine," said Skip.

"Back to you, Amadeo."

"About me? We'll see. The ancients may have been right — whom the gods would destroy, they first deprive of reason."

"Like I said, you have always needed a challenge."

Harry's visit and Gaston's concerns had been a wakeup call. Skip realized he had to normalize his life. He could still live like a human being while slowly putting together the pieces of his new challenge. He changed his routine, and when it all got to be too much, he would stroll down to the Café Olimpico for an espresso or a cappuccino, even if it was after eleven o'clock and therefore heresy to drink frothy coffee. Occasionally, he would indulge in his weakness for Italian pastries. Café Olimpico was not quite like his favourite haunt in Rome's Piazza Navona, but it had fine coffee, excellent pastries, and a discreet staff. It soon became his café of choice.

Wild Bill's desire for a new offshore subsidiary slowly began to take shape. As Skip sat savouring an espresso early one afternoon, Bill rang him up.

"How's it going, Skip?"

"Bill, good to hear from you. It's slow, and there's still a lot of groundwork to prepare."

"As long as you're making progress," said Bill. "I notice you haven't cashed my cheque yet."

"Soon, buddy. I'm almost there."

Upon his return from Germany, Skip's first order of business had been to incorporate the firm. No one in Quebec used the name, so that made it easy. The second order of business was to acquire an office. Spaces were available in the 1300 block of Boulevard René Lévesque in Place Maisonneuve. It was a nondescript steel-and-glass office tower wedged between the Wells Fargo building and the nineteenth-century Cathédrale Marie-Reine-du-Monde. The Fairmont sat nearby, as did the train station.

"Bienvenu, Monsieur Schiaparelli," said the building manager, motioning Skip to a chair. He was anxious to please his prospective new client. The occupancy rate in the building was low, and any new client, however minor, was welcome.

"Good day, Monsieur Archambault. Thank you for seeing me on short notice."

"Of course, monsieur, of course. I understand that you would like to lease an office. C'est correct?"

"Not exactly, monsieur. I need an entire floor."

Skip could see a sudden change in Archambault. He obviously didn't play poker.

"Excellent, monsieur. I believe we can accommodate you. The tenth floor is completely vacant for the moment. I could have it cleaned and ready for you in forty-eight hours, monsieur."

"No," said Skip. "I don't think so."

Archambault looked crestfallen.

"I will take the entire floor, but I will need several key changes made before I can occupy it. I need all phone lines to be physically cut and tapped. I need a DS3 fibre-optic cable installed. The elevator must be reprogrammed to require a code/tap card combination to open on my floor. All office walls must come down except for three. The remaining walls will delineate a large conference room, a lounge area, and a guest suite with private bath. I have architectural plans that I can give you."

Skip sensed that the manager was starting to tremble ever so slightly.

"Is there a problem?" he asked.

"*Problème?* Non, monsieur, there is no problem."

Archambault's face could not mask his excitement at what this prospective client was saying.

"But monsieur must appreciate that these changes may be quite expensive."

"Of course," said Skip as he rose from his chair.

Archambault almost knocked over his own chair in rising to meet him.

"I have taken the liberty of making out a bank draft to your corporate office as a deposit." Skip slid the draft across the desk and watched the manager's eyes go wide. "If you will please draft a lease and an estimate for the changes, I will return on Monday to finalize our arrangements."

"*Naturellement,*" said Archambault, awaiting further demands. "Anything else, monsieur?"

"No, that's all. Merci."

Monsieur Archambault nodded discreetly. He escorted Skip through the lobby; they shook hands, and Skip left. As Monsieur Archambault walked away, there was a clearly discernable spring in his step.

Two more features of the building pleased Skip. His office was within a relaxed walking distance of Café Olimpico, and there was a business branch of the Banque Laurentienne on the ground floor, which became his new bank.

There was no listing for Pangratti Group LLC in the expansive marble-clad lobby of the commercial tower, but this was not an oversight. If someone asked, the well-furnished offices on the tenth floor belonged to a private equity firm. There was no receptionist, and admittance was strictly by appointment. The company name was a nod to Skip's love of hidden connections. His paternal grandmother, his beloved *nonna*, had been a Pangratti. Once a proud family of landed Italian gentry, they had been ravaged by the dissolute reign of the *Fascisti*. His nonna was long gone, but Skip still remembered her fondly. He had needed a name for his new venture, and it had been a no-brainer to name it after her.

Next, Skip tracked down one of his RMC classmates who had left the army prematurely to attend McGill Law. In Glen's office, Skip explained that he had registered a name, but he needed articles of incorporation.

"I'd like Pangratti established as a limited liability company. Am I right that LLCs are how law firms and private equity funds are usually run?"

"Yes," said Glen, "usually."

"I'd like to establish the initial worth of the company to be one million dollars, making a senior partnership worth one hundred thousand. Junior partnerships will cost fifty thousand. The remainder will be associates who will get dividends, but not have any voting rights. I'll buy two senior partners' worth of ownership for myself, then let others buy in. There'll be two more senior partners. I guess that leaves room for twelve juniors. Does that make sense to you?"

Glen tapped his pen as he did some mental arithmetic.

"Four seniors, with you holding two, makes four hundred thousand, twelve juniors for the other six hundred thousand, and unlimited associates. That works, Skip."

"Thanks, Glen."

"This will take several weeks," said Glen as they shook hands.

"That works perfectly," said Skip.

Next came corporate banking. Madame Marie-Claire Lagasse showed her prospective new client into their reception area. She was a handsome middle-aged woman who, like most Québécoises, didn't try to hide her years, instead dressing fashionably for her age.

"Bienvenu, monsieur Schiaparelli," she said, pronouncing the Italian name like she had been raised in Florence.

"Merci, madame," said Skip.

He accepted a chair from her.

"I understand from my assistant you have new offices in this building and wish to open corporate accounts with us. Is this correct?"

"Oui, madame, c'est ça."

"Would you be offended, monsieur, if we continue in English? I ask because I must practise. If I am not mistaken, you are an allophone, n'est-ce pas?"

"Yes, that's correct. My first language was Italian, as you can imagine. Naturally, we can continue in English, madame. As you wish." Skip smiled inwardly; he loved this city, with its new-world setting and old-world manners.

Within the hour, all the papers were signed. Skip used his own money to open the accounts, including a market trading account. He also deposited Bill's generous cheque and initiated the necessary foreign linkages as well as creating the signing authorities.

The next task was to lasso an administrator whom he could trust. The phone rang just twice before it was picked up.

"Hallo."

"*Guten Tag.* May I please speak to Master Sergeant Franz-Josef König?"

"Ja, I am here speaking."

"Hello, old friend."

"*Herr Oberst! Hauptfeldwebel* König standing for attention, Colonel. For what can I be of assistance, mein Oberst? Do you need someone silenced, or maybe a small war started? I am in your debt, Herr Oberst, und I stand ready for receiving the orders."

Skip laughed out loud, and Franz-Josef joined him. Skip then continued, using Franz-Josef's German diminutive name.

"Jupp, I have formed a small company that will be conducting favours, shall we say, for special-needs friends. I require someone who understands administration and international banking. But this man must understand soldiers, and it would be best if he had been a soldier. Mostly, mein Freund,

I need someone whom I can trust completely — with my money and my secrets. Maybe you know someone who might be interested?"

"Herr Oberst, please do not say to me that you would consider forming such a company und not invite your most loyal *Soldat* to join you. It would hurt my tender Ost-Deutsch feelings, Herr Oberst. You know that we Germans are very sensitive peoples."

"Of course not, Jupp, and yes, I recall how sensitive you were when dealing with that British squaddie in Hamburg."

"But that fellow, he was a ruffian. He was not worthy for the wearing of the uniform of *Seine britische Majestät*. I was only doing the Britishers a favour."

"I'm not sure Her Britannic Majesty would have agreed that breaking his legs and giving him a cranial hemorrhage was a favour. And similarly, I'm not sure that my getting you released from the Sankt Pauli police lockup was a favour to Her Majesty. You were fortunate, my friend, that several Polizei Kommissars in Hamburg are friends of mine. The duty Kommissar that night owed me a favour."

"Herr Oberst, I have lost track. How many times did you get this old Ostie out of the prison? But excuse me — I have interrupted you, mein Oberst. Please to continue with the most interesting story you were telling me."

"Knock it off, Sergeant Major. German Hauptfeldwebels don't do sarcasm justice. Can I coax you out of retirement? Can you come to Montreal for a chat '*unter vier Augen*'?"

"This is how it is, ja? We must speak 'under the four eyes' only? *Na gut*, I will come tomorrow. Please tell me where are you hiding."

"I'm not hiding, I'm in downtown Montreal. There's an Air Canada flight from Halifax leaving tomorrow at 16:05. I will pick you up when you arrive and take you home to my place. We can drink and tell each other lies. You should plan to stay a couple of days. I'll make the ticket open-ended, and it'll be waiting for you at the Air Canada concierge counter in Halifax."

"Herr Oberst, I would not want to impose upon your hospitality. Perhaps there is a youth hostel where I could pitch my small *Zeltbahn*. I still have my Ranger blanket."

"Do not dare bring your army hoochie, and I don't want to contemplate what your old Ranger blanket looks like by now. Just get your ass to Montreal tomorrow. Don't miss the plane, Sergeant Major, or I'll be pissed at you."

"*Jawohl*, Herr Oberst."

Skip arrived early at Trudeau International in Dorval and caught sight of Jupp through the glass wall in Arrivals. Waiting at the Tim Hortons for his coffee, he introduced himself to the young Mountie and asked if he was up to helping him pull a little prank on an old army buddy. The gendarme paused for a second, but having served in the Vandoos for a stint, he agreed, even before asking what was involved. Hearing Skip's plan, he flashed a smile.

"Excellent, monsieur."

Jupp had barely come through the sliding glass doors when the RCMP corporal approached him.

"Excuse me, monsieur. You are Mr. Franz-Josef König?"

There was a flicker of panic across Franz-Josef's face.

"Am I back in Ost Berlin? Has the Stasi returned to interrogate me?"

"Relax, sir. There is no need to be insulting. Please answer my question. Are you Mr. König?"

"Yes, officer, but I am only a pensioner living at Halifax. I am coming here for to visit *ein Kamerad*."

"Sorry, Mr. König, but I have a bench warrant for your arrest. You will please come with me, sir."

Jupp was now staring, wide-eyed, and visibly beginning to perspire. Skip let him sweat for a few seconds, then appeared at the Mountie's elbow.

"Excuse me, officer. Is there a problem?"

The young Mountie was now playing his role with gusto. Gently restraining Skip, he said, "Sir, please step away. I am detaining this man on Her Majesty's business."

When Jupp heard that phrase, he spun to face Skip.

"You are a true bastard, Herr Oberst, if the colonel will excuse my language, sir."

The Mountie could no longer keep up the charade, and he stepped back, laughing, so the friends could shake hands. Jupp pulled Skip close and gave him a bear hug.

"*Merci beaucoup, Caporal*," Skip told the Mountie, stepping back from Jupp with a grin. "You are a good sport, and remember, if you are ever in Vieux-Montréal, stop in at Café Olimpico. Tell them to put your order on the tab of *il Colonnello*. Whatever you want, it's on me."

Still laughing, the Mountie waved good-bye as he headed over to talk to his confused-looking partner.

"Herr Oberst, you are an evil, evil man," Jupp said, shaking his head ruefully. "Why would you do such a thing? I was having backflashes to the last time you saved me. In Strasbourg, neh? Mein Gott, I was for certain to be going for the big jump on that day, I can promise you."

"The high jump, Jupp. The expression is 'going for the high jump.' And it's flashbacks, not backflashes."

"Ach, englisch. Who can understand it? You people park on a driveway, and you drive on a parkway. Gott in Himmel, it is completely crazy."

"Pick up your rucksack, old man," Skip told him. "We need to drive on a parkway." He scrutinized Jupp's hand luggage. "And maybe we'll stop at a luggage store on the way home. I can't believe you're still toting that ancient Volksarmee canvas bag."

"Herr Oberst, you wound me. This is the height from fashion in Halifax, especially for the young peoples."

The drive to Skip's condo was pleasant and unhurried, with light traffic. It was Saturday, and they had hit the sweet spot between those returning home from shopping and those going out to party in the city's famous pubs, restos, and brasseries. Jupp monopolized the conversation, earnestly telling Skip over and over again how good it was to see him, and how excited he was at the prospect of working for him. For his part, Skip was delighted to see his rascal of a friend once more. Recognizing the fact that Jupp was nervous, he let him prattle to ease his nerves.

Once in the condo, Skip opened the door to the guest suite. He told Jupp to stow his kit and come into the living room for a drink.

"You have a very fine place, Herr Oberst," Jupp said, emerging from the room a few minutes later. "What a view. Thank you again for inviting me."

"Jupp, my friend, you can relax. All is well, trust me." Skip motioned him to a chair and took the opposite one, setting two opened bottles of beer on the table between them. The two men clinked their bottles in a toast.

"Herr Oberst, I did not expect ever to hear from you again," Jupp said, wiping foam from his lips. "The last time in Strasbourg, I have crossed the line and I know I have done it. You should have left me. You know it, but you did not. One more time, you saved me, Herr Oberst. I have not deserved your help."

"Nonsense, Jupp. Don't say that. Of course, you deserved my help. Since that day in Berlin when you risked your life and your freedom to save me, you have been my friend — and you always will be."

Skip paused to take a drink and recall that day.

"Jupp, you knew that I was working for the German police and that helping me could get you killed, but you did it anyway."

"Herr Oberst, you exaggerate. Anyway, I am old, and I do not remember." Franz-Josef was looking into his beer bottle.

"Jupp, my father always maintained that family was luck, but that you choose your friends. When you decide to call someone a friend, then he is a friend for life, neh?"

"Your father was a good man, Herr Oberst."

Skip nodded thoughtfully and was silent for a moment. "It's time for me to explain why I brought you all the way to Lower Canada for a chat and explain why we needed to speak face to face. You'll understand shortly."

He told Franz-Josef everything, from his sudden retirement to the encounter in Rome to the visit to the Württemberg Landhaus in the Schwarzwald. He didn't keep anything back because Franz-Josef was going to control both the administration and the finances, and Skip was clear that he wanted no secrets between them. The briefing took less than thirty minutes.

"Old friend," Skip concluded, "I need all those financial skills, both legal and otherwise, that you learned while working for that syndicate of gangsters after the Wall came down."

"Those were dangerous days when I met you, Herr Oberst."

"Don't change the subject, old man."

Franz-Josef smiled. He had polished off two bottles of Warsteiner beer, which Skip had been sure to load up on.

"Nah ja," said Franz-Josef, slowly letting out a long-held breath. "It is most interesting."

"What do you think? Will you come aboard? Are you ready to step back into the game?"

"*Natürlich*," Franz-Josef almost shouted. "Herr Oberst, I must be honest with you. I hate retirement. Halifax is beautiful, but it is much too *zivilisiert* for an old Volksarmee dog like me. I would much like to join you, but how can I say it?"

Franz-Josef was stalling. Skip handed him a fresh bottle of beer and waited while his friend took a long pull on the fresh bottle.

"I have no monies to buy my share. I am ashamed, mein Oberst. In Halifax, I do a little bookkeeping for money to pay my rent. Once more, you come to save me. But … how can I buy a share with no monies?" Franz-Josef sat motionless, studying his feet and swirling the remaining few ounces of his beer. "Maybe I work for you on a salary? Is it possible?"

Skip gazed at his friend and thought carefully before he spoke. He didn't want to offend him. Broke or not, the old soldier had his pride.

"Mein Lieber Jupp, working for a salary is out of the question."

Franz-Josef was visibly crestfallen, but Skip quickly continued.

"You will come aboard as a full partner, Jupp. Basta."

"I told you already. I do not have one hundred thousand dollars. I do not even have enough for the rent next month," said Jupp, the emotion welling up in his throat.

"I have made my decision, Hauptfeldwebel. Surely, the Volksarmee did not teach you to question the direct orders of an Oberst? No, you will be a full partner. For now, you can live in the training camp, and I will cover your share. When we take our dividends for our missions, you will pay me back. And I will charge you interest, my friend. Of that you can be sure."

"Danke, Herr Oberst," whispered Jupp. "Danke."

The next day, Skip went into greater detail regarding banking, dividends, and how he was organizing all of the many details. He invited Franz-Josef to stay another night so they could continue discussing the set-up in an unhurried way. He also managed to gently convince Jupp that Pangratti would take care of his Halifax rent.

"Consider it a signing bonus, my friend," said Skip.

The drive back to Dorval the following day was silent. Franz-Josef was unusually subdued, lost in thought. Skip didn't intrude. Pulling over to the curb at Departures, he opted to drop Franz-Josef off instead of going inside with him.

"Close out your life in Halifax, Jupp, and be as quick as you can, please. I need you here. Call me when you're ready to move and we'll work out the details. Have a safe trip, *mein Alter*."

Jupp stared at Skip.

"Herr Oberst, I do not know what to say to you."

"Say 'thanks,' then get the hell out of my car. Move it, or you'll miss your flight."

Franz-Josef got out and turned to look back to Skip.

"Danke, Herr Oberst."

"All good, Sergeant Major."

Pulling away from the curb, Skip felt like he had finally put all the foundation stones in place. Almost all. Structure, mission, offices, finance, and admin were now all set. What he needed now was to recruit some door kickers. First, however, he had an extremely important call to make. The success of that call would determine whether he could carry on with creating his dream team, or if he needed to come up with an alternate plan, a thought that unsettled him.

After supper, Skip eased onto his sofa with a glass of scotch and dialled his friend, but it went directly to voicemail.

"You have reached Colonel Harry Monahan. I am temporarily absent on a board of inquiry. Please leave a message."

Colonel Monahan? The bugger's been promoted. Skip was pleased for Harry, but wondered if the promotion would affect his plan. He wondered where the board was being held. He'd call Jason Wilmot in the morning. In any case, he'd leave a message.

"Hello, Colonel. I am calling from Hussar Escort Services. We are seeking an older gentleman to help us manage our ladies, a sort of avuncular attendant. He might occasionally need to, ahem, *entertain* ladies of a certain age. I have been informed you may be interested. Please call this number at your earliest convenience."

The next day, Skip sat at his desk and reviewed what he had accomplished thus far. When he was in uniform, he'd kept a notebook where he jotted ideas. In those days, it was a hard-back lined book from the unit orderly room. These days, it was a ridiculously expensive hand-crafted, leather-bound *taccuino* he had splurged on at a high-end stationery shop. The Italian leather was like butter, and the hand-pressed paper had a texture that begged for a fountain pen, like the gold Mont Blanc his father had gifted him. Reviewing his notes, he was pleased with how much he had managed to accomplish. He'd seen to offices and banking and had purchased the land needed for a base camp north of Montreal. A team from Eagle was already at work there, which was one reason why Jupp was needed fast. But he still had a few critical tasks.

There was no call from Jason all morning, so Skip dressed and went out for lunch. Over dessert, he perused his notes once more, and checked off a couple more tasks. He felt like he was making progress. Skip rose from the table, left a sufficient stack of bills to pay for his meal, and wandered up the street to his condo. On the way, he felt his phone buzzing.

"Oui, hallo."

"Skip? It's Jason, returning your call.'

"Thanks, mate. How've you been?"

"Better still, how've *you* been?" asked Jason. "There's a pile of folks still pissed at you, buddy. I dare say, if you were to show up downstairs at the security desk, they'd call the MPs."

"Very funny. I'm well, Jason. Thanks."

"You didn't hear about Harry? He was promoted right after getting back from the Gulf. The new Vice Chief tasked him with cleaning up that mess in Trenton with all those pilots who pissed in the pickles."

"No idea what you're talking about, and I don't really care, to be honest. Has Harry got a number in Trenton? That Luddite still refuses to turn on his cell phone."

"Call the base commander. Harry said he's a friend of yours."

"The commander in Trenton? I don't think so."

"Flash Gordon? I thought you mentored the kid."

"Flash is a colonel commanding the largest Wing in the RCAF? Did the world go to hell in the months I've been away?"

"Skip, the world kept turning after you left, buddy. Life goes on. Let me give you the Base Commander's private line. His secretary will track him down for you."

Skip wrote the number on the palm of his hand.

"Thanks, Jason. I appreciate it."

"No worries. So, what are you doing these days? I heard you went to Rome."

"I did, but I got homesick. Now I'm living in Montreal. There's nothing exciting happening, although I'm thinking of getting my broker's licence. We'll see."

"What? Now I'm the one who's surprised. A broker? You?" He gave a dry laugh. "Ha, ha. Take care, buddy." Jason ended the call.

Curiouser and curiouser, thought Skip as he resumed his walk home. Stepping through the door to his condo, he was struck by the mood of his place. Brilliant sunshine poured through the balcony door, lighting up the living space, but it felt somehow cold and sterile. It was much too silent.

RCAF Base Trenton

His desk phone intercom buzzed, and Wing Commander Fred "Flash" Gordon yelled to his secretary in the outer office, "Goddammit, what now, Margaret?"

"Sorry, sir. There's a call for you on your private line. I figured you would want to take this one. It's Colonel Schiaparelli for you. Will you call back?"

"No, no. I'm sorry I snapped at you, Margaret, and I apologize. It's not your fault. Please put the colonel through. Close the door and hold all calls, please, even if it's the division commander. Make up something."

Flash waited a couple of seconds to regain his composure, then picked up.

"Colonel. How are you, sir?"

"Flash, I thought you had to be old enough to vote to be a colonel in the Royal Canadian Air Force. Congrats, my friend, and what's with the colonel crap? Do all you RCAF colonels all call each other colonel? Doesn't it get confusing?"

"Thanks, Skip. Years of habit, I guess. I still don't feel like a 'bird' colonel, even though the air force was crazy enough to hand me promotion *and* command. Honestly, it came from nowhere. When my predecessor got fired, I guess the Chief of the Air Staff got desperate. It was quite a little wreck I got handed, I can tell you. Thank God, your buddy Harry cut through most of the red tape and the bureaucratic chaos. He's nearly finished his board, I hear. He's a solid guy — I like him. You must've trained him because he whipped his board members like rented mules. And he has stories about you I'd never heard."

"Don't believe any of it. The man's a congenital liar," said Skip.

"I'm glad he's here to sort out this mess. God knows, I have enough to deal with already with the loss of my Wing Chief."

"My condolences, Flash. I heard about him being killed in a car accident."

"Actually, the chief's alive, if only barely. The accident happened up on Highway 41. You know how dangerous that road can be. He and his best friend, a warrant officer with 429 Squadron, and their wives, were driving a Winnebago to a fishing cabin. The warrant and the ladies were sitting up front, and the three of them bought it instantly. The chief was in the back having coffee. He broke an arm, six ribs, and his collarbone, and he ruptured his spleen. He's also got a severe concussion."

"Good Lord," said Skip. "He's lucky to be alive."

"Some civilian called 911. The provincial police recognized the chief and called SAR. The boys from his old squadron at 424 Search and Rescue were so fast off the mark that they landed a bird before the locals could even get an ambulance on site. He was technically dead when the SAR techs found him, but they refused to let their old chief die. They revived him twice and air-evac'd him."

"They obviously loved the guy," said Skip.

"He's here in Belleville General, in ICU. The doctors have had him in a chemical coma, and when they wake him up, I have to tell him that his wife and best friend are both gone, not to mention that his career is over."

Skip could hear the younger man's voice getting thick with emotion.

"I've spent the last twenty-four hours trying to figure out how I'm going to tell him," murmured Flash, his voice drifting off.

"I'm sorry," said Skip. "My only advice, my friend, is to soften the blow any way you can, even if you have to shade the facts a little. There'll be time enough for the cold truth later. I assume the others died quickly?"

"A fully loaded gravel truck reverse T-boned them. The cops figure their combined collision speed was north of one hundred and fifty kilometres an hour. It was lights out on impact, and there's nothing left of the Winnebago. It's a miracle the chief survived." Flash was quiet for a moment, and then collected himself. "What can I do for you, Skip?"

"Flash, I've got an appointment with a realtor up north of Marmora tomorrow morning. Can I drop in on you after lunch, assuming army officers are still welcome after Harry's tenure?"

"Not normally, Skip, but I'll always make an exception for you. But Marmora? Why are you going there? There's nothing up there other than rock, scrub, and white pine."

"Precisely why I like it, my friend. Don't tell Harry I'm coming. I want to surprise him."

"You should be aware, I've re-instituted a guard at the main gate for the next while, but I'll clear the flight deck for you. I'll warn the base MPs to keep an eye out for some guy who looks like a mafia don from Montreal driving a car he can't afford."

"Thanks, Flash."

Skip put down the handset and whispered aloud to himself, "Poor bastard would have been better off buying the farm with his friend and the wives."

Like the condo purchase, buying the acreage north of Marmora was a quick and easy decision. Although he already had a base camp being built north of Montreal, near Lac Larin, it bothered Skip that he had no alternate. There was still plenty of Bill's startup cash, and the scrub land he needed was cheap. The young realtor was confused that he would make such a large purchase without taking more than a rather cursory look from the dirt road and spending some time looking at maps, but the land had been sitting there unsold for several years and she wanted the commission.

"I hope you enjoy your acreage," said the realtor as she showed him out.

"I'm sure I will," said Skip.

He bought it with no conditions using a cheque from Pangratti, then he grabbed lunch in the village of Stirling on his way south, opting to stay on the county roads and avoid the highway. He stopped at the security shack inside the ornate black wrought-iron gates at the entrance to 8 Wing RCAF and lowered the car window.

"Hello, Corporal, I'm here to see the Wing Commander."

The RCAF military police corporal came out of his guardhouse and saluted. That was new, thought Skip. Normally the MPs were not known for their military courtesy.

"Sir, are you Colonel Scarparetti?"

"Yes, that's me," said Skip, ignoring the mangling of his family's ancient name.

"Sir, please follow this road around to the front of the Wing HQ building, sir. There is a spot marked 'Wing Commander's Guest.' Park there, sir, and I will phone ahead. You will be met at the door, sir."

Skip knew the way. Nonetheless, he sat stone-faced and let the MP corporal do his duty. Flash had obviously put the fear of God into the base staff. He couldn't remember the last time he had been called "sir" four times in one day on an RCAF base, let alone in one breath.

"Thank you, Corporal."

He laughed to himself and headed for the HQ. Standing next to the allocated parking spot was a young captain. There were no wings on his chest, which struck Skip as odd. Skip figured Flash would have yanked some young pilot to be his PA so that they could go flying together.

"Good afternoon, Colonel."

The youngster saluting him looked fourteen years old.

"Good afternoon, Captain. May I safely assume that you are Colonel Gordon's PA?"

"Yes, sir. I will take you to him, sir."

"You're not a flyer," said Skip, making it a statement rather than a question.

"No, sir. I'm an AERE officer. Air maintenance, sir."

"Is that an RMC ring I see on your right hand?"

The captain nodded.

"College number?"

The captain cringed slightly at the colonel asking him for the last two digits of his RMC college number. A match could be expensive in terms of beer, especially with someone as ancient as this colonel.

"My last two are 'eight four,' sir," said the captain, bracing for the expected blow.

"Pity," said Skip, "mine are 'eight three.' You're home and safe. Isn't the Wing Commander 'eight one'?"

"No, sir. His last two are 'eight five.' I made the bracket."

The kid was relaxing, and there were the makings of a smile on his face.

"Please come this way, Colonel."

When they reached Flash's office, his secretary offered him coffee and asked Skip to please go in and wait. The commander had been called down to Wing Ops because somebody was having a helmet fire.

"Would you like me to stay with you, sir?"

"Sure," said Skip. "Grab a pew."

"The Wing Commander says he's known you for forever. I'm confused. How does a Herc pilot know an armour officer his whole career?"

"I met Officer Cadet Alfredo Gordon when he was a Rook at the college. I was working on a master's, and I found him in the stacks of the Massey Library, looking for someplace to be alone after he'd got dumped by his high school sweetheart. I told him that she wasn't worth spending his angst on. The world was a big place, I said, filled with attractive women who wanted to meet dashing young men from Her Majesty's Canadian Armed Forces. For the rest of that year, I kept bumping into him, and after I left, he used to write to me to tell me how he was."

When the Wing Commander arrived, the PA jumped to his feet and slipped out. Skip and Flash greeted each other with a hug. Not long after that meeting in Massey, and once Skip had learned that Flash was a closet Italian, they had begun hugging each other whenever they met. Few people knew that Fred's maternal grandfather, his *nonno*, Alfredo Marchetti, had been an Italian immigrant. Even at the anal-retentive WASP military college, the two men had shrugged off the odd looks.

"Skip, you look like hell. What's up, buddy? You've got to take better care of yourself."

"Funny," said Skip, "I was about to say that to you. I see your PA has no wings. What's with that?"

"Pilots already run the RCAF. Young flyers don't need a boost to their careers. That kid is probably the brightest captain on the base."

Flash handed his mentor a fresh coffee in a mug with the 8 Wing crest on it.

"Still black, no sugar?"

"Yup, combat coffee, although you could have put it in a proper mug."

Over a couple more mugs, the two friends caught up on what they had been doing since they'd last met. Once the small talk was complete, Flash silently beheld his friend across the table.

"You're making me nervous," said Skip. "What's up? Are you finally coming out of the closet? It's okay now, you know. Was it my manly hugs?"

Flash realized that he had been staring at Skip.

"Hilarious. Can we talk about my Wing Chief for a minute?"

"Of course."

"I heard you just walked away last November and went to Italy. Then I heard some rumour about something going on in Montreal. It's none of my business what you do now, though I have my suspicions."

Flash gave Skip a penetrating look but got no reaction.

"My Wing Chief needs some reason to get out of bed and keep breathing," Flash went on. "He and his wife never had any kids. Now he's left with quite literally no reason to go on. He's a good man, and he's my friend. Whatever it is that you are setting up, I was wondering if you could use an experienced airman like Jules."

Skip smiled warmly.

"Done," he said.

"Don't you want to know what skills he has or what his file looks like?"

"Nope, there's no need. He's your friend and you think he's worthy, that's good enough for me, assuming I can talk him into joining me."

Skip had a small sip of coffee. "Where are you hiding my buddy Harry?"

"His board of inquiry is installed in the conference centre next door. You can't miss it."

Skip walked in and asked the clerk where Colonel Monahan was. The corporal said she'd go and find him.

"Whom should I say is waiting?"

"Skip."

"Skip?"

"That's right, Corporal. Skip."

Harry came rushing out of the work area.

"Arrest this man," he shouted.

The corporal looked momentarily panicked, until the two men shook hands heartily.

"Skip. It's great to see you, buddy. What are you doing here?"

"I'm headhunting for the Hussar Escort Service."

"Is the job of avuncular minder still open? I wasn't sure what avuncular meant, so I googled it."

"Asshole. You never called me back."

The corporal donned her wedge cap and made herself scarce.

"Sorry, Skip. This board has had me putting in eighteen-hour days for weeks. Thank goodness, we're finally done. I'm proofreading the final report over the next couple of days, then I'll hand-deliver it to the Vice Chief and will no doubt be rewarded with a cubicle on the dreaded twelfth floor. Hell, I might even get your old job. Lord knows I've annoyed enough people."

"Sorry — I forgot to congratulate you getting your red tabs. Maybe now you'll stop calling me Colonel."

"Yes, Colonel … maybe."

"Very funny. Can I buy you dinner? Someone said there's a reasonable pub downtown. I think it's called The Furry Fox."

"You mean the Fox and Firkin, and I know it well. It's been my refuge away from the mess here these past weeks. It's a cozy place and the bartender is a young British ex-Para and a bright lad. What if I meet you there at 19:00?"

"See you then."

Skip checked into a local hotel and then made his way over to the pub. He was early, so he took a stool at the bar. The bartender came over.

"Good evening, sir. What'll it be?"

The working-class British accent was unmistakable, though already beginning to fade. What wasn't fading was the tattoo above his wrist.

"What's your bar scotch?"

"We've got a selection. If you're just in the mood for a wee tipple, I would recommend the Famous Grouse. It's the same price as the Johnny Walker Red but smoother for my coin."

"Done, and make it a double, please."

"Ice? Water?"

"Ice, please. Two cubes. No water."

The bartender put the drink in front of Skip and was about to walk away.

"When were you in the Paras?" asked Skip.

The bartender paused.

"Since my seventeenth birthday. I left last year to come over here. My name's Les, by the way."

"I'm Skip. Didn't like it?"

"Pleased to meet you, Skip. The Paras? I absolutely loved it, and I was pretty good at it, too, if I say so myself. It were affairs of the heart what brought me here. What can I say?"

The two men shook hands.

"Are you in the military?"

"Ex. I was a tank driver. So, you came here for a local girl?"

"Aye, she's a schoolteacher here in Belleville. Even my mum loves her and that's saying something, since she hated all of my girlfriends."

Les paused.

"Any road, I've no regrets. None at all."

"The Paras," said Skip, and lifted his glass.

"Cheers," said Les.

Harry was standing behind Skip.

"Hi ho, Colonel," said Les. "The usual, sir?"

"Yes, please, Les. I see you've met Colonel Schiaparelli."

Les froze.

"*Colonel* Schiaparelli? Begging your pardon, sir."

He was looking at Skip and reddening.

"Les and I were having a nice chat till you showed up," grumbled Skip, looking at Harry. "Les, there's no need to apologize. I introduced myself as Skip and Skip it is."

"Yes, sir. I'll be getting Colonel Harry his drink."

"Spoiler," said Skip. "C'mon, let's grab a booth."

The two men moved away from the bar.

"You almost gave the kid a stroke, Harry."

They sat opposite each other.

"Why do you always insist on wandering around in a regimental tie and blue blazer? Haven't you ever heard of relaxed dress?"

"This *is* relaxed dress in my regiment, especially for colonels. I know you Hussars are allowed to wear blue jeans nowadays, but really, no regimental tie? You might as well wander around buck naked."

Les materialized with Harry's drink. The bartender looked like he was about to bolt, but Harry touched his arm.

"Les, please bring us two rib eyes, medium, potatoes, mushrooms, and onions. My usual."

"Aye, Colonel. Some wine?"

"No. Another round of these, please, and put it all on my tab for me."

"Right you are."

Over supper, Skip finally explained what he'd been working on so diligently for the past months. As he had done with Franz-Josef, he took Harry through the 'stations of the cross,' from the meetings in Rome to the discussions in the Schwarzwald, as Harry sat in silence. Without going into details, he kept nothing back. It was important that there be no secrets between them, and Skip told him so.

"Harry, do you remember that German sergeant major I told you about? The guy I met after the Wall came down?"

"That guy was one crazy hard-assed bastard, if I remember some of your stories."

"I just hired him to be my administrator and banker."

Harry looked surprised.

"Really? That scrapper is a banker?"

"I'll tell you more later, but more important than his hidden skills, he's as loyal as a Dobermann."

"Great," said Harry.

"Now the hard part," said Skip."

"Hard part?" repeated Harry, frowning.

"Most military deputies draw their authority from the commander. They're 'the colonel's men.' That's not you, Harry. You're your own man and you carry authority in your own right, which is exactly what I want."

Harry stared at Skip, nonplussed.

"So? Would you be willing to come aboard? Come be my 2IC?"

"Finally," said Harry. "Talk about going the long way 'round the barn. I was beginning to worry that you were never going to ask me to join you. Yes, Skip, absolutely."

"Thank you, Harry. I know you have another fifteen years you could serve."

"There's no way I'd last that long."

Skip extended his hand across the detritus of the steak dinner.

"I'm the one who should be thanking you," said Harry. "With my only kid living in Oz and me facing the prospect of a staff job, I've been trying hard to put a brave face on it, but to be honest, the only thing that's kept me sane these past six weeks was having been shanghaied to crucify some idiot fighter jocks. I've been dreading becoming a staff officer, being trapped in an office. Now I won't have to."

"You would have been fine," said Skip.

"Are you serious? I would have punched out some smarmy general, and without you there to protect me, I'd have been court-martialed. No thanks. I'm thrilled to come work for you, Skip."

"Thanks, Harry, but you're exaggerating."

Harry shook his head from side to side.

"After I hand in my report, I'll visit the Admin Unit and submit an immediate release request. I'll beg the Vice to waive the thirty days."

"No office for you, my friend," said Skip.

"Thank you, God."

Les rang the bell at the bar. "Last call, gentlemen."

Harry raised his hand to wave him over.

"One more round, please, Les. We have something to celebrate."

"On the way, Colonel."

"I like that kid," said Harry. "Do we need door kickers?"

"I like him too, and yes, we certainly do."

"Last question," said Harry. "Do I need to move to Montreal to do this?"

"Not necessarily, but it would certainly make things easier for both of us. Before I forget, is Mary better? Flash mentioned that she wasn't well."

Mary was Harry's only child from his first marriage.

"She called yesterday, and yes, thanks for asking. They figured it out finally. She's home on antibiotics. No worries, she said."

"Excellent," said Skip. "Back to the matter at hand. The housing market in Ottawa is hot. Montreal is still affordable, especially if you buy a condo. Moving there'll put cash in your blue blazer pocket, my friend."

Skip continued and went into more detail on Bill Donovan's motives and his expectations, as well as what he'd offered. Skip explained what he'd already put in place, including the purchase of property north of Montreal and another tract north of where they were sitting.

The ensuing discussions stretched right to closing time, when Les firmly but respectfully threw the two colonels out.

MONTREAL

The next morning, Skip checked out early and drove home to Montreal. Once there, he sat at his table and reviewed his progress over a late breakfast of bacon and eggs. The eggs and thinking of Harry triggered the memory of attending his friend's agonizing change of command ceremony the year previous. My God, thought Skip, what a show that had been — and what a near catastrophe.

Skip had attended the event to ensure Harry wouldn't have a complete breakdown, and he remembered the day with mixed feelings. Harry had been a popular commander, and the Royals had pulled out all the stops for their departing CO. Skip had never seen a battalion CoC with so many general officers in attendance. It was a deep tribute to his friend, and the Wolseley Barracks officers' mess had been filled to bursting. Even so, with Mary unable to attend, Skip was Harry's only personally invited guest. He recalled how deeply moved Harry had been by the occasion, but also how irreconcilably sad.

He and Skip were having a drink after dinner at the bar.

"Honestly, Colonel Skip, this blows."

Harry had already had too many drinks, and he was slurring his words, but it was his night and Skip wasn't about to chastise him.

"All I ever wanted was to command a battalion. I loved this life, every minute of it. What the hell am I supposed to do now?"

Skip worried that Harry's emotions would escape his control, and that he'd say something inappropriate in front of the younger regimental officers. Harry took another slurp of scotch and launched again with renewed vigour.

"I'm never going out on a patrol again, or jumping out of a Herc, or commanding troops on a mission. Skip, I can't exactly explain it, but it wounds me, buddy. I'm still fit. I can still run in the middle of the pack with the young bucks. Hell, I can even shame a few of them by challenging them to pull-ups."

Harry had accepted his gifts and told everyone he was happy to finally be rid of them, and then proceeded to drink till he neared unconsciousness.

"You have a lot of generals pulling for you, buddy," said Skip. "How are you going to command the army if you don't give up your battalion?"

"Who would want to command the army?" said a very drunken Harry.

Harry was getting louder, and several of the generals were looking over at the two of them.

"Nope, not me, Skip. Maybe I could join the French Foreign Legion."

That was it. Skip took away Harry's drink.

The regimental adjutant had been prepared, and two burly young lieutenants were standing by to get their elder regimental brother and ex-commander safely to his quarters. Skip quietly intervened and explained that he'd see to Harry.

"I've got him," said Skip. "You gentlemen may stand down."

The lieutenants looked over to the adjutant for his blessing; the adjutant nodded his approval. Reluctantly, they handed over their charge to the unknown armoured corps colonel. Skip tucked his shoulder under Harry's arm and walk-dragged him out of the officers' mess.

"No, thank you," said Harry. "I don't want to dance."

"Keep your voice down."

Skip felt bad for his friend. Harry had spent his career avoiding the staff at National Defence HQ, but, like Skip, that was where he was headed: a warrior destined to be trapped in an office tower. Skip knew it was not what Harry had envisioned. There were to be no Elysian Fields, no Valhalla.

The next morning, a deeply hungover Harry came out of the shower to find Skip cooking bacon and eggs.

"You look fetching in that apron, but you need to shave," said Harry.

"Shut up and sit your ass down. There's greasy bacon and runny eggs for breakfast. It'll either cure you or have you puking all over the table. I learned

that the hard way during a tour with the Queen's Royal Irish Hussars in Paderborn. God, I have never seen soldiers drink so much. It was a wonder they could function as well as they did, but they did. They were fine soldiers."

Harry did as he was told, and luckily, the cure seemed to be working.

"This is delicious," said Harry. "Who did you sneak in here this morning to cook it?"

"I am sorry to tell you this, my friend, but you are much more charming when drunk. Now drink your coffee and finish your meal. It may not sober you up, but at least you'll be awake, and I can leave knowing that your heart is still beating. Be sure to come see me when you're on in-routine in the headquarters."

"Aye, aye, Skipper," Harry said, and took another bite of toast.

Skip shook off the memory. Everything was falling into place. It had been a huge relief when Harry agreed so quickly to come aboard. He hadn't admitted to his friend that there had been no backup plan should Harry have said no. Sod had already been broken by an Eagle construction crew at the Lac Larin property. Franz-Josef was on track to step across. The incorporation was complete, and he had a growing list of prospects to recruit. But all that could wait. He needed Harry in Montreal, and the sooner the better.

Skip spent the next few days inspecting the work in the new offices and reviewing his plans. His most pressing need was to find the right kind of computer geek. Like Franz-Josef, he needed to be technically competent and trustworthy, and able to understand soldiers. It seemed like a stretch, and Skip phoned his old RSM, Doug, to see if he had any ideas.

After cleaning up the breakfast dishes, he perused his notes and checked off a couple more tasks. His cell phone buzzed. An unrecognized number came up on the display.

"Oui, hallo."

"May I please speak to Colonel Amadeus Scarpetti?"

The voice was oddly familiar.

"If you are looking for Amadeo Schiaparelli, that's me. May I help you?"

"Are you not Amadeus Scarpetti, 'lover of God' in small shoes?"

Skip now knew exactly who the mystery caller was. Scarpetti was the Italian diminutive for 'shoes.'

"Well, you know what they say: small shoes, big dick."

"That's not what they say."

"Harry, what the hell are you doing? Did you steal somebody's phone to make this call? Let me guess: you rolled a nun for it. You still haven't recovered from having your hands strapped at parochial school by those Irish penguins, have you?"

"Hey, show a little respect. It's a sacrilege to insult the brides of Christ."

"Where are you? Tell me so that I can come there and kick your ass."

"That'll be a cold day in hell. I just got off the train at the Gare Centrale. If you were a gentleman, you'd invite me for lunch."

"If I were a gentleman … Never mind. Harry, get your ass over here. We have things to do. Can you stay, or do you need to get back to the Vice Chief?"

"As they so inappropriately say in the admin world, I am on 'terminal' leave. The Vice was impressed with my report, and he agreed to expedite my request. Luckily, the Vice is an admiral, and they're easy to impress."

"Tell the doorman you're Antoine the male escort. He'll let you right up."

Twenty minutes later there was a distinctive knock on the door. When Skip opened it, Harry was standing there with a smirk on his face and a six-pack of Pabst Blue Ribbon.

"Hello, sir. I'm Antoine."

"Get your ass inside before my neighbours wonder what kind of company I keep." He narrowed his eyes. "Again, with the blue blazer?"

"Don't start," said Harry.

Over sandwiches and beer, Skip brought Harry up to speed. After he'd called, Skip had immediately called the bank and warned Lagasse that she would need to amend the paperwork to make Harry a signing authority.

"She has a free couple of hours this afternoon. Pass the mustard, please."

"She?"

"Our banker at Banque Laurentienne."

Harry took a bite of the smoked meat.

"Our banker is a woman?"

"You have a problem?"

"No, no, of course not," said Harry.

"Just one thing," lied Skip. "She's a unilingual francophone, but I'm sure it'll be fine."

Harry took another bite and stared at Skip.

Coming through the doors of Laurentienne, Harry leaned his head toward Skip.

"I'm not sure my Lower Canada College French will get me through this."

Harry had meant to whisper, but heads were turning. Obviously, he'd failed.

"No sweat, Harry. I'll translate."

Madame Lagasse greeted them warmly by in the bank's lobby. "Bonjour, messieurs." She turned to Harry and introduced herself. "Marie-Claire. Bienvenu."

The two men followed her to the glass-walled office.

"Gentlemen, please make yourselves comfortable," she said. "May I offer you something to drink? Mineral water or coffee, perhaps?"

Harry stared daggers at Skip.

"Harry," said Skip, "she would like to know if we want something to drink."

Harry kept up the death stare but said nothing.

"Madame, you will have to forgive my friend. He is a bit slow. He was in a parachute accident, and I promised his mother I would look after him."

Madame Lagasse was momentarily confused. Clearly, there was an inside joke here, but she wasn't certain what it was. Harry turned and smiled at Madame Lagasse, then he took a moment to adjust his regimental tie.

"Please forgive us, madame. My associate led me to believe we would be speaking only French because you did not speak English. I assure you I shall deal with him later. Coffee would be lovely, merci, madame. Black, no sugar."

Harry was quickly regaining his poise, but Skip could restrain himself no longer. He was chuckling softly and cleared his throat.

"*Je m'excuse*, madame. I'll take mine the same way, please."

Lagasse was now smiling broadly. She understood what was going on and thought it was cute that two middle-aged men would behave like schoolboys. She was charmed, in fact. She called to her assistant, raising her voice only slightly.

"Madeleine, trois cafés noirs, pas de sucre. Merci."

She paused and looked at the men.

"Shall we begin? I have all the files for Monsieur Monahan prepared. All I need is a signature in each place where I have put the stickies. Stickies — is this the correct word? I believe so."

Harry pulled his pen from an inside pocket of his blazer and began signing.

Without looking up he said, "Madame, my associate is fortunate that this pen was a gift from my father when I was commissioned. Otherwise, I would have stabbed him in the heart with it. It would have made a mess of your lovely desk."

He ended with a flourish, spun the document around, and pushed it across to the banker.

"I assume you gentlemen are ex-military?"

Harry and Skip looked at each other.

"Pardon me," she said. "It seems to me black coffee and black humour are common among military people."

The coffee arrived. Madeleine served the men and left.

"Were you in the same regiment?" asked Lagasse.

Skip had a mouth full of coffee, and Harry beat him to the punch.

"No, madame. Thank goodness. My regiment has very high standards. Amadeo here didn't make the grade. As with Winston Churchill, Amadeo's father could only bribe the cavalry into allowing him to be commissioned into a Hussar regiment. I am sure you know, madame, that Hussars accept anybody who applies. Right, Amadeo?"

Lagasse was giggling openly by now, and Skip was choking on his coffee.

"Pardon me, madame," Skip rasped when he could speak again. "I was having a little difficulty swallowing. Indeed, I was — I am — a proud Hussar."

Once all the papers were signed, Skip and Harry stood and reached across the desk to shake hands with their banker.

"Merci, madame," said Harry, and Skip added his thanks.

"Mon plaisir, messieurs."

Back on the street, Harry grabbed the back of Skip's neck and gave it a hard squeeze, causing his friend to stop.

"Thanks for making me look like an idiot. She certainly wasn't what I was expecting when you said we were going to see our banker. She's a very handsome woman. Did you notice her eyes?"

"Her eyes? Give me a break. Yes, I did notice her eyes, among other attributes. In any case, stop thinking lascivious thoughts about our banker. Remember our conversation about alimony?"

The two men resumed their walk.

"Skip, you told me about Franz-Josef, but who's going to set up all the computers and phones you've ordered?"

"It's already sorted," said Skip. "I found a guy who lives down in St-Jean-sur-Richelieu. He's an ex-RSM of the Sigs Regiment and did time with the Sig Int crowd. They call him Breaker, and you'll see why when you meet him. We had a long lunch the other day."

"Do you do all your wheeling and dealing over food? Is this a mafia thing? Should I be worried?"

"Exactly," said Skip. "It only took twenty-six years for you to notice, and yes, you should worry."

Their latest addition was Chief Warrant Officer Keith Wilson. The name hadn't meant anything to Skip until his nickname came up: Breaker. Skip had a vague memory of why. Most people assumed Wilson was nicknamed "Breaker" because he was a signaller, but they were wrong. Growing up half-Black in Nova Scotia hadn't been any picnic, and Keith had learned early to use his fists.

"Are you free for lunch? Tomorrow, maybe?"

"When and where, Colonel?"

"Schwartz's Deli, on The Main, at noon."

"See you tomorrow, sir."

Breaker arrived early, and Skip, who was across the street watching, took note. The big man had "army" written all over him, even wearing jeans and a rugby shirt. At five minutes to the hour, Skip crossed the street and introduced himself.

"Let's grab a booth," he said.

Inside, they exchanged pleasantries for a few minutes.

When Skip was a young second lieutenant, Breaker had been a corporal in the Hussars' Regimental Sigs Troop. Skip's prodigious memory finally put the pieces together, and he asked if Breaker was the same guy who'd been hauled in front of the CO for beating the living daylights out of the Airborne Regiment's hockey goalie.

"Yes, sir, that was me."

"I was at that game. I thought you were going to kill him."

"The prick deserved it," said Breaker. He took a sip of water. "Colonel, I'll be honest. I don't remember you from the Hussars, but I know you by your reputation as a commander. Your RSM and I go way back. Doug and me played on the same line on the hockey team. Based on what he told me about you and your leadership style, I'm ready to sign on the dotted line, sir. I'm ready to commit if you'll have me."

"I haven't told you the deal yet."

"That don't matter. Not after what Doug said."

"What did the RSM say?"

"That don't matter either," said Breaker.

Skip smiled and sipped his coffee.

"I need you to be our comms specialist as well as run the downtown office. I'd like you to buy in as a junior partner. If money is tight, I can front you the buy-in."

"Money won't be an issue, Colonel. Giselle has always taken care of the family finances. We don't have a mortgage, and we even have a few pennies set aside for a rainy day. I think I feel a few drops."

Back in Skip's apartment, he and Harry sat with more coffee. There were still lots of preparations to be made, and no time like the present to begin. Several condos were for sale in the building. Skip found the building manager's card and gave it to Harry. Harry called the realtor he had used to buy his place in Ottawa and told him he wanted to sell immediately. Delighted, the broker said he would begin preparing. Harry then called a mover and made the initial arrangements. Things were progressing quickly.

"I guess I'll need to rent a place near here in the meantime," said Harry, putting down his phone.

"You wound me," mumbled Skip.

"Pardon?"

"I assumed you'd be moving in here with me while your furniture and effects made their way to Montreal. If that doesn't suit you, there's always the guest suite in the office. It's spartan but livable."

"I didn't want to impose. If you don't mind having me underfoot…"

"It's settled, then. You return to Ottawa, pack a couple of suitcases, and get back here. We'll figure out what to do with your F & E later, and don't forget your forage cap."

"Very funny. Thanks, Skip."

"Listen. I have a couple of leads on whom we need to recruit. What are your thoughts? I suggest we keep it small, no more than two dozen, including non-operators. As for door kickers, I'm not sure. I was thinking fifteen, maybe sixteen, max."

"That sounds about right," said Harry. "Skip, you know Alex is out, right?"

"Your buddy from the Airborne? That Alex?"

"That's him. He's married again and living with his new wife on Gabriola Island across from Vancouver. He'd really be worth having. Alex was one of the finest soldiers I ever served with, and he did an exchange with US Special Forces, too."

"Excellent idea, Harry. Do you think he'll come east?"

"Let me talk to him."

"If you want him, feel free to make him an offer as a junior partner. The key from my perspective will be not so much to have a wide range of skills, though that would be useful. The most important thing is to have men whom we trust completely, men who will commit to our shared ethos."

"Absolutely right," said Harry, "and that describes Alex."

Skip was in the office with Breaker when Harry came through the door.

"Morning, Harry. This is Breaker."

Harry and Breaker shook hands.

"Why don't you go to the lounge and get to know one another while I make a few calls?"

When Skip walked into the lounge a while later, he found them comparing notes on guys they'd served with in the Airborne Regiment, both good and bad. Breaker and Harry were never in the same commando at the same time, but they'd served together. They were getting along famously, and Skip's anxiety about hiring a relative unknown dropped several notches. He got their attention.

"I just got off the phone with Bill Donovan. He told me when we get our network up and running, he'll send the URL of a website where we'll need to download some software. Bill says it'll allow us to have secure comms with him anywhere, anytime. It's an encrypted VPN, whatever that is. He didn't want to give me the details until you get the hard-wired phones set up."

"Virtual private network, Colonel. It's exactly what we need. Did you get a password?"

"The password is HUTSCHENREUTHER, all caps," said Skip, spelling it out one letter at a time. "Don't ask why. Everything you need to do your magic is over in that room. That'll be our server room and comms closet. Anything you need, just shout. Harry, you and I need to chat about door kickers." He looked at Breaker and back to Harry. "So, you two were in the Airborne together. This is all getting a wee bit incestuous."

Breaker headed for the server room, and Harry followed Skip into his new office. Harry began speaking as he was closing the door.

"I think Breaker will work out great. I didn't say anything to you, but when you told me his name the other day, I rang my RSM to see if he knew him. He sure did. You remember RSM McMillan, in his day the crustiest bastard in uniform? Well, he positively gushed about what a solid soldier Breaker was. He knew him when Breaker was a warrant officer, and for a Royal to have anything positive to say about a sigs warrant speaks volumes."

"No kidding. Like you, I called my old RSM. You should ask Breaker about regimental goalies."

"What?"

"Never mind. Doug feels the same way as McMillan. He told me Breaker understands more about networks and cyber security than anybody in the trade. He did two tours with the Airborne, ironically."

"Why is that ironic?"

"We're back to talking about goalies."

"Gimme a break, Skip. I'm struggling to keep up here."

"Sorry, Harry. Let's get back to business. Breaker also did an exchange tour with a US Special Forces Signals Intelligence Detachment in Afghanistan, which should be useful. I mentioned his Afghan tour when we had lunch, and he just stared back at me. No hint of anything. I interviewed him the day before you got here. He impressed me so much I hired him before lunch was over. He'll be a junior partner."

There was a brief knock, and Breaker poked his head in the door.

"The phone in your office is now live, Colonel."

"What? Really? Is it secure?"

"Yes, sir. Would you like me to explain how I did it, or should we keep pretending that you and Colonel Harry have a clue about what I do?"

Breaker was grinning like a kid. Harry stared at the big man standing in the door.

"Sparky, piss off and go back to work," said Harry.

Breaker laughed and returned to the comms room.

"Yup," said Skip, "he's going to be fine."

Less than an hour later, Breaker had booted up the Apple Mac Pro in Skip's office. He called over to Skip, who was sitting on the couch, deep in conversation with Harry. The two men rose and walked over to him.

"Colonel, first, I'm really glad you went with Macs. This thing is a beast. The security is better, and they're much more stable than anything else right off the shelf. I divided the hard drive in two for you. There's a secure sector and an unsecure one. Logging on with your password automatically accesses the unsecure sector. To access the secure sector, you need to log in a second time through the secure portal. I've set up your passwords based on your college number and army service number with a couple of symbols."

Breaker handed Skip a piece of notepaper. Skip read the slip of paper with the two passwords.

"How the…?"

"C'mon, Colonel, you don't really think those two numbers are secret, do you? Anyhow, once we get serious, I'll create an encryption keychain that'll allow you to use your password and a key. That'll make it virtually unbreakable. Once you log in the first time, please destroy that slip of paper. Eating it would work."

Before Skip could reply, Breaker eyed Harry.

"Colonel Harry, I'll go to the depanneur downstairs and buy some Crayola crayons so that I can explain how you need to log on. Regimental or Airborne colours?"

"Hey, wise-ass …"

"Yes, sir?"

"Okay, I got nothin'."

Harry got up and left the office with Breaker in tow.

Later that day, Breaker downloaded the encryption software. Once that was installed, he downloaded the package including the communications software provided by Eagle. Skip told Breaker to load it onto Pangratti's servers, but three decades of being responsible for military communications security did not evaporate with retirement. Instead, Breaker loaded the two programs onto his test-bed computer first, and then he began a systemic forensic analysis. The analysis raised some issues, and Breaker was frowning.

"Colonel?"

Breaker was standing at Skip's door.

"What?"

"Something ain't kosher. I found a pretty sophisticated encryption protocol buried in one of the sub-routines. I expected some of this stuff. The CIA and the NSA use some high-level crypto."

"So?" said Skip. "You found some viruses?"

"No, sir, not viruses. Coding. Once I found the coding, I did a deeper inspection and found more code buried at the kernel level in both software programs that shouldn't be there. I wasn't going to install either program on the server without debriefing you and warning you of the potential risks."

Skip blinked at Breaker but said nothing for several seconds.

"You have my attention."

"Colonel, this is intentional code buried deep in the software — like I said, in the kernel layer. Coders leave small traces, like fingerprints, if you know how to recognize them. Whoever wrote the code for the encryption also wrote the sub-routines, except that the sub-routines are clearly superfluous to need. If I were to guess, and there's only one place I could test my theory, and I'd need access to tools only available at the Comms Intelligence Service, I would say that these sub-routines are scrapers. They continuously sweep the network and scoop data. All kinds of data. You don't happen to know anybody at CSIS, do you?"

Breaker was snickering at what he thought was a joke.

"As a matter of fact …"

"What?" said Breaker.

"Never mind. I guess we should have expected there'd be data collection software."

"Colonel, you know about this stuff?"

Skip ignored the question. "Is there any way that you can surgically remove the sub-routines, or maybe disable them?"

"Colonel, I'm good at this, but I'm not that good. This is damn near magic. Undoubtedly there's a sub-sub-routine hidden somewhere that'll warn the mother ship when one of the babies is being molested, if you follow me, sir."

"I get it, and here's what I want you to do."

Skip explained more fully what he wanted Breaker to establish and how he wanted it done. Further, only he and Breaker were to be privy to this. No one else, with no exceptions. When Breaker left Skip's office, he was quite impressed. His new boss played dumb, but he understood a lot more about computers and security than he let on. Breaker made a mental note not to play poker with his new boss.

Harry stepped into the office.

"Problems with the software?" he asked, looking back at Breaker.

"Nah, Breaker was briefing me on his deep dive into what Bill sent us. You know these guys. Big Brother is watching you. Don't share your password, don't introduce your friends to attractive bankers … Okay, that last bit was me thinking out loud. No, no worries. He'll have us online soon."

When Harry left the office, Skip immediately phoned downstairs to the bank, hoping to catch Lagasse before she left for the day.

"Bon après-midi. How may I help you?"

"Excusez-moi, Madame Lagasse. I apologize for detaining you so late in the day. Would it be possible for me to see you first thing tomorrow morning? There are a couple of critical changes that I need you to make to our corporate banking arrangements."

"Certainly, monsieur. We open at nine-thirty to the public, but I am usually here shortly after eight. Shall I meet you at the entrance at, let us say, eight forty-five?"

"That is very kind of you. See you tomorrow."

The next morning, Skip arrived punctually at a quarter to the hour. Equally punctually, Marie-Claire reached for the door lock to open it.

"Bonjour, monsieur."

She almost sang the greeting.

"Please follow me."

Walking behind her to the office, Skip thought he detected perfume he had not noticed before.

"I have taken the liberty, Signor Schiaparelli, of ordering in two cappuccini. I hope that is okay."

Skip noted that she had used the correct plural form in Italian.

"How very thoughtful of you, madame. May I ask a small favour before we begin?" Skip hesitated. "Would you mind calling me Amadeo, please? When I hear someone say Signor Schiaparelli, I expect my father to walk into the room, even though he has been dead for several years."

"I would be pleased to call you by your *prénom*, Signor Sch —" She caught herself. "Amadeo. And you must call me Marie-Claire."

"Excellent. Let's begin."

Skip sipped his cappuccino and explained what he needed. The accounts that they had already established were to be restricted. They were to be receivable only. He continued at length, finally asking Marie-Claire if he was making any sense.

She had been quietly nursing her own cappuccino and looked a bit mystified.

"Amadeo, I am not really sure why you are doing this. I am certain I can restrict the series of accounts to accommodate you. But if you are concerned about corporate theft, would not the thief simply move the money first and withdraw it from the so-called mirror accounts?"

"Of course, you would be correct, Marie-Claire, if I were worried about theft, but I'm not. I have no concerns about my colleagues. In fact, I trust them with my life. What I am worried about is something that has only now come to light. Some of the firms we may deal with have the technical means to make our money vanish without a trace."

"I understand, and I assure you, Amadeo, that our security is impeccable. That would not be possible."

Skip took another sip of his coffee. "Is this from Café Olimpico, by any chance? Excuse me, I digress. Are you familiar with the Arab proverb about having a donkey and trusting in Allah?"

The banker shook her head no.

"There was an elderly man with a donkey, and he wished to go into the mosque for prayers. He contemplated whether he could leave his donkey unattended since the animal was not allowed inside. He stood in the street looking pensive, and an imam came by.

"You look troubled, my brother," said the imam. "May I help you?"

"I would be in your debt," he said. "I wish to enter to pray and must leave my donkey unattended. I know that Allah is all merciful, and that we must always trust in Him. I know, too, that He would not wish me to lose my donkey. I do not wish to offend God by tying up the donkey lest He think me faithless. What shall I do?"

The imam pondered the dilemma for a moment.

"Brother, you are a faithful servant to be so concerned. Always trust in Allah, my brother, always, but tie up your donkey."

Marie-Claire almost choked on her coffee as she began laughing aloud.

"I have complete faith in you, Marie-Claire, and also in your bank," said Skip. "However, I think I will tie up my donkey."

"If you will give me a few hours to settle the technical details, I will call you at your office to confirm. Amadeo, I do not think there will be any problems."

Skip rose and offered Marie-Claire his hand.

"I look forward to hearing from you soon."

The two walked to the front door and said good-bye.

At 11:55 that same morning, Skip's phone rang.

"Schiaparelli," he said.

"Indeed, you were correct. The cappuccino was from Olimpico, my favourite café, and I have made all of the arrangements, exactly as you asked. *A bientôt.*"

Lennox and Addington County

It was not by coincidence that early Scots and Irish settlers had felt at home in this part of Upper Canada. Two centuries later, except for towns like Tweed, Marmora, or Stirling, the area was still practically bereft of people. It was a testament to the land's inability to support anything beyond subsistence farming. But such an unfriendly landscape was ideal for the purposes of Pangratti, and it was exactly why this was where Skip was having the auxiliary facility built, otherwise known as the "Ox." Deep in the nearly impenetrable woods, it was more than five kilometres from the nearest dirt road. Any casual driver would not notice the turn-off since there were no signs and the trees and scrub had been intentionally left untouched to hide the entrance.

Broken, rocky, and heavily treed, the thirty-five acres in Lennox and Addington County had been a bargain. The downside was that now Skip had two facilities to secure, but he didn't have to worry about it for long. While an Eagle construction crew was bulldozing some woods, a weathered-looking trapper appeared on site. The crew chief called it in. Alex, who had only arrived from BC the previous day, was catching up with Skip in the mess tent.

"Alex, I haven't had the chance to tell you how pleased I am that you've joined us. I must admit that I was surprised to hear you were out of uniform."

"It's a long story, Colonel. The truth is, I never got over the disbandment of the Airborne Regiment. After my second tour in Afghanistan, I didn't really like where the army was going, then my second marriage broke up, and ..."

"I get it," said Skip. "There's no need to explain."

"When Harry called me, I jumped at the chance to work with him again, and you know I've always had a great deal of respect for you, Colonel. It must have been frustrating for you not to get a command tour over there."

"Afghanistan? You've got that right," said Skip. "I tried, but the Army Commander insisted on infantry units, and having already commanded, the only jobs left for me were on the ISAF HQ staff. I was supposed to be there now, but I pulled the pin before it could happen. The turn of a card, as they say."

One of the construction crew stuck his head into the tent.

"Excuse me, Skip, but there's a stranger walking around down where some of my bulldozers are."

Skip and Alex walked over to investigate. It was immediately apparent that this local was no typical trapper, and Skip could see that Alex was wary of him. Little hints were everywhere. The stranger was relaxed, calm. All the same, there was tension in him like a coiled spring. He was wearing well-worn Canadian Army Mark I combat boots that were highly polished. No local polished his work boots. Moreover, the boots were bar-laced — marking him as obviously ex-military. And finally, the stranger's jeans were tucked expertly into his boots, like a soldier on patrol would do to avoid snagging his trousers walking through scrub.

"Can we help you, sir?" said Skip.

"I'm alright, thanks."

Alex gave it a try.

"We've got a bunch of heavy equipment moving around. There are some small charges set to fell some trees, and we wouldn't want to see you hurt. Would you like us to guide you back to the road, sir?"

"I'm fine, lad, and don't call me 'sir.' My parents were married."

The brogue was distinctive, as was the old military joke.

Alex didn't have time for this nonsense, and before Skip could stop him, he reached out to grab the stranger's jacket. A second later, the ex-Ranger was flat on his back with a shiny, well-worn boot on his chest, a vintage Fairbairn-Sykes commando knife hovering above his throat.

"What the —?" said Alex.

The stranger hushed him with a wide-eyed glare.

"You settle down now, lad. Not a good idea to be reaching for somebody you don't know. It's been a while since I taught unarmed combat to the lads in Hereford, but I still remember how it's done. Age and cunning always beat youth and exuberance, lad." He reached into a pocket with his free hand. "You mentioned charges. I think these here are what you meant."

He threw some coiled detonation cord over toward Skip.

"Easy," said Skip. "We're not looking for trouble, and there was no insult intended. Alex sometimes forgets his manners is all. Too much time yelling at recruits, I suspect. Put the blade away, please." He paused for several beats. "There's fresh coffee on, and the cook's getting ready to lay out some lunch. Come and join us."

The Scot smirked at Alex, lifted his boot, and gave the embarrassed ex-Ranger a hand up. The knife slid smoothly into a sheath hidden inside his jacket as Alex grunted. A sharp look from Skip was his signal to behave. Let bygones be bygones, it said. Alex brushed off his jacket and trousers and stepped discreetly out of the man's reach.

"That Fairbairn looks real," said Alex, working to regain some lost dignity.

"It is," admitted the stranger. "I inherited it from me dad. He used it in Malaya. Mum gave it to me when I joined the Regiment."

"Impressive," said Skip. "Paras?"

"Initially," said the stranger.

"Will you have some coffee with us, then?" said Skip.

"If you don't mind me dog."

He whistled, and a trim and hungry-looking Rottweiler came out of the bush.

"Stirling isn't much of a people dog. He likes to see what happens before he comes out of hiding, but he's a good boy."

He gave the dog a pat on the head.

Over coffee, Skip answered most of the many pointed questions John "Pappy" Wilkinson asked. He was not as timeworn as he'd originally appeared, and he was still fit and clearly still sharp. As they were talking, Harry came into the tent, and walked over to them.

"Well, I'll be damned!" shouted Harry.

Pappy was on his feet in an instant.

"Major Harry, how the hell have you been? I heard you'd run off to join the French Foreign Legion."

The two men were laughing and shaking hands as Alex and Skip eyed one another.

"Major Harry?" said Alex.

"I gather you two know each other," said Skip.

"Oh yeah," said Harry, letting out a long sigh, "but it's a long story and you probably don't want to hear it."

"Small world. I'll leave you two to catch up. Alex, can you come with me, please? There's something I want you to look at."

At supper, Skip, Alex, and Harry sat together.

"What are the odds of bumping into an old mate in the middle of these woods?" said Harry.

"Makes me a little suspicious," said Skip.

"No, Pappy's a stand-up guy. I actually know him well, but I haven't seen him since he did a two-year exchange with us. Seems he missed the great outdoors when he got back to the UK, so he came back. He's lived alone for several years in these woods."

"We need a camp caretaker. Do you think he'd be interested?"

"No idea, but I can ask him. He's invited me to join him at the Fox and Firkin in Belleville tomorrow. If he is, should I offer to let him join us, as an associate, maybe?"

"Harry, as you know, it takes two key elements to be considered: skill set and recommendation. If you think he's a right fit, then I trust you."

"Thanks, Skip. I'll let you know what he says."

Pappy, as it turned out, was delighted to re-affiliate himself with some kindred spirits. He and Stirling pitched a tent at the new facility, and together they became caretakers and security for the Ox. The place couldn't have been safer had it been double enclosed in barbed wire with a minefield perimeter.

Montreal

The next two months were exhausting for Skip as he spent his days interviewing potential new hires. After moving to Montreal, Harry spent most of his time in the offices with Breaker, while Alex and Franz-Josef spent most of their days north of the city supervising camp construction at what Skip had dubbed 'le Chalet.' Pappy kept an eye on the Ox and reported to Alex every other day.

Evenings, when Skip was in town, he and Harry dined together and compared notes. They agreed it was going well, even if they were both feeling a bit rushed. Recruiting a quality crew wasn't easy, but luckily, resources were not a constraint. Eagle's seed money was generous, and as they'd agreed, Bill had dispatched construction crews to establish both training facilities, which was a big help.

"What are we up to?" said Harry.

"What do you mean?" replied Skip. "Pass me the wine, please."

"Numbers. What are we up to? I know you've been buried in files, and I haven't wanted to pester you, but I'm curious. How big is the team?"

"Please don't call it a team, Harry. Forgive me, but I never liked that word. Command team, leadership team, management team, defence team — everything's a damn team. No, let's call it a cohort. The groups within the Cohort will be squads or sections."

"Pardon me?"

"A cohort, like those in a Roman legion."

"I like it," said Harry, as Skip handed the wine back. "So, how big is our *cohort?*"

"Let me grab my taccuino."

Skip stood and went to his desk. He returned with his leather book, tossed it on the table, and retook his seat.

"Harry, for you and me, our lives have always been about two things: trust and loyalty. In the last few weeks, I've been running my ass ragged looking for men like us, and it hasn't been so easy. I've met lots of men with skills, but trust and loyalty are the real issues."

"I've noticed," said Harry, as he took a sip of wine.

"Word has been quietly getting around the bazaars. There's lots of chatter about you and me being up to something, but nobody knows exactly what, and that's good." Skip eyed Harry's plate enviously. "You going to eat those fries?"

"Fill your boots," said Harry.

"I've talked to roughly three dozen people, interviewed twenty-seven and selected eleven. Only those to whom I've offered membership know what Pangratti really is. The rest are in the dark. No doubt that's how the rumours got started. Let's do a review." Skip reached for his beloved taccuino. "There's me, you, Franz-Josef, Pappy, Breaker, and Alex. And that guy Alex wanted — what's his name?"

"Sandy, and he's just joined Alex at le Chalet to help him and Franz-Josef with the construction of the lodge. I took the liberty; I hope you don't mind."

"Not at all. If he's alright for you and Alex, I'm okay with it. Remember, that's been the rule from the start."

"I'm not following."

"Two things: skill set and recommendation. It sounds like Sandy has both. To recap, he was both Airborne and Ranger qualified, right?"

"Check," said Harry. "That reminds me. I've been meaning to ask about Franz-Josef. You had mentioned him in passing over the years, but you've never told me how you got to know an East German senior NCO. I mean, he's a great addition; I just don't know much about him."

Skip looked up from his writing.

"That's true. You don't, and that's how Franz-Josef wants it, but let me fill in some of the gaps for you. You know I attended the German Armed Forces War College, at, shall we say, a tender age."

"Yes, you were the subject of much chatter amongst us junior officers, and I had a lot of street cred just for knowing you personally."

"According to lore, what did I do afterwards?"

"As I recall, you went on exchange with a Bundeswehr Panzergrenadier division for a couple or three years."

"Sort of, but not really. Because of a classmate I got to know quite well during my two years in Hamburg, I was seconded to the German Federal Intelligence Service, the *Bundesnachrichtendienst* or BND, although I did have a duty station at 4 Panzergrenadier Division for appearances. Through the BND, I spent most of my three years working with Interpol as part of the German delegation. Very few people knew I was Canadian, although everyone knew I was military. That's how I met Franz-Josef, except that he wasn't *in* Interpol; he was a target *of* Interpol. And, by the way, whatever Jupp says about owing me, I owe him more. He quite literally saved my life one night in Berlin. I really thought I'd had it."

"What? Are you serious?"

"No lie, Harry. I was in a bad way, but I'll save it for another evening."

Harry was stunned and sat speechless for a moment. "I honestly thought I knew everything about you."

"You and a lot of other people, my friend. Let's get back to counting heads."

"Where was I?" said Harry. "I hired our bartender-cum-Brit-Para, Les. I got to know him well while I ran my board of inquiry, and as it turned out, he and Pappy are mates. I was just never in the pub when Pappy was."

"Excellent," said Skip, "and I found an ex-Patricia named Henry who was recommended by an RMC classmate of mine. Henry then put me on to a friend of his who was a Pathfinder. His name's Bob. He was a master corporal but has lots of experience."

"Check," said Harry.

"I tracked down a guy I remembered from Germany, who left as a warrant officer. He was a loggie and served in the Airborne Service Commando. He retired early to a horse farm west of Toronto. It's funny because he hates horses, but it was his wife's dream. He made a bunch of money consulting on the juxtaposition of logistics and operations. His name's Gord, and he's a very bright guy."

"No doubt, with a word like juxtaposition," said Harry, but looked puzzled. "You want a loggie?"

"Wait till you meet him. Trust me, Harry: he's a stone-cold killer."

"Check," said Harry.

"Next is Terry, who was a combat engineer warrant officer, and one of my ex-sergeants major strongly recommended him. He's a demolitions instructor, and when I met Terry, he suggested another combat engineer, Ray. Terry said he'd trust Ray with his life and when I met Ray, I could see why."

"Check."

"Breaker put me on to a couple of junior NCOs, Jamie and Paul. He knew them both from his time in the Airborne, and both instructed down at the recruit school when Breaker was the school chief."

"Check."

"Les suggested a mate of his. He's another Canadian who served in the Paras with him. Walker's his name, and he lives in Batawa, which is not far from the Ox. By the way, he made the Bisley team twice."

"Check," said Harry. "Always good to have a marksman."

"Breaker recommended another guy called Leo, who did two tours with SOFCOM before becoming an instructor at the infantry school. I also found another Pathfinder, who was a Royal. He said he knew you when you commanded Charles Company. His name's Airdrie."

Skip looked up from writing.

"What is it about guys who were Pathfinders that they can't settle into civilian life?"

"Toughest qual in the infantry," said Harry. "Once you've done that, you get addicted to the adrenaline. I remember Airdrie; he was a master corporal for me. Tough as leather."

"Who names his son Airdrie? I thought Amadeus was tough growing up."

"His dad was a proud Scotsman from North Lanarkshire. He's a good find and a decent man. They all sound top-drawer, Skip. Gimme a sec," said Harry, as he was adding up all the names. "I make that eighteen. Is that enough?"

"I'm not sure. That counts me, Pappy, Breaker, and Franz-Josef, but we aren't front end. So that's you plus thirteen who are bayonets. We're going to need staff for the two camps. Mind you, some of that work can be done on rotation duties, like maybe cooking. Wait, there's one more. I've been holding a place open for Flash Gordon's chief. That'll have to wait until he's out of his coma and I can talk with him, so we could be nineteen. We'll see. In any case, we need to start training. We can't wait any longer."

"Agreed," said Harry. "Let's plan on driving up to Lac Larin tomorrow to see how construction's coming along."

RCAF Base Trenton

"Hi, Skip. My Wing Chief's been eased out of his coma and is being moved to the base hospital."

"I'll be there tomorrow morning," said Skip.

After a couple of days of being awake, Jules had been deemed well enough to be moved to the base facility. There, he could spend time recuperating while the air force began the process of releasing him. The Acting 8 Wing Chief went by every day to brief his predecessor, and Flash looked in on him every day as well. Sometimes Flash and his chief would sit quietly; sometimes they'd talk. After giving him time to grieve a bit, Flash broached the subject of what he was going to do after release. The airman gave his CO an honest and taciturn response.

"No idée, mon Colonel."

"That's okay," said Flash. "I have a couple for you."

Skip arrived at 24 Canadian Forces Health Services Centre on Yukon Street and saw Flash's PA waiting for him by the front entrance.

"Hi, sir," he said as he saluted smartly. "The Wing Commander asked me to escort you to the chief. The boss said something about you having a poor sense of direction."

Skip gave the kid a withering look, which made the broad smile instantly disappear from the captain's face.

"Your boss is a real cut-up. Be sure to ask him about taking the wrong Autobahn exit. He was supposed to meet me in Strasbourg, and he wound up in Stuttgart. Poor sense of direction, my butt."

"Yes, sir. I will," said the captain, swallowing hard. "Please follow me, sir."

As Skip came into the room, Flash was out of his chair with his hand extended.

"Thanks for coming, Skip." He turned to face the patient in bed. "All those stories of drunken debauchery in Germany, France, and Switzerland? Here's the culprit," he announced.

Turning back to Skip, he made the formal introductions. Afterwards, he walked out with his PA in tow.

"*Plaisir de faire votre connaissance, mon Adjudant-Chef,*" said Skip.

"The pleasure is all mine, Colonel, and we can do this in English, sir."

"First, please accept my sincere condolences. I'm sorry about your wife and friends. I'm not sure what else I can say."

"Merci."

"Flash said you are up and even walking a bit now."

"Oui, monsieur. The doctor wants me out of bed each two hours. He is worried for blood clots. They even have a young med tech *caporal* wake me in the night to walk with me. Like a *petit chiot* — like little a puppy."

"Who, you or the corporal?"

The chief laughed, then made a pained sound.

"Sorry. I didn't mean to hurt you."

"No problem. Me, I am the one on a leash," said Jules, indicating his IV feed.

"The *caporal* is a good kid. He is from Alberta, and he has no idée what I am saying when I curse him in French. I tell him he is a crétin from Lac Saint-Jean. The kid, he grins a lot, and he pushes my IV stand when I am trying to walk."

They looked at each other for a minute, until Skip broke the awkward silence.

"I'm not sure what the Wing Commander has told you about my new organization, especially since he doesn't really know much. He thinks you should come join me, and I agree. I read your Unit Employment Record. I think you would enjoy working with us, and you'll find a lot of my guys share some of your skills."

"Colonel Gordon has not told me any details."

"Before we worry about any of that, you need to get healthy. Flash says your medical team wants you out of here in seven to ten days. On the day they discharge you, a driver will be waiting for you downstairs at Outpatients. Flash's PA will go to your house and pack a couple of bags. Don't worry — I'll tell him what you need. Anything he can't find, Pappy will get for you. You won't be too far away, and someone can come back to get it, if they must."

"Pappy?"

"You two are going to be good friends, I think." Skip extended his hand. "Welcome aboard, Chief. My guys call me Colonel or Skip. No more of the 'sir' stuff. Got it?"

"Oui, mon Colonel. My friends call me Jules, mon Colonel."

"I'll see you soon, Jules."

Skip left the room. Flash and his PA were waiting for him downstairs at reception. Skip grabbed the PA.

"Follow me, son. I have instructions for you."

"Is everything okay?" Flash asked.

"I have some chores for your PA. Then you, my flyboy friend, are taking me to the Fox and Firkin for dinner. Over beef and beer, I will explain what's happening."

"I am?"

"Yes, you are. Pay attention." Skip hesitated. "Never mind. You pick the place, and I will buy *you* a steak. As long as it's at the Fox and Firkin. We need to use separate vehicles, though. I have business, and you'll need to go home to your lovely wife."

"Now that's the Skip we all love," said Flash.

That evening, a decent steak and a long chat about Flash's air force career and what might be in store for Jules proved to be a tonic for both men. Toward the end of the meal, Skip idly glanced at his watch and abruptly apologized.

"Sorry, Flash. I lost track of time. I had not meant to keep you this late and I don't want your Lucie pissed at me."

"No sweat, Skip. By the way, she sends you big hugs. There's no rush."

"Actually, there is. I had wanted to be home early. If I leave now, I should be crossing the bridge at Sainte-Anne-de-Bellevue in Montreal before civil twilight."

"Wow," said Flash. "How does an old war horse like you know about civil twilight, anyway?"

"Flash, my young friend, you could fill a book with stuff that you don't know about me." He got to his feet. "Please hug Lucie back for me and remind her that she could have done better," he said as he smiled and hugged his friend.

On his drive home, Skip phoned Harry.

"What's up, Skip?"

"We now have nineteen. I'll see you tomorrow."

On the appointed day, a Yukon SUV with blacked-out windows waited for Chief Warrant Officer Jules Simone outside the entrance to Outpatients. The PA stood with a stranger. The captain had packed Jules's luggage as instructed, and it was already in the vehicle.

"The Air Div Commander called literally while the colonel was putting on his wedge cap to come over. The Wing Commander said to say he'll call you, Chief."

The driver stepped forward.

"Sir, my name is James, but everybody calls me Jamie. I'll drive you up to meet Pappy and the crew. If you'll follow me, sir."

"Stop the 'sir' stuff, soldier. I am not a chief no more. From now on, I am only Jules. *Allons*. It is time to go."

Jules sat up front with Jamie, and neither spoke as they headed north. Pappy had been clear in his instructions, and Jamie kept quiet.

About an hour and a half north of the air base, Jules was caught off guard as the Yukon pulled sharply off the country road. It soon worsened into a barely visible dirt track. Jules thought he knew the area well. He had flown over most of this ground during his time in Search and Rescue, but he was now lost. The first hundred metres of track was rough, and Jules's back and ribs were beginning to complain. Gradually, the track became a well-maintained gravel road. Seeing the look on Jules's face, Jamie apologized.

"The road gets better and smoother as we get closer to the lodge."

Jules nodded but remained silent. Jamie could see he was in pain.

The SUV pulled up to the newly built lodge, where Pappy, having seen the vehicle approaching on CCTV, was waiting to greet them. Stepping out, Jules saw Pappy's hand extended.

"Welcome, Chief. I'm Colour Sergeant John Wilkinson. I beg your pardon — I *used* to be a colour sergeant. The lads 'round here call me Pappy."

"Pleased to meet you, Pappy. I am Jules." He scanned the area as he stretched his back. "I thought I knew these woods. I had no idée you had a camp in here."

"That's exactly the plan, and last time you looked, there wasn't one. Jamie, go and stow Jules's kit in suite number two."

"That is not necessary," said Jules. "I can take care of myself, thanks."

"Colonel's orders, Jules. C'mon, it's time for supper. You and me have a lot to discuss." Pappy turned back to the driver. "What's your problem, lad? Move now."

Jamie jumped slightly and reached for the bags as Jules stepped back and away from the vehicle.

"Follow me, Chief," said Pappy.

"Pappy, please call me Jules. I am not a chief no more. Those days, they are gone. Time for me to move on."

"Excuse me — Jules."

Pappy could hear the pain in the new man's voice. He knew the whole story, and he'd been around enough grieving soldiers to know not to pry. When Jules was ready, he would share what he wanted to share. If not, then not.

"This is very nice," said Jules.

"I agree."

Pappy led Jules to the dining room. There was a large open space that looked to be a cafeteria. An adjacent private dining room was reserved for the colonel and his guests. However, when the colonel was away, Pappy was the top dog at the Ox and Jules was his guest. That was where he was going to have his first meal.

Over the next ninety minutes, Pappy brought Jules up to speed: why it was called the Ox, how the place was run, the various emergency drills, security protocols, and procedures, and why there was a construction crew present who lived apart from them. He was thorough in his briefing but was careful to avoid explaining exactly why all this was tucked away almost a hundred kilometres north of Lake Ontario.

"There's also a mirror facility to this one," he concluded, "but bigger, north of Montreal. The colonel calls it 'le Chalet,' but I really don't know why."

"In Quebec we call them that. It is not the size. It is just a name. Like here in Ontario, everything outside the city is a cottage."

"Le Chalet is the main site, so you'll likely be based there, but the colonel will decide."

Pappy noted that Jules was a quick study, asking only the occasional question. Mostly he listened, sipping from his coffee mug, while Pappy spoke. Pappy was impressed.

"You were Search and Rescue?"

"Yes, almost twenty years, but I started as an aircraft tech before I applied to go SAR."

Pappy's experience with most air force folks had not generally been positive, but this guy seemed different, probably because he had been a SAR tech, and Pappy took an instant liking to him. After supper, the cook came in to ask if they wanted any dessert. More coffee, maybe? Jules looked up at the cook inquisitively.

"*Vous êtes francophone, vous?*"

"*Oui, monsieur. Je m'appelle Michel.*"

"From where?"

"From Chicoutimi, monsieur."

"No, monsieur. Call me Jules. You were in the army?"

"I was *caporal* in the Royal 22nd, *les Vandoos*. Then I transfer to become a cook."

"Good supper, Michel. *Délicieux*, and excellent café."

Pappy saw the youngster beaming at the compliments.

"Merci, monsieur — sorry, I mean merci, Jules."

Pappy grew more impressed. Jules spoke like a Battalion Sergeant Major. He was direct and had a commanding presence. He had a way of eliciting respect, even from strangers. Pappy thought to himself that the young cook had not been with them long and this was probably the most he had spoken at one time since joining. Pappy dismissed Michel and turned back to Jules.

"He seems like a good kid, the cook," said Jules.

"Aye, he is."

Jules was showing obvious signs of fatigue, so Pappy feigned a yawn.

"I apologize, Jules. I don't mean to be rude, but I was up half the night with my dog. We were tracking a black bear that wandered into the compound. Would you mind if I showed you to your room now, and we called it a day?"

"Oui. Merci."

Upstairs, Pappy opened the door and pointed to a double bed with what appeared to be a new, high-end foam mattress.

"I'll have one of the lads come up and make up your bed," said Pappy.

"No."

Pappy was startled by the suddenness of Jules's remark.

"I am sorry, Pappy," said Jules. "Please excuse me. I did not mean to be rude. No, thank you, Pappy. I would like to make my own bed."

"Of course," said Pappy.

He excused himself and slipped away.

The next morning over breakfast, the ex–colour sergeant continued to brief the newest recruit. Jules and Pappy were alone in the private dining room again, and Pappy filled in the gaps he had previously left.

"That is quite a story. I am not sure what to say," said Jules, when Pappy had finished speaking.

Pappy had been completely honest, though he'd held back on some specific details. Skip had given him freedom to use his discretion, but he had reminded Pappy that if Jules decided that he didn't want to stay, it would be problematic for everyone if he'd been told too much.

"So, now what? Do I have to sign a contract in blood, or something like that? I mean, I am in – do not get me wrong. I am happy to be here with you guys. I am only asking what is next, you know?"

"The Colonel told me that you'll need some time to regain your strength, so we can play it by ear. First, I'll take you to meet with Franz-Josef. He'll tend to your paperwork, and no, you won't need to sign in blood." Pappy forced a smirk. "Colonel Skip works on trust. Franz-Josef König is our admin officer. Don't be put off by him. He's a wee bit standoffish, but he's a wizard at the kind of details most of us hate, especially money, I'm told. He also has an interesting grasp of English. For instance, if you pay attention, you'll notice that Franz-Josef never uses contractions."

"Me neither," said Jules.

"Franz-Josef's from East Germany, so he ain't what you'd call warm and fuzzy. Not too many cuddly Hauptfeldwebels in the East German Volksarmee, I guess."

"I guess so. What do I call him?"

"Franz-Josef. Everybody except the colonel calls him Franz-Josef. The colonel calls him Jupp, sort of like 'Youppi,' the mascot for the Montreal Canadiens. By the way, don't ever call him that — trust me."

Franz-Josef had been waiting in the admin office, and he stood as a mark of respect when Jules entered and immediately offered his hand in greeting. Jules had served with 4 Wing in Baden-Baden on the northwest edge of the Black Forest, so he was quite familiar with German greetings and customs. He shook Franz-Josef's hand firmly.

"Pleased to meet you."

"*Ebenfalls* — excuse me. Me too," said Franz-Josef, bowing his head slightly but remaining deadpan.

He retook his seat and indicated that Jules should take a seat as well.

"I understand there are some papers for me to sign."

"*Ja. Das ist korrekt.* Many papers. Der Oberst has established a trust fund. It is for all of us who are core staff, for the partners only. I am informed you will join as a junior partner. When it is time for you to leave us, you will sell the partnership back to us, and if der Oberst allows it, there will be an annuity for you. It will be paid at your bank until you die. Also, the fund will pay your family a lump sum death benefit."

"This is generous," said Jules.

"Ja, der Oberst is a generous man."

Franz-Josef looked at Jules, expecting a comment, but there was none, so he continued.

"I understand your wife was killed. *Kondolenz. Es tut mir sehr leid.* Excuse me, I am so sorry. Please tell me who, or what organization, should get your monies. I will make all the arrangements for you. I have your banking informations already from your air force pay account. I assume your monthly stipend goes to there. Neh?"

Jules was a bit taken aback that Franz-Josef had his banking data.

"How did you get my…? Never mind. Yes, use the same account. I have a niece in Lac Saint-Jean, and I would like her to get everything when the time comes, but I need to confirm her details."

"*Nah, gut.*" He pushed some papers across the desk and handed Jules a pen. "Here we have a standard Last Will *und* Testament. Here are some other papers to sign. Please fill them in und sign where I have made the marks. There is no rushing."

When he had finished signing, Jules handed the pen back to Franz-Josef.

"*Herzlich willkommen,*" announced Franz-Josef, as they shook hands again.

"Merci bien," said Jules, who stood and turned to leave the office.

Pappy was waiting for him in the lounge.

"See what I mean?"

"I served in Germany, so I am used to how they are. No problem. I always got along with the Germans. I like them; they are no nonsense. What is this trust fund? And we get a stipend? I did not want to ask Franz-Josef, but it does not matter. I do not really care, since my RCAF pension takes care of what I need, especially now since I am alone."

"All in good time, mon ami," said Pappy. "It's time for us to walk the grounds. It'll take about half an hour. Do you feel up to a stroll to see what we've got? See who's who?"

"Yes, please. I need to stretch my legs, and it will be good to walk outside again. I miss it."

They stepped off the porch, and from nowhere a Rottweiler appeared and greeted Pappy. The dog glanced up warily at Jules, blinking and panting.

"Jules, this is Stirling. Stirling, say hello to Jules."

The dog's demeanour changed, and he pushed his massive head into the airman's crotch.

"Stirling! Sorry, Jules. He loves to have his ears rubbed."

"You named your dog after the town south of here?"

Pappy laughed.

"No, mate. He's named after Lieutenant-Colonel Sir Archibald David Stirling, DSO, OBE. He was the lunatic Scotsman who founded the SAS."

"Sorry, no offence."

"None taken, Jules. Easy mix-up."

The two men strolled the grounds, with Stirling trotting alongside, as

Pappy played tour guide. After about forty minutes, he could see the new man flagging.

"Sorry, Jules. I didn't think it would take this long. You look beat. Why don't we call it a day?"

"Non, merci, Pappy," Jules said, pausing to catch his breath. "I must get stronger. Sleeping twelve hours a night is not my idée of getting stronger but thank you for offering."

"So, what do you think of our little installation?"

Jules pursed his lips.

"I like the way you have everything spread around, but it is still logical in the layout. Am I correct? You have positioned everything for all-round security?"

"Exactly so," agreed Pappy.

"Only because I wore the light blue for my career, does not mean I did not pay attention." Jules looked at Pappy, who was obviously pleased. "My tour at Kandahar Airfield taught me a lot of this stuff. We were next to a Royal Air Force squadron, and they were protected by the Air Force Royal Regiment, I think they call it. Air force guys with army jobs?"

"You're talking about the Rock Apes. The RAF Regiment. They take a lot of grief from squaddies like me, but the truth is, they are tough buggers, and they know their jobs. They're equal to any line regiment when it comes to close-combat ops, them. At least any that I've come across."

"Rock Apes?"

"You never heard them called that in Kandahar?"

"It does not sound like a nice nickname to me."

"Well, Jules, it's not, but I'll save it for later."

Jules nodded. "Now what?"

"Now we join some of the lads in the mess hall. I'll introduce you around, and you can start to get to know everybody."

"I have a question. I noticed a small clearing like a helipad. We have helicopters?"

"Not exactly. They come from Eagle. Colonel Bill and Colonel Skip have an arrangement. The Yank pilots deliver what we need, but some items Canada Border Services Agency might frown upon, if you follow me."

"I understand," said Jules. "Supper?"

"Supper," said Pappy.

USAF Base Nellis

Colonel Vigo "Andy" Anderson stepped off the plane. On the tarmac he took the time to thank the general for letting him tag along.

"No sweat, Andy. I'm not sure when I'm going back, but if you talk to Jimmy, he'll give you a heads-up. You're welcome to hitch a lift back to DC, if you need to — and stay away from the slot machines," said the general, chuckling.

"Thanks, again, General. I will."

Inside the hangar, Andy found a phone and called his man.

"Sir, this is a pleasant surprise. I wasn't expecting you until the day after tomorrow. I'll be right over to pick you up."

Major Blaine Lewis pulled his car up to the entrance door of the hangar and jumped out. He spotted the colonel coming out.

"Sir, welcome to Nellis. It's good to see you again. I would have been here when you landed if you had told me. Will you have time to visit Vegas? I can give you a tour, sir."

"It's fine, Blaine. I hitched a lift at the last minute with General Williams, and thanks for the offer, but I'm only here for a day."

"Sir, thank you again for sending me here. I'm loving it, and with Jeannie's folks just across the state line in Barstow, she's got a lot of help with little Tommy. I know —"

"It's all good, Blaine. You worked hard on my team, and I was pleased to help you and your wife. Can we grab a coffee at the O Club?"

Once seated inside, Andy composed himself. He needed to be careful.

He had an ask of this major, and he wanted it to be vague enough that he understood without raising any doubts or suspicions. Just the same, he knew that Blaine owed him. He had requested a compassionate posting because his baby son had medical issues.

"Blaine, you know that drone project of mine that got defunded?"

"Yes, sir. That was too bad. There was a lot of potential there. Lots of high-tech stuff on board that baby, and she just sits in the hangar all day."

"Well, it was *officially* defunded, but I've managed to cobble together enough money to continue some limited testing for your team. Only we need to be discreet about costs, if you follow me."

"That's terrific news, Colonel, and I understand. Actually, sir, that project was why I transferred over to drone warfare. It allows us to punish our enemies without them knowing who hit them."

"Exactly so," intoned Anderson. "Exactly so."

LAC LARIN

It was the first time that the entire cohort was assembled in one place, and they were arrayed around the Great Room of le Chalet, north of Montreal. Michel, the cook, was at the kitchen door looking on intently. The lodge here was bigger and more comfortable than the one at the Ox, since it was their primary home. Skip had recruited almost everyone personally, and he'd explained everything to everyone individually. Now it was time to have a frank, open, and honest discussion in plenary session. Everyone needed to feel he had the opportunity to ask questions and, if need be, to challenge suppositions or policies.

Skip was standing in the centre of the room. "Welcome, everyone," he began. "Special thanks to those who travelled a considerable distance. If you've never been up here to Quebec's hinterland, don't forget to pick up some maple syrup. Contrary to what Vermonters think, it doesn't get any better than what's produced right here in these surrounding villages.

"I'm going to talk for a while, so please make yourselves comfortable. Feel free to interrupt with a question at any time, hit the heads, grab a coffee, or whatever. You've all had a chance to introduce yourselves by now, so I'll cut to the chase."

Skip paused to scan the room and check the body language. All the men were sitting upright, leaning slightly forward. He had their attention.

"Some of you may have heard of something called the 'Forming, Storming, Norming, and Performing Model' created by a Professor Bruce Tuckman. Anybody?"

Two hands went up. Skip looked at them and nodded approvingly.

"The model describes the four psychological stages necessary to create an organization, face its challenges, find solutions, and then deliver results. As I've been assembling our crew, which I have dubbed the Cohort, the 'forming' stage has gone well and is now complete. It has also been quicker and smoother than I expected. It seems that Harry and I weren't the only ones who missed playing in the sandbox."

A murmur rippled through the room.

"Between senior and junior partners and our associates, we are now at our full complement. As you know, if you are an associate, then you don't have voting rights. Harry and I are considering adding voting associates, but not yet. You'll note the legal language, and that's intentional. We can talk openly, if we must, with veiled speech about our so-called private securities investment firm. That's also how we've been incorporated for legal reasons, just like a law firm. By the way, Pangratti also provides its clients with bespoke security solutions."

Once more, Skip paused and took a sip from his coffee mug. The men remained attentive. He glanced over at Harry and Alex, who were standing in the corner of the room, and they nodded to him, indicating all was well.

"We now begin the 'storming' stage, which is where we start to bond with each other and build mutual trust. I also expect this to go well for the simple reason that each of you has been hand-picked by me or by Harry. We used a complex set of criteria that are not important now, except to give you our founding principle. Each of you needed two criteria to get interviewed: You needed the right skill sets and, perhaps more important, you needed someone's recommendation."

A hand went up. It was Gord, the loggie.

"Excuse me, Colonel. Can you please elaborate on the recommendation?"

"Sure, Gord. By the way, you were the only exception. I couldn't find anyone who'd vouch for you."

"Thanks, Colonel," Gord deadpanned. "That's comforting."

"I'm kidding, obviously. For those who don't know, Gord and I go way back. Anyway, my point is that everyone here was recommended by someone whom Harry and I trust. That trust was transferred to you, but that just got you to the interview. That was the key. We considered how you came across, what your attitude was, and whether you could be quickly integrated into a select group of experts like this one. To paraphrase a line you've all heard, many were called, but few were chosen. You are that few."

"Got it, Colonel Skip," said Gord.

"As we proceed through 'storming,' we'll quickly move into the 'norming' stage, where you all learn to accept each other and co-operate for the greater good. You won't be surprised that, from my perspective, we are akin to the Cosa Nostra — with a notable exception that I will get to in a minute. Once you're in, you stay in, even after you retire. We don't discuss what we do with people who are not in this room. Ever. That includes wives and especially includes girlfriends and children. That is for their safety. To the rest of the world, Pangratti LLC invests money for select wealthy clients, and we owe those clients absolute confidentiality and discretion. As my father used to say, *Non parliamo dei nostri affari con stranieri*. We don't discuss our business with strangers."

Skip scanned the room to see if his message was sinking in. This particular aspect of the business was critical to him, and he wanted to see if any of the men showed signs of discomfort. None did, so he continued.

"Naturally, the 'norming' stage will get more intense once we get our first mission and we all find our niches in order to achieve that mission. You won't be surprised to hear that this is the stage when I will turn you over to the tender mercies of Harry and Alex, who've spent their careers training top-notch soldiers like you."

Skip paused and looked at Gord directly.

"Well, most of you are top notch."

"Thanks again, Colonel. I'm really feeling the love."

"We have a lot of rules. All of us have been in uniform, so that should be no problem. Keep your mouth shut. That's rule one. Rule two is we always follow our mission SOPs: no exceptions, no excuses. Harry and Alex are still compiling them, but break that rule and you and Harry will have a chat. Break it twice and you and I will have a serious chat. Rule three is the exception I mentioned. Unlike the Cosa Nostra, we do *not* intentionally kill people. We are not murderers. We are not like the firms that some of our friends have joined to provide contracted security services overseas. That is not why we were formed. If someone gets injured or killed during an op, we will talk it out, and if consequences are warranted, then we will see what those need to be. But …"

Skip took a long pause.

"There will *never* be a mission where we intentionally target someone for death. I say again, *never*."

He paused once more to ensure that his message had sunk in.

"Our missions will always be those that Eagle Investments cannot do. Why won't matter, but when Bill Donovan hands off a mission, I will discuss it with Harry. If it suits us, I'll accept it and we'll move out. Speaking of missions, that is obviously the final stage, the so-called 'performing' stage. The model predicts that if the first three stages are carried out well, then exceptional results can be achieved in the 'performing' stage, and I am confident that we will prove the model correct. Are there any questions so far?"

There were none, and Skip went on in this vein for another few minutes. No one interrupted with a question or got up for coffee or any other reason.

"Let me say in summary that I wish to be absolutely clear on one aspect. Irrespective of what part you may play in our little limited liability firm, in our cohort, your job is important. Door kicker, planner, trainer, squad leader, or banker — there are no exceptions. We are all in this together."

Skip looked at each man directly, once again checking to see that his message had got through. He saw no cause for concern.

"Right. That's enough from me. Take ten and reassemble. Harry needs to have his say."

Coffee was poured; some men headed to the washrooms, and one or two went outside for a quick smoke. Alex passed the word that when Colonel Skip said ten minutes, he meant nine minutes and fifty-nine seconds. Harry kicked off on time.

"As Colonel Skip has said, we are a bound to each other. We're a cohort. Since I am not Italian, let me give you my white-bread take on our relationships. We are a band of brothers. I know it sounds corny, but I don't care since it's how I feel. Some of us were already brothers from when we served Her Majesty. Others have only recently become our brothers. It doesn't matter, because we accept each other, based not on time served or on rank achieved. Rather, our bonds are based on character and on our shared adherence to our unwritten moral code."

As Skip had done, Harry paused for effect. He sipped his coffee and scanned the room. Skip, now in the corner with Alex, gave him a discreet thumbs-up.

"The business end is important, so let me review it. We will each draw our monthly stipend. Each quarter, Pangratti will declare a dividend based on our various corporate earnings. It will pay out at a ratio of one per associate, two per junior partner, and four per senior partner. On December thirty-first of each year, Franz-Josef will issue a corporate statement telling us what the firm is worth. I'm the managing partner, which makes me like the parliamentary party leader. I call the votes, and I count them. If you have an issue you believe we need to vote on, then you bring it to me. If I deem it worthy of a vote, I will call a vote. If not, then suck it up and move on. Colonel Skip did not set up this organization to make us rich. If that's why you joined, though I doubt it, then we need to chat privately. Colonel Skip has always been generous, and I can assure you that you'll be pleased with that side of things. Any questions so far?"

Harry paused again for a few beats, scanning the room once more. The men sat attentively.

"No? All right, let's talk training. Some of you have already commenced. Excellent. Tomorrow at 06:00 we go for our first group run in the bush. Don't be late. We will all run. Colonel Skip has already established his alibi. He will keep Jules company so that our RCAF brother doesn't get lost in the woods. Don't be teasing Colonel Skip. We all know that armoured guys are sensitive about being with us manly men who served with the Airborne and the Paras. Nobody wants to see an old Hussar cry, especially me. There's one exception for our runs, however: Franz-Josef will not be joining us. The Colonel has excused him since some time ago the East German *Stasi* surgically removed Franz-Josef's funny bone, and it hurts when he runs, but he's the only exception."

A disembodied voice from the corner muttered '*Schweinskopf*' a little too loudly.

"Pardon me?" said Harry.

"*Danke*, Harry. *Alles gut*."

Harry scanned the room and stopped when he saw the cook.

"Michel, that includes you, buddy. Just like when you were a Vandoo."

"Oui, monsieur."

Harry turned to Skip.

"Colonel?"

"Thanks, Harry. Nothing to add."

"Okay, ladies, see you at supper," said Harry. He walked over to Skip, who was still standing with his back to the stone fireplace. "Thoughts?"

"I think we're off to a solid start, Harry."

"Indeed," agreed Harry. "I've got some things to attend to, so I'll meet with you for supper."

Franz-Josef approached Skip.

"Herr Oberst. Do you think that it seems bad that I do not join with the running? I can do it, for sure."

"I know you can, my friend, but there is no reason to test how well the Danish surgeons who put you back together did their work. I do not need you to run, Jupp. I need you to count our money."

"Jawohl, Herr Oberst. I understand."

Franz-Josef had barely survived the last brutal beating that he had taken at the hands of some Russian sailors on leave in Copenhagen. Like many Osties, Franz-Josef retained a seething hatred of Russians — all Russians. He had purposely provoked the brawl, and the sailors had obliged by breaking each of his legs in two places. They also fractured his hip and crushed a cheekbone. If a random Danish police patrol had not chanced upon the fight, Franz-Josef would have bled to death in a back alley by the harbour. It took him months to get back on his feet.

Pappy was next to walk over to Skip.

"I had no idea Franz-Josef was busted up. Colonel Harry mentioned it on the QT. I've never taken him for a run, but he seems okay."

"He doesn't like to talk about it, so please keep it quiet. The truth is the man is held together with surgical steel and strategically implanted titanium. The last thing he needs is to go rough-terrain running each morning.

"Aye, Colonel. Mum's the word."

"Jupp's critical skills are administrative and financial. We've got enough door kickers. Amongst us, only Franz-Josef understands international finance, unless you'd like to pitch in, Pappy?"

Pappy raised both hands in surrender.

"I'd rather be shot at dawn," he announced as he chuckled and wandered away.

The next morning before the run, Skip scanned the crowd. He saw almost two dozen different types of wristwatches, and it put his teeth on edge. He didn't think he was a pedant, although he had to admit that he let small things get under his skin. As he aged, the tendency seemed to have become cemented into his psyche.

When the men started out for their run, Skip held Jules back.

"Jules, let's you and I take a moderate pace. I know what route Harry's using and we'll trail them. When they pass us coming back, we'll turn about and follow them home. I know that you SAR techs are very fit, but for now, you and I will log time, not distance. We have nothing to prove."

"Oui, Colonel."

The two men stepped off, and Skip kept the pace intentionally slow. He knew that, despite his pain, Jules would want to demonstrate that he belonged, so Skip kept him talking.

"Sorry, Jules. I don't think I mentioned this before, but if you're willing, I'd like you to be the Cohort RSM. You have the most experience in that regard. In the air force, you dealt with multiple ranks and multiple specialists. More importantly, you did it without physical threats, and that is what I want."

Jules looked across at Skip as they ran and cocked his head like he understood.

"If I wanted old-school yelling and threats, which I do not, I would ask Breaker or Pappy. I've already discussed it with both of them, and with Harry. I want you."

"Merci, Colonel," said Jules, slightly out of breath. "I am honoured."

As expected, Harry's group was on its way back long before Skip and Jules got to the turnaround point. Skip had used this technique with troops for years and it worked well. Everyone began together and mostly ended together so they could warm up and cool down as a single unit.

The men were doing their cool-down stretching, and most had removed their shirts, exposing an interesting collection of ink. Practically all of the jumpers had some variation of parachute wing tattoos. Several had regimental crests, and others had symbols. One tattoo caught Jules's eye, and he strode over to the man. Skip was a pace behind him.

"Walker, is that a Chinese tattoo on your chest, la?" said Jules, pointing.

"Yes, RSM. It's the Chinese character for China," Skip confirmed. He was standing directly behind Jules.

"Bien," said Jules. "Now I have to ask why Walker has a symbol of China on his chest. He is not Chinese."

Walker was starting to get visibly nervous, and a number of the men were obviously enjoying his obvious distress. The Colonel and the RSM were arguing over Walker like he wasn't even there. Skip sensed Walker's discomfort.

"Well done, Walker," said Skip. "Let me guess. You think China is a major threat to the West and that they are our next big enemy. Am I right?"

Walker was noticeably relieved to be allowed to speak, finally.

"Yes, Colonel, that's right, but nobody ever gets that. How did you figure it out?"

Skip looked over at Jules, then back at Walker.

"You have it inked over your heart. It tells me that you keep your friends close but keep your enemies closer, right?"

Walker began to laugh.

"Yes, Colonel, that's it exactly. In my defence, I was pretty drunk. The Paras were in Hong Kong on an exercise. Les was there. Me and a couple of the lads thought it would be cool. Even pissed, I gotta admit that it hurt like hell, I can tell you."

"I'll bet it did. Hong Kong? I'm surprised you didn't end up with hepatitis," said Skip.

"Actually, my mate Joe did get sick. The rest of us were lucky, I guess. The upside was that the tattooist was really hot, and she took me —"

"Enough," said Skip, cutting him off. "The RSM and I already know more than we need to."

Les elbowed Breaker.

"Aye, Colonel, I was there. She weren't that cute, if I'm honest."

Jules shook his head in disgust and walked inside with Skip.

"These kids today. I do not even understand them a little bit, *tabernac*."

After breakfast, Skip asked Jules to drive into Montreal and told him to buy nineteen identical Casio G-Shock watches. He wanted them all to be black. He pushed a slip of paper to Jules.

"Here's the model number. What I would prefer is nineteen Omega Speedmasters, but for now, the Casios will do. Go see Franz-Josef for the money, and feel free to buy them anywhere convenient. Before you issue them, please make sure you and Pappy synchronize them all to the same second."

Pappy overheard this last bit and began to raise an objection, but Jules stilled him.

"No problem, mon Colonel," said Jules. "We will be back in a few hours."

On the drive into Montreal, Pappy wondered aloud why the colonel was being so anal about such a little thing.

"Mon ami, it is not a little thing. When the men go on an op, every second will matter. The G-Shock is a good utility watch. We issued them to our pilots when they deployed to the Gulf. They are inexpensive, accurate, rugged, and simple. Even a fighter pilot could operate it."

The two men shared a laugh.

"What did you think about Walker's tattoo?" said Jules.

"I ain't sure what's odder. A Para complaining about the pain of a tattoo or Colonel Skip figuring out why it was there."

They shared another laugh.

"Pappy, please remind me in the store. We need twenty watches, not nineteen."

"Twenty?"

"Oh yes," he said. "You forget Michel. The cook needs a watch also. Remember what Colonel Skip said. We are all together. We are brothers, mon frère."

Training for the Inaugural

September – November 2012

WASHINGTON

Bill was standing in Senator Fredericks' office and the situation was getting heated.

"Senator, I don't like it. I don't like it one bit."

"I don't give a good goddamn what you like, Bill. If this thing goes pear-shaped, we need to have top cover. Your Canadian friends will provide that. Am I clear?"

"Yes, sir, but I —"

"But nothing. That's enough from you!" blurted Fredericks, now exasperated. "I need go up to the Hill for a committee meeting. Stop acting like the leader of a Cub Scout pack and do what I told you, dammit. I have enough trouble with the Senate Whip and that idiot general over at the NSA without you adding to my grief. If this mission fails, we are all going to be in deep shit, and I for one am not willing to let that happen. For the last time, Donovan, do I make myself clear?"

"Yes, Senator, you do."

Bill was dismissed from the office with a perfunctory wave. He hated working for Senator Robert E. Lee Fredericks, but these were the cards he'd been dealt. Bill was an experienced enough poker player to know that it wasn't about the cards you held. It was how you played them, and that was what made poker the game of strategy most people didn't appreciate. He was passing through the outer office when he was halted.

"Colonel Donovan, sir."

"Yes, Miss Loretta. May I help you, ma'am?"

The long-suffering secretary, who mothered the Senator and who had done so since he had first come to Congress a quarter-century ago, obviously had more instructions from her lord and master.

"The Senator asked me to remind you that next Wednesday there is a budget hearing before the Intelligence Committee. He will need your briefing note no later than Tuesday at noon, Colonel."

Bill was about to tell Miss Loretta that this was not his first rodeo but thought better of it. She was completely loyal to the bastard for whom she worked, and being sassy with his Southern belle guard dog wouldn't win him favour with either her or Fredericks.

"Of course, ma'am. Please assure the Senator he will have it well before then."

Bill nodded, turned on his heel, and walked away.

He exited the building and walked out onto Constitution Avenue. His driver was waiting at the curb, but Bill waved him off. He needed to walk off his anger lest he do something he'd regret. Constitution became Maryland Avenue as it crossed 2nd Street NE. Walking by the headquarters of the Veterans of Foreign Wars, Bill wondered if he should find a local bar. No, it was too early. Anyway, there wasn't one within walking distance. Fifteen minutes later he strode up the steps of the nondescript brownstone that was home to Eagle Investments. Not meaning to, he slammed the door behind him.

Gunny glanced up, startled.

"Are you okay, boss?"

"Sorry, Gunny, I didn't mean to slam the door. Yeah, nothing's wrong. I'm just having one of those days, is all. I'm going for a walk. I need to clear my head."

"Aye, aye, sir."

Out on the street again, Bill took a couple of deep breaths. He decided to walk back toward the Mall. The Reflecting Pool and the Washington Monument always calmed him. His phone began to buzz in his pocket. It was a number he almost never saw but recognized immediately.

"Donovan here."

"Colonel Donovan, can you please engage your security app and redial?"

"Immediately," said Bill, and did as he was told.

"Hello, Bill."

"Hello, General. Is something wrong?"

"Not necessarily. I'm checking on you because I am aware that you've just had a testy conversation with our friend the Senator."

"Sir, I only just left his office. How did —"

"Never mind, Bill, but I need to confirm that the Senator doesn't know the real reason we need to collect our friend in the jungle. I had hoped that Eagle could handle this mission discreetly, but that option seems to have been removed by him."

"Yes, sir."

"Yes, sir, what?"

"Sorry, General. Yes, the option is no longer open to Eagle, and yes, the Senator is ignorant of why we need to go to the jungle. I have no doubt that he sees it as too risky and that's why he wants me to hand this off to the Canadians."

"Are they capable on such short notice?"

"Honestly, sir, I'm not sure. I will approach Colonel Schiaparelli and report back to you either way."

"Alright, Bill. Do I need to remind you that the reason we need this guy remains close hold?"

"No, General, you don't. I fully understand, sir."

"Get back to me soonest."

The line went dead. Thinking that his day had just gone from bad to worse, Bill decided to cancel his walk and return to the office.

Gunny stood as Bill came through the door.

"Sir, I wasn't expecting you back so soon. There's a Colonel Mackenzie waiting in your office. I offered him a coffee, but he said he didn't want anything."

"Thanks, Gunny, I've got this."

Bill stepped into his office with his hand outstretched.

"Great to see you, Mack. What can I do you for?"

Dougal Mackenzie stood to shake Bill's hand, stared at Bill's face, and frowned.

"Bill, you look like a truck ran you over. Is the Senator being a prick again?"

"Not 'again,' Mack. Still. Sometimes I wonder what it would be like to live in South America where politicians don't screw with iron colonels like me and you. Or how about that KGB colonel who threatened to bring down the whole Politburo if he couldn't take his family out of the USSR? What was his name again?"

"Kirov. Colonel Petrov Ivanovic Kirov. That's a great idea, Bill. Let's go live in a country where you need to line up for toilet paper. There's a wish you really don't want to come true. Sounds like the Senator's being even prickier than normal. And that's saying something for the Senator from Butt Falls, Arkansas. Only, you know what? I think I can help you with that."

"Don't get funny, Mack, and that's *Butte* Falls, which is in Oregon. Don't be a jerk. And he's not from Arkansas, so stop maligning my home state. Exactly how is me buying more guns from some arms manufacturer going to help me get the Senator off my back?"

Mack gave Bill a knowing grin and tapped the side of his nose with his index finger in the ancient conspirator's signal.

"Let me take you for a steak dinner, so we can discuss it.

"Sure."

Bill looked toward the outer office.

"Gunny, Mack, and I are heading out the back door. Close up shop for me, please. I'll see you in the morning."

"Aye, sir."

Bill and Mack walked up Maryland Avenue. The day was pleasant, and Bill still needed to walk off his frustration.

"There's a decent place off 8th Street," said Mack. "We haven't been there in a while."

"Sounds good," said Bill.

Although they'd been classmates at West Point, they hadn't had much to do with each other until they'd become Firstics. Then, each had become a cadet battalion commander in the 2nd Regiment. They'd hit it off immediately, despite coming from completely different backgrounds. Bill had grown up the privileged youngest son of a moneyed family in Arkansas, whereas Mack was the son and grandson of Pennsylvania coal miners.

"Feelin' any better yet?" said Mack.

"Keep walking," said Bill.

The best friends were chalk and cheese. Bill had gone to West Point because men in his family had attended either The Citadel or USMA since before the Civil War. Mack had attended to escape the coal mines and the gritty working-class life of central Pennsylvania. After graduation they went their separate ways, but in its inimitable way, the US Army kept sending them to the same posts — and to the same conflicts. They stayed close even after Bill moved to Army Intelligence and Mack climbed the greasy pole of Special Forces before leaving to become an arms broker.

"Good," said Mack, "the place is empty. Let's grab a booth at the back, away from prying eyes and ears."

The waiter came over with menus. Bill had never seen him before, making him suspicious.

"Greetings, gentlemen. What can I bring y'all to drink?"

"You look new," said Bill. "How long have you worked here?"

"Almost a month, sir. I started —"

Mack interrupted him.

"Never mind him, son. We'll have two Jim Beams. Rocks, with water on the side. My friend will have a broiled striploin, medium well, and I'll have a porterhouse, medium rare. We'll need a big bowl of your sweet potato fries on the side. There's no hurry; we have things to discuss. How's about bringing a platter of nachos to start us off? Only one check, please, and keep the JBs coming until I tell you to stop."

The waiter repeated the order back and got Mack's nod of approval, after which he headed to the bar. The first two whiskies were on the table promptly, exactly as ordered.

"Why'd you interrupt me?"

"Because you're in a foul mood and it's not likely that baby-faced kid's a spy for your boss, that's why. Cheers."

Bill stared at Mack and then smirked.

"Yeah, you're right. Cheers."

Both men took healthy slugs of their whiskies.

"What did the Senator do to piss off my battle buddy?"

"You remember me telling you I was exploring the possibility of setting up a subsidiary of Eagle?"

Mack nodded.

"I found a guy, and it's done. His name's Skip and I like him, Mack. He's ex–Canadian Army and armoured cav. He left the service early, as what we would call a colonel (P), on the fast track to general. He's a bit older than us and graduated from RMC when you and I were Plebes. He's head-hunted a group of ex-SOF guys, mostly Canadian."

"So far this doesn't sound like a problem," said Mack.

"I gave him my word that he'd have a minimum ninety days' notice to move. The Senator is forcing me to give them a no-fail mission that has to launch in about seven weeks from now. I wanted to hand it to an Eagle crew, but Fredericks vetoed it and I smell a rat."

The waiter approached, so Bill waited while he put two fresh drinks and the nachos on the table.

"The drinks are neat this time, gentlemen. Here's a bowl of ice for you when you're ready."

The waiter didn't wait for a reply.

"The kid's on the ball," said Mack.

Bill finished his first JB and grabbed the fresh one.

"We've been looking for a certain scumbag for reasons that don't matter, and he recently popped up on the radar. It's a routine job for Eagle, but Fredericks says it's trial by fire for the Canucks. I explained to him that they've barely got set up, but he didn't give a damn. He said it was perfect. If it fails, they will take the fall with no connection to us. For him it's a win-win."

"Not that I'm siding with the Senator, but I'm not seeing the problem here. How long have you known this guy? A few months, maybe? Sounds like he's been around the block. I know you were a Boy Scout, but this is the game you're in, my friend."

"No, Mack, it's not. I may not have known him very long, but he's one of us. When he comes to DC, you'll see what I mean. It sounds like he's put together a real A-team, so maybe I'm worrying for nothing, but here's the problem. This mission gives his guys no 'out' if they get stung. The Canadians will disown him and so will we. In fact, the nut-job running the country they're headed for will probably line them up and shoot 'em all."

"Where the hell are you sending these guys?"

Bill stared across the table at his friend and said nothing.

"Sorry. Forgot who I was talkin' to for a sec, there."

The two men nursed their drinks in silence for several minutes, Mack swirling the ice cubes in his glass to encourage them to melt.

"Listen," said Mack, "how badly do you want to be free of this Senator?"

"What are you talking about?"

"Your buddy Mack can make this Senator problem go away, but it's a question of how badly you need it done. Only thing is, it's a one-time, non-reversible event."

The waiter reappeared with two plates of grilled AAA American beef and a heaping bowl of sweet potato fries. He had included a large side of fried mushrooms with onions on his own initiative.

"In case you need something to offset the fries," he offered, placing the steaming plates between the two men. "Enjoy."

"Son, you have earned yourself a spot in heaven," said Mack, "or at the very least, a sizable tip."

The waiter was grinning from ear to ear as he headed back to the kitchen.

Bill cut into his striploin and took a bite. He closed his eyes for a moment to savour it, before opening them to stare at Mack.

"You have my undivided attention," said Bill.

MONTREAL

"Oui, hallo."

"Skip, it's me, Bill. I'm coming to Montreal to discuss something urgent."

"Sure, when are you coming?"

"Tomorrow, on the first flight I can grab. I'll text you when I'm boarding and call you when I land."

"Harry and I'll come get you."

"There's no need. I'll meet you at your office. Anyway, it needs to be private — only the two of us."

"What's wrong?"

"I can't talk. I'll see you tomorrow, Skip. Remember, just you and me."

"Okay, I hear you."

At breakfast in the main dining room, Skip explained the call to Harry, then drove down into the city alone. Skip waited for Bill in the lobby of the office tower.

"Hi, Skip. You didn't have to be standing here. I could have found my way up."

"I don't think so," said Skip as he held up a key card. "You need one of these. You also need a code to punch in for the tenth floor."

When the elevator doors opened, Bill asked if there was anybody else in the offices.

"Just you and me, Bill. Everybody's up at le Chalet being beasted by Harry."

"Sorry, Skip. This is about your first mission, and I don't mean to be so secretive, but it's highly sensitive. Once we hammer out some details, you can issue orders for your guys to commence the planning. Just not yet."

Skip guided his guest to the staff lounge and flipped on the high-end Faema coffeemaker. With so many coffee addicts, Skip had decided to spring for the two-thousand-dollar machine. It soon produced two cups of black coffee as Bill stared at the machine.

"Well, if snatching bad guys doesn't work out, you can always open a coffee bar."

"I'm glad you like it, because you bought it," said Skip. "Why do I feel like I'm being sandbagged?"

"I don't have to explain to you that the inaugural mission is key to our future together."

"Clearly," agreed Skip as he took a sip of his espresso. "Bill, you're making me nervous."

"I have a target," said Bill. "It's a relatively straightforward job, but behind the scenes, there's more to it, a lot more than I can share. Apart from wanting the target, this mission's a proof of concept for me. It's my way of proving to my superiors that bringing you aboard was worthwhile. It's a small job, but it's critical, and my team can't do it."

"Why not?"

"I can't say, but it's complicated," said Bill as he finally took a sip of coffee and paused. "The bad news is I need it done within the next seven weeks."

Skip put down his cup.

"What? You promised me ninety days minimum to prep for the first op. I've just barely assembled everybody. Are you serious, Bill? The camp isn't even fully built."

"I know, I know, and I'm truly sorry. The target's been silent for over a year. He's finally where he's vulnerable, and it's the first time in almost two years we've had any eyes on the guy. The trick is we need him alive. He's a Colombian named Lopez, and he grew up with Miguel Rodríguez Orejuela."

"The guy you have in prison? The head of the Cali Cartel?"

"Yes. Lopez was sent to Mexico through some kind of a deal and quickly rose in Sinaloa, but then things went sideways. The bottom line is his old boss in the Sinaloa Cartel put a price on his head. If he goes dark again, there's no telling when or where he'll be the next time we find him."

Bill hesitated.

"Or find pieces of him."

"I'm confused," said Skip. "I thought the cartels were done."

"Yes and no. It's not the Wild West anymore, but they're still a problem. They may even have reached their high-water mark, but this guy is important for other reasons. For starters, he's in hiding because he was a rat — sort of like the Joe Valachi of the drug families — and we want him bad. Again, I can't go into details."

Skip's face was clouding over as Bill spoke.

"He's spread money around and bought protection in a very remote locale. It's remarkable what you can buy when you bribe people with truckloads of untraceable US cash. I don't care about the money he's got, quite frankly, but he's got secrets locked in his head and we need to know what they are. That's where you come in."

Skip didn't speak, but Bill could see his jaw muscles clenching and unclenching.

"Skip," groaned Bill, "my balls are on the line here. Seriously, no bullshit. You can say no, although if I go home empty-handed, I have no idea how the Senator will react. Our whole joint venture might just be stillborn."

It was the first time Bill had mentioned he was working for a US senator, though it wasn't clear whether it was on or off the books. Skip let the comment slide and sat silently.

"Thoughts?" said Bill.

Skip looked pensive.

"I can see why you needed to fly up here. Give me more details and we'll talk about it. When do you fly back to whatever rock you crawled out from under?"

"I'm booked back to DC tomorrow morning on United 6052, leaving at eleven o'clock from Dorval. That should give us enough time to hammer out what you need, don't you think?"

Skip glanced down at his watch and scowled while Bill sat in silence.

"I'm not fucking happy, Bill. There's a lot of stuff here you keep telling me is critical but can't tell me about."

Bill was taken aback by Skip's sudden profanity.

"I understand, Skip, and I'm being as open with you as the situation will allow. You've got to believe me."

Skip pondered his coffee for a long moment.

"I believe you, Bill, but that doesn't mean I'm happy about it."

"Do we carry on, or should I just go back to DC?"

"I'll order a pizza and you can convince me that I haven't wasted the last four months of my life and my entire reputation."

He reached over for the house phone and ordered some food, then called down to the security desk to tell them to pay for it and have someone bring it up. That done, he began giving Skip some idea of why the target was so important, being careful to give him only what he needed to know. A short time later, the elevator buzzed loudly. Skip walked over and punched in a security code. The door opened and one of the security guards stood inside holding the pizza. Skip didn't invite him in. He grabbed the box and handed the young man a fifty-dollar bill.

"Non, monsieur. That is too much."

Skip patted him on the shoulder and pushed the button to close the elevator door. He walked back to the lounge and dropped the pizza on the coffee table.

"Speak," he said to Bill.

The discussions went later than expected. They wrapped up just after midnight and it only then occurred to Bill that he hadn't booked a hotel. Skip told him not to sweat it and they walked over to his condo in silence.

On the way to the airport the next morning Skip broke the tension.

"Obviously I don't like this, and I have to study it. My gut tells me we can pull it off and that there's too much invested to let it all go away. But my brain tells me to be careful. Either way, I have some calls to make and some favours to ask for."

"I'm sorry," said Bill. "I'll help in any way I can. I know the time is short — too short. Really, I do."

"I'm not sure exactly how to put this, Bill, so I'll just say it. You mentioned you did a deep dive on me, so you must know that I have a lot of contacts in a lot of interesting places."

"I do," said Bill. "That's one of the reasons I wanted you to form the team."

"That's what I figured. We've known each other a while, and I like you, but I have only a vague idea who you're working for. I'm taking you at your word, but I need to tell you that if this is some kind of a set-up, I won't forgive or forget."

Bill looked at Skip, and a shadow crossed his face.

"Are you threatening me?"

The atmosphere in the car grew suddenly cold, and Skip didn't answer immediately.

"No," said Skip. "But you're a serious man and I want you to know that I am too."

Skip took the A20 to the airport, and there was a deafening silence for almost ten minutes. He eyed his passenger.

"I believe you're being straight with me, Bill, and I'm proceeding on that basis. I really want to trust you, so I'll pull out all the stops to get this rolling. But let's be honest. The risks here are all on me and my guys."

"You're right," said Bill. "Like I said, I'll help any way I can, but my fingerprints can't be on this. I hope I can explain why later. One last thing: please keep the target location close hold until you agree to accept the task."

Skip pulled over to the curb at the departures level.

"Give me twenty-four hours with no interruptions. I'll call you after that and brief you in broad strokes, whatever I decide."

Bill looked across at Skip, then leaned over and shook his hand without speaking. He left the car and walked into the airport.

On the drive back into the city, Skip's mind was racing. He tapped the steering wheel.

"Hello, Mercedes," he said.

"Hello, Skip," mimicked the car's disembodied voice.

"Call Jules," he said.

"Calling Jules Simone."

"Colonel. Qu'est-ce que c'est?"

"RSM, send a vehicle to my condo ASAP. Tell Harry and Alex I need them both to be ready for mission planning, and recall anybody who's not there. No exceptions, including anybody who's at the Ox. Effective immediately, the Cohort is confined to le Chalet."

"Oui, Colonel."

Skip killed the connection and slipped into the traffic stream leaving the airport.

$$\text{❦ ❦ ❦}$$

Bill sat in the departure lounge waiting for his flight to board. He reached for his phone and opened a secure app. There was only one number in it, which he dialled.

"Yes, Bill."

"Sir, I am in Montreal, waiting to board. I believe we are a go, sir. I will confirm in twenty-four hours."

There was no reply, and the line went dead.

Le Chalet

It was shortly after noon when the black SUV arrived in front of the main lodge, where Alex and Harry stood waiting. Skip stepped out.

"Before you bombard me with questions, let me tell you I've spent most of the last eighteen hours talking with Bill Donovan. We have our first mission, if I'm willing to accept it. We launch in just over six weeks, and there's no use in bitching about it. There's a five-day window based on solid intel. Not before forty-six days and not after fifty-one days. That's all the freedom of manoeuvre we have."

Harry and Alex saw the look on Skip's face and kept silent.

"Let's go inside so we can talk about this."

Most of the men were gathered in the Great Room. Skip dropped his canvas attaché bag and scanned the room slowly.

"Gentlemen, I know I said we'd have ninety days to prep for the launch of our first mission. We don't. We have just under fifty."

The men started shifting in their seats and murmuring.

"Quiet," said Harry.

Skip waited for silence.

"I won't go into details yet. I need to have a hard look at the options and then analyze this. In the meantime, I ask you to do only one thing: decide if you are in or out. Anybody wanting out gets his full share of money back, with no questions asked and no shame in the decision. I asked you to join us under certain conditions. I've just broken a major condition. If you want out, please tell Franz-Josef."

The men looked around the room to see how others might be reacting.

"Harry, Alex, and I are going to my office and are not to be disturbed. I'll have more to say by supper. Jules, please have Michel make some sandwiches for the three of us and have him bring them into the office. The rest of you, go eat."

The three men separated themselves from the group and walked to Skip's office. Skip shut the door.

"This is absolute crap," blurted Alex. "Are we planning a kid's birthday party? What gives, Skip?"

Before Skip could reply, Harry stepped in.

"Jumper, sit your ass down and shut the hell up. What's wrong with you? Colonel Skip will brief us, then we'll have a chance to discuss. And watch your tone. You know better."

Alex looked chastened.

"Sorry, Harry. Colonel Skip, I apologize. No offence."

Skip was both taken aback and bemused.

"None taken, Alex, and you're right: this is crap. If it helps, I agree with your sentiment. However, I told Bill we would do our best to execute the mission. So, unless we see a showstopper or discover that everyone except us has bailed, we will do our best to execute." He unzipped his attaché bag and pulled out some papers. "Listen up."

When Skip finished bringing his two deputies up to speed, he asked if there were any questions. Alex shook his head no.

"Alex, I can see you're annoyed," said Skip, "and you have every right to be, but do you see any showstoppers?"

"Not at this point."

Harry spoke up. "I have only one question. Can we trust Bill?"

"Good question, Harry," said Skip. "Damned good question. I hope so."

The three men worked as they ate lunch. They took a fifteen-minute stretch in mid-afternoon and by supper had most of an outline concept, in spite of the fact that Skip had given them only a vague idea of where they were headed. They agreed that the hard part would be building the confidence required within the Cohort to allow the men to work closely with each other. Building trust took time, and it was the one missing ingredient.

"The stakes are high," said Skip. "An operation like this has to be perfectly executed. One stumble could bring the whole thing crashing down. But this is what everybody signed on for."

What was left unstated was that since they were no longer working for the Crown, failure could mean prison in some foreign hole in the ground. The pressing question was how many members they would have available for the mission. They agreed that whatever the numbers, if someone was not deemed ready before deployment, they would be scrubbed. It was too risky not to.

"I'll make that decision based on recommendations from the two of you, but don't discuss it with the others."

Harry and Alex nodded.

"Last point," said Skip. "We wear our game faces starting right now. There can be no hint of negativity. A little doubt means we appreciate the risk, but no negativity. You two know we can do this."

"Got it," said Harry.

"Agreed," said Alex.

The trio stepped out of the office in time for supper. Most of the men were idling around the lounge area and a couple were outside. Skip caught Franz-Josef's eye. Franz-Josef cocked his head. Skip raised both eyebrows and his chin — an interrogative well known to the German. Franz-Josef smirked and shook his head slowly side to side. No takers on Skip's offer to step away. It was an excellent start. Skip asked Harry to gather everyone.

"Listen up. Jules, please call in the guys who are outside. The Colonel's got something to say."

Skip waited in silence for the men to come inside and for everyone to settle.

"First, I want to say thank you. Franz-Josef tells me no one wants out. I'll take that as a vote of trust. We have a lot of details to pound out and precious little time to do it. At least we now have a solid concept. I have complete confidence you are all up to this challenge."

Skip paused and scanned the room to gauge the response.

"Here's what you need to know for now. We're going on a snatch mission. There is someone who has been in hiding, and we need to go get him. We'll form two squads, Red and Green. Harry will lead Red. Alex will have Green. In the next day or so, Harry will assign each of you to your squad. We start tomorrow with in-briefings."

Skip stopped for a sip of coffee as the men looked at each other. He could see them wondering which teams they'd be on.

"Here are two fundamentals you need to make part of your understanding of how we will operate. First, although we will carry small arms, there'll be no shooting except to save the life of a squad member. Second, we will communicate exclusively by hand signals. No talking. Jules, Breaker, Pappy, and Franz-Josef, you won't deploy this time. That's enough information to get your minds in gear. It's time to eat."

After supper, Skip called Breaker to come to him.

"Yes, Colonel."

"Phone Colonel Donovan on a secure line. Tell him I don't have time to talk, but say we are a go and that I'll call him back soon. Also, tell him to be ready for requests."

"Requests, Colonel? What kind of requests?"

"Just tell him. Off you go."

Skip grabbed a coffee and asked Alex, Harry, and Pappy to join him in the lounge. Scanning the room, he saw Jules and waved him over, too.

"Gentlemen, small arms are not my forte. All squad members need to carry side arms, so what do you recommend?"

Alex spoke first.

"I'm not a fan of the Browning. It's too ancient for my money. Then again, I'm not a pistol expert. Harry knows more about this than I do."

"I'm with Alex, Skip. If we're going with pistols, then we have lots of choice, but we need stopping power, especially if the target's wearing body armour. It gets worse if he has an assault rifle to shoot back. Pappy, the SAS carry a variety of pistols. What do you think?"

"Well, it's usually based on the mission. For what we're looking at, my suggestion is the SIG-Sauer P228. It was always the weapon of choice. It's solid, reliable, and has reasonable stopping power. That's the ticket for us, Colonel."

Harry and Alex both agreed.

"Right. We need a bunch of 228s. Pappy, talk to Eagle. They'll provide. That's enough from me. Harry, this is your show. I have a bunch of calls to make and some serious favours to call in. Let's have a drink tonight and a chat. You can brief me then on what you're doing."

"Right, Skip."

Skip rose and walked to his office, shut the door, sat, and tried to clear his head. He needed aircraft, a staging area, a command centre ... He grabbed his taccuino and pen and began making notes. Then he shouted for Breaker.

There was a rap on the door. It opened and Breaker stepped in.

"Did you call Eagle?"

"Yes, Colonel. I spoke with Colonel Bill and he's a happy man."

"Good. I need to make a secure call to Colombia. I've got the number here. Can you set it up for me, please?"

"No problem."

Skip slid the piece of paper across his desk.

"Give me ten minutes then establish the call. Please shut the door again on your way out."

Back in the lounge, Harry continued with the array of tasks that needed to be done to get them rolling. Pappy spoke up.

"Leave the weapons to me, Harry. I'll call back to the Eagle team that's still working at the Ox and also contact Gunny. Tomorrow morning, Jules and I will establish a field firing range. We should have what we need in a day, maybe two days."

"Make it one," said Harry. "How fast can we get those weapons?"

"The lads making the helicopter runs from down south have been pretty good getting stuff here quickly."

"Good, because we need them here *fast*. I need everyone fully comfortable with their personal weapons ASAP."

"Aye, Harry."

Pappy stood and Jules joined him.

"Anything else?"

"Thanks, gentlemen," Harry said, then turned to Jules and Pappy. "Wait. I know we're in the middle of nowhere up here, but what about the noise? Won't we attract visitors?"

"I do not think so, Harry. I already took care of that," said Jules. "Hunting is a big deal here, and a lot of the local boys have small arms and target rifles. The police around here do not worry too much about it. We were planning an indoor range, but there is no time yet to build it. Last week I applied for a permission for a private shooting club. There are lots of them up here and I have already phoned to some of them. We also joined la Fédération Québécoise de Tir. I call us Club de Tir Léopard. We are very private and not open to the public. Signs are being made for the gate."

"Good," said Harry. "That's all for now."

They stepped away, leaving Harry and Alex to speak privately.

"What do you think?" said Harry.

"I'm okay," said Alex.

Harry paused for a moment.

"Me too, for now, but there's a hockey sock full of stuff to do."

The next morning Skip called Bill on a secure line to confirm that they were a go, but there were some issues he needed to ask about.

"Like what?" inquired Bill.

"I've reached out and confirmed I have enough connections to get us in and out of where we're going, but it won't come cheap, and we haven't talked about money."

"That is the least of your worries, Skip. I'll arrange to put a large draft of cash into your corporate account. If you need more, have Franz-Josef say so. I appreciate that I have made this harder than it should have been and that keeping my fingerprints off this mission comes at a premium, but I really only care about two things: get me Lopez and do it before we run out of time."

Skip did not respond.

"You still there, Skip?"

"I'm still here. Confirm that we're headed for Colombia."

"I confirm. And also Brazil."

"Brazil?"

Bill could hear the chill in Skip's voice.

"The target is on the border. Listen, Skip, I know I put you in a bind, and I'll make it up to you. I promise."

"Bill, you do know I'm still tracking all your promises, right?"

"Ack that," said Bill.

The following two weeks were busy but highly productive. Intel was updated daily, but none of it changed the overall plan. Eagle was quick off the mark with the weapons. As well as the pistols, Harry asked for assault rifles, and Eagle sent four LWRC Ultra-Compact Individual Weapons, which were 5.56mm assault rifles developed especially for Special Forces. They also sent bulletproof vests so the men could accustom themselves to wearing them. Last, Eagle provided four shotguns, modified for door busting. Skip expressed concerns about the amount of firepower they were amassing, and Harry assured him it was absolutely necessary. Skip kept any further concerns to himself.

The preparations, which initially focused on fitness, soon shifted to drills. Harry and Alex assembled the two squads. Harry also established a third, smaller squad. Harry initially called it "Reserve," but Skip renamed it the "Quick Reaction Force." Once the three squads began to gel, Harry and Alex introduced Skip's concept of battlefield jazz, only to be told that word had already spread through Pappy, Breaker, and Jules. The men had been discussing the concept for several days, although there were some skeptics.

One morning at breakfast, Alex had asked Skip about the third squad.

"I may regret asking, but why change the name? What's the big deal?"

Alex could see Harry's face lighting up.

"Alex, it isn't a big deal, but a reserve is not a QRF. However, a QRF can be a reserve."

"Harry, you are enjoying this way too much," said Alex.

"I warned you that working for Skip was like being on course."

"Alex, I'll spare you the staff college explanation for now, but it'll be clear soon. Harry, on that subject, I see that you've assigned Les to lead it. That's a critical task. Are you sure?"

Harry was chewing on some bacon and looked at Skip silently for a moment.

"Yes, Skip, I am. Alex and I have been watching Les closely and he'll be fine."

"I agree," said Alex.

"Like I've said, tactically, it's your show, Harry."

Jules had built a surprisingly challenging field pistol range. Ingeniously, he'd had the men rig a series of large tarps to create a semi-enclosed space. The effect was a reasonable muffling of the sound at a distance. Breaker and Pappy had gone to the edge of their property and done a test. The pistol shots were audible but surprisingly faint. Pappy also supervised the construction of a mock-up of the target building, or at least what little they knew of it.

"It looks good," said Skip, "but the décor lacks a certain something."

"Aye, Colonel. Not exactly Balmoral Castle."

The benefit of careful recruiting now paid dividends. Terry, the combat engineer, was a hobby modeller and he rose to the challenge of creating a scale model of the target area, including the river and the landing zone. He had an eye for detail and spent his non-training time using Google Earth to get as many features as possible. He constructed the building from scratch as well as a variety of trees common to the locale. Skip teased him about Pangratti going into the architectural model business. Terry laughed it off, but he nonetheless looked pleased to be praised for his efforts.

In passing, Skip asked Pappy to get a couple of blackout bags they could use for hoods when they grabbed Lopez, eliciting quizzical looks from the younger soldiers. Skip made a face, so Alex explained.

"They're amused because you're a Cold War dinosaur, Colonel."

"I beg your pardon?"

"Black hoods are Hollywood, but I wouldn't expect you to know that. Hussars drink sherry in their tanks and deal death at three klicks. Hoods are out. In Afghanistan, we came up with a better solution. We used a large, twisted kerchief to stop the target from making any noise while allowing him to breathe, and we used tight-fitting welder's goggles with the lenses spray-painted black. We also had heavy-duty industrial ear defenders."

"Explain this to me, please," said Skip.

"We'd grab the guy, gag him, put on the goggles, and slap the ear defenders on him. The sudden loss of vision and hearing inevitably caused severe vertigo in most of them. The poor buggers would wobble, and many couldn't stand upright on their own. It was perfect for disorientation. Before they knew it, they were face down in the back of a LAV and headed to Kandahar Airfield."

Skip grunted and muttered something about young Turks.

"Pardon me?" said Alex.

"I was merely commenting on how damned clever you Afghan vets are."

Harry had made judicious use of the expertise available to him. Pappy conducted daily lessons on close-quarter unarmed combat. The sessions were short and usually painful, particularly for those whom Pappy selected for his demonstrations. Pappy ensured there was enough discomfort to make the men remember the lesson, but without lasting damage. True to Skip's direction, the focus was on incapacitation, not killing. Pappy's direction was clear:

"Kill if necessary, but not necessarily kill."

Alex directed daily drills in complete silence using only hand signals, both close up and at a distance. He proved to be a demanding taskmaster, but the men worked hard to please him. It was a valuable refresher for the ex-SOF members and highly demanding for those not accustomed to working in silence.

"I feel like I'm learning a new language," said Terry.

Harry drew upon his love of small arms to refresh everyone's shooting skills, usually calling upon Walker when he wanted a demo. Harry had asked Eagle to include Simunition ammo and conversion kits with their weapons package since close-quarter shooting was the focus. That got the men sensitive to being accurate while not being hit themselves. Finally, Harry moved everyone to the field firing range, which he'd modified for intensive snap shooting based on the British Army instinctive shooting manual.

Jules had refreshed everyone on combat first aid, focusing on stabilizing wounds for rapid extraction.

As for Skip, he was making calls to people he hadn't seen in years and to one man in particular. Eventually, he thanked his old contacts and said he didn't need their help, because one course of action had been confirmed.

In the evenings, Skip could see the men were exhausted. More importantly, though, the squads were gelling. Cohesion was growing and the three squads were spending more and more time in each other's company. Still, Skip worried about overtiring everyone and discussed it with Harry.

"Skip, you're right to worry. Trust me — Alex, Jules, Pappy, and I are keeping a close watch. Nobody's showing any signs of distress, either mental or physical. Their tails are up, and tomorrow we're conducting a short live-action drill. Pappy mocked up our target area in half-scale, and Alex and I will take our two squads through in a timed run with the QRF as enemy force. Why don't you come along and see how they look?"

"Thanks, Harry. I'll do that. What time?"

"That's the rub, Skip. It will be a very un-cavalry hour before dawn."

Pappy was far too cheerful.

"How can you be so bloody pleasant at this hour?" grumbled Skip. "It's miserable out here."

"Is the Colonel ready to come along, or is he returning to the officers' mess?"

"Shut the hell up and let's get going."

Jules was waiting in a small clearing representing the landing zone. Squads Red and Green knelt a few metres apart. Once Jules saw Pappy and Skip, he said, "Go." The two squads moved off. Pappy kept Skip close enough to see what was happening but sufficiently back not to influence any behaviour. The squads moved with precision and confidence. At the mock target building, two members of the QRF stepped out unexpectedly for a smoke. Harry's squad subdued them without a sound.

Les and another QRF man appeared with weapons drawn to rescue them. Alex's men took them out before either one loosed a round. Then Alex's squad immobilized their prisoners, while Harry's went inside to grab their target, in this case a full-sized training mannequin. The dummy was bound, gagged, and fitted with goggles and ear defenders. Everyone took up positions to return to the landing zone. When Harry gave the signal, off they went. The drill was complete as the sun began to break through the trees.

"Impressive," said Skip, "even at half-scale."

"Careful, Colonel. You don't want to be swelling their heads," warned Pappy.

With the men headed to the showers in preparation for breakfast, Skip took Harry aside.

"It's been a month of hard training. What do you think about a stand-down weekend? Can we spare the time?"

"I think we can," said Harry. "They've been going at it hard. We could all use a break, even if only a short one."

"Done," said Skip.

During breakfast, Skip rose and asked for everyone's attention.

"Impressive morning, everyone. I can see all your hard work paying off. Harry is getting soft in his dotage, and he's asked me to give you guys a stand-down weekend — a couple of days to escape le Chalet. I have acceded to his request, so here's the deal. Enjoy Montreal or someplace nearby. My only stipulation is that no one travels alone. Squad members must travel in pairs or greater. I don't care whether you're headed to a brasserie or to a library. With apologies, Pappy, Franz-Josef, I need you to stay here. I'll also need a few volunteers from the QRF to stay as security with them."

All four men raised their hands immediately.

"Thank you. Finish your breakfast."

Skip remembered how important these events were when he was at RMC. Once per term, the commandant would announce a stand-down weekend. Cadets were encouraged to go home to clear their minds. Skip usually took the Bishop and one or two of his mates whose families lived too far away to make the trip worthwhile. They'd inevitably return to the college raving about Mrs. Schiaparelli's cooking and complaining that they'd need a month to burn off all the calories.

Franz-Josef pretended to be crestfallen when Skip told him he was confined. Between the nightlife downtown and the pretty Québécoises that abounded, Skip had visions of having to bail Franz-Josef out of jail — again. Besides, Jupp had introduced the German three-man card game known as Skat to Pappy and Jules, and they were quickly becoming addicted. Jules opted to remain, but Breaker went home to Saint-Jean. With all of that decided, Skip tucked into his breakfast.

MONTREAL

Skip, Harry, and Alex drove to Montreal together. Harry had finally bought a condo in Skip's building, and Alex was going to bunk with him. On the drive, Skip suggested they have dinner at his place. They could enjoy a meal together and casually review their progress in the privacy of Skip's apartment. Harry and Alex instantly agreed. Skip was demanding in command, but in the comfort of his own home, he was both generous and unflinchingly hospitable.

On the drive south, Alex asked Skip a question.

"Why do we do so much business over meals?"

"Better stop that line of questioning before Colonel Skip makes you an offer you can't refuse," said Harry.

Alex looked at him and then at Skip with puzzlement. He was about to speak when Skip and Harry began laughing. On arrival, Skip told them he'd see them at 19:00 and not to be late.

At the appointed hour, Skip could hear voices in the corridor, and he opened the door as Harry raised his hand to knock.

"How do you do that?" he said. "Do you lurk? Do you have video surveillance of the corridor?"

Skip laughed and let the two men in.

"It's good to see you laugh," said Harry, holding out a bottle of wine. "You've been quite dour of late. This is for your table. I know you're too cheap to buy good wine, so Alex and I bought you a bottle from your homeland."

He handed Skip a bottle of Ruffino Chianti Classico Riserva Ducale. Harry knew his friend well enough to know that, at about thirty-five dollars a bottle, it was more than double what Skip would normally pay for any bottle of wine.

"This is very generous. Did you ask Franz-Josef for an advance on your quarterly dividend? Thank you both."

Skip's penchant for cheap wine was one of his well-known and more puzzling quirks. Alex had heard the rumours but wasn't convinced of their authenticity. He had once been present when Skip had cracked a two-hundred-and-fifty-dollar bottle of single malt scotch for a bunch of friends. Could this man really drink ten-dollar wine?

"Skip, is it true you prefer cheap wine, or is Harry taking the piss?" Alex asked.

"Go ahead, Skip," Harry urged. "Tell him about your wine fetish."

Unruffled, Skip invited his guests to sit. Seemingly to make the point, he opened a new bottle of 1998 Lagavulin Double Matured single malt scotch, costing somewhere between two hundred and two hundred and fifty dollars a bottle.

"Please help yourselves. Ice is in the regimental ice bucket over here. I won't offer you water, so you won't inadvertently offend me." As Alex reached for the bottle, Skip said, "Am I to explain my so-called fetish?"

Harry nodded while Alex poured three glasses of nectar from the Isle of Islay.

"Harry, it's not a fetish. It's my conviction that wine is one of the world's great scams. Of course, there's a difference between a fifty-dollar reserve and a ten-buck jug of table wine. However, any difference there may be between a twenty-five-dollar bottle and a two-hundred-dollar bottle is lost on me."

Skip paused and took a small sip of whisky.

"When I was CO, my 2IC and my adjutant were both wine snobs, who tried endlessly to convert me. Their constant prattling about bouquet, nose, and body drove me to distraction, and I told them so, repeatedly. It merely encouraged them to try harder."

Skip stopped and took another short sip, enjoying both the whisky and the memory.

"They even enrolled me in a London wine society. I've been a member for decades and haven't bought a single bottle. I was never going to pay twenty-five quid for a single bottle and then have the privilege of paying to have it shipped. After a while, it became a challenge to buy the cheapest bottle of plonk I could find, then serve it to them at dinner parties."

Skip stopped once more as he chortled at the memory.

"I once served a bottle of Beaujolais I picked up in a French commissary for under two dollars a bottle. The 2IC gagged and the adjutant made a face, while their wives laughed so hard, they wept. The woman I was then dating didn't share the wives' amusement. That was my first clue. I removed the offending bottle and produced something more fitting."

"Wait one," said Alex. "First clue?"

"About the woman," said Harry.

"What woman?" asked Skip.

"The one you were dating. What ever happened to her?"

"It didn't work out. Like many women, she didn't get the army or why we all loved it so much." Skip stood. "Time to eat. *Tutti a tavola per mangiare.*"

Over dinner, the three men reviewed the training thus far. Skip offered that the squads had gelled much more quickly than he'd expected. Harry felt it was due at least in part to all the members having taken great pride in being soldiers. Regardless of why they had taken off the uniform, they were all eager to be back among comrades. Alex agreed, but Skip sensed there was something he was holding back.

"What's the matter?" said Skip.

"Colonel, I don't want to sound like a suck-up is all, but …"

"But? But what?"

"A bunch of the guys have mentioned to me they appreciate your leadership style. You trust them and treat them like men. Frankly, it drives them to work harder because they don't want to disappoint you."

There was a moment of awkwardness, and Harry broke the silence.

"Too late, Alex. You do sound like a suck-up."

Skip burst out laughing, barely managing to refrain from spraying everyone with the delicious Riserva Ducale.

"Enough," he said. "Thanks, Alex. I appreciate it. What do we do next to sharpen the men's skills?"

The question opened a discussion on some close-combat drills that both Alex and Harry were familiar with from training with SOF. They described them to Skip. The training would build trust within the squads as well as hone some shooting and situational awareness skills. Harry finished describing one particularly harrowing extraction drill as Skip's phone rang. He excused himself from the table. Picking up the phone, he yelled over his shoulder.

"Harry, there're some pastries in the fridge. Alex, are you qualified to run my coffee machine?" He turned his face to the phone. "Hello."

"Hey, buddy."

It was Bill's unmistakable twang.

"Time for a chat?"

"Perfect time. I'm having dinner with Harry and Alex. We've been reviewing the training. Can I put you on speaker?"

"Skip, wait. I can give you more, but do you trust these two guys to know all the details already? Maybe I can tell you, and then you could filter the data to them."

"No," said Skip, placing the phone on the table. "You're on speaker. Say hello to Harry and Alex, my two deputies."

There was dead air for about three seconds while Bill recovered from what amounted to Skip giving him a slap.

"Hey, guys. Nice to talk to y'all. How are things up there?"

Harry, despite his years of experience with the US military, had never been comfortable with the innate American condescension toward their supposed best friends north of the border. He coughed.

"No worries, Bill," said Harry, "although there's a bit of an ill wind blowing in from south of the St. Lawrence River."

Alex looked at Skip but held his tongue.

"Whatever that means," said Bill. "I'm just calling to confirm some details."

Skip held up his right index finger in front of Harry.

"Ready our end, Skip," Bill said. "Your request to have all of your equipment delivered to that specific location is arranged, so leave all your stuff behind. I have a buddy who's done this several times, and all he needs now is a date and twenty-four hours' notice."

"Roger that," said Skip.

"He's familiar with the base you chose and has delivered items there before. By the way, I have some contacts there.”

“No, thanks,” said Skip. “Fingerprints, remember, Bill?”

“Yes, Skip. I’m just trying to help.”

Skip looked at his two dinner companions. Neither man had any questions.

“Thanks, Bill. Talk soon.”

Skip ended the call, flipped over the phone, and removed the battery. Looking up, he saw Harry and Alex staring oddly at him.

“Okay, so maybe I have trust issues. Where’s my espresso?”

Alex continued to have an odd expression on his face.

“What’s wrong?” said Skip.

“Nothing’s wrong. I just didn’t track all of that conversation.”

“That’s my fault,” admitted Skip. “I haven’t brought you up to speed on ingress and egress, mostly because it depended on Bill being able to arrange delivery of our weapons. And my contact finally confirming his ability to help. I mentioned a name in passing a couple of weeks ago. Coronel Augusto Maria Corrido di Tomasino. He’s an old friend of mine from my days with Interpol and he’s now the head of the special anti-drug unit in Colombia.”

“Interpol? Isn’t that police?” said Alex.

“I’ll fill you in later,” said Harry.

“I reached out to him for help as soon as Bill dropped the mission on us. He said yes immediately, but needed time to work out the details, especially since I wanted as few people involved as possible. He just confirmed that he’d worked out all the details a few days ago, and I called Bill regarding the equipment drop.”

“Sorry, Alex,” Harry said. “Skip’s been keeping me in the loop, but I wanted you concentrating on your squad.”

“That’s fine, Harry. I get it. So, Skip, does that mean we’re going to Colombia?”

“Exactly,” said Skip. “We’re also paying a short visit to Brazil. At least you two are.”

“Two countries?”

“Now’s as good a time as any to bring you both fully up to speed, assuming nothing changes in the next few weeks.”

Skip grabbed his espresso and began to give the men the finer details of how they were going to get to their area of operations. The briefing took another ten minutes.

"So that's it in a nutshell, like I said, unless there's a change," Skip concluded.

The three men sat quietly sipping coffee for several moments.

"By the way, Colonel," said Alex, "you never answered my question."

"Which one?"

"About the meals and doing business."

"Shut up," Harry interrupted, "before Skip orders me to put a horse's head in your bed."

Le Chalet

The men returned fresh and ready to be put through the new paces that the three men had discussed. Skip found a secure message from Bill waiting for him. Among other things, it fleshed out details of both the house and the compound, causing Terry and Pappy to modify the model and mock-up, respectively. Breaker deciphered the coded text immediately after it had arrived and brought it to Skip.

"Welcome back, Colonel," he said. "I've deciphered a coded message for you and put it on your desk."

"Thanks, Breaker."

Skip read the message twice. It took him thirty-five minutes to go through it in detail. He made notes, then did another mission analysis before heading off to dinner. On his way to the dining room, he stopped to speak with Harry.

"Gather the O Group in my office at nineteen hundred, please."

"How about Les?"

"No, not Les. We'll read him in closer to the mission. I think my office is big enough."

"Skip, are you having doubts about Les?"

"No, but he's quite junior, and I want him focused on leading the QRF. I'll include him if you insist."

"It's all good, Skip. I'll stage it for you. Mind if I don't join you for supper? That meal you gave us yesterday will take me a month to work off. Your mom would be proud."

"See you at nineteen hundred," said Skip, grinning. He walked into the dining room and saw Franz-Josef sitting with Jules and Pappy at a table for four. He went over.

"Mind if I join you gentlemen?"

"Herr Oberst, bitte," said Franz-Josef, pulling back the chair next to his own.

"You gentlemen have a mini–UN General Assembly going on here."

"Und now we have the Italian ambassador to make our delegation complete. Did you have a good weekend in Montreal?"

"Yes, thanks. It wasn't really a break, though. Harry, Alex, and I worked, but a change is almost a rest, even if only for two days. What about you three? All quiet?"

"Ja, very calm."

"Has Franz-Josef skinned you two at Skat yet?"

"Not quite," said Pappy. "It seems that our young airman here learned to play the game in Baden-Baden. If I'm not mistaken, Franz-Josef has not yet got over the shock."

Jules displayed a toothy smile. He was the proverbial cat who'd eaten the canary, and Skip was pleased to see him fitting in so well.

"*Ach du Lieber*. I should have smelled a mouse when Jules said, 'What do you call this game again?'"

Jules and Pappy startled to laugh. After a moment, even Franz-Josef had to agree that it had been a smooth con.

"Smelled a *rat*, Franz-Josef," said Pappy.

"Pardon?"

That made the two men laugh louder.

When the laughter died away, however, the three ex–senior NCOs could see that Skip was preoccupied with what the secure message had passed on. Breaker hadn't breathed a word of its content. The men kept the conversation light. Pappy extolled Jules's bush skills, expressing surprise that a flyboy could snare, skin, and roast a rabbit over an open flame.

"Our friend here is also a decent stalker," said Pappy. "We took a long walk through le Chalet's acreage on Saturday and spotted a white-tailed buck. Listening to gunshots in the distance, I was a little worried that we weren't wearing Day-Glo vests. Anyway, if we'd been carrying anything more than pocketknives, there would have been venison for supper."

"I gather you didn't drag Jupp into the bush with you," said Skip.

"Herr Oberst, you make the fun? Why would I want to walk in the woods? I was able to hear the game between Leverkusen und Bayern-München on der Deutsche Rundfunk."

"Franz-Josef," Pappy interjected, "you are not like any Deutscher I've ever known. I thought all you blokes loved the woods."

"Yes, you are right. But you are forgetting that I grew up in Ost Deutschland. When I was a boy, if you went to the woods, the Stasi would have many questions for your neighbours. *Und so, mein Freund,* we created inside because outside was *nicht gut.*"

Skip stood abruptly, and the three men rose from their chairs. "Please excuse me. I have to prepare for my O Group," he announced, and walked away.

"The Colonel don't look so good, if you ask me," said Pappy quietly.

"Do not worry," said Jules. "Le Colonel will be fine."

Skip went into the office and shut the door. He knew that he was being distant and sending the wrong signals to his men. He needed to shake it off. He sat and closed his eyes. He could hear his Squadron Sergeant Major's voice in his head.

"Major. We need to chat. Come to my tent."

Come to his tent? Who the fuck does he think he is? thought Skip. He waited ten minutes before visiting his new SSM.

"Have a seat, Skippy."

The SSM sounded drunk.

"I beg your pardon?" said Skip.

"Sit, sir." The SSM pulled out a bottle of rum and poured a shot into a cup, which he passed over to his new major. "You and me need to clear the air. I know you're the new hot-shot squadron commander in this regiment, but you need to listen to me."

Skip could feel his blood rising. He had been told that this was the best SSM in the regiment, yet here he was lecturing him like he was a new lieutenant.

"You're an arrogant son of a bitch, aren't you?" The SSM paused. "Sir." Another pause. "The RSM warned me. He said he knew you as a lieutenant. He

said you were a strong personality but a good leader. In these two weeks we've been together, I've seen the strong personality, but I'm still looking for the leader."

Skip was stunned. He wasn't quite sure what to do, so he took a sip of rum. "Is that so?"

"He speaks," said the SSM. "Yes, that is so. I've been patient, and I can see some things I like in you. I see lots of potential, but this morning you crossed the line. I figured you and me had better clear the air, else I'll have to go to the RSM and ask for a new assignment."

Skip sat in silence, waiting for the other barrel.

"Listen to me, Major. You are the commander — you need to act like a commander. The troops don't need you to be their friend. Yesterday you called your driver by hist first name. I fucking near shit myself. Never do that. He's a corporal. Anyway, you know better. I know you do."

The SSM emptied his cup, then filled it again. He looked across at his major. "Another tot?"

"Sure, half a shot. What did I do today that sent you over the edge?"

"Corporal Raymond."

"What about him?"

"That incident in the tank park. You lost your temper with him and threatened to cut his nuts off. I was standing there with you. Imagine how humiliated I was. You want someone de-nutted? Fine. You turn to me. I'm your bayonet. You are the commander. You shamed me in front of the men, sir. Christ, you did my job. It erodes morale and discipline, and I can't live with that."

Skip stared into his cup. He knew that the SSM was right. Skip had been so eager to take command of the squadron, to prove he was worthy. He had behaved badly, and he knew it.

"Sergeant Major, I'm not sure what to say, other than you're right. I do know better, and this won't ever happen again."

"Sir, the men look to you for leadership, and it don't matter if it's in the tank park, or pushing the squadron across an obstacle, or even in the mess hall. You are their commander, and they want to be proud of you. They want to know that you will lead them. Got issues with the men? Tell me and I'll sort it. That's my job." The SSM took another slug of rum. "You need to do better, sir."

"I got it, Sergeant Major." Skip was deeply ashamed. "Thanks for the talk, and for the rum."

Skip rose and returned to his own tent. He had unwittingly humiliated his

SSM, and now it was his turn. He thought about what the SSM had said and how much courage it had taken to do what he did. That explained the rum.

In the morning the Sergeant Major was all business. At breakfast Skip invited him to join him at his table. The two men ate in silence for several awkward minutes.

"Sir." The SSM cleared his throat. "About last night. I wanted —"
Skip cut him short.

"SSM, I want to thank you for last night. You were right, and I needed that slap in the face. It hurt, but I appreciate it. Honestly, I do."

The two men went on to be fast friends. The SSM even asked permission to follow Skip to his new command when he relinquished the tank squadron. He was the best SSM Skip had ever known.

The O Group was set to arrive, and Skip needed to get his head in the game. It was time to become the Colonel again, and not Skip, the guy who'd put together a small, dangerous business venture. There was a rap at the office door and Harry poked his head in.

"Sorry, Skip. Alex and I would like to stage the office."

"I'll go grab a coffee."

When Skip returned with his steaming mug, the door was open. Inside, the men were seated, awaiting his entrance. He stepped into the office and Harry, who had remained standing, called them to attention.

"Gentlemen."

The men sat to attention as Skip rounded the desk. He stood facing them. Skip noted that Harry had staged his orders in the classical manner. In the front row were the tactical commanders; behind them were supporting arms. Harry's and Alex's places were up front, while Jules, Breaker, Franz-Josef, and Pappy were seated behind them.

"As you were," said Skip.

Harry moved silently to regain his chair.

"Before we begin, I want to say again how pleased I am that this group has gelled so quickly. It's hard for me to believe that most of us have only been together for several months. Gentlemen, you have my thanks for your roles in our success thus far.

"One small note, if you'll indulge me. I will be giving orders in a moment, remembering that we still have a couple of weeks to go before deployment. Some of the information is already known to some of you, but I'm doing this to put all of us on the same page and to allow each of you to make whatever arrangements you must. It's a bit out of the ordinary, I know."

He lingered for a moment and felt something that he didn't think he'd feel again: it was the joy of command.

"Gentlemen, orders. First, I will christen the ground." Skip unfurled a blow-up sketch of the area where the casa was located. "Note how close the two international borders are. We can practically hop from Columbia to Peru and into Brazil. The target house is on the south shore of a large triangular island in the Amazon. Across the water to the north is the town of Leticia-Tabatinga, a single city split by the international border. Remarkably, there are two small international airports in Leticia-Tabatinga, one either side the border, so the sound of aircraft will not raise any suspicions …"

Skip paused to indicate the city.

"The river is almost two kilometres wide on the north of the island, which is heavily wooded …"

Over the next half hour, he gave orders in the standard NATO format. Everyone took notes and listened intently. The target was a fugitive from American justice, a drug lord named Lopez with powerful friends. He was hiding in a Brazilian jungle, on the island indicated. They would fly in pairs to El Dorado International Airport in Bogotá using various routings and airlines. Special Colombian police would meet them and accommodate them at a military police facility, which was at the northwest end of the international airport. That was where they would marry up with their weapons, tactical clothing, and equipment.

Skip went on for another few minutes, and then concluded, "Take two minutes to review your notes. I will then accept questions."

Skip started his watch timer. The men sat in silence, looking at their notes. At the two-minute mark, Skip spoke again.

"Harry?"

"No questions, Colonel."

"Alex?"

"None, Colonel."

"Jules?"

"Pas de questions, mon Colonel."

"Breaker?"

"No questions, Colonel."

"Pappy?"

"None, Colonel."

"Jupp?"

"*Keine Fragen*, Herr Oberst."

"Very well, gentlemen. We still have much to accomplish, and there's limited time to get it done. I wanted to say again, you all have my complete confidence." Skip paused. "When I was in uniform, it was always my habit to give the last word at orders to my sergeant major. Please wrap it up for us, Jules."

"No points, Colonel."

"Orders end," said Skip. He looked at the assembled group and felt a growing sense of pride. "Who will join me for a drink?"

Everyone rose and followed Skip to the lounge. Breaker and Jules took their seats and began discussing something quietly.

"Did I not tell you le Colonel would be fine?" said Jules.

"Aye," agreed Pappy. "He's back."

A couple of the other men spoke softly to each other as Skip stepped behind the bar and invited his O Group to pick their poisons. After Skip had poured out the drinks, he leaned on the bar with both elbows, appearing lost in thought. He stared out over the lounge where the majority of the men were sitting and relaxing in twos or threes.

"Colonel, you look pensive."

"Pappy, I was contemplating how well everyone has coalesced into a unit in such a short time. You men have done great work."

"Aye, the squads are runnin' like them Swiss watches you like. That they are."

Skip took his elbows off the bar.

"God, I hope not."

Pappy was startled at the comment and Harry attempted to intervene.

"Now you've done it, Pappy. We're going to spend the rest of the evening discussing jazz."

Pappy, not to mention everyone else, was puzzled.

"I don't know what the hell you're talkin' about, Harry."

"Gentlemen, please grab your drinks," said Skip. "The O Group will reconvene in my office in five."

Harry grabbed his glass and looked at the bewildered men with a grin as Skip headed back to his office.

"What did I tell you?" he said and followed Skip.

As the men settled back into their chairs, Skip booted up his computer. He began to play a song at very low volume and didn't speak. It was a live jazz performance. Jules began to speak, but Skip raised his hand to quiet him as he slowly raised the volume. Everyone sat and listened for several more minutes, after which Skip lowered the volume, letting the music play on.

"Question or comments?"

Pappy had begun this whole process, and he wasn't about to put his foot in it twice in a row. Jules finally spoke.

"Mon Colonel. I am not a big jazz guy. I recognize the song, I think. Something about taking the train, maybe, but I do not see why we are listening."

"It's actually called 'Take the "A" Train,' by the late Duke Ellington," said Skip, "although this is not his band. This is a 1964 recording of the Charles Mingus Sextet. Mingus is on bass, with Eric Dolphy on alto sax. Johnny Coles is on trumpet. Dannie Richmond is on drums and Cliff Jordan on tenor sax. Obviously, you can't see any of the musicians, but if you could, you would see that none of them are reading from musical scores. They are all sitting on a stage and jamming with each other. If you listen, you can hear each of the artists come in and go out of the song almost at random. Did anyone notice that at one point everybody stopped playing to let the pianist, Jaki Byard, play solo? Then the drummer stepped in, and soon all six musicians were jamming again."

Skip surveyed the group.

"This, gentlemen, is the opposite of a Swiss watch. It's what synergism is all about."

Alex and Harry were both notably silent. They had been down this road with Skip before, and they each decided to let the others commence their own voyages of discovery. Breaker spoke up.

"Okay, Colonel. So what? Those names mean nothing to me, and I'm not sure exactly where you're going with all this, to be honest. Sorry."

"No, don't apologize, Breaker. There's nothing to be sorry about. If you aren't into jazz, then chances are you've never heard of Chuck Mingus, and you don't know that he was one of the greatest jazz musicians of the twentieth century. But this is not about Mingus, or his band. It's about unit cohesion and ops."

"Unit cohesion?" said Breaker.

"I'll explain."

Skip looked at the men and thought for a few seconds. He needed an easily relatable analogy.

"There are two ways to look at a military operation. The first, and more conventional, is that everyone in the op has a part to play, and they each do exactly what they're told. The Soviets took this to ludicrous extremes, not allowing any initiative or discretion. George Patton described combat in terms of a symphony. He called it the music of Mars, where each weapon system played its part of the musical score and the commander conducted it, so to speak. Decades later, the US Army dubbed this synchronization. Further, they developed a synchronization matrix so all the combat power could be coordinated to create this synchronization. Roger so far?"

Everyone nodded. Harry and Alex shared a knowing look.

"The second way to look at an op is that it is like playing jazz. Each musician knows his own instrument, and he doesn't need the conductor to tell him when or how to play. He listens to the music and feels the rhythm, the tempo, the emotion, and joins in when, where, and how he sees fit. There are several key elements to appreciate. Each player needs to understand the whole, but he must also subordinate his own playing to the goal of synergy, to the beauty of the melody. See the difference?"

Skip looked at his O Group.

"Sorry, Colonel, but no, I don't," said Breaker.

"Breaker, there's still no need to apologize. Let me try it another way. In the first methodology, the synchronization is planned or even forced: it's a program, a process. In the second, it isn't a procedure. It's an *outcome*. If jazz doesn't do it for you, think of hockey or any other team sport. We've all played or watched a sports team that was in the moment. Athletes call it being in the zone. Every pass works. Every shot scores. In music, this happens when every player submits to the tune. Every individual is in synch with every other player and building synergy, where the whole is greater than the sum of its parts. It's rare, but it happens."

Heads were now nodding.

"Okay," said Breaker. "I think I'm beginning to get it. So, why isn't that like a beautiful Swiss watch?"

"Because a finely tuned watch can only function if every aspect of its mechanism works *exactly* as predicted. That's fine for Swiss watches. They live in a closed environment. But that's practically impossible for combat operations. Absolutely nothing in an op is completely predictable. You're all experienced soldiers. You know that. To return to the watch analogy, a single grain of sand will stop a ten-thousand-dollar Rolex, and in our case, we're trying to run those watches in a sandstorm with no backs on them."

Skip could see that his message was sinking in. He was impressed that all the men assembled here had the mental agility to reconsider decades of military indoctrination.

"It wasn't my intention to lecture you all on the Zen of Operations," said Skip, shutting the laptop. "Let's call it a night. Alex, Harry, please stay behind."

The rest of the men filed out of Skip's office, and Skip closed the door.

"Sorry, guys," he said with a wry smile. "The nutty professor escaped from his straitjacket, and I lost control of him again. I hope I haven't messed with their heads, which was not my intent."

"Don't sweat it, Colonel," said Alex. "They get it, believe me. I'm sure Harry agrees with me. The men are much closer to being a jazz sextet than they are to a parade square formation, trust me. Even if they never heard of Chuck Mingus."

"Alex is right," said Harry. "Besides, the nutty professor needs to escape now and again, and I, for one, always learn something new when he does." He was grinning.

"Thanks, you two. I'm going to have a quiet nightcap. I'll see you in the morning."

Skip watched Harry and Alex leave, then put his office in order and headed out. In the lounge he found Les sitting alone and walked over to him.

"May I join you?"

"Of course, Colonel."

Les started to rise but Skip stopped him.

"Are you, okay, Les?"

"Yes, sir."

"I'm not convinced. What's up?"

"Colonel, if I'm honest, I'm wondering what I've done to upset you."

"Upset me? You haven't upset me. What gives?"

"Sir, Colonel Harry made me the reserve squad leader. Sorry — I guess it's the QRF now, but you haven't invited me to join your O Group. Do you not trust me, Colonel?"

"I see," said Skip. "Wait here."

He went to the bar, poured two glasses of Famous Grouse, signed the chit, and returned. He handed one to Les.

"*Slansche.*"

"*Slansche,*" said Les.

"Listen. I apologize if I gave you that impression. Nothing could be further from reality. Harry picked you as the QRF leader because we need someone whom we can count on to lead the charge if this op goes pear-shaped. He and I discussed it. We had lots of experienced men to choose from, and we chose you. That's point number one. Point number two is the O Group. I felt that based on your experience, bringing you into my O Group this early might be counterproductive. Maybe I was wrong."

"Colonel, I'm not questioning your judgment."

"I know that. Let me finish. You and your squad need to be as razor-sharp as the members of Red and Green. But you have a completely different function. You'll be carrying assault weapons, and you'll only be deployed if Harry calls for you. If that happens, it'll be the proverbial mad minute. You'll go in blazing, with the only object being to get everyone out. You follow?"

"Yes, Colonel."

"I felt that joining the O Group now would split your focus. For now, you and your men need to be ready to step up and replace any member who can't deploy. Once we're ready to launch, you, me, Harry, and Alex will go over your mission in fine detail, but I don't want it practised. I want no seeds of doubt planted in anyone's mind, although I see that I have inadvertently done it to you, Les, which wasn't my intent."

"Colonel, I'm fine, and I apologize for doubting you. I should have known you had your reasons. Now I feel foolish, sir."

"Absolutely not. Commanders often have to withhold info, but constant questioning is what good soldiers do. It's part of mission analysis. You were right to doubt me. Feel better?"

"Aye, Colonel, much. Thank you, sir."

"Good night, Les."

"Good night, sir." Les drained his drink, stood, and headed out of the bar.

Harry had observed the pair but waited for Les to leave before joining Skip.

"Everything okay with Les?"

"It is now. I raised doubts in his mind by not including him in my O Group. He's okay now, I think. What about you, Harry? Have I raised doubts in your mind?"

"Not at all, Skip. I've known you long enough to realize that you always have a reason for what you do, even if it isn't always clear to me. You're accumulating and assimilating."

"Pardon?" said Skip.

"I've been watching you do it for years, buddy. It's how your mind works. You accumulate data and you slowly assimilate it all, subconsciously. Eventually, you make all the connections and linkages."

"You make me sound like some kind of a freak," said Skip.

Harry smirked and shrugged his shoulders.

"Thanks, Harry. Time to call it a night."

WASHINGTON

"Thanks for dinner and listening to me vent, Mack." Bill raised his glass to his old friend.

"Hey, what are army buddies for? And I was serious about my offer," said Mack.

Bill swirled his JB and listened to the ice cubes clinking.

"Tell me more about your offer."

"As you know, my business has made me a lot of private contacts, both legit and otherwise. One of these contacts, a guy who straddles that divide, is an ex-FBI investigator."

"Straddles the divide?" said Bill.

"Not the way you're thinking, but don't worry about it. He's top notch and extremely discreet." He was quiet for a moment. "I don't know if you realize it, but you've been grousing about the Senator for months. Maybe it was just you letting off steam, but to me it sounded like a cry for help from my oldest and best friend."

"Mack, listen. I didn't mean —"

"Don't sweat it. Anyway, I decided to call my guy for a deep dive on your boss. I explained that it had to be very discreet, and I was, shall we say, generous. After two weeks of digging, I got a call. My guy had struck gold. Listen …"

Mack went into detail on the Senator's unusual preferences while Bill sat speechless at what he was hearing.

"He's what?" blurted an incredulous Bill when Mack had finished.

"Yes, dear friends, the Senator likes them young. The darker the better, so long as they are boys. Leather, whips, studs, the whole deal."

Bill was stunned. "I don't believe it."

"Believe it," said Mack. "I have proof."

Bill wasn't sure what to say, exactly, and sat stone-faced, holding his now empty glass.

"Are you okay?" said Mack. "Need a refill?"

"I'm fine, thanks, and no, I'd better not. It's getting on and I need to get home."

"Are you sure? I can always drive you."

"I appreciate it, but right now, all I want to do is go home."

The two men shook hands and parted.

After his second divorce, Bill had ached for seclusion, and he'd found it in a small cabin on seven bucolic acres in rural Virginia, which was where he went now. It was his escape from the madness and toxic politics of Washington, his refuge against the venal men and women whose bidding he was obliged to do, especially in the past few weeks.

Mack's offer had rattled him. He'd initially thought that it was an offer to kill the old man. What was perhaps worse for Bill was that for a minute he had considered it, thinking that it mightn't be such a bad idea. Bill was ashamed of himself but chalked it up to mental fatigue. Luckily, he had misunderstood his old friend, for what Mack had actually given him was an even better solution.

Bill stared into his fireplace, sipping his whisky and pondering how best to leverage what Mack had told him. Slowly, he felt a gentle warmth grow inside him.

"Morning, sir," said Gunny. "You seem better this morning."

"Gunny, today is going to be a be a fine day."

Bill picked up the handset of his STE phone and punched a speed-dial button.

"Senator Fredericks' office. How may I help you?"

"Good morning, Miss Loretta. It's Bill Donovan. How are you this fine morning, ma'am?"

"Good mornin', Colonel Donovan. I am very well, thank you. The Senator is in a meeting and cannot be disturbed, I am afraid."

"No, of course not, Miss Loretta. Please tell Senator Fredericks that I called. Also, please tell him I have an urgent need to speak with him at his earliest convenience."

"Colonel Donovan, I will surely do that once he is free."

Bill returned the phone to its cradle. He perused the overnight intel traffic that Gunny had put on his desk. It was the usual. At least Lopez was sitting tight. Gunny came through the door.

"Hey, sir. I got you an apple fritter."

He dropped the fragrant sugar bomb next to Bill's cup.

"Gunny, if I have a heart attack brought on by diabetic stress, I will hold you personally responsible."

"Yes, sir, got it. I hope you like raisins. I got you one with raisins because the calorie count was too low on the other ones."

Bill's phone rang. "Remind me to finish chewin' your ass later," he said as he turned to grab it. "Eagle Investments."

"Colonel Donovan, I have the Senator on the line for you, sir."

There was a short pause while she transferred the call.

"Donovan, what is so important that you interrupt my day? I am a busy man."

"Yes, sir. I know that you are busy, and I apologize, but I have something to discuss with you that cannot wait. I also do not believe that we should discuss it in your office. I suggest that we meet today for a ten-minute chat before lunch. I'll be sitting on one of the benches on the north edge of the Botanical Gardens. Shall we say eleven o'clock?"

"Listen here, Donovan. I don't have any intention of meeting you —"

Bill cut him short.

"Senator. You either meet with me, or I will make an appointment with Miss Loretta so that you and I can discuss your dear friends Enrico and DeShawn."

Bill let the pregnant pause build. He heard the Senator swallow loudly.

"Son, you are playin' with fire."

The Senator slammed the receiver so hard that Bill was sure it must be in several pieces by now.

Bill wandered out to the coffee machine and noticed that Gunny had a strange look on his face.

"What's up, Gunny?"

"Nothing, sir. Never heard you humming before, is all."

"Humming?"

"Yes, Colonel."

"I don't hum, Gunny."

"No, sir."

The walk from Eagle's offices to the Botanical Gardens took twenty minutes. Bill rounded the corner toward the benches and saw the Senator standing there, perspiring profusely.

"Senator, thank you for meeting with me here on such short notice."

"Donovan, what the hell are you playing at?"

"No one is playing here, Senator."

"Son, are you looking to blackmail me?"

"Absolutely not, but I do need you to understand that I will never hang any of my personnel out to dry, and that now includes the Canadians. Sir, you're the boss, but I need to see some changes in our relationship."

The blood was beginning to rise in the Senator's face. Bill continued.

"What I need is a little less dismissive rudeness, and no more telling me how to suck eggs. I would like our relationship to be professional, respectful. That's all, sir."

The Senator was beginning to tremble.

"Senator, I know what goes on during your so-called AA meetings, and we both know what would happen if video footage were to be sent to the *Washington Post*."

Bill was measuring his words, being careful not to overplay his hand.

"Sir, I have no intention of smearing you, but we need to understand each other. I don't want much from you, sir. All I'm asking you to do is let me do my job. You're a powerful man with powerful friends, but Senator, I am sure that you remember Jimmy and Tammy Faye Bakker …"

He let the implications hang in the air between them. The look on the Senator's face told Bill that he had gotten through to him. For a minute, Bill feared that Fredericks might have a stroke right then and there.

"How do I know that you'll keep your word?"

"My daddy raised me to keep my promises. Other than that, you'll just have to trust in the Lord."

Bill wished the Senator a pleasant afternoon, then turned and strolled back toward the office. He noticed an ice cream truck stopped on 1st Street off Independence Avenue. The kids were lining up for their cones, and he decided to celebrate with a cone of his own. He joined the line with the other joyful youngsters.

MONTREAL

"Caller ID Blocked." Skip had an inkling of who it might be and debated letting it go to voicemail. After the third buzz, he accepted it.

"Hey, Bubba," said Skip.

"How'd you know it was me?" said Bill.

"Because you blocked your ID. I don't know anybody reputable who does that. What was the worst that could happen? Some guy from Nigeria trying to scam me would be caught off guard because I called him Bubba?"

"You sound better this morning."

"I'm feeling better about how preparations are proceeding. What's up?"

"Not a lot, but I thought I'd check in."

"Like I said, no issues," said Skip.

"All good, buddy. Well, time is money, as they say down here where we worship Mammon. Gotta go."

"Wait," said Skip, but the line went dead.

Skip rubbed his chin. *What was that about?* The call had unsettled him. The comment about Mammon set bells ringing. Whatever bad habits Bill had, Skip knew him to be serious about integrity and duty. The last thing Bill ever seemed to worry about was money. He was signalling something. It was subtle, maybe even subconscious. He was still looking at his phone when Harry came in from his morning run.

"Morning, Skip. You know, instead of filling your gut with bacon and eggs with Pappy and Franz-Josef, you should be out on the trails in the morning with me and Alex. Even Jules comes out occasionally. It'll keep you young, buddy."

"Been there, done that. You forget, but we cavalry officers are actively discouraged from even walking too quickly. It frightens the troops. Anyway, I'm not actually hitting the beaches with you and your snake-eaters, remember? I'm the guy in the château looking at maps and making important calls."

"Right," said Harry. "I'll bugger off and leave you with your deep thoughts."

"Deep thoughts? What deep thoughts?"

"Skip, when something is rattling around that big brain of yours, you always rub your chin, like you're doing now. Accumulating and assimilating, right?"

"I guess," said Skip.

"I'll see you for lunch. Alex and I will give you a SITREP then."

"Thanks, Harry."

Skip made a mental note about his tell, and wondered what other tells he had. Harry's observation about how his thought process worked had never occurred to him.

Skip sought out Jules and found him outside with Pappy discussing how to mock up a helicopter so the squads could practise boarding and exiting.

"Excuse me, gentlemen."

Both men straightened as Skip approached.

"Sorry to interrupt you."

"Not at all, Colonel. How can we help?"

"Harry and Alex are giving me a SITREP at lunch. I figured I'd gather the whole O Group in my private dining room and have Michel lay out sandwiches. Jules, can you set it up for me at twelve o'clock, please?"

"Oui, Colonel. Pappy, we can discuss this further in a little while."

Jules began to walk away and stopped.

"Colonel, did your friend in Colombia confirm what kind of helicopters he will get for us?"

"Not yet, but Hueys, I suspect. They have a lot of them, but no, I'm not sure."

Jules nodded and walked away as Skip turned back to Pappy.

"How's our RSM doing?"

"Colonel, I'll be honest, the man's a marvel. I can see him getting stronger every day, and he's even running some mornings. Bringing him on board was a win-win. His sense of humour is back, he's smiling and laughing, and he's brought some first-class skills from his time as a SAR tech."

Skip was smiling as he listened.

"Good. I was sensing as much."

"He also has a light touch with the lads. He's earned their respect and their trust, which is saying something about both Jules and our jumpers. He and I make a good pair. I bludgeon 'em, and he pats 'em on the back with a look that says, 'Do this or I'll give you back to Pappy.' But there's a wee bit of madness in the man."

"What do you mean?"

"Did you know that when he was a sergeant, they were looking for a downed aircraft up in the woods near North Bay? The cloud cover was at two thousand feet and the SAR Herc couldn't see through it. Jules got the loadmaster to hook him to the winch cable and jumped out the back. The loadmaster let out as much cable as he dared, and Jules 'flew' below the clouds so he could search the woods. I saw some insanity when I was with the Paras, believe me, but you couldn't pay me to do that."

"Did they find the aircraft?"

"Pardon me, Colonel?"

"Did Jules find the downed bird?"

"As a matter of fact, yes, he did."

"Well, there you go."

Skip walked away grinning, leaving Pappy wondering if these Canadians he had joined were all lunatics.

At 11:50, Skip headed to the private dining room. The door was open, and his O Group was standing around waiting for his arrival. Once again, Harry called everyone to steady up as Skip entered.

"As you were. Breaker, Jules, Franz-Josef, and Pappy, kindly begin to make yourselves lunch."

When they hesitated, he reminded them of the Canadian Army's longstanding tradition of soldiers getting into the chow line in reverse order of rank or seniority.

"You all know the drill. I'll eat last, so please don't wait."

Once all had been seated and begun eating, he nodded to Harry to begin with his SITREP. Harry, true to his decades of experience, gave a succinct five-minute report of how all the training was going. He finished with a short recap that focused on his own squad. Next, Alex did likewise for his squad, after which he similarly did the QRF, for which Harry had made him responsible during the training phase. Once Alex had finished, Skip asked Breaker for an update on comms, then turned to Pappy for weapons and drills. Next came Franz-Josef with admin. Last, he turned to Jules.

"Non, merci, Colonel."

By 12:30 everyone was fully up to date.

"Very well," said Skip. "One thing that I haven't discussed openly is who will be going. I have decided that it will be myself and the three squads, so Jules, Pappy, Breaker, Franz-Josef, and Michel will remain."

He regarded the four men.

"Pappy, I'll need you to return to the Ox when we go. The remainder will maintain a rear link here."

"Aye, Colonel."

"I am sorry if you are disappointed, gentlemen, but I need people here whom I can trust to put the wheels in motion should we suffer a mission failure. I put a sealed envelope in my office safe with detailed instructions. It's a signed operations order, and I've given it a name: Op Valkyrie."

Franz-Josef looked stricken. He turned to look at the others.

"If ever I give that code word when we are deployed, then Franz-Josef will open the safe. You senior men will read it together and carry out the orders. RSM, you'll call Pappy on secure means and brief him in."

The room was still. Skip let the silence grow.

"What's in the order is not important right now. What is important is that I need people I can trust to fulfill the instructions if they have to. That's enough for now. We still have seven or eight days before we fly, so there's still time for adjustment of some of the coordinating instructions."

Pappy lifted a finger and cleared his throat.

"Colonel, I wanted to confirm that you were good with the weapons and tactical equipment delivery arrangement. All I know is that Colonel Donovan says it's in hand. I must tell you, sir, that I find not knowing the details is worrisome, especially for the question of weapons."

"Thanks, Pappy. I have a decent idea, but I'll confirm. Breaker, please set up a secure call with Colonel Donovan after we finish here. No time like the present for him and me to discuss that."

Breaker nodded.

"Other questions or issues?"

Skip paused.

"Almost forgot. Jupp, are accommodations and travel all confirmed?"

"Ja, Herr Oberst. *Alles gut.*"

"Alright. Harry, please stay behind. Everyone else, give us the room."

The small crowd filed out of the dining room.

"Harry, I want you to sit in on the call with Bill, please. I'm a bit anxious based on some of the things that Bill has said. I'm getting an odd sense from him. Having you listen in will help."

"What about Alex?"

"No, Harry. Just you."

"No problem, Skip, and what's with Valkyrie? You know that was the code word for the plot to assassinate Hitler. Did you see Franz-Josef's face?"

"Yes, I did. With a bit of luck, nobody will need to read the order."

Skip picked up his coffee mug. Turning, he saw Harry still standing in front of him, staring blankly.

"What's wrong? You look upset," said Skip.

Harry tilted his head inquisitively. "What's wrong?" he said. "Are you going to tell me about Valkyrie?"

"I'd rather not."

"How the hell can I be your 2IC when you won't tell me what's on your mind?"

"Harry, it's a set of comprehensive instructions on how to help us if we have a mission failure: lawyers, banking, individuals who owe me favours. You need to be focused on the mission and not what might happen if it goes pear-shaped. You want details? I can give them to you, but it's meaningless to you right now. After all, you can't execute. You'll be the guy everybody's helping me to retrieve."

"I can walk and chew gum at the same time," said Harry.

"Of course, you can. I know that, Harry, but I'm trying to let you stay focused on the tactical mission. Let me worry about the rest, will you, please?"

Harry was only partly mollified. He turned without a word and walked out of the room, brushing past Jules and Pappy, who had been standing outside the office. They looked at each other quizzically.

Skip returned to his office, where Breaker was setting up a new secure phone that had been delivered from Washington.

"Colonel, the new STE is all set. Colonel Donovan is waiting for your call, sir." Breaker stepped away from the desk. "Anything else?"

"Thanks, Breaker. Please call Harry. I suspect he's on the porch."

Breaker left. In a couple of minutes Harry came in, still sullen but calmer. He shut the door and took a chair. Skip put an index finger up to his lips and made the call.

"Donovan here."

"Hey, Bill. I have you on speaker. Between paperwork and coordinating details, I missed lunch. I'm eating a sandwich, so if you don't mind, I'll mute the mic when not speaking and get some grub into me."

"Sure. No problem, Skip. Is everything proceeding apace? I gather you want to talk about equipment."

Skip unmuted, audibly smacked, and swallowed. He saw Harry beginning to relax.

"Yes, please. Sorry, had a slurp of coffee."

"What's the problem, Skip? As we discussed, my buddy Mack will deliver everything on your list to your Colombian contact. Mack knows the guy and they've worked together before. Do you have a better way to get everything there?"

"No, I was just confirming, that's all. So long as everything on the list is there."

"It'll all be there. Trust me, Mack is a solid guy. Want to review the list?"

"No, that won't be necessary, thanks."

"Is there anything else, Skip? I'm sensing you have more questions."

"I'll remind you that surprise is a principle of war, *not* a principle of administration."

"I'll write that down," quipped Bill.

"I won't keep you. I'm sure there's a senior citizen waiting for you to help her to cross Constitution Avenue."

"Out here."

The next few days proved hectic. Franz-Josef re-checked all the flights and confirmed the rooms. The Courtyard Marriott Airport in Bogotá was large enough that it easily accommodated everyone. Franz-Josef insisted that due to the size of the booking, the hotel give him a special rate and that they upgrade Skip's room to a large suite. The hotel was almost empty, and the manager, not wanting to lose the booking, acquiesced.

For his part, Skip had not been sleeping well. It was one thing to prep for an op. It was quite another to know that he would be sending his men somewhere he wouldn't be going. It went against his leadership ethos, and no amount of rationalization could ease the disquiet that he felt. He'd spent his career sharing whatever perils he exposed his troops to. However, he knew that he had neither the experience nor the necessary skills to join in the raid, and that he would've been a burden, but he took comfort in the fact that he had done everything possible to ensure success. Still, Skip remained unsettled.

Franz-Josef broke in on his thoughts.

"Excuse me, Herr Oberst. I have now for you the travel arrangements as you asked me. Les will fly with you."

Skip scanned the travel itinerary.

"No flights from Montreal to Bogotá?"

"I am sorry, Herr Oberst, but the train to Toronto is most comfortable, no?"

"Absolutely, Jupp."

Skip sensed that Jupp was hesitating.

"What's wrong, old friend?"

"Nothing, mein Oberst. I am only sorry not to be able to go with you."

"I understand, Jupp. I feel similarly about not going forward with Harry and the squads. We are old soldiers, and we want to see action, but you and I would only be in the way. Besides, I need someone here whom I trust unconditionally in case anything goes wrong. You, my friend, are that man."

"Valkyrie," said Franz-Josef.

"Exactly," said Skip. "When I get back, we can destroy the document together, neh?"

"You are not so old, Herr Oberst. Many commanders still in the uniform are older than you."

"That's true, but I'm not the right man to lead the squads. That man is Harry. A commander must be where he can best do his job. For Guderian, it was at the front; for Montgomery, it was in his headquarters; for me, it will be in a command post."

"Yes, Herr Oberst."

Skip hoped that travelling together from Toronto to Bogotá would give him a chance to get to know Les better. He had been too busy to spend sufficient time with him. The young Brit had easily slipped back into his routines as a soldier. Skip got the sense he'd had a storied career and that he missed it. Working at the pub in Belleville paid the bills, but it wasn't what he loved. Skip was confident that being a platoon sergeant in the legendary British Army Parachute Regiment was what Les had loved.

Two days before their departure, Skip insisted that Les go home to his wife, Lorraine. He'd ride with Pappy back to Belleville, then grab the train to Toronto. They'd link up at Pearson Airport.

"Colonel, I shouldn't get a special favour just because I'm one of the few who're married."

"You're right, Les, so let me make it simple. Staff Sergeant, put your heels together. Tomorrow morning, be in Pappy's Yukon."

"Aye, Colonel."

That evening, Skip asked Harry, Alex, and Les to join him in his private dining room.

"Gentlemen, I'll begin with an apology. I've left this discussion a bit late, but I've done so partly on purpose. It's time to discuss the QRF. As I've said, I needed you three laser-focused on getting everyone up to speed. Discussing the QRF would have distracted you. As it is, you've all done an extraordinary job of prepping the squads in so short a time."

The three men sat quietly.

"When Harry assigned individuals to the squads and I changed the name of the reserve, I did it for a reason. A reserve is to exploit success, and that isn't an issue here. Success will be binary. We grab Lopez alive, or we don't. I have complete faith in you grabbing Lopez, but if it all goes to hell at the casa, I want a force there to extricate you. That's the QRF."

Alex looked at Harry, who nodded but didn't speak.

"Okay," said Alex, "but we haven't practised extraction under fire."

"Skip and I have talked it out," said Harry. "We figured the disadvantage of not practising would be outweighed by the advantages, in terms both of morale and of focus on the mission."

"So, what's the plan?"

"Harry, over to you," said Skip.

"Les will have his own bird. The QRF will depart the RV sixty seconds after us and keep that separation. When we move into the jungle toward the casa, he'll be landing his squad on the beach. He'll wait there until we're gone, then the QRF will move to the jungle's edge. He'll have eyes on us from there since it's about a hundred metres. The QRF will wait, and if all goes well, they won't move."

Harry paused to see if Alex or Les had any questions. They did not.

"Returning with Lopez, Red and Green will pass back through the QRF and get airlifted out. If there's any shooting, the QRF will come to the rescue with assault rifles. Les will then have different rules of engagement than us, Alex. His only mission is to extract us back to the beach. All of us. Either way, he'll exfil sixty seconds behind us, just as with the infil. Simple."

"Seems straightforward," said Alex.

"Exactly," said Harry, "but you can see that Les has to shift his and his squad's focus as of right now." He looked at Les. "Understand what I'm driving at Les?"

"Absolutely. Like Colonel Skip just said, we're the fire brigade. I'll gather the men as soon as I leave here and begin the process."

Inaugural Mission

November 2012

Belleville

The next day, after Pappy drove off, Skip sat drinking coffee with his stay-behind crew. He ran through final details with Jules, Breaker, and Franz-Josef. There were no issues. Alex and Harry were heading off on a short run to shake off some nervous energy, and they poked their heads in to say good-bye.

"Got a minute, you two?" said Skip.

They started walking over, and Skip rose to meet them halfway.

"Does it bother you two that I don't join you for your morning PT?"

Harry looked at Alex, then at Skip.

"Skip, we know you're busy, and anyway, you don't have to keep up with all these young bucks like me and Alex have to. To answer your question, no, not at all."

Skip nodded, satisfied. "Then I'll see you in Colombia, and I'll be at the airport to meet your flight."

Jamie pulled up in the Yukon to take Skip down to the Dorval train station.

"Bon voyage, Colonel," said Jules, as Skip rose and walked over to the vehicle.

"Merci, Jules."

"Colonel, have a good one. We'll be here waiting to hear from you, sir. Day or night."

"Thanks, Breaker. SITREPS from me as promised. Remember, once we launch, I'll be on radio silence."

"Herr Oberst. *Ich drücke Dir die Daumen.*"

Franz-Josef held up his two fists with the thumbs tucked inside.

"Danke, Jupp. I appreciate you pressing on your thumbs for all of us. And I was serious about Valkyrie."

Breaker and Jules looked at each other. Skip got into the SUV, and the vehicle drove off.

Skip had always preferred trains to planes. He could watch the countryside slide past, walk the aisles, and visit the bar car, if there was one. Today he didn't like the choice of scotch, so he opted for a Rémy Martin.

"Will there be anything else before supper, sir?"

"No, thank you. I'm fine," Skip told the bartender.

Supper was going to be after the Belleville station stop, which wasn't far off. He sat and flipped through the morning Montreal papers and sipped the Rémy. The train began to slow and, looking up, he saw they were pulling into Belleville. Once the train fully stopped, he put the papers and empty glass aside and left the bar car. He walked up to first class, and, stepping through the car doors, he saw someone familiar sitting in the seat next to his.

"Cheers, Colonel," said Les.

"What are you doing here? You weren't supposed to meet me until tomorrow at the Airport Hilton."

Skip took his seat as the train lurched into motion.

"Aye, Colonel. Lorraine could see that I was on edge. She didn't press me to know why, just told me to get a move on and call if I could. I phoned Franz-Josef, and he made the changes, so here I am. Would you prefer that I sit elsewhere, Colonel?"

"Not at all, Les. Sounds like Lorraine is a keeper."

"Yes, sir."

"Grab yourself a pre-dinner drink and we'll get to know each other a bit better."

The trip to Union Station was a few minutes shy of two hours, and the two men filled the time with talk. Skip tried not to be too prying.

"Where'd you grow up, Les?"

"Originally, I came from a working-class neighbourhood near Croydon. Tough town, Colonel, and I ran with a bad lot."

"Is that how you pitched up in the Paras?"

"Yes, sir. One of my mates got into trouble. The magistrate gave him the classic choice — prison or the army — so he ended up in the Paras. He came home after he got his wings and wore his uniform, complete with maroon beret and parachute badge. Joe was down the pub bragging about how tough it was. I knew I were tougher than him and that it were only a matter of time before I got myself nicked, so I enlisted straight away."

"Smart move," said Skip.

"Aye," agreed Les. "Best part was that I loved it. By the time I made lance corporal in the 2nd Battalion, I got selected for the 1st Battalion, the one permanently assigned to Special Forces. I made staff sergeant in no time. I was on the fast track to being a warrant officer when I met Lorraine in a pub."

"You should have been a professional gambler with your luck."

"I were gobsmacked," said Les. "She went back to Belleville, but I couldn't get her out of my head. I visited twice in six months, and the rest is history."

"Lucky for us," said Skip.

"Lucky for me. This way I have real mates again like I did in the Paras — and I have Lorraine."

The train pulled into Union Station right on time, which surprised Skip, based on his experience. The two men went down the stairs to the bowels of the massive station, then up through the connecting ramps to the dedicated monorail to the airport. By 21:00 they were checked into their rooms.

BOGOTÁ

Franz-Josef had booked Skip and Les through Houston, figuring that travelling through New York would be less attractive to Skip. He figured correctly. Skip and Les were not together on the first leg, but on the second, they managed side-by-side seats. Both flights were long. Thankfully, they were boring, which was exactly how Skip preferred them. Sending everyone business class had been wise; the comfort was worth the expense, and unlimited access to liquor always helped ease Skip's dislike of flying.

El Dorado International was busier than expected, and like many South American airports, an armed military presence was everywhere. Skip saw what looked like scores of military aircraft at the northwest end of the airport. Before they reached the passport barrier, he spotted his old friend. Coronel Tomasino was standing to one side of the checkpoint, accompanied by two fit-looking young men in uniform.

"Mi Coronel," said Skip as he extended his hand to shake Tomasino's.

The senior policeman pulled Skip close and gave him a hug. Les looked at the two escorts, who appeared more than mildly surprised.

"Amadeo. It is so good to see you again, mi amigo," said Tomasino. "It has been too long since our time in Berlin."

"Augusto, you look fitter now than you did then. So good to see you, too. Thank you so much for helping me out." Skip held his old friend at arm's length and regarded him approvingly.

"I look forward to talking to you more about this, but first we must collect your bags and move you to the hotel."

"Allow me to introduce you to my colleague, Leslie Tidder," Skip said, turning to his friend. "Les, this is Coronel Augusto Maria Corrido di Tomasino. He is the Commander of the Colombian National Drug Enforcement Unit."

"I'm honoured to meet you, sir."

"The pleasure is mine," said Tomasino.

The commander turned and directed everyone to a side door. His two escorts moved quickly to open it and allow the three men through. On the other side was another police officer who Skip assumed was a senior officer from the airport police, based on his uniform.

"*Bienvenidos, señores.* Please follow me. I will take you to the baggage area."

At the carousel, Les spotted their bags and reached for them. The two escort policemen intervened and lifted them off the conveyor.

"That's all we have," said Skip.

"*Excelente,*" said Tomasino. "Please come this way."

Outside, a minibus awaited with a driver and another policeman, who, based on the gold on his uniform, Skip assumed was yet another officer.

The drive to the hotel took all of five minutes.

"We could've walked," muttered Les under his breath.

"We have taken the liberty of checking in your men already, Skip," said Tomasino as they exited the vehicle. "Let us go to your room. I have a small surprise for you."

"Thank you, Augusto. As you know, I have more colleagues arriving today and tomorrow. Is it possible to have use of this van for the next —"

"Amadeo, do not worry. The vehicle, driver, and escorts are at your disposal for your entire time. Major Fuentes," he indicated the officer standing with the escorts, "is your liaison officer and will be available to expedite the arrival of all of your men."

Skip took two steps to shake hands with the major.

"Pleased to meet you."

"Colonel, the pleasure is mine. Colonel Tomasino has briefed me, and I am at your disposal, day, and night."

Skip shook his hand and noted the complete lack of a Spanish accent.

"Thank you, Major Fuentes."

Skip turned to Les.

"Settle yourself, then go with the major back to the airport. Please call me when Harry's flight lands. I promised to meet him personally."

"Yes, Colonel."

"Augusto, shall we go and see your surprise? Should I borrow a sidearm from Major Fuentes?"

Skip's remark elicited a laugh from both Tomasino and Fuentes. Tomasino headed to the elevator, followed by Skip and one of the escorts who had Skip's bag.

His room was on the top floor, and when they reached it, the door was ajar. Tomasino took the suitcase and dismissed the escort as the door swung open.

"Hey, buddy. Good to see ya," called a familiar voice.

"Bill. Are you under house arrest?" said Skip dryly.

Bill laughed and greeted the two men as Tomasino deposited the suitcase.

They all shook hands.

"Does this mean we're roommates?" asked Skip.

"No, but I did put on a fresh pot of coffee. Shall we?"

The three men took seats at a table by the window, and Bill brought mugs of coffee for all of them. The room was silent while they sipped their drinks. Augusto finally spoke up.

"Gentlemen, first I wish to tell you how honoured I am to have you both visit me. It is a pleasure to see you again."

"Augusto, you never mentioned that you knew Bill."

"That's on me, Skip," said Bill.

"Yes, Bill and I have worked together several times already. We have an important American presence here." He paused momentarily. "Both in the open and not."

Bill shrugged his shoulders. "How about you, Skip? You never let on that you knew Augusto well, although I knew you did."

"Is that so?"

"I seem to recall that you were part of a large undercover Interpol operation in Berlin some years ago. You know, the one where you had your mishap."

"Mishap?" said Augusto. "I do not think that being in surgery for eight hours to have a pelvis reconstructed is a mishap."

Skip tried to smile benignly but looked uncomfortable. Augusto saw his discomfort and changed the subject.

"Amadeo, I must leave you, but I can tell you that everything we discussed is ready for you. The day after tomorrow, you and your men will be moved to a special operations centre at the Brigada de Aviación No. 33, on the military side of the airport. My brother is the commander and has put one of his hangars at your disposal so that you will have a space separate from us."

After seeing Tomasino out, Skip returned to Bill. His cell phone buzzed as he sat.

"Yes, Les."

"Colonel, I just wanted to tell you that we've retrieved four more. Harry arrives this evening. His flight was delayed, but he and Alex should be here just before twenty hundred. I'll bring the vehicle round to the hotel and call you when I'm in the lobby."

"Thanks, Les." Skip killed the call and turned his attention back to Bill. "So, after all my calling in of favours, you could have done this for me."

"I could have done it all," said Bill, "but it was a matter of fingerprints, my friend. Plausible deniability, remember?"

"Of course," said Skip.

"You should take a quick dip in the pool before supper. Wash off some of that concern you're wearing."

"Is it obvious?"

"It is," said Bill.

"I might do that," said Skip.

By 17:00, Skip had unpacked and made a quick call to Franz-Josef on an unsecure line using a German phrase they had agreed upon. Afterwards, a visit to the outdoor pool helped, just as Bill had suggested. In a fresh golf shirt and chinos, Skip was now ready to meet with Bill. There were several issues still bothering him, and now was the time to run them to ground. He grabbed a stool at the bar and ordered a Cinzano Rosso with ice and a lemon slice.

Bill appeared about twenty minutes later and caught sight of Skip sitting at the poolside bar.

"Admiring the local wildlife?" he said, taking the stool beside him. He looked down at Skip's feet and grinned. "Did you forget to pack socks?"

"These are hand-stitched Italian loafers, and they deserve bare skin. I've been sitting here trying to recall what it felt like to be fit like some of these kids in the pool. I've spent too much time in offices and not enough time with troops in the last decade."

"I know the feeling, Skip. Come, let's grab a table in the corner." He indicated a secluded table under a magnificent royal palm.

Skip finished his drink, got the waiter's attention, and pointed to the table. The waiter nodded back at him. Skip and Bill made their way to the table, where they sat opposite each other and relaxed. The waiter appeared.

"Buenos días, señores. May I get something for you?"

"Yes, please," said Bill. "A beer for me and another Cinzano for my friend."

The two men sat quietly until the waiter returned and deposited the drinks.

"Gracias," said Bill. "Nothing else for now."

The waiter bowed slightly and departed.

"Well, Skip, here's to a successful inaugural." Bill raised his drink.

"Amen," said Skip, doing likewise.

"Happy with your plan, your team?"

"The Cohort is the best I could have hoped for."

"What?"

"Cohort. I don't like the word team. It's just a pet peeve. Yes, they're talented, professional, loyal. No worries there …"

"But…" said Bill.

"But stitching this thing together in six weeks was painful. I would have liked more time. That said, the men have all risen to the challenge. What about you?"

"What about me?" said Bill.

"I was wondering if all was okay with you, and why you're babysitting me."

"I'm not babysitting you."

Skip could see the muscles in Bill's jaw clenching. "Sorry. Bad choice of words. Why are you here?"

Bill sipped his beer. "If we want to be clinical, I'm protecting my investment. I've spent a lot of effort to get this off the ground. But it's also because I like you, and I'm not entirely convinced the Senator isn't working against the two of us, somehow."

Bill paused and took another pull on his beer.

"Eagle works for the intel community; the NSA, to be precise. Because of how it's funded, my boss is a powerful senior senator. Since I brought up the idea of creating a Canadian version of Eagle, he has been riding my ass, and it has got progressively worse. I'm not entirely sure what his problem is. I told you that he forbade me from using Eagle for this op."

"Yes, you did."

"About two weeks ago he summoned me to tell me to have a plan in place should this mission fail."

"Makes sense," said Skip.

"I agree, but that's not what he meant. After I briefed him, I thought he was going to have a stroke. He wasn't looking for a backup rescue plan; he meant a plan for how we would sweep away any evidence that we had anything to do with y'all. That didn't sit with me, and I told him so. I thought things were bad then, but I was wrong. It got worse."

Bill went on at length, like he was on his therapist's couch; he clearly had to get this out. It struck Skip as odd, considering he was someone accustomed to keeping secrets. Bill didn't go into detail, but he did say enough for Skip to have some sort of idea that Bill had dirt on his boss. He listened quietly and let Bill speak until he had it all out of his system. When Bill finally seemed spent, Skip suggested they eat.

"I have to keep an eye on the time," he explained, picking up his menu, "because I want to meet Harry and Alex when they land."

"Mind if I tag along?"

"Not at all, but we haven't yet discussed why you're here."

"Like I said, just in case, but I won't interfere. I promise."

"Isn't it odd for you to be in country at the same time I am?"

"No, not at all. I come down to visit the drug enforcement guys routinely and inevitably spend a lot of time here and at the airport."

Skip nodded and scanned the restaurant. "I'll grab the waiter by the bar."

Bill sat quietly sipping his beer as Skip went to order supper. In a couple of minutes, he was back.

"Food and booze are on the way. You look weary, buddy."

"I wasn't brought up this way. My father is an old-school kind of man who believes in honour, duty, and country. I grew up to believe that a man's word was his bond."

"I don't know your father," said Skip, "but he sounds like he would have got along with my own father. I'll bet your father would be pleased to hear of his son keeping his promise to a friend, even at the risk of his own future. That's what I think."

Bill stared at the table. "Thanks," he said.

"By the way," said Skip, "I'm keeping track of all those promises, and you still owe me for the lunch tab in Rome."

The quip finally put a smile on Bill's face.

Supper arrived and the two men ate in silence. Sometimes silence was what was needed. Out of the corner of his eye, Skip spotted Major Fuentes approaching.

"Sir, please excuse me for bothering you. I want to inform you that all of the equipment you ordered is now safely under guard in the hangar at 33 Aviation Brigade."

"Thank you," said Skip. "Would you care to join us?"

"Thank you, Colonel, but no. I have duties to attend to. I will see you in the morning, perhaps?"

"Yes," said Skip. "Please join me for breakfast here in the hotel."

"Gracias mi Coronel. I will see you at 07:00."

The major departed quickly.

At 19:45, Les appeared at their table. "Good evening, gentlemen. Colonel, the vehicle is at reception whenever you're ready."

"Thanks, Les. By the way, Les, I'd like you to meet Colonel Bill Donovan, the founder of the feast. Bill, this is Les Tidder, one of my best snake-eaters."

The two men shook hands, and Les went to wait for Skip at the van.

"Skip, I've got the check. That'll take care of at least one promise," Bill said, chuckling. "I'll meet you in a few minutes."

At the airport, Les guided the two men to the security area. He now had the routine down pat, and the police knew him from the day's comings and goings.

"I see them," said Les. "I'll be right back."

Five minutes later, Les, Harry, and Alex rejoined them.

"I'll see to the luggage," said Les.

Alex excused himself to go help.

"I finally meet the disembodied voice of Skip's right-hand man. My pleasure," said Bill.

"Likewise," said Harry, and extended his hand.

"I suggest we move to the vehicle," said Skip.

By the time they arrived, the luggage was stowed with everyone else seated and ready to go. The driver put the van in gear and they set off for the hotel.

Once they had all reassembled in the hotel lobby, Skip took Harry and Alex aside.

"I want you to know that I had no idea Bill would be here, but it doesn't change anything. I'll be in the command centre, and you two are at the sharp end. Bill has no role to play."

"I was going to ask," said Harry.

Skip momentarily considered sharing Bill's concern about senatorial subterfuge and quickly decided not to. His two deputies were focused, and he wanted them to stay that way.

"Let's meet in the pool bar at 22:00 to chat. Tomorrow is a recuperation day. We still have a half-dozen guys arriving, but they'll all be here by lunch. As planned, we gather tomorrow evening, and the next morning we move to the staging area, which is now confirmed to be back on the airfield, so only five minutes away."

"All good," said Harry.

Alex nodded his agreement.

"If you're too tired to meet me at 22:00, no worries. Like I said, we have tomorrow."

Skip walked off, and Alex looked at Harry.

"What's up, jumper?" said Harry.

"What's with Skip? I'm getting a Captain Ahab vibe."

"Pardon?"

"You know, from *Moby Dick*. The obsession with the whale."

"No, Skip's not like that. Sure, he can be overly focused sometimes — you know he lives in his head — but obsessed? No, whatever is under his skin, we'll find out soon enough — if we need to know. See you at 22:00."

Alex grimaced. "Sorry, supper on the flight didn't agree with me, so I'll pass. See you at 07:00 in the breakfast room."

Harry came down to the pool bar a few minutes early, spotted Skip sitting at a table, and walked over.

"Hi, sailor. New in town?"

"Harry, what can I get you?"

Skip waved the waiter to come over and Harry ordered a beer. As the waiter left, Harry explained that Alex had begged off.

"Are you OK, Skip?" he prodded. "You seem to be elsewhere."

"I'm fine. Bill showing up threw me, that's all."

"There's something else," insisted Harry.

Skip looked his friend in the eye.

"You know I trust your leadership, and I promise to let you run the tactical op …"

"But…" said Harry.

"No 'but,' Harry. The truth is that I'm struggling knowing that you're going into harm's way and I'm sitting it out. Some part of me thinks I might just as well have run this op from Montreal."

The waiter appeared with Harry's beer and quietly left.

"Very funny," Harry said, taking a sip of his drink. "Skip, we've discussed this. You'll be at the command centre in Leticia. It's no different than you being in regimental headquarters and sending two tank squadrons into a fight."

"Not exactly. In your scenario, I could be a tactical bound back in overwatch and ready to deploy resources immediately."

"Same thing, buddy. I'm counting on you having our backs once we leave the airstrip. The only thing missing will be that one-hundred-and-twenty-millimetre phallic symbol you armour guys love."

"Now you're just being weird." Skip was laughing, which was a relief to Harry.

"Did I miss something?" said Bill, who had appeared behind Harry.

"Hey, Bill. Pull up a chair," said Skip. "Harry was just implying that I was gay."

"No, I wasn't."

Bill waved for the waiter. "Maybe it's just as well I missed the conversation," he said.

"Harry, our LO from the Colombians is a Major Fuentes. He's joining me for breakfast at 07:00. I'd like you there unless you have other things planned."

"Roger that."

"Our supplies arrived and are under guard at 33 Aviation Brigade, which is also our staging area. I want to run over after breakfast, check the equipment and the set-up. Harry, I need you and Alex to come along. We'll work out the details at breakfast with Fuentes."

"Good," said Harry.

"I think that's enough business for one day," said Skip. "No, I'm wrong. Les has been wrangling everybody. I want to make him our acting sergeant major, or do you want a more senior guy, Harry?"

"You read my mind," said Harry. "Did you have a good talk during the trip?"

"It was a very good talk. I'm now entirely confident that we picked the right guy to lead the QRF."

"That's excellent," said Harry.

Skip nodded, drained his drink, and yawned. "Gentlemen, I am fading," he said, "so I'm heading for bed." He stood and saw Les standing at the entrance to the bar. "It's been a long day, and tomorrow's going to be busy. See you at 07:00."

Skip headed toward the door and as he met Les, he said, "Please come with me."

The two men rode the elevator in silence, and when they reached their floor, Skip asked him to join him in his suite. Inside, Skip invited Les to sit.

"Did I put my foot in it, Colonel?"

"Not at all, Les. Quite the opposite. You're doing a great job, and I wanted to tell you so. I also wanted to tell you that it was a mistake not to make you part of the O Group for this mission, and I apologize. Also, I'd like to lean on you to be Acting Sergeant Major in Jules's absence."

Les had never had a colonel apologize to him, and it was a bit disorienting.

"Colonel, there's no need to apologize, sir."

"Are we okay?"

"Yes, Colonel. We're fine, sir."

"Good. Tomorrow morning Harry, Alex, and I are going to check our kit and the facilities at the air base. Keep everyone here in the hotel. No exceptions. Don't let them gather in groups bigger than four men. Tomorrow evening, have everyone come here to my suite. It's big enough for a bloody battalion."

"Aye," agreed Les, "that it is."

"I'll give everyone an update then. Any questions?"

"No, Colonel.

"Good. Now go get some kip, *Sergeant Major*, and I'll see you tomorrow."

Skip rose and offered Les his hand.

Harry left the bar shortly after Skip did, but once in his room, he realized he was still wound up from the travel. He decided that a walk around the pool deck might relax him and headed back downstairs. Passing through the door, he waved off the waiter.

Bill was still at the table and beckoned Harry to join him. "Can't sleep?"

"Nope," Harry said, taking a seat. "I figured a short walk would do the trick."

"Drink?"

"No, thanks."

"Listen, I know you've spent a lot of time with the US Army. The team that you and Skip — excuse me, the Cohort — have assembled is unique in my experience. I'd love to slowly reshape my own organization, and Skip has given me some great insights. How about you, Harry? Do you have any thoughts you can share?"

Harry pursed his lips.

"As with every unit, the commander's personality sets the tone, so it's no surprise that Skip's personality is what's shaped the Cohort. You did your homework. You knew he wasn't a Special Forces guy when you approached him."

"True. I wasn't looking to duplicate Eagle; I was looking to augment it. I needed someone with exceptional characteristics, and Skip was the only candidate who had them all."

"Let me tell you about my old friend," said Harry. "Skip's unique in several ways. I've known him since I was a Subbie, or what you guys call a Shave-Tail. He always had a reputation as a serious professional with an incisive intellect, and a temper best not tested. Trust me, he knows how to go ugly, and when he does, you do not want to be in the room."

"I've seen a hint of that," said Bill.

"You'd expect that since almost everyone else is some kind of airborne killer, a guy like Skip would struggle to be accepted, but that's not the case. He's the leader, but he works at not always being the centre of attention. As you know, trust is something that is either found or earned, and you know that to men like us, that is the essential quality required of a leader. Skip has made it clear that if you trust him, then he'll trust you. To be fair, we haven't been together as a group long enough for a lot of that to show, so —"

"Sorry to interrupt," said Bill. "So how do the men know they can trust each other?"

"Partly it's Skip's reputation," said Harry. "They've all heard stories from guys like me, Alex, and Franz-Josef, our East German bad boy. Partly it's the individual relationship that he has slowly been building with each member. Skip recruited practically every member personally, and that helped him to establish a personal bond with each man. Partly it's the pressure cooker environment you put us in. But with so little time together, a lot of it's based on faith. The truth is that the men want to please him."

Harry paused. "No, that's not it; not please him. The men don't want to disappoint him."

"I'm sorry about the short notice, by the way," said Bill. "I know how hard that made it for all of you."

Harry gave him a crooked smile and continued.

"We all defer to Skip and his vision for our organization. Maybe it's because he's had the most command experience, but it's also because he works to maximize people's strengths and minimize their weaknesses. Bill, for guys like you, me, Alex, and Skip, our lives have been about two things: trust and loyalty. We all trust Skip, and we're all loyal to each other. Like I admitted to one of the guys not long ago, I have a very short list of men that I trust completely. Skip is on that list twice."

Harry looked at his watch. "Well, I have a thing to do tomorrow morning, so I'd better go try again to get some sleep."

Bill looked pensive as Harry stood to leave. "Thanks, Harry. I appreciate you sharing all of that with me."

Harry nodded. "Good night, Bill."

Courtyard Marriott Hotel

At breakfast the next morning Skip sat with Major Fuentes, Harry, and Alex. As they were getting settled, Bill appeared.

"Join us," said Skip.

"I don't want to intrude."

"Not at all. Anyway, since you're the link with Mack, maybe you should join us on the airfield."

"Sure thing."

Bill grabbed a chair from the adjacent table. As Skip was about to be seated, he saw Les sitting with Walker, Henry, and Paul, his QRF.

"Please excuse me a minute. I need to speak to Les."

As he approached the table, the men rose.

"Please sit, gentlemen. Good to see you three," he said, looking at each man in turn. "Les, I'm taking the van away shortly, but will send it back right away."

"No worries, Colonel. The next pair arrives at 09:40."

"Good. Enjoy your breakfast."

Skip returned to the first table and sat. Breakfast conversation was light and trivial.

Afterwards, Skip and his colleagues set off to the airfield. Having a police driver and a uniformed senior police officer made accessing it fast and easy. It took only minutes to arrive at 33 Aviation Brigade. The airfield was loaded with various types of aircraft, most of which were marked with the Colombian flag. Some announced that they were Colombian Policía

Nacional. There was even a USAF Herc tucked away discreetly in another hangar.

As they stepped out of the van Major Fuentes said, "Colonel, the brigade commander is absent, but his operations officer is here. I will take you to him if you will please follow me inside."

Inside the hangar, Skip saw an array of cots, topped with pillows and blankets, lined up as if on parade. There was a door leading to a room that appeared to have comms gear, and opposite that was what appeared to be a temporary quartermaster store. Some soldiers were milling about, and a tall officer strode over to them. Major Fuentes saluted him.

"Mi Coronel," he said to Skip, "may I present Teniente Coronel Gasparro. He is the operations officer of the army aviation brigade and our host."

Gasparro saluted Skip. "Welcome, Colonel Schiaparelli. It is my pleasure to meet you. I am sorry that the commander is away on duty."

"Colonel Gasparro, the pleasure is mine," Skip said, then introduced his entourage.

"Bill, it is nice to see you again," said Gasparro.

"Likewise," said Bill. "How did you enjoy army staff college?"

"I prefer flying, to be honest, but it really helped my English," he said, laughing, "and Kansas is much too dry for me. Colonel Schiaparelli, let me take you to see your equipment."

The men walked over to where the soldiers had been a few moments earlier. Gasparro spoke briefly to an NCO who barked a command at several soldiers. Moments later, a series of tactical footlockers were brought in and opened.

"These two contain all of your weapons. This one contains your ammunition, and the tactical vests are in the remainder," said Gasparro, indicating the array of cases.

A soldier ran up to Gasparro and saluted, and a stream of unintelligible Spanish ensued. All that Skip was able to make out was something about *Americanos.*

"You must excuse me, gentlemen," said Gasparro when the man had finished. "I am needed urgently. Major Fuentes is fully briefed and can answer any questions." He saluted and was quickly gone.

"Over to you Harry," said Skip. "Have a look."

He stepped back with Bill while Harry and Alex went through the boxes and checked the contents against a bill of lading. Major Fuentes and the soldiers watched in silence.

"I'm sure it'll all be there," said Bill. "Mack didn't get rich by annoying his clients."

Skip smiled at Bill but stood silently with his arms folded across his chest. After ten minutes, Harry came over to him.

"All present and correct," he said. "It all looks brand new."

"Almost," said Bill. "Everything Mack delivers has been proved on a range and zeroed in, based on the weapon's most effective combat distance, then his guys clean it all up and repackage it. Like I said, Mack likes to keep his clients happy."

"Excellent," said Harry. "I'll have them re-stow it for us."

Major Fuentes came over. "Is everything alright?"

"Yes, thank you," said Skip. "Is there somewhere we can we sit and talk?"

"Once Colonel Harry and Alex are satisfied, I will take you to a secure office that the commander ordered to be set aside for you, mi Coronel."

"Skip, I'm going to beg off," said Bill. "There's a US Army LO here and we go back a ways. My phone works here if you need me. Otherwise, I'll see you at the hotel."

"Thanks, Bill," said Skip absently.

A few minutes later, in the secure office Major Fuentes had arranged, Skip noticed a military map of the target area. He walked over and inspected it.

"This is much appreciated," he said.

"You are welcome, sir."

Skip continued looking at the map.

"Major Fuentes, please tell me more about Leticia and the area."

"Certainly, mi Coronel. The airport there is like here. It is half civilian and half military. We have both a police and a military presence because it is on the border, but we enjoy reasonable relations with the Brazilian and the Peruvian authorities."

"Reasonable?"

"Si, that is the best description. Peru and Brazil are very close, but Colombia and Peru are sometimes not quite so close. At our lowest local levels, we get along better. Probably because we all have the same job. We stop smugglers and control contraband fishing and mining. El

Comandante, who also apologizes for his absence, has arranged for you, me, and a small signals detachment to be in the airport control tower."

Fuentes put his finger on the map.

"The tower closes to civilian traffic at midnight, but my staff are already there and will secure the tower and do radio checks for us before we arrive."

"Excellent," said Skip. "So, no need for a radio van as Coronel Tomasino and I had discussed previously."

"No, mi Coronel. Mi Comandante decided this was a better option."

"I agree. The Herc will take us to Letitia, and then the squads will use helicopters?"

"As you asked. Three utility Huey helicopters with no markings will arrive there tomorrow during the day and be prepared and waiting for you. We have helicopters there frequently, so no one will notice anything unusual."

"You have no permanently stationed forces there?"

"Local police, yes, and we have our federal police in the small harbour. They have two zodiacs to patrol the river. Sometimes they work with the small detachment from the Peruvian federal police in Santa Rosa de Yavari, which is across the river." Fuentes touched the map again.

"Interesting," mused Skip. "No one mentioned the harbour before. Harry, Alex, any questions, or concerns?"

Alex shook his head no.

"All good," said Harry.

"One more question," said Skip. "Is the harbour detachment always manned?"

"Si. It is very small, but since most smuggling is at night, they are on shift duty, twenty-four-seven."

"What's this pin here on the map? It looks like it's in the Amazon River."

"It is. It indicates the place where the borders of Colombia, Peru, and Brazil meet. It is called '*el trípode*,' the tripod, by the locals, and there is a river navigation buoy anchored there."

Skip rubbed his chin and seemed to be digesting the information.

"I see. Thank you."

That evening after supper, the three squads arrived at Skip's suite.

"Nice digs, Colonel," said Gord. "RHIP, I guess."

"Problem with rank having privileges Gordo?" said Skip, lifting his eyebrows.

"Not at all, sir. Not me."

Skip broke into laughter, quickly followed by the men. Skip glanced over at Harry and nodded.

"Listen up," piped Harry. "Colonel Skip."

"I hope everyone is rested and ready," Skip began. "You all look like you are. I wanted to take this last opportunity to tell you how impressed I am with all your preparations and give everyone one last chance at questions. Remember my brief description of Professor Tuckman's four-part model? The first three phases have gone exceptionally well. All that is left is the 'performing' phase. After tonight, I step away and it becomes Harry's show as the tactical commander. The plan is solid. You're all ready, and our Colombian friends have pulled out all the stops to support us. Any questions for me?"

Skip looked around the large room. Everyone was looking straight at him, but no one spoke.

"Good. Normal breakfast tomorrow, after which we'll be taken to the airfield. I remind you to pack your bags and bring them along. Your rooms will be cleaned and waiting for you when we get back. Harry, any points?"

"No, Colonel."

"Les, you get the last word this evening."

"Nothing to add, Colonel."

Skip turned to Gord. "Gordo, get out of my room and take this rabble with you."

"Ha, ha, ha. Yes, Colonel."

As the last of the men filed out, there was a rap on the door. Skip opened it to find Bill standing in the corridor.

"Come in."

"I don't mean to disturb you. I just wondered if there was anything you needed before I turned in. You won't see me tomorrow, but I'll be waiting here with Tomasino for your return. I gather you and Fuentes are going to be at the Letitia airport."

"That's right." Skip stepped aside and held the door open, gesturing for

Bill to enter. "Sorry, Bill, come sit down."

Bill entered and plopped himself on one of the large couches.

"Drink?" said Skip.

"I'll pass."

"Any last-minute intel? said Skip.

"No, same as it has been for weeks. The situation is ripe to go in and grab Lopez."

"I hope you're right," said Skip. "His obsession with his personal safety really helps us. His refusal to have armed guards in the house overnight is a blessing."

"It's more than that. It's a paranoia about being assassinated in his sleep. Not sure I'd make my security detail stay in a small settlement fifteen minutes away by dirt road, though."

"I'm with you," said Skip. "You really have to ask yourself what use it is to have half a billion dollars in cash stuffed in mattresses. He lives in self-isolation like a prisoner. I don't get it."

"Me neither, but you don't have to be a criminal to live that way. Look at how Howard Hughes ended up."

"No kidding."

Bill stood up.

"I'll let you get some sleep. Tomorrow's going to be a big day, and a long one. And thanks for the chat by the pool, my friend."

"Likewise," said Skip.

33 Army Aviation Brigade

The next day at the hangar, the men were busy trying on tactical gear. There were knee and elbow pads and tac vests reinforced with Kevlar body armour. All the vests were matte black with semi-reflective black lettering that said 'POLICIA.'

Skip walked over to Harry, who was staring at an assortment of clothing at his feet.

"Issues?"

"None," said Harry. "Les, come here, please."

Les jogged the dozen paces to Harry.

"See to the issue of the weapons, then ensure that Red, Green, and the QRF are fully kitted. Once that's done, assign a bunk space to each man and have them stand by them. When everything is ready, come and get me."

"Aye," said Les, and jogged back to the men.

"He was a find," said Harry appreciatively as he and Skip watched Les. Skip nodded his agreement. "I'm going to grab Alex and run through our drills one last time, then an equipment check, then make sure that everyone is bedded down. It's a big day tomorrow, and it's an early start."

"Absolutely," said Skip. "I'll leave you to it. It's your show now, my friend."

Skip patted Harry on the shoulder and walked to the office space. Major Fuentes rose to his feet as Skip entered.

"Is there anything you need, mi Coronel?"

"No, thank you. I'm just staying out of everyone's way until they bunk down. Colonel Harry Monahan is the tactical commander."

"I see," said Fuentes.

It was pitch dark when the Colombian duty watch came around to wake the Canadians. The hangar was slowly coming to life, and Skip spotted Major Fuentes walking toward him with something in his hand.

"Good morning, Colonel. Coffee, sir?" He extended a steaming mug.

"Thank you," said Skip, as he took a sip. "This is very good. Did you get some sleep?"

"Colonel, we are in Colombia. Of course the coffee is good," said Fuentes, smiling broadly. "Yes, sir. I got a few hours, thank you."

Skip took another sip. He and Fuentes looked around and saw the men preparing themselves. Each checked his own gear, then pivoted to check the gear of his battle buddy. Men were tightening straps and jumping up and down to ensure that nothing rattled, was loose, or made noise. Alex was checking each wristwatch to ensure that it was set to silent, so that there would not be any surprise beeps or chimes. Les was walking from man to man with a canvas bag in his hand.

"What is that bag for?" asked Fuentes.

"Last-minute check to ensure that everyone is clean. No papers or ID that would indicate who they are or where they're from. Looks like his bag is empty."

The hangar had achieved about fifty percent illumination, and Harry directed everyone to walk out toward the waiting Herc.

"Come," said Skip to Fuentes. "It's time to go."

The men loaded onto the Herc, seemingly indifferent, much like businessmen changing trains on a morning subway commute. Les gave Harry a thumbs-up, which he passed to the crew chief, who then spoke to the pilot. The Colombian Air Force C-130 Hercules began its taxi to the runway.

Within minutes the venerable bird was lifting off with the engines screaming at full pitch. The plane banked sharply to the left, then began its climb to nine thousand feet. Most of the ex-jumpers on board were fast asleep before they even reached their cruising altitude. Skip was not one of them. He may have been parachute qualified, but his dislike of flying ran deep.

The weather gods shed their grace on the Cohort, and the trip was smooth with little to no turbulence. They hit a small patch of moving air as they were leaving the rough terrain surrounding Bogotá, but once over the vast Amazon water catchment area and its dense tree canopy, the flight was smooth, with no bumps or sudden drops. Skip was thus spared the indignity of being airsick in front of his men.

From Bogotá to the airport at Leticia was over a thousand kilometres by air. This model of Herc cruised at just over five hundred kilometres per hour, and in little more than two hours the plane was making its final approach to Letitia International.

The Herc landed, and the pilot started dropping the ramp as it slowed to a stop. Skip turned and watched his men stand and deplane. Wordlessly, the three squads moved to their waiting helicopters. Skip felt a strong sense of loss, but he had given his word to Harry, and he would not interfere. Harry waited for all the squads to deplane and then leaned over to his old friend.

"See you in a couple hours, Skip. I wanted to thank you for giving me this gift, my friend." He tapped Skip on the shoulder and headed for the choppers before Skip could reply.

Major Fuentes waved over a small staff car to take him and Skip to the control tower. There was no elevator, and it was a long climb. Once in the tower, Skip saw that the military controllers had taken over and there were two police officers manning the radios. One of them handed Skip a headset with a boom mic.

"Major, I need you to do something for me," Skip said as he donned his headset

"Yes, Colonel?"

"Deploy those two zodiacs to the tripod now, please, and put them on zero notice to move."

"Colonel?"

"Do it now."

"Si, mi Coronel."

Amazonas

Three nondescript helicopters were parked at the end of the runway at the northeast end of Alfredo Vásquez Cobo Airport-Leticia. Two of the birds began to turn their rotors. Although the airport was now shut down for the night and they were isolated, Harry used hand signals to indicate that the QRF was to follow Les. He then indicated that Red and Green were to mount up.

The first two helicopters lifted off and gently banked toward the river. Harry looked over his shoulder to see the rotors on the QRF chopper beginning to turn.

From the airport, the helicopters made a short hop to the expanse of slowly moving blue-brown water. The trip to the LZ was just over twenty kilometres, and the helicopters flew nose to tail with no lights and disturbingly close. They hugged the river's southern shore. Technically, this put them inside Peruvian airspace for half the journey, crossing into Brazil where the river split around the target island, due south of Tabatinga.

The last leg of the journey was always the one that made Harry the most nervous. He trusted the pilots, of course, but all the same, skimming the water at eighty knots on a moonless night made him tense. Like the majority of infantrymen, Harry was happiest when on his own two feet. Being ferried about, whether in an armoured vehicle, a helicopter, or a plane, made him feel helpless and out of control. Harry pushed these thoughts out of his mind to concentrate on the upcoming mission.

As the two aircraft skimmed above the lazily moving river in the dark,

Harry became fully disoriented. With no running lights on the helicopter, the only thing visible was the soft green glow from the instrument panel. He could see the pilots had their night vision goggles on, and Harry hoped they could see each other because he had no idea where anything was. Harry and Alex had opted to have their squads don their goggles once they were on the ground. There was nothing for Harry to do but wait and listen to the rotors.

The lyrics to Billy Joel's "Goodnight Saigon" came to mind, with its haunting images of whirling rotors evoking the troops waiting below, wondering about their fates... Another thought to push from his mind, as the sudden flaring in preparation for landing jarred him back to reality.

The two choppers swept up out of the riverbed at full speed and came to a soft landing between the beach and the jungle's edge. The pilots slowed the rotors until the squads had all exited, then powered up again and headed out of the area, headed back to Letitia airfield.

The men loped silently up the rough ground toward the trees. It was time to activate their own NVGs. Each man did so, then stood still for the sixty seconds required to allow their eyes to adjust to the eerie green haze. The pre-dawn noises of the jungle had swallowed the sound of the departing aircraft. Harry nodded across at Alex and gave him a thumbs-up. Harry stood, and immediately the two squads were up and moving. Harry looked over his shoulder and saw Les and the QRF exiting their own bird, right on time.

Alex and Harry knew that it was now time to slow down the pace. They all had adrenaline in their systems and needed to dump some of it to get their bodies down to a more normal metabolic state. Harry's watch indicated eighty-four minutes until the start of civil twilight. There was ample time.

Pathways had been cut into the jungle from the beach to the open field in front of the casa, but the squads avoided them. The jungle was thick, though surprisingly passable. Harry took his squad left and sent Alex to the right. They then approached the casa on converging axes. The men soon found themselves on the edge of the jungle. Everyone dropped to one knee and listened for any unusual noise for a full minute. The jungle was alive with sound, but none of it was even vaguely human. Again, Harry stood and waited for everyone to regain their feet.

The clearing up to the house was not exactly a lawn, but the footing was solid. The vegetation had been kept cut down, and it was only a hundred metres or so to the main building. The squads approached cautiously, the last man of each squad walking backward every ten steps. Within several minutes, they were on the patio edge. Les and the QRF had waited the allotted sixty seconds before they moved through the jungle to their overwatch positions. Les gave each man an arc to scan, then dropped to one knee and surveyed the entire area.

The patio doors were open, which was unexpected. They had been told that Lopez locked himself into the building each night before retiring.

The first deviation from the intel.

They could see the sheer curtains that covered the patio doors wafting in the pre-dawn breeze. Harry froze and raised his hand to stop the squad. Alex saw the signal and did likewise. He then signalled to Alex: Problem. Harry motioned that he heard voices. Lopez was supposed to be alone.

The second deviation from the intel.

The men concentrated on slowing their breathing, opening their mouths wide to help them hear. Music. Someone was singing in Spanish. Was there a party? Lopez was supposed to be asleep.

The third deviation from the intel.

Harry made a snap decision. He signalled Alex to hold while he took Squad Red onto the patio. They approached the open doors, and Harry could now make out the voice. Goddamn. It was Julio Iglesias.

"What next?" he thought.

Les saw the unexpected halt and held his breath. When Harry moved again toward the house, he relaxed slightly.

Harry peered through the doors to see if there was anyone listening to the crooner. The room was clear, so he entered and dropped to one knee. He could hear a second voice singing in another room, and it was getting closer.

Bésame, bésame mucho …

Harry froze. Seconds later he recognized Lopez walking into the lounge with a glass in his hand and singing badly at the top of his voice. Harry was committed. He had to get to him fast, before he could raise the alarm.

Harry leapt toward Lopez but inadvertently hit a lamp, sending it crashing to the floor. Lopez turned to see Harry hurtling toward him, dropped his drink, and pulled a pistol from his waistband just as Harry hit him like a linebacker sacking a quarterback. The two men fell to the floor and the pistol went off. Harry kneed Lopez in the groin, then punched him once in the face. With his boot, he pushed the pistol across the tiled floor to the far wall. Lopez lay motionless.

The gunshot obviated the need for silence, so Harry turned and shouted to his men.

"Snatch Section, move now!"

Harry heard movement behind him and turned to see Lopez up and lunging for what looked like a small panel on the wall nearest to him. He leapt at Lopez and the two of them hit the wall — and the panel. It was the alarm. Harry landed a solid punch to Lopez's solar plexus, sending him breathless against a chair.

"Get in here!"

Harry barely got the words out of his mouth before strobe lights began flashing and a loud claxon began to wail. Outside, the entire building was being lit up by powerful floodlights.

"Subdue this fucker, and let's get out of here."

Les heard a shot from the building, followed by shouting. Then a claxon ruptured the silence and there was a series of flashing strobes inside the casa. Almost immediately, the exterior of the building was bathed in a harsh white light. Alex and his team were now fully illuminated.

"Red, this is Quebec, over."

No response.

"Red, this is Quebec, over."

Harry was not answering, but Les could see movement in and around the casa.

"Quebec, this is Zero. Send SITREP, over."

"Quebec, single shot fired at target location. Red not responding. I see movement. Holding and ready. Wait, over."

"Zero, roger. Lift now on its way. Prepare to exfil, over."

"Quebec, wilco, out."

The need for hand signals and silence was now gone. Les started his timer. They had less than fifteen minutes to get out before Lopez's protection party from the north of the island arrived and —

"Quebec, this is Green. Stand by. Moving to you now. Red is following, with target, over."

"Quebec, roger. Lift is on the way, out."

"Walker, you're with me. Henry, Paul — move now and secure the LZ. Remain weapons HOLD. Prepare to receive Green and Red in that order."

"Roger, Les, we are weapons HOLD."

The two men disappeared toward the beach as Les moved out beyond the edge of the jungle with Walker and told him to scan the area around the casa for any sign of intruders. Les could see both squads moving toward him.

"Walker, we are weapons TIGHT. Safety on."

"Roger, Les, we are weapons TIGHT," repeated Walker.

Walker shifted his position and remained standing to better scan the entire casa grounds. There was no more firing, but the casa was ablaze in lights, making their night vision goggles useless. In less than a minute, both squads had arrived with Lopez. Les spotted Alex out front.

"Alex, I have Henry and Paul securing the LZ. Move when ready."

"Roger," said Alex.

Alex paused momentarily to check his squad before leading them to the landing zone. His men were all down on one knee, and he was holding them for thirty seconds to regain positive control. Alex stood.

"Green, follow me."

Alex started walking briskly, followed by his squad.

"Red, this is Zero, over."

No response.

"Red, this is Zero, over."

Still no response.

"Quebec, this is Zero. Stand by for orders …"

Skip gave Les short, sharp instructions. Thirty seconds later, Harry appeared at the head of his squad. Terry, Sandy, and Jamie were carrying Lopez, who was tied, gagged, goggled, and wearing ear defenders. He was also sweating profusely.

"Harry, did you hear that lift is inbound?"

"No," said Harry. "I broke my headset tackling Lopez."

"Green is at the LZ with two of my guys."

"Good work. C'mon, follow me."

"Sorry, mate. You keep your squad moving to the LZ. I've got orders from Skip."

"Orders? What orders?"

"Go talk to Alex. I can hear choppers, Harry. I'll join you in two minutes. Now go."

Harry looked like he was going to say something but didn't. He shouted to his men. "Red, to the LZ. Move now."

As Red moved into the foliage, Les grabbed Walker's shoulder and dragged him forward.

"Listen, mate. I have to go back to the casa. Stay here and keep me in your sights. If Lopez's boys arrive, then do what you have to do."

"What does that mean?"

"Walker, you're my best mate and our best rifle shot. You know why I picked you to do this. Save your last two rounds."

"No fucking way! I'm not going to —"

Walker didn't finish his sentence because Les was already sprinting back to the casa to do what Skip had ordered.

About fifty metres from the house, Les stopped, stripped off his tac vest, and put his assault rifle on top of it. Then he dashed for the patio. He immediately saw what he needed. He pushed the BBQ halfway through the patio door and lit all five burners, then he ripped some curtains down and threw them onto the flames. He looked around quickly. Floodlights, strobes, and claxons were everywhere, but still no rescuers. He ran back to his assault rifle.

"Quebec, this Zero. Send SITREP, over."

Les lay on top of his vest, gulping air. He was surprised at how composed the colonel's voice sounded — and how calming.

"Zero, this is Quebec. Fire lit. Red and Green at LZ. Moving to join. Out."

Having regained his breath, Les rose and took careful aim at the BBQ. It took four shots. The last one found the propane tank, and a fireball engulfed the side of the building. He didn't wait to see any more. Clutching his rifle, he began his race back to Walker.

At the edge of the jungle, Walker waited as Les approached at a dead run.

"You scared the shit out of me when I heard the shots. I've been scanning, but no sign of the cavalry yet."

"C'mon, mate. We need to get to the beach. Now."

The two men moved as quickly as the foliage would allow, and in less than a minute, they saw helicopters. Harry was beside one of them, shouting into a handset.

The problem was immediately clear. There were two helicopters, but only one was one of the birds that had dropped them. Red and some of Green were aboard that one, and the rotors were beginning to gain speed. The second helicopter was a tiny civilian craft that looked like it was used for tourists. Aboard were the pilot, Alex, and one other in back. Both birds were now full, probably over-full.

Harry was shouting something at Les, but the rotor wash drowned him out.

Les was shouting and signalling to the birds. "Lift off! Go!"

Harry stood motionless for an instant, then clambered into the larger helicopter. He was barely aboard as it began to rise from the beach. The chopper lifted off, followed immediately by the smaller one. The two aircraft turned, dipped slightly toward the water, and fled to safety.

"Zero, this is Red, me, and Green returning to your location. Quebec, holding on LZ."

"Zero, roger, out to you. Quebec, this is Zero, over."

"Quebec, over."

"Zero, move to the water, now. Figures two zodiacs on their way. Echo Tango Alpha, figures 'fife' minutes."

"Quebec, I confirm figures two zodiacs in figures 'fife.' Exfil by water."

"Zero, out."

Skip's continued calmness reassured Les as he gathered Henry, Paul, and Walker.

"We're being taken out by two zodiacs," Les said. "They're on their way. Everybody pull out your torches … I mean flashlights. We won't turn them on until we hear the boats on the river. Move to the water's edge and load a round in the chamber. We are now weapons FREE. Let's go."

The men jogged down to the water and picked positions they could defend if they had to. Les looked at his watch. It had been four minutes and there were no boats yet. For that matter, there were no vehicles either. Henry interrupted his thoughts.

"Listen," he said.

The men stilled themselves and opened their mouths, listening. Someone was shooting at the casa.

"The cavalry has arrived," said Paul.

"No," said Les. "That sounds like rounds cooking off. Single shots at random."

"Wait," said Walker, pointing to the river.

The men turned to face the water. In the gloom, they could make out two faint shapes moving toward them at speed. Two "V" shapes could now be seen in the water as the sound grew louder. It was the sound of water and outboard engines.

"Lights on," said Les.

In seconds, two searchlights illuminated the beach as the zodiacs raced toward them. Then they heard the sounds of vehicles and automatic fire coming toward them from the far side of the jungle.

"Get into the water!" shouted Les.

Two men met each boat as they waded waist deep into the river. The crews on the zodiacs killed the searchlights, pulled the men into their boats, and turned to head out into the darkness. As they picked up speed, Les turned to see headlights moving into the beach area. Then he could see muzzle flashes, but it didn't matter. They were well out of range already.

The helicopters sped back up the shallow Amazon River valley, and Harry could feel the second wave of adrenaline leaving his system. He screamed at the co-pilot for a headset.

"Zero, this is Red. Confirm you have Quebec, over."

"Zero, I confirm I have Quebec. See you in figures three. Out."

Harry was now feeling a bit nauseous. He knew from experience that this was a perilous time. The mission wasn't over. They still needed to get back to the airport and then to Bogotá. Dropping their guard now was dangerous. He scanned the helicopter and could sense the fatigue in the men's faces. He reached above the bound and gagged body to slap each man on the arm, followed by a thumbs-up.

Once on the tarmac, Harry jumped off the chopper. He spotted Skip standing next to Fuentes. At the end of the runway, the Herc was now idling with the ramp down.

"Welcome back," said Skip.

"Where's Les? You said you had him."

"Patience, Harry. We do have him and his QRF."

"Mi Coronel," interrupted Fuentes.

A police van was driving across the darkened runway apron. It pulled to a stop in front of the men, and the sopping-wet QRF jumped out. Skip looked around and did a nose count.

"Mount up," he shouted, waving at the idling Hercules. "Sergeant Major, well done. Count them all onto the Herc and let me know when we're good to go."

"Aye, Colonel," said Les as he stepped off, shepherding the men across the darkened airport and toward the plane.

"Come on, Harry. We have a plane to catch," said Skip as they walked quickly toward the idling Herc.

Les gave Skip the thumbs-up, and Skip patted the loadmaster's shoulder. He could see him talking to the flight deck on the intercom as he stepped aboard. Moments later, he was jolted against the bulkhead as the pilot applied full power then released the brakes. They were halfway down the strip with the ramp still down. No one cared; everyone had experienced this dozens of times when they'd flown with Canadian Herc crews.

Skip staggered over to Harry as the plane climbed above the jungle canopy. He heard the ramp snap closed and audibly lock as he tapped Harry on the shoulder.

"Everyone should put their heads down," he shouted.

Harry stared at him blankly and turned to look into the cavernous fuselage. Lopez was fully immobilized, and the men, not needing to be told, were scattered all along the floor, prone and already asleep. The two men laughed. Harry gave him a thumbs-up and Skip returned the gesture.

33 Army Aviation Brigade

Getting off the Herc upon their return to the airfield, it was obvious to Skip that the troops were all exhibiting signs of adrenaline exhaustion. Fatigue was scribed on all of their faces, but they remained organized and silent. It would have been easy to declare victory and head for breakfast, but that was the furthest thing from Skip's mind. He ordered everyone to hit the showers and wash off the fatigue. He also wanted everyone back into fresh civilian clothes.

As he watched the men stripping off their gear, he saw Tomasino and Bill approaching. With them was a small squad of police officers in tactical gear.

"Augusto, Bill, isn't a bit early for you two?"

Tomasino smiled easily and waved his officers toward the bound and gagged Lopez. Fuentes was with the prisoner, and once they took possession, Skip walked over to greet his commander.

"Congratulations, Amadeo," said Tomasino. "Well done, my friend. I must apologize for the two failed helicopters. I am not happy, and heads will roll, I can assure you."

Fuentes joined them, saluted, and then headed toward the hangar.

"Thank you, Augusto," said Skip. "All is forgiven. We both know that helicopters are not nearly as reliable as the pilots insist that they are."

"Nonetheless —"

"Nonetheless — you are the commander and I know you will do what you must. I want to commend Major Fuentes, however. His quick thinking saved my men. Stealing the tourist helicopter and dispatching the zodiacs was what saved us."

"Mi Coronel, I did not —"

Skip silenced him with a raised hand. "Major do not be modest. I offer you my most sincere thanks."

Skip reached over and shook the major's hand. Tomasino smiled coldly and waved the major off.

"Amadeo, you are too generous. The major has already reported to me what occurred in the tower, old friend. It was not *his* quick action that saved your men, *mi amigo*."

Bill looked on, a bit puzzled.

"Who knows? Maybe someday, when you are retired and I am falsely accused of shoplifting during a holiday in Colombia, a future Coronel Fuentes will come to my rescue."

"Amadeo, I am not as old as you think."

"No, but I am not the one who has drug lords for enemies, my friend."

"That may just have changed," said Tomasino.

The three men began to laugh as Major Fuentes returned to inform them that there was a bus waiting outside the hangar to shuttle the men back to the hotel at their convenience.

Courtyard Marriott Hotel

Before allowing everyone off the bus, Skip asked for their attention.

"Harry, Alex, Les, I offer you my congratulations. Our inaugural mission is a success, and you all deserve both great credit and a long rest. However ..."

"Colonel, please don't say we all have to go back and get the vest that Les lost."

The bus erupted in laughter.

"Our sock-counter speaks," Skip deadpanned. "No, Gordo, we can write that off. What I wanted to say was that today I want you to rest and refresh yourselves, but we will all be confined to the hotel. Jot down your thoughts for the After-Action Review that we'll conduct back at le Chalet, but do not talk publicly about the last thirty-six hours."

Skip looked down the length of the vehicle.

"Good work, gentlemen. I am proud of all of you. Now, get off my bus."

Most of the men went to get some sleep, but Skip was still wound up and he was starving. Luckily, the breakfast room had just opened, so he went to get something to eat. As he was walking in, he heard someone call him from behind. He turned to face Les.

"Colonel, may I have a quick word?"

"Of course, Les."

"I wanted to thank you for what you did."

"Like you, Les, I did my job, that's all. By the way, I know what you told Walker when you returned to the casa."

"That bugger. Did he grass me up?"

"Not at all, Les. You had a hot mic. We'll keep it between us, shall we?"

"Colonel, if you can't ask a mate, then who can you ask?"

"Go get some kip, Sergeant Major. You're going to have to be on your toes with all the lads trapped here today. Keep a lid on their drinking."

"Aye, Colonel, I will. See you later, sir."

After breakfast, Skip retired to his room to make notes on the last few days. He had filled almost two pages in his taccuino when there was a knock at the door and Bill stepped in.

"Hi, Bill," said Skip, pausing in his writing and getting to his feet. "This is becoming a habit."

"Sorry, Skip. I wanted to say good-bye. Tomasino and I have handed Lopez over to my guys, who have already loaded him onto a non-existent flight to a non-existent location, and it's time for me to head back. We have lots to talk about, but all that can wait. By the way, if you keep an ear cocked, you'll start to hear discreet media reports that the Colombian National Drug Enforcement Unit has made an extraordinary bust."

The two men shook hands.

"Congratulations again, Skip. I'll talk at you real soon. Promise."

Skip gave him a quizzical look. "Bill, wait. You weren't here just to watch this show."

"What are you talking about?"

"How many men did you have standing by if it all went south?"

Bill paused momentarily, then patted Skip on the shoulder, smiled, and left in silence.

Skip saw Harry sitting by the pool bar and joined him. "Enjoying the company of all your friends?"

Harry didn't respond. Skip pulled out a chair and sat down.

"That was a joke. What's wrong?"

"I'm feeling guilty about how I reacted to Valkyrie. I was annoyed, but I should have trusted you."

"I'm sorry you were annoyed, Harry, and I didn't take it personally. I know you trust me, and I trust you. Think back to when you commanded the battalion. As commander, there's some stuff you just need to keep to yourself. That's all this was."

"Still …"

"Harry, we've known each other for decades, but you've never actually worked for me. We've never been in a tactical situation, not even on an exercise. Considering what we've built in such a short time, and what you pulled off yesterday, I'd say we did pretty well."

"You're right, Skip. I don't mean to mope," Harry said, seemingly mollified.

"May I join you?" intruded a voice behind Skip.

"Alex. I didn't see you there. Of course. Please pull up a chair. Did you two get any sleep?" said Skip.

Both men nodded.

"When do you fly back?"

"Tomorrow morning at ten o'clock. How about you?"

"Les and I fly out at nine-fifty to Chicago."

"Skip," said Harry in a low voice, "visitor approaching on your left."

"Major Fuentes, hello again," Skip said, getting to his feet.

"Good day, gentlemen. I am here to pass on Colonel Tomasino's respects and ask if you could join him in his office."

"All of us?" asked Harry.

"Actually, the colonel asked for Colonel Schiaparelli, but he would certainly welcome anyone you wish to bring along, mi Coronel."

"Excellent," said Skip. "Finish your drink, Harry. We're all going for a ride. Alex, can you leave a message for Les at the front desk telling him we're breaking curfew, and then join us out front, please?"

Colonel Tomasino stood as the men entered his office. He dismissed Major Fuentes and asked his guests to be seated. An orderly brought in a porcelain coffee service and departed.

"Gentlemen, please serve yourselves. I only wanted to receive some immediate feedback from all of you before you depart. Normally, I would ask for a written report, but not under these circumstances, I think."

"Congratulations, my friend," said Skip. "I just heard that your unit has captured a notorious drug lord who has been in hiding. By the way, anything on the news from Brazilian radio?"

Tomasino took the comments as intended and began to laugh.

"Thank you, Amadeo, and no, there is nothing on Brazilian news and I do not expect anything, because they have been insisting for over a year that they do not know about where he is."

The subsequent discussion didn't last long, with both Harry and Alex remaining mostly silent. At an appropriate pause in the conversation, Skip rose from his chair.

"Augusto, thank you again for all of your help and for your generous hospitality. I'm sure you have much to do, and as for us, we must prepare to return home. Let me be absolutely clear. We could not have succeeded without your assistance and your resources, my friend. I am in your debt."

"Amadeo, again I want to apologize about the helicopters, and I am sorry that your visit was so short. Next time I hope you visit longer so that I may introduce you to my wife and family. It is good that, unlike Berlin, you are leaving in good health from my country. *Vaya con Dios.*"

The two men embraced, and Skip left the office with Harry and Alex. On the way downstairs to the waiting vehicle, Alex paused on a landing.

"Berlin? What was that about?"

Skip was about to reply when Harry interrupted.

"Jumper, stop asking questions. Remember what I said about the horse's head."

Skip laughed out loud and continued down the stairs.

Le Chalet

Before leaving Bogotá, Skip ordered all of the weapons and tactical gear cleaned and left with Fuentes. It was a small gift to Tomasino, and there would have been no way to get any of it to Canada in any event.

The men took a day to rest at the Marriott and then began leaving the way they had come, once more travelling in pairs and by multiple routes. Being safely out of the area of operations didn't mean all the risk was gone, however, but the return to Montreal was thankfully uneventful. It took several days to re-gather everyone, and once the group was together again, Skip insisted that the entire cohort reassemble in the Chalet for at least twenty-four hours to decompress as a unit. He had learned from watching the mistakes made with redeploying troops from Bosnia and Afghanistan. They needed to stay together, and unwind together, before being left on their own. The adrenaline-fuelled sense of unity that they had experienced on the operation needed to be brought back to normal levels under controlled conditions. Besides, he needed to do another hot wash and then a full After-Action Review, which proved highly valuable. The need for more training on mental agility, branches and sequels, emergency rescue procedures, and other considerations had all been reinforced in Skip's mind, and he made extensive notes.

Within minutes of the men being dismissed, the lounge was mostly empty. Breaker, looking for Skip, stepped outside the lodge, and saw him standing with Harry and Franz-Joseph.

"Harry, the lighter, if you please," said Skip as Breaker approached.

Harry handed Skip a disposable lighter, which he ignited. He then produced an envelope from his pocket, clearly marked 'Valkyrie.' "It deserves an appropriate Wagnerian funeral rite," said Skip. Brandishing the lighter, he dipped one corner of the envelope into the flame and set it alight.

"Colonel, there's a call from Colonel Donovan on your secure line," said Breaker.

Skip placed the burning envelope on the ground, made his apologies, and went inside. He shut the door and punched the speaker button.

"Hey, Bill. What's up? I have you on speaker but I'm alone."

"I just wanted to touch base with you. We've been putting our new friend through the gears, and I thought you'd like a quick update. Are you interested?"

"Indeed, I am," said Skip.

"Well, the intel was a little off, but you already know that, and that's on me to fix. Looking back, it was stupid of me not to assume that even with his paranoia about being assassinated, he'd have one or two weapons around. It was also a lapse on my part not to assume every room had a panic button."

"I'm as guilty as you," admitted Skip. "We live, we learn."

"We've got coverage of your guys going in and coming out."

Skip felt his stomach do a flip and was silent for a moment. "From the house security cameras? Did they hear us speaking?"

"No," said Bill. "The fire destroyed most of the building. We had separate eyes on you from several miles up."

Skip was silent again. "You diverted a satellite just to watch us? Not worried about deniability?"

"I have friends at Nellis."

"I have no idea what that means, but continue."

"The infil was really smooth. You know more about the exfil than I do, although the fireworks were spectacular. I am a bit curious why Les ran back to the house, though."

"Because I ordered him to."

"Why? What did that accomplish apart from almost setting the Amazon jungle on fire?"

"Once mission stealth was blown, I wanted an extra minute or so because it caught the pilots off guard. I figured the rescue force would rush to the house first if it was on fire. Of course, the pilots pooched it anyway when two of the birds went non-serviceable. That was an interesting few minutes in the tower."

"I can imagine," said Bill. "Your diversion worked. The footage shows them racing right up to the house and dismounting. Then they all go for cover and start shooting at the burning building. Any idea why?"

"My guys didn't see it, but based on what they heard, they figure the fire started cooking off rounds in the main lounge about the time the rescue force arrived."

"Looks like they returned fire for maybe thirty seconds before somebody gripped them."

"That's likely when they heard the helicopters coming up the river and went to investigate," said Skip.

"That makes sense based on where the birds were relative to them when they suddenly abandoned the house and raced for to the beach," said Bill. "Les took one hell of a risk going back."

"I know," conceded Skip. "I know."

It was Bill's turn to be silent now. "I have an interesting tidbit about the tactical vests," he said at length. "You'll recall that Les left his vest about fifty metres from the building. It's led to a bit of a witch hunt."

"My guys all wore tac vests that clearly said POLICIA. Won't that lead the Brazilians right back to Colombia?"

Bill chuckled. "You underestimate your old friend Tomasino. I guess you don't survive long enough to be an iron colonel in Colombia without street smarts. Those vests were *Brazilian*. I spoke with Mack, and the vests he provided were plain and nondescript. Seems like Tomasino had them all replaced but never said anything to anybody. The folks from Brazil's *Força Nacional de Segurança Pública* are now conducting an internal investigation."

"I knew Tomasino was clever, but that is a stroke of genius. I must send a discreet note to him. Thanks for the update, Bill. Is there anything you want me to pass along to the men?"

"Only my gratitude for a job well done."

"One question. Did that USAF Herc get home alright?"

There was a moment's silence. "Don't know what you're talking about, my friend."

"I'll be in touch," promised Skip, as he terminated the call. He stepped out of his office and grabbed Breaker.

"What's Nellis?"

"The US Air Force Base?"

"Probably."

"It's in Nevada, and it's where they watch drone feeds and have lots of other high-tech stuff. Why?"

"I was just curious. It doesn't matter."

Everyone was assembled in the lounge when Skip walked in. Harry called the room to attention.

"Relax, please," said Skip. "That was a particularly useful AAR this morning. Just like the quick AAR we did right after the op, we seem to agree on the need for more consideration regarding mental agility, branches and sequels, and emergency rescue procedures. Harry, Alex, and I will review all of these points later." Harry and Alex both nodded their agreement. "I wanted to say a few more words to everyone before you head home. First, let's talk about changes. We don't need to change much. One thing I do want to see changed, though, is I don't want all of you coming to attention for me. It's bad enough that I couldn't come along and play on the beach in Brazil. Everybody knows how much I love helicopter rides."

There was some snickering.

"Making like I'm the CO of a line unit doesn't feel right, so we'll drop that," Skip went on. "Speaking of Brazil, Colonel Bill sends his thanks for a job well done. Our friend Lopez is spending a lot of time under a hot light. Also, it seems you are all on video. There was some kind of 'eye in the sky' on site, it seems. Anyway, it confirms what Les and Walker suspected about the rescue force arriving at the casa and then shifting to the beach. Also, the Brazilian police are stumped. It seems the tac vests you all were wearing were Brazilian, not Colombian."

There was open laughter now, and a voice on one of the sofas said, "Those clever Colombian bastards."

"My sentiments exactly. Talk about a deception plan." Skip paused, then grew serious again. "I want to publicly acknowledge the great work done behind the scenes by Pappy, Jules, Breaker, and Franz-Josef. What the squads accomplished in the jungle would not have been possible without all the work they did to prepare you, not to mention taking care of all the hundreds of details that allowed all of us to get in, do our jobs, and get home cleanly."

"And for you to get that suite at the hotel," quipped Gord.

Skip laughed out loud and extended his open palm toward the four men. "Gentlemen, Bravo Zulu."

There was spontaneous applause, and the four ex-soldiers looked appropriately embarrassed.

"Your hard work and training paid big dividends, and you have proved the validity of Professor Tuckman's model. Just as important, in the back of our minds, we all knew that no matter how much planning and rehearsal we did, we were well aware of the old adage that no plan survives first contact might bite us in the ass, and it sure did. But each and every one of you rose to the challenge. As we all learned from our earliest days, adapt and overcome."

Skip paused for several long seconds.

"I am proud of you."

The men sat in silence. Skip knew he'd made them uncomfortable, but he didn't care, and he let the silence linger.

"Listen," he said at last, "if Bill tries to headhunt any of you, I need to know, immediately."

There was more gentle laughter.

"That's it from me. You all deserve a long rest, and I promise no drills or rehearsals for several weeks, at least."

The room broke out into whoops and cheers.

"Enjoy your break and spend time with people you love."

Skip looked over to Jules. The last-word tradition was now well established. Jules shook his head with a firm no.

"Be safe," Skip said. "Go home."

Harry jumped to his feet and called the room to attention, and everyone braced. Skip glared at Harry, who beamed and shrugged his shoulders as Skip walked out.

Rest, Refit, and Re-Launch
December 2012 – April 2013

Montreal

Almost six weeks after returning from Colombia, Skip was enjoying a quiet Sunday morning in his condo when his cell phone buzzed. He picked it up and saw that, true to his word, it was Bill calling.

"Hey, Skip. How's everything up in the frozen north?"

"Bill, don't you ever get tired of being a jackass? You do realize that Montreal is south of most of the state of Maine."

"Wait, what?"

"What's up?" said Skip.

"First, I wanted to tell you that the Senator has been taking credit for assisting in the successful capture of one of our most detested drug lords — even though we've been putting it out that the Colombians brought him to justice on their own. I wanted to check and see if the money got deposited into your accounts. I was also wondering what y'all had planned for the next couple of months or so."

"Yes, Bill, thank you. Franz-Josef reported that there was a big deposit to our current account the day after I returned. I must admit, I don't recall the sum being quite so large when we agreed on compensation. Thank you for that. It was generous of you. Regarding our schedule, I assume you're talking about after Christmas. For now, I have everyone on rest and refit. Harry and Alex have established a rotating duty watch with some small arms shooting, now that the indoor ranges are both built. It's a light training schedule. The lads went at it hammer and tongs for almost fifty days straight and ended with a twenty-four-hour adrenaline parade."

"No kidding, and yes, I meant after Christmas. I don't need to be the Grinch that stole Christmas on top of everything else," said Bill.

"The door kickers all need to ease back on the throttle, but not me and the support crew. There's lots to keep us busy."

"Of course," said Bill. "I was wondering if you might be interested in a bit of joint training with my guys. They've been the big dogs on the block for too long and they're a bit cocky. Word has been trickling back about how good your guys were. I sure would like to see your guys bring them down a notch — gently, of course."

Skip wondered how word had been "trickling back" but didn't ask.

"Gently for real, or gently the way we play you guys for the Olympic gold medal in ice hockey? Also, I assume we're talking about us coming south to train with you, unless you're thinking of teaching all your guys how to use snowshoes."

"Ha, ha. No, snowshoes are not really an option right now. Maybe you could think about it. Call me in the next day or so."

"Sounds good, Bill. I'm sure my guys would enjoy a little force on force with your guys somewhere with no snow. I promise to get back to you within forty-eight hours."

"Talk at you soon," said Bill, and hung up.

Skip needed more coffee and went into the kitchen for an espresso. As he watched the machine create the perfect cup of coffee, he wondered why he hadn't indulged in this toy years earlier. When the demitasse was full, he took it over to the house phone, where he buzzed Harry's condo.

"Did I get you out of bed?" said Skip.

"What the hell are you babbling about? It's thirteen-fifteen. Are you experimenting with LSD again?"

Skip chuckled and took a sip of his coffee. Perfect. "If you can spare a half hour, come on up. I got a call from Bill, and we need to discuss something."

"Mary and all the saints, please don't tell me he's got another attack from the line of march."

"No, no, it's nothing like that. Come on up, and don't forget to wear your regimental blazer and tie. You know, the one from *the* RCR."

"Piss off, Skip."

Ten minutes later, Skip replied to the rap at the door. Harry stepped in wearing his well-worn Airborne Regiment hooded sweatshirt, looking for all the world like a maroon Smurf.

"You look very fetching," said Skip.

Harry pushed past him and headed for the Faema coffeemaker. "Does this thing work?"

"Step aside and let me do it. What'll it be?"

"Expresso, please."

Since Skip liked to rib Harry about *the* RCR, Harry liked to add the "x" to 'espresso,' knowing that the WASP-y affectation put Skip's teeth on edge.

The two men went to the living room where they could sit comfortably. They sipped their coffees and watched the sun reflecting off the windows of the towers down around Place Bonaventure. All seemed right with the world.

"I'm listening," said Harry.

"I assume that since I haven't heard anything to the contrary, everyone is okay and that the training schedule is working. Speaking of which, does Alex really intend to continue living on Gabriola Island and flying out here whenever required? Wouldn't it make sense to move?"

"Not a topic of discussion for now, my friend. Like me, Alex hasn't had the best of luck with wives, but my experience pales by comparison. His current wife is willing to put up with him disappearing with no explanations, but only if she doesn't have to leave her beloved island. She's a bit of a nature freak — talks to the trees and sings to the eagles and the orcas."

Skip looked up from his coffee. "She sings to the eagles?"

Harry went on.

"I've made one concession for him. He's promised to take a ferry over to the mainland every two weeks to shoot. There's a private club in Burnaby that's almost exclusively retired RCMP. That's how Alex stays sharp. He has a buddy there from his days of working with the Special Emergency Response Team."

"I didn't know he worked with the SERT," said Skip, giving a barely perceptible nod of appreciation. "Anything else?"

Harry pondered for a moment.

"Franz-Josef mentioned that Eagle was generous with its compensation for our excursion."

"Bill and I had an agreement regarding how much Eagle would pay for the job. Franz-Josef said that more than a million extra went into the account. Breaker got an encrypted note saying all accounts were paid in full. I asked Bill about it, and he told me not to worry. I guess when you have an unlimited draft on the US Treasury, you can afford to be generous."

"Must be nice," said Harry.

"The reason I asked you up here was to discuss whether we want to accept an invitation from Bill to conduct some joint training. There are no details, no dates or locations, other than it won't be here in the snow. He just wanted to know if we were interested. I told him that I'd think about it and get back to him within forty-eight hours."

Harry sipped his coffee. "I like the idea of a JOINTEX," he said. "I can't think of any reason not to. I suspect we could learn a lot from them."

"I agree," said Skip. "And I think it would be useful to keep everyone's skills sharp. There's nothing like some friendly competition for bragging rights to motivate high-testosterone boys with toys. As for learning from them, well, it's for the *opposite* reason that Bill made the offer. I told you he was impressed. Tomorrow I'll have Breaker set up a secure call. In the meantime, you and I can put our heads together and look at what we'd want to achieve, then we'll see what's on offer from Bill."

"Okay with me," said Harry. "You got any plans for supper? I owe you at least one dinner by now. How about some ribs down at the Fairmont? The walk will be good for us both. I'll book a table and meet you downstairs at eighteen-thirty."

"Sure," said Skip. "I don't suppose I can talk you into going dressed like a maroon Smurf?"

The next afternoon, Harry and Skip met in the corporate offices. Breaker had set up the call, and when they walked in, he was chatting on the phone with Gunny. Bill was on another line with someone. Harry headed for the kitchen, and Skip caught Breaker's eye and made a slashing movement across his throat.

"Hey, Gunny, can you excuse a me minute?" Breaker said. "I gotta step away." He hit the mute button.

"Afternoon, Breaker. Anything I should know before we start?"

"Afternoon, Colonel. No, there's nothing new or unusual. Colonel Donovan's on another line and promised Gunny he'd end that call quickly. You're all set, sir, so I'll step out. The line is already secure."

"Stay, Breaker. I'd like you to listen in. It's always worthwhile to have an extra set of ears."

Harry returned with two mugs of coffee and handed one over to Skip.

"Sorry, Breaker. I didn't bring one for you."

"No worries, Harry. I've got a cup already."

Skip took his seat and reached down to unmute as the two men settled into chairs.

"Gunny, it's me, Skip."

"How's the colonel this afternoon, sir?"

"I'm very well, Gunny. Thanks. Is Bill still on the other call? Who's he talking to, anyway?"

"Sorry, Colonel. Yes, he's still on the call and, um, I, um… I don't know who he's talking to, sir." Gunny sounded oddly nervous.

"No problem, Gunny. I'm going to mute again but stay in the room. Let me know when Bill's ready."

Skip muted the phone and looked to Harry.

"He's gone all squirrelly for some reason," mused Skip.

Harry and Breaker shrugged and continued sipping their coffees.

The speakerphone crackled to life again. "Hey, Skip. Apologies, buddy. I had to take the call."

"Good afternoon, Bill. I have you on speaker, with Breaker and Harry sitting with me. Harry and I have discussed your offer, and we agree that it would be worthwhile, for lots of reasons. Where do you want to start?"

"I'd rather do this face to face. Let's see… Today is Monday. How about I come up on Friday morning? I'll bring Gunny with me. He has another software package update for Breaker, then you, me, and Harry can spend a few hours together. It'll be a welcome break from DC for us."

Skip shrugged at Harry and Breaker. Both shrugged back.

"Would you like me to meet you at the airport?"

"Thanks, Skip, but that's not necessary. We'll show up at your offices shortly after noon on Friday. Does that work for you?"

"Sure. See you then."

PARIS

His prayers complete, Qassem bin Nakbah al Jezayry proceeded down the urine-stained corridor to an equally filthy washroom. He barely noticed the other residents as some nodded deeply and muttered "Sheikh" respectfully and others lowered their eyes and tried to pretend he wasn't there. He hated this despicable government housing in this vile neighbourhood, but he had been told to occupy it by his handler. His burner phone buzzed in his pocket.

"Oui, hallo."

"Salaam, my brother."

Qassem recognized the voice of his handler.

"The peace of the Prophet be upon you."

"Are you alone?"

Qassem stepped into an open-air stairwell and looked around.

"Yes, I can speak. Do you have news for me?"

"Patience, my brother. Have you changed your appearance?"

"Yes, I have begun by shaving my beard. And the cream you provided is removing my *zabiba*."

"Good. The infidels remain suspicious of men who bear the forehead callus of the devout. It is well that you are removing it. You will need to look French if you are going to blend in where I am sending you next."

"Am I finally going to bring the vengeance of Allah upon them?"

"Patience, Qassem, I know that you burn to avenge your dead brothers in Panjwa'i, those killed by the Canadian soldiers, but first I have work for you in Paris."

"But brother, I —"

"Enough! You will obey me, Qassem. I know you hate them, and that you yourself carry the scar of a wound from a Canadian soldier, but Allah has a plan for you. Like you, I too am his instrument, and I will guide you."

"Forgive me, brother."

"Of course. I need you to continue to prepare yourself. Money will be provided for new clothes, and in a few weeks, you will be given new accommodations in a better part of the city. Have patience, and pray for humility, Qassem."

"Thank you, brother. I am a servant, and I will obey."

The line went dead, and so did Qassem's desire to kill French infidels. He would wait for the money and the new apartment, and he would play the role of obedient servant, for now. He would also adopt a new Jihad name. He would be Abu Alaintiqam, the Father of Vengeance. Those Canadians in their faraway wasteland of snow and ice would learn to fear Allah's wrath at his hands.

But he knew he could no longer stay in Paris, and he would pray for patience. A path would be shown to him, for was he not the one chosen by God?

SAINT-PIERRE-ET-MIQUELON

Qassem landed at the airport in Saint-Pierre and was astounded at how small and backward this rocky outcropping in the Gulf of St. Lawrence appeared. He had been told that the islands were in the Atlantic Ocean, but that was not correct. How typical of the French, with their Euro-centric view of the world. He recalled having an argument with a stupid teacher in a Paris café regarding the size of the Atlantic.

"Of course, the Atlantic is the largest ocean in the world," the man had insisted.

"Non, monsieur," said Qassem. "You are mistaken. The Pacific is twice as large."

The idiot teacher would not listen. How could a man who was supposed to teach children believe that the Atlantic was bigger than the Pacific? What a moron! Better that the children should study the Holy Quran in a madrassa. At least there they would learn the truth.

In a taxi on the way into town, Qassem's phone buzzed. He recognized the clipped Parisian voice immediately.

"Where are you?"

"I am where I must be."

"What does that mean? I have been trying to reach you for two weeks. You did not move to the new apartment. Enough of this foolishness. Tell me where you are."

Qassem hung up, then he opened the back of his phone and removed the battery. The call was not unexpected, and the journey had not begun well. Was this an omen? Was it a warning from Allah, perhaps?

The taxi dropped him at the address where he was to meet his realtor.

He stepped out of the cab, and a moment later the realtor hurried up to meet him.

"No, no, no, monsieur, the flat is not at all what was promised by my agent in Paris. No," Qassem said, perhaps too loudly. "It is intolerable. My agent mentioned nothing of it being above a discotheque. I am an academic, and I must have quiet to write my book. How am I to pursue my studies of the Fortress of Louisbourg?"

"Please excuse me, monsieur al-Zawawi. I understand completely, and I am so sorry you do not like the flat, but you are in luck, monsieur. I have another available in le Centreville. Please allow me to drive you to this second apartment, which I am certain will be more to your liking."

Qassem was surprised at how accommodating the landlord was, but he maintained his semblance of aloof displeasure as they drove to the second flat together. The two men stepped out of the car and the landlord led Qassem up to the flat.

"Here we are, monsieur," he said, opening the door and stepping aside to let Qassem enter. "This apartment will certainly please you. It is smaller, yes, but as you see, it is in a less busy quartier of le Centreville. Below us is the neighbourhood boulangerie, and only a few steps up the street there is a petit café."

"The boulangerie," said Qassem. "Is it very busy?"

"No, monsieur, not really. Although they fire their ovens before dawn, they are quiet, hard-working people. The bakery opens to the public discreetly at seven. The clientele is mostly the local grandmothers doing their morning shopping. And of course, it is closed all day on Sunday. No matter whether we are close to le Canada, we remain French and do not worship the dollar on Sunday. *Le bon Dieu* must have His due and His day, n'est-ce pas?"

"I see," mumbled Qassem, who was beginning to deeply dislike this little man. "You promise me that it is quiet?"

"Oui, monsieur. That is what I understand from the neighbours. Might this smaller apartment be suitable?"

Qassem considered the situation in silence. It was clean, and the rent was lower, which was a bonus. Having disobeyed his handler and fled, he needed to watch his expenses, for now.

"Yes, I will take it. At least I will have fresh bread," he said lightly.

And do not worry, you crétin, he thought. Le bon Dieu will indeed have His due — and very soon.

It took Qassem a week to settle into his new routine. There was no mosque on the island, so he prayed quietly in his rooms. Apart from having a little too much curiosity about him, the locals left him alone. He was careful to build slowly upon the legend he had created for his alter ego and was always pleasant and polite to the shopkeepers and locals. Within a few weeks he overheard the old women, the *grands-mères*, gossiping under their breaths in the boulangerie.

"Did you meet our handsome young professor, Marie, with his stylish Parisian clothing and accent?"

"I certainly did, Francine. Such a well-mannered young man."

Qassem smiled inwardly. He was quickly becoming invisible.

After another week, Qassem reassembled his phone, and within twenty-four hours, it buzzed anew.

"Oui."

"Qassem, I am losing patience, my brother. I have tasks for you, but you do not make yourself available. I ask you again, where are you?"

"Where I am is not important. I am studying the Holy Quran more deeply. And planning my attack on the Canadian homeland."

"What?" exclaimed the handler, in a raised voice. "I told you that could wait."

"No, it cannot, but I am delayed because I am waiting for the papers I will need. In the meantime, I plan."

"Qassem, you must stop. Tell me where you are, and I will come to you so we can discuss this further. I can help you, but you must —"

Qassem killed the connection, removed the battery, and put the phone aside. He decided to write a short note to the forger in Paris telling him to email him at a new address when the documents were ready. In the end, it would not matter. Allah would provide His servant with all that was needed. Qassem reached for his Holy Quran.

Montreal

"Most people don't know this, but France still owns a small and very French piece of its once vast North American empire. It's a mere vestige of its former possessions, now a mere ninety-four-square-mile overseas territory, or more properly, the Overseas Collectivity of Saint-Pierre-et-Miquelon."

"Kilometres," said Skip.

"What?"

"It's French," he said. "They don't use miles, and Bill, when you say most people, you mean most Americans."

Bill chose to let this pass. "The collection of eight small islands at the entrance of the Gulf of St. Lawrence is an integral part of France," he continued, "like Burgundy or Lorraine, and the capital, Saint-Pierre, with six thousand inhabitants —"

"Fascinating," interrupted Skip.

"It's not size or culture that make the islands interesting," said Bill, ignoring the interruption. "It's their location, a mere six nautical miles southwest of Canada. The collectivity is a veritable dagger aimed at the loins of the confederation."

"Seriously? Is there a point coming?"

Bill pretended to look wounded but continued, undeterred.

"The US Navy has a base nearby. Placentia may now be inactive, but —"

"Bill, stop. I'm feeling a brain cramp coming on."

Bill remained undaunted. "The cold, damp climate of Saint-Pierre means that tourists avoid it. It's perfect."

Skip stood suddenly, scowling. "Enough already. Perfect for what? Pneumonia? Bill, is this a long-winded lead-up to you wanting to train in the Gulf of St. Lawrence? Am I even close?"

"Actually, Skip, we have a stop-drop. I'm sorry — it's my fault. It happened while we were on the way to the airport, so I figured we'd keep the appointment and talk about what's next. Where's Harry?"

"Harry begged off this morning, and it's just as well considering your news of a stop-drop. Right about now, he'd be ready to leap across the table to choke you."

"Really?"

"Harry takes all of this completely to heart."

Bill pursed his lips. "Is everything alright?"

"His daughter Mary surprised him with a call from the airport. She apologized for the no-notice call. You probably passed each other at Arrivals."

"Is his daughter okay?"

"She's fine. She's got an unexpected six-hour layover and called to see if he could come out and spend time with her. I said I'd entertain you on my own. Of course, that was before I knew you were going to lecture me on the perfection of Saint-Pierre-et-Miquelon."

Bill noted an edge in Skip's voice and gave him a quizzical look.

"Bill, you didn't fly to Montreal to give me a regional geography lesson regarding Canada's Atlantic provinces, so what gives?"

"I've been trying to ease my way in. I came to give you and your boys another mission."

Skip kept his expression calm. "Bill, if this is another no-notice op, you can forget it. Anyway, without large indoor training facilities, we can't do any running-and-gunning training, unless you have some guy hiding up in the Yukon that you need me to grab. Has someone decided to mess with the Iditarod, maybe?"

"Very funny. Skip, I wouldn't do that to you twice. I'm here to discuss a *potential* mission. There's no running-and-gunning involved, and we have plenty of time. The target is hunkered down, and from what we know, he's not moving anytime soon. Naturally, that might change, but the bottom line is you hold the cards this time."

"I'm not sure I like the sounds of this," said Skip.

"Let me lay it out for you. Then you can discuss it with Harry and get back to me. You can set a date for the op, and I'll conform my timings to you — all assuming you agree to accept the task. If you still want a JOINTEX, then fine. However, I suggest we put that aside until we discuss the potential mission, and I say again, *potential*. Once I describe it, you'll see that it's a win-win for both of us."

"What do you mean you'll conform to me?"

"This op will be in two phases. Phase one is your half; phase two is mine. Thus, when you work it out, I'll make my plans so that they dovetail with yours. Like I said, you hold the cards."

"What's the Senator think of this? I gather you're on better terms lately."

"We are," said Bill, "but this op is off the books. The Senator is out of the loop, and, for reasons I can't share, he needs to stay that way, at least for the time being."

"Speaking of your boss, was he aware that you had a Herc on standby in Bogotá?"

"First, I report to the Senator, but he is not my boss. I work for the director of the NSA. It's complicated. And second, there was no Herc."

"Aren't babysitters taught to always have an escape plan in case of emergency?"

Breaker and Gunny returned from their donut run as Skip was needling Bill.

"I'm taking Bill for a quick supper downtown," Skip told them. "You two make yourselves comfortable. We'll be back well before you need to leave for the 22:00 flight back to DC."

Spring had come early to the city, and since Bill had anticipated cold weather, they decided to walk into the old quarter. Bill explained that the travelogue was more than idle chatter. It was why he'd come to see Skip.

"The target is in the capital city," revealed Bill. "My guys could go after him, but it would be better and easier if Pangratti did it."

"I'm not sure I see why."

"It's only six miles offshore, so Canadians visit all the time. You have French-speaking members, which means you'll be virtually invisible among the tourists, plus this target is hypothetically an easy op and has a high payoff financially. What's even more important, it has a lot of political juice. I've got more details, but let's eat first."

Skip stopped walking for a moment and turned to Bill.

"You seem unusually anxious for my guys to do this."

"Not at all," said Bill. "It just makes so much sense, that's all."

"And the Senator doesn't know."

"Not yet, but I'll tell him eventually. After it's finished."

"And your *real* boss?"

"Oh, yeah. He knows."

There were several steakhouses nearby, so Skip chose his favourite, guiding his guest wordlessly inside. A waiter immediately came over to seat them.

"Bonjour, messieurs. May I offer you something to drink before dinner?"

"Thank you," said Skip. "A Cinzano Rosso, ice, and lemon slice for me, and my friend will have a Raftman."

The waiter nodded and left.

"What did you order for me?" asked Bill, watching him go.

"I ordered you a decent bottle of local beer. Trust me, you'll like it."

Once they had their drinks and had ordered their food, Skip asked what the deal was with Saint-Pierre. Did this have anything to do with fishing violations in the disputed boundaries at the mouth of the St. Lawrence?

"I can't imagine any other reason to go to that postage stamp of an island," said Skip.

Bill sipped his beer. "Do you remember the riots and fire-bombings in Paris last November?"

Skip nodded.

"Well, those attacks were the work of one nasty little man named Qassem bin Nakbah al Jezayry. Ever hear of him?"

Skip shook his head.

"The guy's an arrogant little prick, to the extent of giving himself quite a grandiose new name. Maybe you know him better by that name — Abu Alaintiqam."

"I'm still drawing a blank," confessed Skip.

"It literally means the Father of Vengeance."

"Wait," said Skip. "That rings a bell. There were riots in one of the Parisian banlieues. Let me think… Saint-Oren-la-Seine. Is that right?"

"Almost. It was Saint-Ouen-sur-Seine, a half-dozen klicks north of Paris. The riots damn near brought the northern half of the capital to its knees. This guy, let's call him Qassem, is a vile piece of work. He's originally Algerian, and until recently, he was quite western in his outlook. He's highly educated and was a solid citizen. He's multilingual, grew up as a moderate though observant Muslim, and held no strong political beliefs."

"I don't understand. How does he suddenly become the scourge of Paris?"

The waiter appeared with their food and placed it on the table. "Anything else, messieurs?"

"Thank you, no," said Skip. The waiter departed and Skip turned back to Bill. "Please go on."

"A little over a year ago, he was visiting some family in Iraq for a wedding. When he discovered that it was going to be a bit of a drunk fest, he made his excuses and opted not to go. Instead, he attended daily prayers in an old mosque. Well, we got some bad intel, probably intentionally bad, that one of the wedding guests was on our hit list. A drone strike killed almost a dozen people in the wedding party, including Jezayry's cousin and a couple of children."

Skip took a bite of his steak. "That's bad," said Skip.

"It was nothing short of a disaster. The US government apologized, and even made a substantial reparation payment to the family. The idiot who authorized the strike is probably cleaning toilets in Quantico."

"So, the deaths flipped a switch in this guy's brain?" asked Skip.

"Exactly," said Bill. "Qassem convinced himself divine intervention guided him away from the wedding. In his mind, he'd been spared by the hand of Allah, and the deaths were a message from God that Qassem should become His weapon of vengeance."

"*Vox Dei.*"

"Pardon?"

"The voice of God," Skip translated. "It's Latin."

"Right. So, he went to Saudi Arabia and joined a militant Wahhabi sect and swore on the blood of his cousin that all infidels would pay. Then he went off to fight."

"Bill, wait — how do we get from the wedding to Paris and then to Saint-Pierre?"

"I'm getting to that," said Bill. "After Saudi, he went to Iraq, then to

Afghanistan with the Taliban, but it didn't satisfy him, so he went back to Iraq to work with ISIS, but he wasn't much of a soldier."

Skip nodded.

"Qassem then goes back to Afghanistan again. He's offered martyrdom, but he declines, which raises doubts in the minds of his Afghan leaders. He also seems to have a knack for leaving the scene of a fight moments before the door kickers show up. The truth is his little terror cell in Panjwa'i was, shall we say, insufficiently zealous. Most of his cell were more interested in selling drugs and committing rape than in re-establishing the caliphate."

The waiter stopped by to see if all was well. "May I take your plates, gentlemen? Coffee? Dessert perhaps?"

"Just coffee," said Skip, and Bill nodded his agreement.

"Panjwa'i was where the Canadian battle group was stationed," said Skip, taking a sip of freshly deposited coffee. "I was supposed to be there during their rotation, but I pulled the pin before it could happen."

"I know," said Bill. "In fact, the Canadians almost killed him, but he saw his close call as another affirmation that Allah was singling him out, guiding him along a new path, so he bolted. Since he's well educated and speaks French like an upper-middle-class native, his handler sent him to Paris and settled him in Saint-Ouen-sur-Seine."

"I hear those banlieues are hellish," said Skip.

"Some of them are so bad the French gendarmes won't even go into them. Anyway, Qassem is seen as a freedom fighter who's there to liberate downtrodden North African Muslims. Initially his bombing spree went well, but it didn't last long. His arrogance and willingness to sacrifice others for his own gain caught up with him. Again, he saw the writing on the wall and slipped away quietly, under the radar."

"To Saint-Pierre? Why? And how do the French gendarmerie know that?"

"Why? To target Canadians, we think. How? They don't. The gendarmes lost him. So did the DGSI, the General Directorate for Internal Security. But I had eyes on him separately from the DGSI. The Cultural and Trade attaché in the Paris embassy is a pal of mine."

Skip smiled benignly and took a sip of his coffee.

"My pal noticed he'd gone, spread a few euros around, and what did he find? Qassem had a hard-on for Canadian soldiers, especially the

French-Canadian snipers that were so murderously effective in Panjwa'i. He shaved his beard, cut his hair, and cleaned up. He bought some new clothes, acquired some fake papers — but no passport — and headed to Saint-Pierre-et-Miquelon."

"Strangely," said Skip, "it all fits."

"Fits?" wondered Bill. "Fits how?"

"Nothing," said Skip. "Just an idle thought I had. Please continue."

"Without a passport, he's now locked in place, at least temporarily. He just got there and is living in a small apartment above a bakery. The Black Dog, or whatever that is in French. His cover is he's doing research for a book on the Fortress of Louisbourg. He's stuck where he is for the moment because, as far as we know, he's disobeyed his handler, and without a passport ..."

"*Le Chien Noir*," said Skip.

"The bakery? Have you been there?"

"No," said Skip. "I was telling you what the translation of 'black dog' would be. Do you still have eyes on him?"

"We do. Our source there isn't an official operator, but she's trained and discreet. She's retired and likes to keep an eye on things for us. My stipend supplements her small government pension, and she's worth every penny. Talk about ear to the ground."

Skip rubbed his chin. "It sounds simple enough. Excuse me for asking, but aside from grabbing another homicidal terrorist, where's the payoff? More precisely, why involve us, exactly? I mean, I think I get it, but lay it out for me."

"I don't need to remind you that sometimes the US and France do not play nice with each other. If we can bring this murdering psychopath to the French, we get 'atta-boy' points, although probably not publicly. You have much easier access to the guy, and no Canadians get targeted. We act as the bird dog. You go bag him, then hand him to me. The source is mine and privately maintained, so there's no issue regarding the Senator — or the reward, for that matter. You can have most of it."

"You didn't mention a reward."

"Sorry. France has a two-million-euro bounty on Qassem, but they want him alive. Otherwise, I could have used a shooter." He regarded Skip thoughtfully. "What do you think? Is this something for your guys?"

Skip started to rub his chin again but stopped. He reached across the table and offered Bill his hand.

"Deal. How about an eighty-twenty split?"

Bill nodded his assent. "Sounds good."

After supper there was a growing chill, so the two men grabbed a taxi back to the office. Breaker and Gunny were sitting chatting in the lounge. They'd eaten early in case Skip and Bill returned unexpectedly. Breaker had treated Gunny to a classic smoked meat supper at Montreal's renowned Schwartz's Deli. He'd then taken him to Tim Hortons for dessert, which comprised Gunny's beloved maple glazed donuts.

Bill looked at his watch and then over at Gunny. "It's coming up to 19:00, so I think it would be best to head to the airport," he told Skip.

"Okay, Bill. I promise to get back to you as soon as I speak to Harry."

The four men shook hands, and Bill and Gunny left.

"Breaker," said Skip, "is there was anything that can't wait until Monday?"

"No, Colonel."

"Close up and head home, then. I'm off."

On the walk home Skip called Harry.

"Hey, mate. I'm walking home. Give me ten minutes, then drop by."

A few minutes later, Skip opened his apartment door and handed Harry a glass of sour mash as he entered.

"How is young Mary?" Skip asked, closing the door behind him. "I don't think I've seen her since before you took battalion command."

Harry took a sip and moved to the couch. Skip took a seat opposite him and set his own drink on the table between them.

"Bourbon," Harry said. "This must be work. Mary looks terrific, thanks. She's tanned and fit. Living in Oz obviously agrees with her. She sends you her love and a big hug, so consider it delivered. We had a great visit, but she sounds like a bloody Australian."

"I wonder how that happened, Harry? She married an Aussie and lives in Brisbane. One of those deep mysteries, I guess."

Harry exhaled loudly. "Shut up. You know what I mean. Anyway, it was a lovely surprise. Sorry to beg off on such short notice. What's up with Bill, and when's the JOINTEX?"

Skip had a taste of bourbon. "That is another deep mystery. Allow me to fill you in."

"Mystery? I thought we were planning a JOINTEX."

"That changed about the time you headed to Dorval. Bill called a stop-drop. However, there is a ripe plum, and it's a low-risk task with a big payoff. Actually, it's exactly the kind of op I had originally envisioned when I formed Pangratti."

"You have my full attention," said Harry.

"It's another politically sensitive situation, only this time much closer to home." Skip outlined the situation, who Qassem was, and why Bill felt it was best handled by Pangratti. When he finished, he stood up and went to grab the bottle of Woodford Reserve and the ice bucket. He put the bucket and bottle on the table between them and resumed his seat.

"So?" said Skip.

"Sounds to me like a no-brainer," said Harry. "We fly to St. John's, rent a van, drive to Fortune, and take the car ferry to Sainte-Pierre. We meet this Qassem fella, ask him politely to pack an overnight bag, and then convince him that he'd really like to join us. Then we take him home. Easy peasy."

"Harry, you are an operational genius, my friend. All those years of military planning were not wasted. So, why would we go to Fortune, and where the hell is it?"

"Newfoundland," said Harry. "Great place. You need to visit, but I don't recommend it in the winter, especially for delicate flowers like you. Fortune is southwest of St. John's, and it's where the ferry terminal to Saint-Pierre is. It's about an hour and a half drive one way — in summer."

Skip took another sip of bourbon. "Even if we have no problems," he continued, "we can't just throw him in a car and head back to Newfoundland. That's what worries me. It's inevitably the simple-looking problems that can trip you up. What did Defense Secretary Donald Rumsfeld call them — the unknown unknowns?"

Harry nodded.

"Remember the Airborne problem, Harry? The one we all did when we were captains at the army staff college? It looked straightforward until you got into the details and realized that it was a proverbial swamp full of alligators. So, we need to think this through and have a couple of contingencies in place to boot. If it taught us nothing else, Brazil taught us that."

"Too right," said Harry. "It does look simple, perhaps deceptively so. So, we should be looking at multiple options and even multiple squads. The big advantage of Saint-Pierre being small and isolated becomes a major disadvantage if something goes wrong. We could find ourselves trapped. Sound familiar?"

"Islands," moaned Skip. "What is it with us and islands?"

"Well, since we're in agreement," said Harry, "I suggest we stop there, and let your subconscious mind chew on this problem." He examined his empty glass. "Is it time to move from bourbon to scotch?"

"Harry, you read my mind."

"Accumulate and assimilate," said Harry, laughing softly. "Accumulate and assimilate."

The next morning Skip caught up on some personal administration, did some housekeeping, and generally rested. At noon, he decided to wander down to Café Olimpico. As he walked, Skip wondered if his oldest friend was free. He pulled out his phone and called him.

"Amadeo, I was hoping you would call," said the familiar voice. "I have been here for five minutes already, anticipating your arrival."

Although they had only shared a room in their first year, he and Gaston had remained best friends during their remaining years at military college. After graduation, Gaston had served two years in the Royal Canadian Engineers but was mustered out due to an injury incurred while working with a German engineer unit on a NATO exercise. Through his father's considerable connections, Gaston was allowed to transfer from the army to the Royal Canadian Mounted Police, Canada's famed federal police force.

The big man was hard to miss, and Skip spotted him straight away. As expected, his friend was seated with his back to the wall in the rear of the café and had a commanding view of the whole establishment.

The waiter approached Skip. "Nice to see you, Colonello."

"I'm meeting a friend," he said, indicating the table where Gaston was sitting.

The waiter nodded and discreetly followed him to the table.

"Mon cher Amadeo," said Gaston, rising to his feet with his hand extended.

"You could have called me," said Skip. He took the Bishop's hand and was pulled in for a bear hug.

Feeling his friend's strength, Skip wondered absentmindedly if there really were a bishop of the Roman Church built like this mountain of a man in whose death-grip embrace he was now being held.

"It has been too long, but I know that you have been busy. Honestly, it has been months and no call. I have not seen you since you first arrived. Are you angry with me, mon vieux?"

Skip grunted, and Gaston released him from the hug with a short laugh.

"I wouldn't dare be angry at you, Gaston. You are too dangerous for anything like that."

His friend appeared momentarily hurt, then gave Skip an easy smile as he waved him to the seat opposite him. Skip turned and scanned the room, wondering which of the other patrons quietly having coffee were the Bishop's close protection detail. Probably the tall, fit-looking man two tables over.

"No, my friend, I'm not angry with you." said Skip. "I've been wrapped up in my new venture and haven't had time for anything else. Please forgive me."

Gaston finally looked past Skip to the waiter. "*Due espresso e due panino, por favor.*" The waiter, scowling at the failed attempt to speak Italian, nodded and walked to the bar.

Skip shook his head in mock consternation. "How can you have grown up in this city, spoken French your whole life, and still not be able to order two coffees and two sandwiches correctly in Italian? How many times do we need to have this talk?"

"I do not know how many times you have corrected me, Amadeo, and I do not care. Maybe I *want* people to think that I cannot speak Italian. Did you ever think of that? Or maybe I do it just to annoy you." The big man winked.

"I see. Maybe I should stop picking up the tab whenever we meet. An important guy like you, not doubt, has an expense account."

"Skip, as I have always said to you, I am a humble civil servant, a government employee trying to scrape by."

"Indeed, Gaston, and the prime minister rides the number ninety-five bus to Parliament Hill every day. By the way, mister 'I am a humble civil servant,' tell your close protection team to stop being so obvious. They're embarrassing."

Gaston laughed out loud and nodded his approval.

"I'm sorry for not calling you sooner," said Skip, growing serious again. "Apart from being busy, I was out of the country for a while as well. I haven't had time for my usual *caffè e pasticcini*. Totally my fault."

"Naturellement. I know that you have been busy. Pangratti Group seems to have a lot going on these days, and the coffee is probably better in Bogotá."

Skip froze in his chair. He had no idea that Gaston knew anything about Pangratti. He struggled to regain his composure.

"I should have known you'd be tracking what I'm up to. Are we on everyone's radar?"

"Not at all. Just mine, Amadeo. You need not worry, trust me."

"Of course I trust you, but since when does the deputy director of operations have eyes on investment firms?"

"He does not, but then I am not DD Ops, and Pangratti is not an investment firm. I am the special assistant to the director." The Bishop grinned. "You have not been keeping track of me like I have been keeping track of you, my friend."

Skip's heart missed another beat, but he pushed on. "I didn't know the director had a special assistant."

Gaston held his old roommate's gaze blankly. "He does not, and before I forget, a friend of yours from the German Intelligence Service asked me to say hello."

"I don't know anyone in German Intelligence," said Skip.

"I am certain that Dieter would be hurt to hear you say that."

"Dieter who?" said Skip.

"Does it matter? You do not even know anyone in the Bundesnachrichtendienst."

Skip stared impassively at his friend. "Why do I feel like I'm in a Kurt Vonnegut novel? Remind me, Gaston, when did you transfer from RCMP Intelligence to the Canadian Security Intelligence Service?"

"Not long after CSIS formed, and too long ago to count," he said.

"New topic," said Skip. "How's your dad? Is the old RSM still the spider sitting in the middle of his corporate web? Is he still the oldest teenager in the Gaspé? And your dear mother — how is Mamma?"

"Mon Dieu, you said it. I have told him that you have a new job here in Montreal and that you will call soon, for sure. I did not want to see him send someone to break your legs for not paying him an overdue social visit. We must all kiss the ring, mon cher Amadeo. Anyhow, since Mamma passed, he has been spending a lot more time at la Grange in the Gaspé."

Skip froze a second time. "Gaston, your mother passed? I didn't know, I swear. I'm so sorry, my friend. Honestly, I didn't know."

"It is okay, Amadeo. It was very sudden. She said she had a headache and went to bed. When Papa joined her a few hours later, she was dead, and already cold. I did not put a notice in the alumni newsletter. It was a shock, oui. But also, a blessing that she slipped away quietly in her sleep. Papa had her cremated and discreetly took her ashes back to her village north of Chicoutimi. C'est bon. Really, it is. I did not tell anybody. You were occupied in the south, and I kept it very quiet on purpose, so please do not apologize."

Skip sat stricken. "I am so sorry, Gaston," he sighed again, and gave his friend's hand a brief squeeze.

WASHINGTON

Andy sat in his office wondering idly what the day might bring. He picked up the ringing phone.

"Anderson."

"Good afternoon, Colonel. Major Blaine Lewis, sir."

"Hello, Blaine. It's good to hear from you, son. Is there a problem with Tommy?"

"No, sir. No problem. Thanks for asking. But there is something interesting I thought you'd want to know. One of the watch commanders here is a classmate from the academy, and last night he and his wife came to dinner. Frank had a bit too much of my homemade beer and asked me why in hell he would be assigned to watch a USN submarine. It's sitting alongside in Norfolk. It makes no sense."

"You're right, Blaine. It doesn't, but I appreciate your call. Don't talk about this with anyone, understand?"

"Absolutely, sir."

"This is not a secure line, so I do not want you to answer me. Send me a secure email on SIPRNet, son. I need a name. Got it?"

"I've got it, sir. Email in ten minutes."

Andy stood and stretched his legs. Who did he know at Sub Force Atlantic, he wondered … It took him an hour of looking through some staff lists, but he found someone he knew. They'd done a tour together a few years back on the joint intelligence staff and had become chums. Andy made a call. The two men chatted amiably for a few minutes.

"It was good catching up with you, Andy," said his contact, making wrapping-up noises, "and congratulations on making colonel, by the way. I promise to ring you next time I'm in the Pentagon, though I do my best to stay away."

"I wish I could do the same," said Andy, laughing at his own joke. "Oh, maybe you could do me a small favour?"

"Sure. Fire away."

Andy couched his request in terms of having some anal-retentive general breathing down his neck and chewing his ass about some small issue.

"Sure thing, Andy. How'll I get it to you?"

"How about a short SIPRNet email?"

"No harm in that."

"Thanks, buddy. Don't forget to call when you're in DC," said Andy.

"Ha, ha, ha. Okay, but don't hold your breath."

By the end of the day, there had been no email. Oh well, he thought. He'd tried.

The next morning, Andy booted up his secure computer and scanned the overnight traffic. There was something from his friend. As promised, it was short: some guy named Donovan and a USN sub. The same sub that Blaine had sent: USS *Thunder*. He deleted the email and then cleared his trash folder. He rebooted the computer and defragmented the hard drive.

When Andy had been promoted to colonel, he had discovered that one of his new tasks was to be a dogsbody for the Senate Intelligence Committee. Tasks were intermittent and inevitably menial, but occasionally, he got to sit in on an interesting briefing. At one such briefing, he had been introduced to the Chair, a Senator Robert E. Lee Fredericks.

At this morning's meeting, during a coffee break, Andy dropped Bill Donovan's name and made a slightly disparaging remark.

"You know Bill?" Fredericks asked.

"Not really, Senator. We had a disagreement over a drone project I was running, but I do find it interesting that he is now involved with the USN submarine fleet."

The Senator showed no reaction to the comments, and Andy said nothing. It was worth a shot, he thought idly.

Upon returning to his office, Fredericks stopped by his secretary's desk.

"Yes, Senator?"

"I'm trying to remember the name of an air force officer who had a high-tech drone project that was cancelled last year because I re-allocated his project money to Donovan. His name won't come to me."

"I believe that was Lieutenant-Colonel Anderson, Senator."

The Senator put the pieces of the puzzle together in an instant. He pushed the intercom button and asked his secretary to hunt down Vigo Anderson, now a colonel and on the Air Force Intelligence Staff in the Pentagon.

"Please schedule a meeting in my office for next Monday."

"What should I tell the colonel that the meeting is about, Senator?"

"Drones, Loretta. Tell him I want to talk to him about drones."

The call from the Senator's office could not possibly have been random, Anderson thought. There had to be something going on with Donovan. He didn't know what it was, but he had to figure it out somehow. Maybe the Senator would tip his hand.

"Welcome, Colonel. The Senator has been looking forward to your visit, sir. Please go right in."

Anderson stopped at the door, saluted, then entered the office.

"Senator, I know that you are an extremely busy man and I appreciate you seeing me, sir."

"Colonel, I have a small task for you. May I call you Vigo?"

"Of course, Senator."

"Vigo, I have cleared it with your boss, and he understands that you will be temporarily assigned to my office, for as long as I need you."

"Yes, sir."

"I need you to investigate something, and it requires a very light touch and a great deal of discretion. That said, everyone will know that you will be doing it for me, even though my name will never get mentioned. Are you following me, Vigo?"

"I understand completely. I am your man, sir."

"Good. Here's what I need you to do ..."

MONTREAL

Bill's request for assistance with Qassem was cause enough for Skip to recall everyone to le Chalet for planning and pre-deployment refresher training. He told Harry and said he'd tell the RSM and also call Alex. Alex asked for a few days' indulgence, saying he'd be there on Saturday morning, if that was okay.

"That'll be fine, Alex. I intend to brief the whole cohort on Sunday after breakfast, so any time Saturday will work. Be sure to let Jules know what flight you'll be on so Jamie can drive out and collect you in Dorval."

"Thanks, Colonel," said Alex.

Next, Skip phoned Jules and told him to initiate a Level 3 recall — report no later than seventy-two hours from notification. He also told him that Alex had an extension. He wanted everyone to be ready to receive a mission briefing on Sunday at 10:00 in the Great Room. Jules acknowledged and Skip hung up.

The next morning, Harry came to Skip's condo after breakfast. The two men sat looking at Google Earth images of the tiny French islands. The men agreed that it was astounding technology, certainly a long chalk from how they had been trained to plan, with dated maps and photos of only marginal quality.

"Skip, the more I think about this Qassem guy, the less I like this job. Sorry, but it seems too simple, like I said earlier. Something's not right here. Are you sure that Bill is being square with us? I still have trust issues with him."

Skip nodded. "I understand, but I don't think Bill's playing us. Think of what he did for us in Colombia. I know he denies it, but he had an extraction team on standby, I'm sure. All the same, it does seem deceptively cut and dried. For now, let's play it straight. We'll need to really think about this in terms of phases and having branches and sequels. This won't be like the Brazil op. In fact, it's the opposite." He looked at his watch. "I'm beginning to regret letting Alex arrive late. He's quite skilled at planning this kind of stuff."

"So how do you want to start?"

"Let's put ideas down and let our subconscious minds start to connect the dots."

"I assume that since this will be a non-combat op, and the fact that Jules is a native speaker, you'll want him along."

"Also, I know that Leo was a Vandoo before he joined SOFCOM, so maybe we need him paired with Jules. Better yet, let's put one francophone in each squad so we'll always a have a native speaker. Each squad will thus have a point man, so to speak. Do I recall correctly that we have a couple of ex–Airborne Pathfinders? Was it Alex and Henry?"

"Actually, we have four guys who were Pathfinders, all from the Airborne Regiment. Alex, Bob, Jamie, and Airdrie," said Harry. "Airdrie is the most experienced. Why do you want Pathfinders?"

"I'm thinking out loud," mused Skip. "Advance, Main, and Extraction. Maybe even a fourth squad, but I'm not sure yet."

"I think I see where you're headed. Send in the Pathfinders and put eyes on, then send in Main and have Extraction right behind them. Am I following your train of thought? Alpha, Bravo, and Charlie?"

"Check, and maybe Delta. We'll see. Like they say, the devil is in the details. How far ahead should the Pathfinders go in? What separation do we need between Main and Extraction? What about a reserve or a QRF? I'm not sure what use a QRF would be if we drop the ball, to be honest. We need to chew on this, but these questions are a good start."

"Aren't you the guy who always preached that a commander must have a reserve at all times?" Skip made to reply, but Harry cut in. "Never mind. This is all good, Skip. I'm warming up to it. Let me make some notes."

Harry scribbled while Skip looked more closely at the terrain displayed on his large iMac. He stopped and looked over at Harry.

"Something Bill said … That's it," declared Skip. "Argentia — that's the pivotal aspect we were looking for. More correctly, Placentia Bay."

"Argentina? I'm not following you, Skip," said Harry, looking up.

"No," said Skip. "Argentia. I'm not sure I have it worked out yet. Let me run this by you. We send in a squad to put eyes on …"

Over the next ten minutes Skip explained what his flash of insight had revealed to him. Harry listened intently, occasionally looking up at the screen.

When he'd finished, Harry said appreciatively, "I like it, Skip. I like it a lot."

WASHINGTON

Anderson had finally put the puzzle together. It had taken weeks of discreet phone calls to the full range of staffs and some awkward conversations, but it now made sense to him. Andy was reminded of the shocking degree to which intelligence was kept in organizational silos with few or no crossovers. The key to the puzzle had come almost by accident when he was talking to a friend in the air component of the Naval Intelligence staff.

"It's all routine traffic, Andy. I don't see why anyone is curious about it."

"Thanks, Colin," said Andy.

"Mind you, I do find it unusual for a sub the size of *Thunder* to be looking at Placentia Bay, especially since they are supposed to be in the Faroes Gap for most of the summer, but what do I know? I'm a naval aviation analyst. Who am I to question what a sub skipper wants?"

"Placentia Bay?" said Andy.

"Yeah. Weird, right?"

It was time to brief the Senator and put a stop to Donovan's game. Anderson called the Senator's office, and to his surprise, Miss Loretta told him that the Senator would see him immediately.

"Good morning, Senator. Thank you for seeing me so quickly, sir."

"Come in, Vigo. Come in and have a seat. Loretta tells me you have important news for me that you couldn't share on the phone."

"Yes, sir. I believe I have figured out how Donovan is connected to the USS *Thunder*. If I may explain …"

Even the Senator wasn't ready for what he heard. When Andy finished briefing him on what Bill Donovan was up to, Fredericks struggled not to let his fury show.

"Thank you for your excellent work. Naturally, I was aware that Colonel Donovan had an operation ongoing, but it would seem he was attempting to shelter me from some of the grittier details. As you can imagine, I am somewhat troubled. Nonetheless, you have been a great help to me, Vigo, and I won't forget it."

Anderson rose to say farewell, feeling like he had hit a home run.

"Thank you for your time, Senator. Is there anything else I can do for you, sir?"

"No, thank you, son. Time to let this play out, and I remind you how sensitive this information is."

"Of course, sir."

"Vigo."

"Yes, sir?"

"I will need any and all records of your investigation, please. Absolutely nothing of this can be shared for reasons I am sure you understand."

"Of course, Senator. I'll deliver them later today."

"Excellent, and please include a one-page fact sheet on that drone project of yours. I'd like to have a rethink on that funding."

"Yes, Senator. Thank you, sir."

Anderson stood to leave but paused.

"Senator, one more thing, sir. Did you know that we had an unscheduled visit of a USAF Hercules aircraft to a military facility in Bogotá last November? It came to my attention when I was looking into Director Donovan's activities, but there are no details on the visit, sir."

"Is that so?" said the Senator, whom Andy thought was looking suddenly even more annoyed. "Oh, yes, that's right. Now I recall. Thank you, Colonel."

As Anderson shut the door behind him, he thought that he might actually weep with joy at the prospect of being able to pay back the feckless Donovan.

Le Chalet

The men were gathered in the Great Room, some sitting, some standing. The aroma of black coffee permeated the space. Chatter over breakfast had been subdued yet animated, much of it speculation about why Colonel Skip initiated a recall. A drill? It didn't feel like a drill. Whatever the reason, everyone was well rested and itching for another op. Skip walked in and the room fell silent. Several of the men rose from their seats.

"As you were," said Skip, feeling the tension in the room. "Welcome back, everyone. You're all looking well. No, this is not a drill. There's a real op on the table. That's why I recalled everyone. This one will be an interesting challenge for us. Let me say this up front: it's a non-combat mission. It's top secret and more complex than it might appear at first blush, but in a nutshell, we're going to snatch a terrorist off the streets of a small French town. We'll probably need to do it in broad daylight, posing as tourists. I'm not sure yet. We'll then have to exfiltrate this guy without alarming either the authorities or the general populace. Let me be clear. The chances of this individual coming along voluntarily are nil."

Skip waited to let everyone absorb his message.

"Later, I'll be meeting with the O Group to formulate a plan, but for now, let me give you the broad strokes. The nature of this op will call for multiple branches and sequels because the target is a free runner. He has no known routine. We, however, have a lot of restrictions. For now, what you need to know is that practically all of us will be travelling for this op. Once again, we are on foreign soil, but there will be no weapons. I say again, no weapons this time, not even for self-protection."

"Are you nabbing some bloke at Euro Disney?"

There was a bit of chortling in the room.

"No, Pappy, we are not subsidizing your holiday plans." He waited for the laughter to die down, then continued. "We will deploy identically to the previous op. We'll assemble in multiple squads, and once we reach a certain stage, Harry will take tactical command. Our methodology this time, to use the Russian term, will be *maskirovka*. In English, it's the art of deception.

"That about sums it up. You are free to go and do your normal workouts or go for a run. No special instructions for today. Questions?"

"Sorry, Colonel," said Les. "I have one. I'm not really clear what branches and sequels are."

"Les, there's no reason you should be familiar with the term, and I apologize for not explaining it sooner. It's what you would have probably called officer-talk back when you were a Para. You know what branches and sequels are, Les, even though you may never have heard the term before."

"I do?"

"Yes, you do. In every operation there are critical junctures where a plan can go left or right or stay on the track that you foresaw. In other words, a branch is a contingency plan, an option built into the base plan. A sequel is a follow-on operation based on the potential outcomes of the current plan. Think of a cat chasing a squirrel up a big tree, where the squirrel can change the path of his escape every time he comes to a fork. The cat has to be ready to go up the various routes, wherever they lead. Conversely, the cat needs to be ready to leave the squirrel's path and take a different route in order to trap the squirrel. If the cat isn't thinking ahead, the squirrel escapes."

Skip could see that his example had done little to clarify the concept. "That's not exactly right …" He was quiet for a moment, searching for a better example. "Think of Brazil. Lopez was supposed to be asleep, and you guys were supposed to have to break in. If there had not been a branch plan, it could have unhinged the whole op. Squad Red had branch plans in place should there be any developments. Granted, the branches were not exactly what Red faced, but there was sufficient flexibility that Harry could suddenly deviate from what was expected, and you all executed without having to stop and have it all re-explained to you. But a sequel, irrespective of how Red grabbed Lopez, was to get him back to the LZ."

"Sorta like the difference you explained between orchestra music and jazz, Colonel?" Breaker called out.

Skip grinned. "Yes, Breaker, that's it exactly."

"Lopez was dropping grains of sand in our Swiss watches," said Breaker. "Did I get that right?"

"Absolutely," confirmed Skip. "Is the concept becoming clearer now, Les?"

"Aye, Colonel. It is now," said Les.

A disembodied voice called out, "Colonel, if we're using deception, should we all brush up on our Sun Tzu?"

It was Terry, their demolitions-expert-cum-modeller.

It was Skip's turn to laugh.

"I like it, Terry." Skip looked up and began quoting from memory. "'Let your plans be dark and impenetrable as the night, and when you move, fall like a thunderbolt.'"

He scanned the room. Skip could see there were plenty of questions, but nobody wanted to ask one that would certainly be addressed later by orders. Since time did not seem to be pressing, everyone remained silent.

"Very well. We'll stop there for now. Harry, kindly gather the O Group in my office at ten-fifteen, please."

"Wilco, Skip."

As the men dispersed, Jules approached Skip. "Colonel. *Avez-vous une minute?*"

"Of course, Jules. I always have time for you. But before I forget, I have a question for you about Michel."

Jules looked a little startled.

"I want your opinion about taking Michel with us. I don't mean as an operator, but to make him feel closer to all of us, to emphasize that he's one of us now. You have bonded with him more than the rest of us. What do you think, RSM?"

"Colonel, you read my mind. I wanted to ask the same question. He is a solid kid, but he is all alone here in camp. He was a soldier, and he sees all these soldiers around, only he is not one of them, no more."

"Exactly," said Skip. "It would be good for him to feel more useful."

Jules nodded approvingly. "Do not worry. I will watch out for him."

Skip smiled. "Jules, I can't believe we came to this conclusion at the same time, but I'm glad we did. Let's go talk to him."

The two men went to the kitchen.

"Bonjour, Michel," said Jules.

"Bonjour," said Michel. He was chopping vegetables rapidly, and hadn't looked up to see who was with Jules.

"Michel," said Jules. "*Fait attention, toi.*"

The young man looked up and dropped his knife on the cutting board with a loud clatter. Excusez-moi, Colonel. I am sorry, Colonel. I did not see you there. Je —"

Skip cut him off. "It's fine, Michel. It's my fault for interrupting you in your kitchen. There's no need to apologize, son."

Michel looked puzzled.

"Le Colonel, he has some news for you, Michel," said Jules.

"Informations for me?"

"Yes, Michel," said Skip. "I need you to accompany us on our next mission. Not to be our cook, but to be a member of one of the squads. You are too valuable to leave behind, so you'll accompany us to Saint-Pierre. Pappy and Stirling will be fine here without you."

The young man's eyes were like saucers. "Moi?" he said, stunned. "Thank you, monsieur."

"Harry will assign you to a squad later so that you can train with them. For now, Jules will bring you up to date and explain how this will work. Naturally, you'll continue to feed us before we go." Skip smiled broadly to indicate the gentle ribbing about being dual-hatted. "Agreed?"

"Oui, Colonel. Thank you again, monsieur."

Michel stood mute as Skip turned to leave the kitchen. Jules patted Michel's shoulder, then turned and followed Skip.

In Skip's office, the scene was a repeat of previous O Groups. After they had all settled into their chairs, Skip began with christening the ground. On the wall there was a sketch of the south coast of Newfoundland, Saint-Pierre-et-Miquelon, and the surrounding waters.

"As you have already heard, this op is a bit different. You will note the sketch map behind me. Yes, that's where we are going. Harry and I have been chewing on this problem for a couple of days, and I am satisfied that we have a workable plan. Even if only in outline form. Alex was not brought in on it until yesterday, so he is still letting it all soak in. Now

I want to bring the rest of you into our deliberations to see if we have any gaping holes, so that we can begin the many minor preparations and administrative arrangements needed before we can launch."

Skip paused to read the room. Interest appeared high.

"First, we have the target. His full name is Qassem bin Nakbah al Jezayry, but he goes by his Jihad name, Abu Alaintiqam, which is Arabic for Father of Vengeance. Rather than mangle the pronunciation of either of his names, a process that I have some experience with, we will simply call him Qassem. Just for your info, he has chosen a second alias during his stay on the island. He is calling himself Professor Omar al-Zawawi."

Skip noticed Harry and Alex smirking.

"He's an Algerian Muslim by birth, a university-educated engineer, and literate. He is a late convert to terrorism. He's been very lucky so far. It's almost like he's got a sixth sense. He can feel it when he's in danger." Skip paused. "He's also a cold-blooded, murderous psychopath."

Skip reached for his cup of coffee to let the last sentence sink in.

"This guy is not to be underestimated. Obviously, we can't go in with guns blazing. I remind you that the island of Saint-Pierre is sovereign French soil, and thus, we need to do this by stealth. As the Scottish say, 'Softly, softly, catchy monkey,' right, Pappy?"

"Aye, Colonel."

"Our intel says the French authorities don't know where he is. As far as they know, he's still hiding somewhere in Paris. They want him badly. Moreover, they want him *alive*. He has much that they want to know, and corpses tell no tales. But, like I said, he's wary of anything that gets his wind up, so when we move, it must be deftly and with great precision."

Skip was looking at his notes, and someone said something he didn't hear.

"Pardon?"

"Sorry, Colonel," said Breaker. "I said this sounds more like a casino heist than a snatch mission."

Skip pursed his lips and nodded his agreement. "What we have so far is that we'll send in an advance squad to get eyes on him, a main squad to do the grab, an extraction squad to get him off the island, and a QRF that will stay out of the way and be kept on standby for special tasks. I'll pause now for questions."

"Mon Colonel, I assume that you will need me because I am francophone?"

"Yes, Jules that's right. Am I right in thinking that Leo is also francophone? He's done a decent job of hiding it, but if memory serves, his father was from the Gaspé. If he has to, can Leo switch over to Québécois French? I need you to start speaking only French to each other because I want you both comfortable sounding like two Québécois tourists. Other questions, Jules?"

"No, Colonel."

Pappy spoke up. "I'm assuming, Colonel, that you will want me and Stirling to stay behind to keep an eye on the silverware. After all, somebody's got to watch Franz-Josef, here."

"Almost right, Pappy. Hang on — remind me who's at the Ox?"

"Colonel, we still have about a half-dozen men from Eagle finishing the camp. The crew chief's name is —"

"Thanks, Pappy, I don't need his name. He works for you. Yes, you and Stirling will stay here, but Franz-Josef will be in Halifax, so you don't have to worry about losing your next dividend to him at Skat. By the way, we are taking Michel along, so you'll be making your own peanut butter sandwiches."

"Ach, Herr Oberst, you will allow this old Ostie to accompany the troops?"

"Yes, Jupp. I have a special job for you, my friend. I need someone who knows Halifax, but don't get too excited. You won't be alone. Breaker will be along to keep you on your best behaviour. He will lead the Halifax detachment, and you will assist him."

"Herr Oberst, you speak about me like maybe I am a bad boy."

Skip stared at his friend but said nothing for a long ten seconds.

"*Natürlich*, Herr Oberst. No problem. Please excuse me."

"Anyone else? Breaker, what about you?"

"One question, Colonel. Do you want me to see if I can break into Qassem's computer or his router?"

"No, Breaker, I don't think we should try it. First, it really doesn't matter a whole lot, and second, I'll lay even money on Qassem using an onion server. I suspect it'd be a waste of your time."

"Roger that," said Breaker.

Harry couldn't help himself. "Onion server? What the hell is an onion server, apart from some kid at Burger Shack?"

"Harry, I'd explain it to you," said Breaker, "only I'm worried it'd hurt your head."

Harry glowered at the big man and Skip jumped in.

"Good time for a short break. Everybody, take ten."

The group broke up, and Skip held Harry and Alex back.

"Harry, Alex, concerns so far?"

"Other than what the hell an onion server is, no," said Harry.

Alex shook his head and looked pensive.

"Colonel, I don't see any real problems," said Alex. "I think what may be giving you some odd feedback is our body language. We're all door kickers. What you're talking about here is going to a foreign country and abducting some guy off the street. It's the opposite of what we were trained to do."

"Exactly, Alex."

Skip was rubbing his chin as Alex continued.

"I think we all need time to wrap our heads around this idea and exactly how we'll execute without tripping over each other. Guys like me would be inclined to fly in, punch him in the forehead, then put him in a large hockey bag. Naturally, that's a dumb idea, except we spent our careers doing frontal attacks, so finessing the solution is something we need some time to get used to."

"Alex is right Skip, but no worries. We'll get there," promised Harry.

In the Great Room, Breaker, Jules, Pappy, and Franz-Josef were huddled around a coffee table.

"Qu'est-ce que c'est?" said Jules. "Why do you all make faces? You want to do a para drop in black pyjamas, break into his house, and snatch him? All of this complicated deception — what did the Colonel call it? Maskirovka? It has you uncomfortable, yes? Like you said, Breaker, this is like stealing from a casino. You do not go in with guns. You distract them, then you take their money."

Franz-Josef sat bolt upright.

"Mein Lieber Gott, that is why the Oberst wants Breaker und me in Halifax: to rob the casino."

Breaker stood, shaking his head. "For pity's sake, I think you've been kicked in the head too many times. C'mon, we need to get back into the office, and don't even think about asking me if I own a tuxedo, and don't say nothin' to Colonel Skip about any casino."

The others stood, and the four men moved back to Skip's office. After another hour of discussions, the plan was nicely roughed out.

"I'm happy with how far we've come thus far, and it's time for some detailed planning. Harry, you break down the groupings and tasks. Alex, you need to study the time and space issues."

"Got it," said Alex.

"Breaker, I need you to rough out the command and signals paragraph, and I'll write the intent paragraph and the general outline," said Skip.

"Und for me, Herr Oberst?"

"Jupp, please work with Jules and write the administration and logistics paragraph. Right — nobody worry about formatting, spelling, or that kind of stuff. Please submit all your thoughts to me no later than noon tomorrow, even if it's only in bullet form. I'll compile all the paragraphs, then Harry will proof my work. Last time around the room."

Skip looked at each man in turn as the members of the O Group shook their heads.

"Jules, any last thoughts?"

"Merci, Colonel. No points."

"Thank you, everyone. Can I have the room, please?"

"Skip, do you need me here?"

"No, thanks, Harry. I'm just going to give Bill a quick SITREP. Last time we spoke he mentioned that the more lead time he could have for the hand-off details, the better."

"Makes sense. I guess grabbing a submarine isn't quite the same as hailing a cab."

Harry saw Skip punching in Bill's secure number and shut the door as he left the office.

OTTAWA

"Monsieur, you have a call from Washington, but the caller refuses to give his name."

Gaston nodded slightly, indicating to his aide that he would take the call. He raised the receiver on his STE desk phone. A voice on the line said, "Go secure." Gaston did so, and there were three telltale beeps on the line.

"Hello, Marmot. How've you been, my friend?"

The codename instantly told Gaston who the caller was. Only one person used that name.

"All is well, Traveller," he said, returning the favour. "It has been a long time since I have not heard from you."

The caller could now be certain that it was Gaston to whom he was speaking. Nonetheless, the two men always spoke like they were on an open line. Such habits were hard wired, especially in their business.

"How is the weather on the island today?" said Gaston.

"Lots of storm clouds. More than usual, in fact, but you know how variable the weather can be here."

"Yes, I certainly do. I understand that you have news for me about something important?"

"I do, but it's a bit too delicate to describe over the phone. I would be much more comfortable if we could sit together. But the news is time sensitive. Are you coming to the island in the next couple of days?"

"You are in luck," said Gaston. "I had a short vacation planned, so I can see you tomorrow. Are you free for lunch?"

"Tomorrow is good. Are you taking your usual flight? I can meet you at the Blue Crab Café near the beach, like always."

"That would be perfect, except that this time it is my turn to pick up the check."

"I will be at our customary table. Would you like your usual order?"

"Yes, please," said Gaston, then replaced the receiver.

"*Philippe, un instant.*"

Gaston's aide appeared at the door.

"Yes, sir."

"Please book me to Baltimore Washington International. I need it to be tomorrow morning, and leave the return leg open."

"Oui, monsieur."

BALTIMORE

Gaston stepped off the American Eagle CRJ 700 regional jet at BWI and walked into Arrivals. It pleased him somehow to ride a French-Canadian plane into the heart of the American republic. He turned and headed toward US Customs and Border Protection. A clean-cut young man in a light-coloured Brooks Brothers suit intercepted him.

"Welcome, sir. I'm Ed Philipps. The director assigned me to be your escort officer today for your visit to the headquarters. I'm aware you've been many times, so please consider me a staff aide, sir."

Gaston offered his hand. "Hello, Ed. That is a nice suit. Are you ex-military?"

"No, sir, not ex. I'm regular Army Intelligence, sir."

"It is most courteous of your director to send you, Ed."

This ritual repeated itself with every visit. It was the NSA's way of recognizing Gaston's high-level credentials. It also allowed the organization to keep a close watch on him, since it would be unwise to have a man like Gaston wandering around the HQ unaccompanied. He always enjoyed the little pantomime.

Ed handed Gaston a security pass, then flashed his own to the airport security officer. Without even waiting for an acknowledgement, Ed guided his VIP guest past the usual screening and into the executive security lounge.

"Can I get you a cup of coffee, Mr. Levesque? Your car and driver are waiting in the VIP parking lot for you. You're free to go to the Agency at your leisure, sir. I can accompany you, or, if you prefer privacy, I have my own transportation, sir."

"Thank you, Ed. I will be going to the Agency in about forty-five minutes, but there is no need for you to wait. If you would be so kind, please inform the driver of my delay so that he is not worried about me. I have some business of a personal nature here in the airport, and I think I will grab a quick sandwich while I am here."

"Sir, the food here isn't that good. I'd be pleased to take you to the VIP dining room at the Agency instead."

The young man was looking concerned.

"Ha, ha, ha. Thank you, Ed, but my French-Canadian palate has been looking forward to the Reuben sandwich the way it is put together in one of the kiosks on the other side of security. You do not need to tell me that there are better restaurants in DC, son. I am well aware." Gaston smiled at his young escort. "Sadly, I have become addicted to the one here at BWI," he said, pointing vaguely over his shoulder. "It must be the bread. I do not know, but what can I tell you? It is a weakness."

The humourless escort officer showed no reaction.

"No problem, sir. If you have nothing more for me, I'll tell the driver that you'll be delayed and then I'll head back to Fort Meade. I'll be waiting for you in the lobby at the front entrance to the Agency, sir."

Ed turned to leave but stopped.

"I nearly forgot. The director sends his apologies, sir. He's trapped in the West Wing all day. The chief of ops is on standby for when you arrive."

"Thank you, Ed."

With that, the two men stepped out of the lounge, and Ed walked off. Gaston watched the young man leave, then slipped into the crush of people moving through the crowded airport. Occasionally, he wondered if it would not be easier to take a government jet down to Potomac Airfield, but, in truth, he preferred it this way. He liked the idea of being swallowed by this ocean of humanity in a public transportation hub. Anonymity was important in his line of work, and besides, if he used Potomac Airfield, he would not be able to meet discreetly with Traveller.

After giving Ed sufficient time to leave, Gaston stepped onto the escalator going up to Departures. At the top, he turned left and headed into the public restrooms, washed his hands, and left. Looking across to the escalators, he did not see anyone who was pretending to ignore him.

He took the escalator back down to Arrivals, scanning his surroundings for a tail. At the bottom, he walked straight ahead for about one hundred metres, then abruptly doubled back, hesitated momentarily to look at the front page of *The International Tribune*, then quickly entered a service door to a stairwell. His secure phone vibrated.

"Oui."

"Are you on your way?"

"I am thirty seconds out."

He ended the call, walked back up one flight of stairs, and paused. Reasonably assured of not being followed, Gaston pushed his way through the door back onto the departures level and made his way to the coffee shop. There, he saw his contact seated in a booth with his back to the wall. The preferred booth was three steps from the emergency exit that led to a fire escape and an employee-only parking lot. Gaston walked directly to him and sat down opposite him.

"Hello, Joe."

"Hello, Gaston. I ordered the Reuben for you."

A waiter came over and deposited two cups of black coffee. "Your sandwiches will be along in a few minutes," he said, then left the two men alone.

"Well, Joe, what is so important that we could not discuss it by phone? Please do not tell me that your guys are about to invade some small, defenceless country again. That is getting old."

"Actually, it's much more serious than that. Your friend Colonel Schiaparelli is about to be caught in a wide net. If Senator Fredericks gets his way, Skip's organization will be crushed, burned, and buried."

Gaston betrayed no emotion as he took a sip of coffee. He could feel the muscles in his jaw tensing and began to grind his teeth slowly.

"One question only," he said at last. "Is Bill Donovan part of this treachery?"

"No. In fact, your friend is not the real target. Donovan's the target, and your friend is merely collateral damage."

The waiter was back, bearing two Reubens with sides of slaw. He put the plates on the table and left without speaking.

"*Merde*," cursed Gaston. "Joe, fill me in and please give me all the details you can."

Gaston picked up the sandwich and took a bite. He needed something to absorb the acid that he could feel spilling into his stomach. Joe laid out what he knew and how the situation was likely to unfold unless there was some kind of intercession. Further, he explained Senator Fredericks's involvement in the plan.

"That does not sound promising," said Gaston.

"There's an understatement," said Joe as he bit into his own sandwich.

"Time is very short," said Gaston.

"I'm sorry, but I called as soon as I could confirm the details, which by the way, are very close hold."

"Yes, of course. I am not criticizing you, Joe. I appreciate what you have done. Unfortunately, I am struggling to see how I can help at this late stage."

Gaston was working hard to keep calm even though his mind was racing. Joe stared at him across the table.

"What can I do to help you, Gaston?"

The Bishop was silent as Joe slurped the dregs of his coffee and took a last bite of his sandwich. He looked at Joe, then nodded and smiled.

"Nothing, my friend, nothing, but if I think of anything, I will call. Thank you."

Joe wiped his mouth with his napkin, then stood and wordlessly slipped away through the emergency exit. The waiter appeared an instant later.

"My companion had to leave," Gaston said. "How much do I owe you? I have a flight to catch, and I am running a bit late already."

The waiter pulled out his pad and inspected his slips.

"That's thirty-three fifty," he said, putting the check on the table.

Gaston handed him two crisp American twenties.

"Thank you very much, and please keep the change."

As Gaston headed back to the American Airlines counter to get on any flight that had space available, he used the speed dial to call the NSA switchboard. He punched in the four-digit extension to the duty desk and explained who he was. He momentarily considered asking to be put through to General Paul Spenser, the commander, but quickly pushed the idea away.

"I will not be visiting the headquarters today. I have been ordered to return immediately to Ottawa."

Intelligence officers never asked why. It saved them from lying to each other.

"Please recall my car and driver. He is sitting in the VIP parking lot at the airport. I do not need him, thank you. Also, an escort officer named Ed Philipps is waiting in the lobby at the main entrance to the headquarters. Please tell him to make my apologies personally to the director of operations."

The duty officer acknowledged the message and hung up.

Le Chalet

The preparations for the Saint-Pierre mission had taken on a completely different character to the Brazilian op.

"How's it coming?" said Skip.

Several of the men were sitting in the lounge on a break.

"May I join you?"

"Of course, Colonel."

Terry slid over on the couch to make room.

"You're all looking deep in thought," said Skip.

"Colonel, this is different," Les offered. "I gotta say, it's a refreshing challenge for the majority of us. Except for you, Harry, and Alex, we spent our military careers as NCOs. Brazil focused us on fitness, shooting skills, and rapid close-quarter combat. Hard work, but easy for us to understand. It was skills and drills."

"And I've thrown a curveball at you all by accepting this mission."

"Sort of," said Les, "but really interesting. Saint-Pierre is forcing all of us to look at the problem in terms of multiple options, misdirection, and stealth. What did you call it?"

"Maskirovka?" said Skip.

"More like Russian roulette," said Les. "This op is emphasizing the intellectual considerations of chance, probability, and deception. We were just discussing the fact that the key condition here is rapid thinking, not rapid shooting."

The men were nodding their heads in agreement.

"But it's all good, Colonel. I understand that many of us were recruited because we understood violence. But now we're being asked to put aside that violence, and a couple of us have found that sort of confusing, at least I have." Les paused for a moment. "No, not confusing. That's not the word."

"Do you mean disorienting?" said Skip.

"Aye, Colonel. That's it — disorienting. But a couple of the more senior fellas, like Jules, they put us on track. The best way to put it is that you've dragged us all into your world, Colonel."

"Ha, ha, ha!" Skip was laughing out loud as he stood. "You are all very welcome to my world, gentlemen. And don't forget to check and see how many chambers of the pistol cylinder are loaded before you spin it."

After the initial days of hammering out the details, the plan was finally fully developed. Skip converted the plan into an order, and then delivered formal verbal orders in the Great Room to the entire cohort. Then everyone wargamed and rehearsed the operation multiple times, going through all of the various high-probability branches and sequels. Skip insisted on including those branches and sequels that led to mission failure. Michel, who had left the army as a junior corporal, was both intimidated into silence and wide-eyed in fascination as he sat and watched the proceedings.

"Colonel Skip, excuse me, but I'm not sure why we're wargaming sequels that we know lead us to mission failure," said Walker. "This is the third time we've run one of these to ground and I'm sorry, but I don't get it. Why bother when we know it'll fail?"

"That's a fair question," agreed Skip. "Does anybody want to answer Walker?"

The room was silent, and Skip stood waiting with his hands in his pockets. He didn't come to the rescue; instead, he let the tension build.

"So," he said, when the silence had become deafening, "Walker has the guts to ask why, and none of you can offer him a reason? Really? You're all playing along because you have nothing better to do?"

"Colonel, that's not it," said Gord. "I can't speak for the others, but I figure you have your reasons, or you wouldn't be pushing us through it. That's all."

"At least you're being honest, Gord." Skip slowly scanned the room and stopped at his RSM. "Jules, you've lived your life with drills, routines, and checklists. I'm sure that you were in more than one flight simulator where the pilot flew it into the ground. Any thoughts you'd like to share?"

"I have crashed eleven times in simulation and one time for real," he said. "What did save us for real was the pilot knew he was going to crash. He did it in the simulator, so he knew what was coming but could not stop it. He was young and overconfident, and he thought that he knew better, *tabernac*. It was too late to keep us airborne, but the time in the simulator did prepare him, you know. He finally got it, and he knew what he had to do. It was not how to save the plane. No, it was how save the crew. It hurt like hell, by the way, but everybody survived."

The room broke out in light laughter.

"Merci, Jules," said Skip. "You have it exactly right. We are doing all of the branches and sequels in case we get ourselves into trouble. One of you will surely have a memory of what we wargamed, and it might just save us all. Mission failure doesn't have to be catastrophic. Does that help you, Walker?"

"It sure does, Colonel. Thanks."

"Thank Jules. He was the one who had to survive the crash."

That got more chuckles.

"Time for a break, everyone," said Skip. "Take thirty, so back here in twenty-nine."

The break wasn't over, but some members of the group were re-assembling around the mission terrain model. Once again, Terry's eye for detail had been put to good use. Skip was admiring the work.

"This is a beauty, Terry."

"Thanks, Colonel. Jules and I went to a high-end hobby shop in North Montreal. I decided to use mostly 'T' scale railroad buildings and trees for this model so we could capture a lot of the city and the island. It was a challenge to find enough pieces for this scale, and Google Earth really helped."

"Well, as the wargame coordinator, it makes my job easier, I can tell you."

Skip patted Terry on the back, complimenting him again on his extraordinary efforts, then went looking for Breaker.

Spying him across the lounge, he called Breaker over to him.

"Breaker, I have a couple of special tasks for you. Grab a coffee and meet me in my office, please."

"Be right there."

A few minutes later, Breaker stood at the doorway, mug in hand. "Colonel, what can I do for you?"

"Well, I need you to smuggle some toys in from the US," said Skip.

"Pardon me?"

"I need you to slip across the border from Saint-Jean and go to a Walmart or some such store in Vermont. I'd like you buy the four smallest tasers you can find, carefully disassemble them, and bring them across the border in small unrecognizable pieces. Then show Terry and Ray how to reassemble them and hand them off to the two of them."

"Seems like a lot of trouble, Colonel Skip. Can't I just go to a Canadian Walmart?"

"I'm afraid not. Owning an operating taser in this country, if you aren't a law enforcement officer, is an offence under the criminal code."

"I didn't know that. No problem, Colonel. I'll take Giselle with me. Like most cute Canadian housewives in Saint-Jean, my wife bats her eyes at the Canada Customs agents at the crossing, and they wave her through. I'm always the dumb lump sitting in the passenger seat. Anything else, Colonel?"

"As a matter of fact, Breaker, yes there is. As you know, I need you to go home to Halifax with Franz-Josef. Let me tell you why. Please shut the door."

When Breaker exited the office a few minutes later, Harry was waiting outside. He tapped on the doorframe and stepped into the room.

"Hey, Skip. Everything okay?"

"Fine, Harry. Why do you ask?"

"I saw Breaker come in and wondered what was up. I'm not really clear on his task. He can't get to us from Halifax in time to save the day. I know you did that for the men's morale. Are you going to share the real task in Halifax?"

"Don't worry about it, Harry. It's all good."

"No, Skip, it isn't. You did this to me before with the Valkyrie file, and now you're doing it again. What's going on? I feel like you're hiding something, and I don't like it."

Skip stared at his friend. He didn't want to be dismissive like he had been before, but he hadn't planned to discuss the issue with Harry just yet.

"Have a seat, Harry," he said, decision made. "I was going to talk to you about this later, but since you're here, we can do it now."

Harry shut the door and sat in one of the leather armchairs.

"Have you lost faith in me?"

"What?" Skip said, genuinely astonished. "No, Harry not at all. Listen, I need this to be close hold, please. Even Breaker doesn't have the full picture, so it has to stay between us — just us."

"Understood," said Harry.

"I've told Breaker to charter an ocean-going speedboat. He still has a boyhood contact ..."

Skip spent a few minutes laying it out for Harry, who listened intently. As he finished, there was a rap on the door and Jules opened it a crack and stuck his head in.

"Colonel, everyone is seated, monsieur."

"Thanks, Jules. We'll be right there." Jules nodded and closed the door again.

Skip looked at his friend. "All good, Harry?"

"No worries," said Harry.

After days of this routine, Sandy, one of the ex–Airborne Rangers, was commenting over supper that he had never appreciated how mentally fatiguing it was to prepare for this kind of mission.

"Looking back on my army career," he said, setting his fork down, "I have to admit that I always admired the fact that the officers I worked with not only learned all the physical skills and drills, but they also shared the physical hardships with us. On top of that, they also had the added burdens that I've only begun to experience in the last few weeks."

Several of his mates nodded their agreement.

"Good thing they never asked me to take an officer's commission," confessed one of them.

The general mood of the group remained positive, however. Everyone was pleased to be back in harness, and eliminating a terrorist was a noble pursuit. That said, much of the usual adrenaline was missing this time. There was no tactical gear to stow, and no weapons to check. Harry still dragged everyone out of their bunks at zero dark thirty each morning and rode their butts through the woods on morning runs, this time usually with both Skip and Jules in the pack. But now, it wasn't about fitness. It was about clearing all the mental cobwebs. It was also to stretch muscles that had grown stiff from physical activity that mostly comprised standing around a terrain model. In fact, most of the men voluntarily went out again in the late afternoon for the same reasons.

As everyone prepared for deployment, Skip gathered them in the lounge one last time.

"I'd like to review the travel. I know that Franz-Josef has given each of you your travel arrangements. Terry and Ray, since you're driving with Terry's so-called little 'Frankenstein monsters,' you're heading out tomorrow, correct?"

"His what?" interjected Harry.

"His little remote-controlled explosives," said Skip.

"Check," said Harry. "Sorry to interrupt."

"No worries," said Skip. "So, Terry and Ray, are we on net?"

"Yes, Colonel."

"Pathfinders also leave tomorrow, is that right?"

"Yes, sir, but we're flying, so we'll be first on the ground."

"You'll be in the small pension across the street from the bakery, and immediately begin round-the-clock surveillance."

"Yes, sir," said Airdrie.

"Pappy, please confirm we still have a small Eagle crew at the Ox."

"Aye, Colonel. I've given them their instructions and I will stay here with Stirling."

"Breaker and Franz-Josef, you'll be the last to leave le Chalet. Let me know as soon as you're set in Halifax."

"Wilco, Colonel," said Breaker.

Franz-Josef nodded, and Skip could see the excitement on his face at the prospect of deploying on a mission.

"That's it from me. Any questions?"

There were none, so Skip passed it over to Jules.

"I will see you all in Saint-Pierre, messieurs," he said.

Skip looked at his watch and tapped his inside pocket to check for his passport.

"Leo, we are two oceans away from Italy, but we have just crossed the Rubicon, mon ami."

They were boarding the Air Canada flight from Montreal to St. John's, Newfoundland, and Skip could tell by the puzzled look on Leo's face that he had no idea what Skip was talking about but didn't want to say so to his face.

"Oui, Colonel," replied Leo quietly.

Saint-Pierre-et-Miquelon

Jules and Les wandered the streets of Saint-Pierre's Centreville in apparent nonchalance for two days. They visited almost everything there was to visit in the tiny capital. In reality, the seemingly casual tourists seen strolling through the streets were part of a three-section, closely choreographed surveillance operation that was part of Squad Main. Two of the three sections were constantly moving among the sparse crowds of tourists and locals, occasionally stopping at their pensions to change their clothes.

"Jules, you look like someone who bought his wardrobe from the Salvation Army Thrift Store."

Jules gave the ex-Para a withering stare while changing his shirt. "Come with me, smart guy. We have more walking to do."

Although he pretended to be irritated with Les, Jules was enjoying working with the sharp ex-paratrooper. "We do not need to look fashionable, mon ami," he said. "We only need to be not too obvious."

"But we're obviously not locals," said Les.

"Clearly, we are *étrangers*, others, but we need to be forgettable others. Keep walking."

In addition to the mobile section, another of the three sections was always perched temporarily either at the bookstore or at the small café, both situated across the street from the boulangerie. Stefan, the café's owner, chief cook, and waiter was a late-middle-aged, balding man trying desperately to appear younger than his years. His focus on the young women walking by in their skirts and shorts was so intense that it became a matter of routine for customers to place an order at least twice, even if it were a simple black coffee.

"I wonder how big Stefan's collection of surreptitious photos is," said Skip, sipping on yet more caffeine. "I'll bet that we could all leave the café without paying and Stefan wouldn't notice — as long as we did it while some leggy young thing was swishing by."

"Colonel, this sitting around waiting for Qassem is driving me nuts," said Gord. "Maybe we should cross the street, kick the door in, go upstairs, and grab the little psychopath."

"That is a brilliant idea, Gordo" said Skip, deadpan. "I'm not sure why I didn't think of it before. I'm sure none of the locals would notice us."

"Sorry, Colonel. I wasn't being serious. I'm just a bit bored."

"I know. Me too, but we've gamed this out and we need to be patient. Think of it as another typical day in the army. Look busy, drink coffee, and wait."

The men all nodded their agreement. Still, it was now day three, and except for a single brief sighting the day they'd arrived, no one had seen Qassem. A couple of them speculated that perhaps he was no longer there.

"Colonel," said Gord as he stirred his café au lait, "how do you stand it?"

"Sorry, Gordo. Stand what?"

"The waiting. How can you get all charged up and then sit calmly for days watching an empty building?"

"It's no worse than counting socks, Gord."

"Ouch, that stung," said Gord, making a face while mimicking that he had been stabbed. "I'm wounded, and anyway, somebody has to know how many socks there are."

"I'm kidding, Gordo," said Skip, giving him a friendly tap on the arm. "I guess it's a question of training. Like almost everyone here, you were a jumper, and a SOF guy as well."

Gord shrugged.

"Your military experience was all about action and making things happen, mostly with violence. That's all good, all necessary. I get that, but my early days in the army were in armoured reconnaissance."

"I remember," said Gord. "It was all about 'sneak and peek' in those days."

"Exactly," said Skip. "We had no armoured vehicles and no heavy weapons to speak of. We would establish an observation post, then sit there day after day with no fires, no noise, no light … Our job was watch and wait, then watch some more."

"Much like right now," said Gord.

"I didn't go to tanks until I was a major, and it was a totally different life. Like you, I went from mostly passive, mental work to almost exclusively violent action. So, this is really a return to my roots."

Gord didn't say anything.

"Besides, I'm an old dog now, and drinking coffee and watching the pretty girls go by ain't so bad. Just don't tell your lovely wife Janet we're doing that. I don't want her mad at me for leading you astray."

The rest of the men laughed along with Gord.

"Gotcha," said Gord, smiling broadly. "She knows where you live, Colonel."

"My turn to say ouch," replied Skip.

A short time later, Les and Jules arrived for their shift at the café, sending two other men for a break.

"Good day, gentlemen," said Skip as they took their seats.

"Bonjour, Colonel," said Jules. We are back for more coffee and more watching."

Les nodded and signalled the waiter for two more coffees.

"Jules," said Skip, "I was wondering about your dislike of tattoos. What do you have against them?"

"Simple, mon Colonel. They are stupid, especially for women who have beautiful skin."

Les became suddenly animated and looked like he was about to jump in, but Skip quieted him by raising his hand.

"I see," said Skip. "That leaves us with two good Canadian options: silence or the weather."

No one spoke up.

"Silence it is," said Skip.

After another half hour of sipping coffee and nibbling on croissants in silence, they saw the door to the apartment open.

"It's Qassem," said Skip. "Finally."

Jules checked his watch. It was about a quarter past eight. A few moments later, Qassem walked through the open door to the bakery. There was no fear that he was headed to the ferry because Skip had planned their "assault" upon the island to coincide with a week-long maintenance period when the ferry service to the deserted village was suspended. The timing had worked out well since the ferries were scheduled to recommence in the morning.

Jules stood, stretched, and left the café, then quickly crossed the cobblestoned street. Les followed, but loitered outside the bakery, pretending to look at his smartphone. Skip watched quietly from across the street and quickly texted Harry.

Jules stepped into the dimly lit bakery. "Bonjour," he said to no one, a bit too loudly.

It was quite confined and crowded, but Jules immediately spotted Qassem standing in line near the back, behind some older women. He also spotted Michel, who was somehow back by the ovens discussing breadmaking with someone. How did he manage that, Jules wondered? He pulled out his phone, pretended to examine the screen, and carelessly plowed into Qassem.

"Pardon, monsieur."

Qassem turned and waved him off.

Jules switched to his broken English. "Excuse me, monsieur. Are you not the young *professeur* who is writing a book about la *forteresse* de Louisbourg? Le *Professeur* al-Zawawi? Madame at the bookstore, she described you to me. I am so fortunate to meet you, monsieur."

Jules paused, but not long enough for Qassem to dismiss him.

"Have you visited the abandoned fishing village *musée* on Île-Aux-Marins?" Jules went on. "Is it not fascinating?"

Qassem was quickly becoming annoyed with this foolish busybody. All he wanted was to buy his daily baguettes and be away. Now, with all of his neighbours staring at him, he realized he must engage the idiot tourist or run the risk of exposure. He had only a vague notion of what this *crétin* was talking about.

"Oui, monsieur," said Qassem. "I hear that it is truly beautiful. I did not yet make the trip, no."

"You should, monsieur. In the Archipélitude Museum in the village there is a strong connection back to the Fortress of Louisbourg. It is a must, and such a short trip from the ferry terminal. They say that Île-Aux-Marins is the soul of the community here. It tells the full story of the *patrimoine* and *histoire*, back to the days of *Nouvelle-France*."

By now, everyone in the small shop was a party to their conversation. The *grands-mères* surrounding the men were clucking their agreement. Yes, it was true, the grandmothers were saying to each other. A visit to the village is a must, they all agreed.

Qassem became wary of this abrupt intrusion on his privacy. There was something about this man that was making him nervous, but he was unsure of what it was. The stranger had a certain presence. Scanning the shop discreetly, he forced himself to be calm. Nonetheless, he needed to careful. Clearly, the stranger was not French. In vain, he sought to place what he thought was perhaps a Languedoc accent. He spoke like an ill-educated peasant. Was he French-Canadian, perhaps?

"You are not a local, monsieur. You are perhaps Franco-Canadien from the mainland?"

Puffing himself up and squaring his shoulders in mock indignation, Jules replied, "*Non!*," once again a little too loudly.

Qassem stepped back, suppressing his sudden urge to flee the shop.

"Excuse me, monsieur, I mistook your accent. I meant no —"

"Ha, ha, ha. Forgive me, *Professeur*. I am cruel to you. No, I am not *Franco-Canadien*. I am proud *Acadien*, monsieur, not *Franco-Canadien*. I visit from New Brunswick."

The women in the bakery all nodded approvingly at the stranger's fierce expression of Acadian uniqueness.

"You will forgive me, *monsieur*," Jules said, grinning amiably. "I make a joke at your expense, and I am sorry."

Qassem relaxed slightly. This peasant was undoubtedly a descendant of the sheep thieves whom the French had banned from Europe two centuries ago. That explained much.

"Yes, yes, of course. There is no harm in a small *geste*," said Qassem. "*Certainement*, you are correct, monsieur. It is on my list to visit the village soon. Unfortunately, I became so immersed in my research that the days have slipped away. You understand."

"*Naturellement, monsieur. Naturellement.*"

It is time to disengage, thought Jules. He sensed the intense scrutiny to which Qassem was now subjecting him. He needed to leave the shop, but Qassem beat Jules to the punch. He paid for his bread and quickly walked away.

"Au revoir," said Qassem over his shoulder, stepping outside to return upstairs. Up until today, he had thought that only those Canadian Vandoo soldiers were worthy of his vengeance. He now considered adding these so-called Acadians to his list.

"*Au revoir, Professeur*," said Jules to Qassem's back, and a couple of the women chimed in.

Au revoir, indeed, thought Jules. I look forward to our next meeting, you murderous little coward. A voice was attempting to break into his thoughts. Someone was talking to him.

"*Monsieur? Monsieur?*"

It was the saleslady behind the counter, attempting to get his attention.

"I am sorry, madame," Jules said, turning to her apologetically. "I was remembering le musée … I was lost in my thoughts."

"*Comment?* I am sorry, monsieur. My English is not so good."

"*Excusez, madame. Deux croissants au chocolat, s'il vous plaît.*"

The woman passed the two pastries across the glass-topped counter. Jules paid for the still-warm chocolate confections, then stepped outside, where Les had stood watching.

"Bugger me," quipped Les. "I was getting ready to burst into the shop. For a minute there I was afraid you were going to go into an impersonation of Chief Inspector Clouseau. Peter Sellers spoke better French than that, mate, and he was from bloody Middlesex. Here, hand us one of them choco-croissants."

Jules stared down the ex-Para coldly without speaking.

"Listen to me, wise guy. You obviously never met any Acadians. I worked with a few when I was on the squadron in Shearwater. Hard workers, and good soldiers, but their French, *caliss*." He shook his head ruefully. "They are a unique group in Nova Scotia and New Brunswick, with a bizarre dialect."

Les looked puzzled as Jules walked away with both pastries firmly in his hand. He crossed back to the café and stepping inside, returning to the table where Skip and Gord had been watching.

"Gord, you sit tight with Les," Skip said, getting to his feet. "Jules, you and I are going to our pension to talk."

Back in Skip's room in the small bed and breakfast, the two men sat to discuss what had just transpired. Jules handed Skip one of the croissants.

"Did it go well, Jules?" Skip said, biting into a pastry.

"Oui, mon Colonel. We got lucky, for sure. I think I set the hook, but to be honest, I cannot be certain. I am a little worried that maybe I spooked him. I am not sure, but we need to be ready, Colonel."

"Yes, I agree, but ready for what, exactly?"

"Les checked some websites on his phone," said Jules. "The museum on Île-aux-Marins re-opens tomorrow at 09:00 and closes at 17:00. There is a ferry again every hour beginning in the morning at 07:00."

Skip interrupted. "I thought the first sailing was at 06:00."

"*Normalement*, but tomorrow, they start again at 07:00."

"Good," said Skip. "We'll pre-position Bravo's vehicle behind the church first thing in the morning."

"One thing more, Colonel. I think Qassem is now worried about me. I could see it in his eyes. Maybe I pushed him too hard. I do not know. I think I should not go to the island tomorrow. If he sees me, he may be suspicious because I told him I already visited the museum. Time for a branch plan, maybe?"

"No, Jules. Everything is fine, and we'll stick with the plan. I'll just change the watch rotation a bit. You go grab Les and the two of you lay low for the remainder of today. We don't want to run the run the risk that he sees the two of you again. Go get some rest, and I'll send another man to the café. Everyone holds in place for now. Harry and I will work out a new duty watch rotation on the apartment. With luck, tomorrow will be a busy day, and our last one."

Skip looked at Harry and Alex, who were sitting next to him in the tiny but surprisingly well-stocked bar of the Hôtel Robert, a small inn near the harbour.

"Now that Jules has set the hook, we need to put Bravo on the first ferry in the morning over to Île-aux-Marins. You need to be prepared to spend the whole day on the island if necessary. I've decided to consolidate all the other men to ensure we keep eyes on Qassem's place so he doesn't slip away. If you need more manpower, you can have it."

"No thanks, Skip," said Harry. "I think the squad is in solid shape, even without Jules. Any more men and we'd be tripping over each other on that small island."

"I'll give Angus Crosbie a call," said Skip, referring to the fisherman whom Harry had engaged in Fortune, Newfoundland. "We'll need his boat sitting at anchor somewhere between Île-aux-Marins and Île-aux -Vainqueurs by tomorrow morning."

"Roger," said Harry. "Let's hope we don't have to repeat this for too many days. Alex, we need to go grab the lads and wargame tomorrow one more time."

Skip raised his hand in a slight wave as the two men left the bar. When they'd gone, he pulled out his phone and opened his taccuino. He made a few cryptic notes, then called the number for Angus.

"Hello."

"Good morning, sir. Am I speaking to Captain Angus Crosbie?"

"Aye, that's me."

"I am Commander Black from the Royal Canadian Navy. I believe that my associate, Colonel Hardiman, mentioned I would be calling you regarding our secret joint forces exercise this week."

"Aye, Colonel Hardiman did say that you'd call. I was beginning to wonder."

"Captain, I apologize for not calling sooner. It's been quite a week. I'm sure Colonel Hardiman explained that this combined RCN/RCMP/ Army/Canadian Coast Guard exercise had some flexible timings. I'm sorry we could not have been more specific."

"No worries, Commander. I did a short stint in the navy. Aside from all the drinking, what I remember is how we was always grumbling to the petty officer about having to rush like mad and then wait for three days to do nothing. It's alright by me, Commander. Let me know when you want me."

"That's why I'm calling, Angus. May I call you Angus?"

"Yes, sir, 'course you can."

"Angus, it looks like we'll be doing the prisoner transfer tomorrow, or at least we hope to be doing it then. It may be the day after. I'm not the exercise director. He's an admiral aboard HMCS *Assiniboine* alongside in Halifax. I think it would be wise to have you at anchor somewhere between Île-aux-Marins and Île-aux-Vainqueurs in anticipation. Forgive me — I'm not trying to tell you your job, Captain. You know these waters better than I do, but looking at the charts, it seems to me there's a protected bay on the south side of Vainqueurs."

"Aye, there is. There's a small cove, with a nice sandy bottom."

"Pick your own anchorage, Captain. All I need is assurance that you can be at the beach on the east side of Île-aux-Marins within thirty minutes of us calling. We'll need you at anchor no later than tomorrow around 09:00 hours. Can you manage that?"

"Aye, that'll be no problem at all. I won't cross into French water until tonight, and you can be sure I'll be no more than thirty minutes away when you shouts for me."

"Excellent," said Skip. "I'll be sure to pass to the admiral how helpful you've been. Bye for now."

Skip killed the call, then punched in another number. He had one last call to make.

"Breaker. All set?"

"Yes, Colonel. Do you want the boat deployed?"

"Yes, please. Send him to the RV, now."

It was a long night of watching a silent and darkened building. Thankfully, one of the pensions that housed the sections was only a few paces up the street from the bakery, and Qassem's entrance door was clearly visible from the window. One-hour shifts, two men at a time was the routine. Both men were fully dressed and ready to rush across the street at a moment's notice should Qassem appear looking like he was ready to run.

Airdrie and Paul had the night shift.

"Maybe we'll luck out and he'll make a run for it in the night," said Airdrie, yawning.

"That would make life easy, but we'd better be careful what we wish for," said Paul.

The pre-dawn sun was beginning to brighten the sky.

"If he makes a run for it now, we could bump into the baker and his crew."

"Wait, what's that?"

The two men saw a light come on in the apartment.

"I'll be right back," said Airdrie.

He slipped out and jogged the few steps to Qassem's door, then looked up and down the street to ensure he was alone. After about two minutes, he returned at a brisk pace, but didn't run.

"He was beginning his morning prayers, but we'd better call it in."

The duty shift reported to Skip what had happened. There was no doubt, however, that Qassem was still inside.

There were no more shifts. They were fully expecting Qassem to visit the museum, so everyone was awake and ready. Jules offered to sit first watch so that Les could join Skip for breakfast. Harry told all the members of Bravo to get to the nearest café for their own breakfasts, and then to RV at the Place du Général de Gaulle, where the van would gather them and drive the last few hundred metres to the ferry.

"Got it," said Alex. "I'll meet you at the de Gaulle Plaza."

The van with Harry's squad was at the ferry terminal an hour before the first crossing. The men were sprawled inside the white Ford Transit drinking coffee from their thermoses. They had worked out in detail how they would grab the target, and they were quietly running through the branches and sequels again. Coffee cups, lids, and sugar packets replaced Terry's meticulously built terrain model.

"Remind me again — are the coffee cups the shops or are the sugar packets?" asked Walker.

"Don't be a jerk," said Paul. "Just shut the fu —"

"Hey!" said Terry, giving the men a withering look.

They fell silent. The question was moot; the layout and the procedures were all deeply ingrained in their minds.

Alex and Harry stood in front of the vehicle and watched the queue slowly grow behind them.

"It was the right call to be extra early," said Alex.

"All we need now is for Qassem to actually head to the island. Otherwise, we're back to square one," said Harry.

"Not much of a crowd waiting," said Alex.

"True," said Harry, "but look at the size of the ferry."

"I see what you mean."

The van and maybe a dozen cars would be the extent of the load, plus the pedestrians. There was no sign of Qassem, but that was good. The squad needed time to carry out their critical first step. They had to get the van into position on the island. Harry was hoping Qassem didn't get on the first ferry. If he didn't make this one, then the squad would have at least an hour to establish the net.

Alex shaded his eyes with one hand and looked uneasily over at the island. "Not for nothin', but looking over at that postage stamp of land, I —"

"Alex, shut the hell up. I know what you're thinking, and now is not the time. How many variations did Skip drill us on, each with its own branches and sequels? We're fine."

"Sorry, mate. You're right. I'll shut up."

Harry didn't say it aloud, but he understood Alex's anxiety. This was like predicting the outcome of a chess match after only one pawn had been moved. The possibilities were endless. The tiny island, with its deserted village, its empty, beautifully maintained church, and its museum, was both blessing and curse. With so few people to witness an abduction, it might be possible to wait until Qassem was momentarily alone and hustle him into the van. By the same token, even if only one or two people witnessed the snatch, it would take only a scream or a quick emergency call. Trapped as they'd be on a small island, the whole operation could end badly, possibly very badly. Harry had dark visions of scrambling aboard Breaker's fast boat from Halifax before the police could get there, assuming the boat even found them.

"I'm going inside for the tickets," said Harry.

"Why bother? You can just pay the deckhand."

"Trust me."

The line for the ferry was beginning to grow as Harry went inside to the ticket counter. He wanted to make a point of buying their tickets from the clerk instead of from the deckhand.

"Bonjour. I need to buy tickets, please."

"Yes, monsieur. How many do you need?"

Harry verbalized as he calculated. "Let me see… I have a van, a driver, myself, plus two passengers in the back. I need four adult tickets, please."

The clerk shook his head.

"It is not necessary for you to buy four tickets, monsieur. The driver, he is included for the vehicle. I give to you one ticket for the vehicle and three for the passengers."

He held up his thumb and two fingers, in the European fashion.

"Sir, your English is very good. I wish I could speak French that well."

"Thank you, monsieur. Cash or credit?"

Harry passed some euros to the clerk, and received his tickets. "Merci," he said as he pocketed them.

"You are welcome, monsieur. Enjoy your visit."

Harry returned to the vehicle, hoping that his little farce would save him if things went sideways. Like Qassem's hated snipers in Afghanistan, Bravo would leave the island with two fewer men than they took across. If they got inspected upon loading, Harry planned to claim that he had misunderstood the ticketer. He observed that this morning's deckhands seemed completely disinterested. So far, no vehicles were being checked. Everyone looked hungover, thought Harry.

"Martin!" The lead deckhand shouted to one of the younger men, who walked closer so the two could speak.

"What's happening?" said Alex.

"The boss just told the junior hand to inspect the white van. That's us. Sit tight."

The young man turned around and frowned. He began walking toward the van. Harry stepped out to greet him.

"Is something wrong?"

"*Non, monsieur*. I must inspect inside your *véhicule*. At the back. Please open it."

Harry paused. There was nothing for it, so he prepared himself to explain why the van had too many passengers. Slowly, he reached for the latch. The young man's phone rang.

"*Oui, hallo.*"

The deckhand started to groan and laugh. Harry was able to make out something about too much beer the night before.

"Inspection?" said Harry.

"C'est correct, monsieur. No, it is fine."

The youngster waved Harry off as he turned and headed back toward the ferry.

Harry got back into the van and Alex looked over.

"That was close."

"God protects drunks and fools, as Sister Margaret used to say."

"So, which are we?" said Alex.

Once they had driven aboard, Harry left the van and stood on the deck, carefully positioning himself to observe all of the passengers and vehicles as they boarded. He confirmed that Qassem was not on the ferry. Once the vessel cast off, Harry rejoined Alex in the van, then pulled out his phone and checked in with Skip.

"We're on with no problems," said Harry. "Qassem is not on this ferry, so that's good."

"Roger that," said Skip. "We haven't seen him leave yet. Let's hope today is the day. Break a leg. That reminds me — I told Breaker to launch the fast boat several hours ago. It'll be in the channel between Langlade and Saint-Pierre by ten o'clock."

"Roger that, Skip. Fingers crossed it doesn't come to that."

The ride across the harbour to the small, uninhabited island was short. Thankfully, the day was clear, and the ocean lay slowly undulating like blue-green molten glass. In fact, the crossing was the shortest portion of the excursion. It had taken longer to load and unload the ferry than it did for the ride.

Harry returned to his spot on the deck and watched the details of the little island come slowly into focus.

Île-au-Marins

Once they docked, Alex drove off the ferry, through the ruins of the abandoned village, and directly up the road to the white wooden church on the dominating high ground. Notre-Dame-des-Victoires was surrounded by several small outbuildings, all equally empty. Alex drove to the east side of the church and tucked the van into its shadow around the corner on the south side.

"This is ideal, Alex," said Harry. "We're in a blind spot from everywhere except the open sea. This'll be my command post. The high ground ensures communications and just by walking around, I can survey most if not all of the island, including the sandy cove where Angus will bring in his trawler — or our escape vessel."

Alex said, "I'm a bit concerned about the approach to the beach. I'll send Paul and Walker down the footpath to check it out. I'll be right back."

Harry stood looking down toward the cove. So far everything was going well, but… Harry pushed that concern from his mind.

Alex returned shortly. "Looks good, Harry. It's about ninety metres down the path to the water, and Walker says it's ideal for a trawler to enter. Paul thinks it might be possible to get the van down the hill, but he wasn't sure."

"No," countered Harry, "it's too steep. We don't need to run the risk. Qassem's not that big. They can carry him down to the water with no difficulty."

The two dozen tourists who had come across with Harry's squad began their various explorations. Here was the challenge facing Bravo. Not only did they need Qassem to wander relatively close to the van, but, more importantly, they needed to somehow separate him from the other visitors. Harry watched the tourists disperse in various directions upon departing the terminal. Alex regarded him thoughtfully.

"What's wrong, Harry? You look troubled."

"Nothing really, Alex. I just don't like not having the initiative."

"I know what you mean."

"I've been playing out the branches and sequels in my mind all morning. Our challenge boils down to timing. I can consider all the convoluted options I like, but until Qassem steps onto the island and begins his walking tour, we are all in a reactive mode, and I don't like it."

"So, how do we seize the initiative?" said Alex.

"I guess we're going to have to think like Chuck Mingus and his boys."

Alex just grinned and went to check on the rest of the men.

While Alex was directing everyone to their initial positions in the village, Harry decided to call Skip.

"Anything happening over there?" said Skip.

"All good so far. Everyone is moving into position."

"Has Terry found the spots to put his toys?"

"He has. He's just finishing up and walking up the hill to me, if you want to talk to him."

"No need," said Skip. "Like I said, it's your show now, Harry."

"Are you still at the café?"

"Les and I are lolling over some *caffe latte* and *pasticcini* — excuse me, I forgot where we were. I meant to say *café au lait* and *croissants*."

Skip's feeble attempt at humour elicited a soft snort from Harry. At least Skip is trying to stay lighthearted, he thought. I'll be glad to get this over with. Skip has been wrapped too tight for too long.

"Harry, you have a lot to attend to. I'll tell you when our friend decides to go for a stroll. Bye."

Terry arrived just as Harry was putting the phone back into his pocket.

"Did you manage to find suitable spots for all of your little Frankenstein monsters?" said Harry.

"I did," said Terry. "I did laser range checks from over there." He pointed to where he had an unobstructed view of all the locations.

"It's two hundred seventy-eight metres to Boris, two hundred ninety-nine metres to Bella, two hundred eighty-seven metres to Abbot, and three hundred twenty-one metres to Costello. They're all perfect line-of-sight shots," declared Terry, looking quite pleased.

"What's with the names?"

"They're from the Frankenstein movies," said Terry. "You know, Boris Karloff —"

"Stop," said Harry. "Sometimes I wonder about you." He shook his head wryly. "I'm curious, though. I know you're a demolitions instructor, but those IEDs you created are not usually what you guys work with, are they?"

"You're right, Harry. They're not even close. Terrorists, from the IRA to the Jihadists, are famous for these things, but they didn't invent them. Farmers have been making improvised explosives for over a century."

"What?" said Harry, surprised.

"Sure. They use fertilizer mixed with various fuel oils to blast stubborn tree stumps and rocks. We took that technology and developed it into an art form."

"From the look of your little 'toys,' I'd have to agree," said Harry.

"I must admit," said Terry, "I really enjoyed fine-tuning these devices. When Colonel Skip told me what he wanted, I had quite a lot of experimenting to do."

"I seem to recall a lot of bangs and smoke."

"I had to get very specific with the mixes," said Terry. "I eventually created charges that wouldn't be too loud but would create great plumes of dark smoke without being lethal beyond a couple of feet. I remember Michel teasing me, saying that I looked more like a sous-chef weighing cake ingredients than a combat engineer blowing things up."

"I recall that joke going around the camp."

"For me, the icing on the cake was the triggers. I used components cannibalized from a collection of radio-controlled model plane parts, and managed to build IEDs that I could trigger at will."

"Yes, Doctor Frankenstein," said Harry. "You're sure about the ranges of the triggers?"

"Absolutely. I confirmed them through repeated trials, and I have an effective range of four to six hundred metres. Here on the island, I set the devices no more than three hundred and fifty metres from where I'll stand to be sure of detonation."

Although it took a bit of lateral thinking, Terry had assembled the IEDs without adding either the gasoline or the diesel. He had bought the fuel once he and Ray got into Saint-Pierre. It was then a simple matter of topping them up and adding the detonators. The risky part was crossing from Newfoundland with them. He had disguised them in tattered carboard boxes that were then put inside more used boxes filled with odds and ends that wouldn't raise suspicion if casually observed. The detonators, however, had taken more care. Those he had placed in a small shockproof tin and then into a specially concealed compartment that he installed under the back seat of the rental vehicle. In any case, his toys were neither large nor lethal. They were moderately loud, however, and by design, very, very smoky.

"You're ready to go?" asked Harry.

"All set," confirmed Terry.

"Now we play tourist and wait," said Harry, just as his phone buzzed.

"Hi, Harry," said Skip tersely. "He's left his apartment and is now walking down toward the ferry site."

"Thanks," said Harry, and hung up.

After his morning prayers, Qassem considered his upcoming day. He did not want a repeat performance of yesterday in the bakery. Today was clear and sunny, a good day to visit Île-aux-Marins. That way, if the women asked how he'd liked it — it was a near-certainty — he could honestly say that he had made the journey. Checking the ferry schedule, he decided to take the nine o'clock crossing, wander through the village, and return for his midday prayers.

Approaching the quay, Qassem saw the ferry departing for its second run. It was of no consequence. He would board the third sailing. He had taken care to look a little dishevelled, just as he imagined an academic author would look. It was refreshing to leave the apartment for a day in the sunshine. He bought his ticket and sat on one of the benches, pretending to study the tourist guides that were available for free. The sun began to warm the island. Qassem could feel Allah smiling upon him again.

The third ferry was almost empty. Most of the day's tourists had crossed earlier. Qassem boarded and stood on the deck looking out at the water.

The boat cast off its lines and began its journey.

Skip, who had followed him at a discreet distance, called Harry. "He's aboard and moving toward you."

"Roger that."

The ride across the channel to the island made Qassem think of his native Algeria. There was a similar sort of barren beauty to the landscape, especially where the sea met the rocky shore. Once at the arrival dock, his contemplative mood ebbed slightly; he was annoyed to have to fight the crowd attempting to get onto the ferry for the return. Was anyone left on the island, he wondered? He hoped not. It was bad enough that these were faithless infidels. These idiot tourists were also rude.

Sandy, who was standing outside La Maison Grise, to the northeast, immediately spotted Qassem. He was pushing his way through those anxious to reboard the returning ferry. Sandy phoned Harry.

"He's with us."

"I see him," said Harry. "Ignore him from a distance."

"Wilco," said Sandy as he returned the phone to his jeans pocket, and became fascinated with the peeling paint on the ancient grey house where he stood.

Finally free of the press of annoying tourists, Qassem once more sat on a bench to study the simplified tourist map. He looked up to orient himself, then back down at the map. He realized that he had miscalculated. The distance to the museum could not be more than one hundred and fifty metres. He would take his time and wait for most of the tourists who were headed there now to be headed somewhere else. Then he could walk up the hill with no intruders around him. In the meantime, he could loll among the few buildings between the terminal and the museum. If he timed it well, he might have the museum to himself. He would have a quick look, and then return to the ferry.

ⲧ ⲧ ⲧ

Terry and Harry stood by the church and pored over the tourist map. Terry took pictures with his phone, while Harry checked in with Sandy.

"All good, Sandy?"

"All good, Harry. I'm about fifteen metres behind him but out of sight."

Alex, who had left the van with the keys in it, was now between the museum and the church. He checked in with Walker, who was inspecting the weathered cruciform monument at Calvaire, southwest of the church.

"Any issues, Walker?"

"All good here."

Harry looked at his men. He could see the tension that had been building in the way they stood, the way they walked. They were skilled at many things, but idly waiting for an opponent to make the first move wasn't one of them. It was the same challenge for them all.

He stood motionless, surveying his domain like an eagle waiting for the right moment to fold its wings and dive for the kill.

"Patience," he said softly to himself. "Patience."

Qassem moved slowly up from the houses and toward the museum.

"Ray, I need you to head up toward the church," Harry said. "Close the distance, but do it slowly so you don't spook him."

"I'm on my way," said Ray.

Next, Harry called Walker.

"Walker, head for the church, but do it slowly."

"Wilco," said Walker, and started to move.

Terry looked over toward Harry, who shook his head to indicate "No, not yet." He could see that Terry was getting antsy. Harry kept slowly shaking his head.

The main door to the museum opened, and a small crowd came flowing out. It made Harry think of an elementary school ending classes for the day. The crowd soon expanded in all directions away from the museum. Qassem arrived at the museum door and went inside. Harry picked up his phone.

"Ray, position yourself at the shop adjacent to the church."

"One step ahead of you, Harry. I'm just about there."

Ray pocketed his phone as he moved to the shop window and began to study the various pieces of tourist ephemerae in the window. A couple materialized next to him, admiring some of the souvenirs. Qassem came out of the museum alone and scanned his surroundings. He pulled out his map and appeared to study it. The street was deserted. He glanced at his watch, then looked briefly up toward the church. He turned in the opposite direction and set out downhill, back toward the ferry, headed directly for Ray. At that moment the couple standing next to Ray went inside the store. Ray put his hand into his pocket and gripped his taser. At the perfect moment, he stepped back unexpectedly from the window, directly into Qassem's path.

"Excuse me, sir."

Qassem dropped like a sack of potatoes, caught completely unaware by Ray, who without warning had tased him with one quick jolt to the neck. Alex was less than fifty metres away, watching the museum door. Seeing Ray's impromptu move, he sprinted to join him. Harry called Walker.

"Get the van down to the souvenir shop as fast as you can."

Miraculously, no one saw the hit. If they could drag Qassem's limp body behind one of the small sheds, they could keep him quiet until the van arrived.

Ray gripped him under both arms and began dragging him. Qassem was groggy but still conscious as Alex appeared.

"Grab his feet!" Ray ordered.

Within seconds the three of them were tucked behind a wall. Alex pulled out a small roll of duct tape. He put a strip across Qassem's mouth. When he began to struggle, Ray showed him the taser and put it on his neck. Qassem's eyes went wide with fear. He stiffened as Ray pushed the device into his flesh but refrained from shocking him a second time. It was a simple but effective warning.

No more than two minutes later, Harry and Terry appeared on foot with the van close behind. Harry took a quick look around. The street was still empty. The van's side door slid open.

"Get him inside!" said Harry in a loud stage whisper.

Alex and Ray tossed Qassem roughly into the van, and Harry threw himself on top of him, while Alex grabbed the side door and started to close it. In seconds, Qassem was bound hand and foot, gagged with the bandana, goggled, and capped by heavy-duty ear defenders. Now completely disoriented, he made a feeble attempt to kick his captors and was rewarded with a sharp punch to the solar plexus. Walker began driving before the door was fully closed, and at that instant, the couple who had gone into the shop stepped back outside to see Ray patting the side of the van as it drove away.

"Bonjour," said the woman.

"Bonjour," said Ray, smiling.

The van drove toward the church, and Ray began his unhurried stroll to join the rest of Bravo.

Angus answered his cellphone. "Aye, Colonel."

"Hello, Angus. Can you come to the beach, please?"

"I'll be there in about ten minutes."

"We'll be waiting," said Harry.

The trawler came straight into the cove and let the keel settle gently into the sand.

With Harry and Alex on the trawler taking Qassem to the RV for the hand-off to Bill, Terry was left in charge of Bravo, and he now faced a small dilemma. Boris, Bella, Abbot, and Costello were sitting unexploded on the island. Qassem's antisocial desire for privacy had created a sudden, narrow window of opportunity, and Ray, acting on instinct, had taken it. That obviated the need to create any diversions. There had been no need to use the noisy explosives to herd the tourists in any particular direction.

Walker saw Terry looking puzzled. "What is it?"

"The IEDs are all still in place, and they're all armed."

"Oh, shit." Walker thought for a moment. "Let's just abandon them and get the hell out of here."

"No, Walker. We can't do that," said Terry.

"Why not? Eventually, someone will find them. Without the triggers they're inert, right? Anyway, they can't be traced to us."

"It's out of the question. They still have live detonators. What if some kid finds one or somebody with a radio-controlled boat inadvertently triggers one? How do you think Colonel Skip would react to us leaving them behind?"

Walker looked suddenly contrite.

"Sorry, Terry. That didn't occur to me. You're right. I wasn't thinking.

So now what?"

"I have to go back to the four IEDs and disarm them one at a time," he said. "We'll have to drive to each location, wait until the area's clear, then I'll disarm them, and we can dispose of them. Let's move."

Terry grabbed the four radio-controlled remotes he had so carefully built and removed all the batteries. He jumped onto a large rock at the water's edge, then threw all four controllers, as well as the batteries, into the cove as far as he could. The ocean's salt water would make them useless in a matter of minutes. Slow corrosion would do the rest.

"What was that about?" said Ray, puzzled.

"There's now no fear that any IED will inadvertently go off while I'm disassembling them," said Terry. "That reminds me," he said, handing his taser to Ray. "Throw all the tasers into the ocean, now."

Ray collected the rest of the devices and, one by one, tossed them out into the water.

Driving the van to each position in turn and waiting for Terry to empty the fuel, remove the triggers and detonators, and disassemble the devices took much longer than expected. Each time, they had to wait for the area to be free of tourists. With each device, Terry drained the fuel, then took it down to its component parts. He then handed the various pieces to Walker, Ray, and Sandy to drop into nearby waste containers. Where no container was available, the parts were returned to the van for later disposal. Ray then drove to the next location, while Terry walked the distance to clear his head and settle his nerves.

"You look tense," said Sandy as he watched Terry work. "I thought they were inert."

"I've handled hundreds of detonators over the years. I never take any for granted," Terry said. "I know a half-dozen guys with missing fingers. These things may be inert, but they're still dangerous. I always remembered what my instructor taught me: treat the caps like a girlfriend. The minute you take the little darlings for granted, they'll blow up in your face."

"Interesting," said Sandy. "If you don't mind, I'll wait for you at the van."

After the last IED was dismantled, Terry gathered up the various bits and walked back to the van.

"Ferry's loading, Terry," said Ray.

"All done. Drive on," he ordered, climbing in.

"What's in the tin?" said Ray, looking over at him.

"The detonators. It'll be fine. I have a plan."

"I don't think I can make the ferry."

"No worries, Ray. There's one more before they shut down for the day. This way we'll be at the head of the line for the last ferry."

The return trip was different from the one coming over. There were no students on shift, and the deckhands seemed more diligent for some reason. Prior to boarding, Ray parked the van where the deckhand indicated. The worker stepped next to the passenger side and asked Terry to please open the rear doors. In halting English, he explained there was always some fear of leaving someone on the island overnight. It occurred to Terry that although the deckhand didn't say so, there was obvious concern that the van might be taking something off the island from the abandoned village or church. In spite of the many bilingual signs on the island warning visitors against it, Terry suspected that tourists had frequently smuggled away small souvenirs.

The young man called over to his boss at the ramp and said something to him, after which his crew chief gave him a thumbs-up.

"What'd he say?" said Ray.

"He told them there were two men in back and nothing else," said Terry.

The deckhand nodded at Terry, who showed him the three ticket stubs — two men in back plus him and Ray up front. The deckhand gave him a thumbs-up and waved the van onto the waiting ferry. Although the crew was attentive, they all seemed rushed to end their workday.

Terry waited until the ferry was approximately halfway to the Saint-Pierre dock. He left the van, walked over to the starboard side and leaned on the salt-encrusted rail. Terry saw the city slowly turning on its lights as the ferry gently arced its way to the government wharf. Looking slowly left and right, he nudged his small, half-opened metal box off the railing. It fell the fifteen feet to the waterline and was swallowed by the bow waves extending from the hull. He then pushed himself back off the rail and returned to the van.

"You, okay?" said Ray.

"All good. I gave the last of Doctor Frankenstein's toys a burial at sea."

Halifax

Breaker sat looking at Franz-Josef. The two men were sitting in one of Halifax's most famous fish restaurants and were thoroughly enjoying their elegant supper. The restaurant was off Barrington Street, and they could see the lights of Casino Nova Scotia through the large plate glass window. This restaurant held deep significance for both men. Neither had been able to afford even a pre-dinner drink in this fine establishment before coming to work for Skip. Breaker's savouring of his steak and lobster was tinged by the regret that his mom had not lived long enough for him to bring her to a place like this. Jupp, having always frequented the cheap bars in the city's large student ghetto, was feeling like at any moment the maître d' would appear and ask him to leave.

"I like this city," said Franz-Josef, "but too much temptation for me."

"Not me," said Breaker. "Too many bad memories."

"I did not know. You have served here, in the army?"

"No, I was born here. My father was a US Navy petty officer who took advantage of a foolish girl, then left her pregnant and alone. I know your childhood was no picnic, Franz-Josef. But believe me, neither was mine."

Franz-Josef stared at his friend. "I am sorry, mein Freund. I did not mean to upset you." He changed the subject. "You are familiar with the casino?"

Breaker kept telling him that there was no such plan, but Franz-Josef didn't buy it. In his heart, he knew what was going to happen, but not how. He felt like he had on the feast of Sankt Martinstag when he was a boy.

Breaker felt the phone buzzing in his pocket.

"Hello. Yes, sir. I'll confirm.

"Was this important?" Franz-Josef looked wide-eyed at Breaker.

"That was Colonel Skip. The fish is in the net. Harry and Alex are taking it to the market for sale."

Jupp could not help blurting out an excited whisper. "*Hervorragend!*"

"What?"

"I am sorry, Breaker. That is outstanding news," he said. "Do you now make the call?"

"Now I make two calls."

Franz-Josef looked puzzled. "The casino?"

"Quiet," said Breaker, and put the phone to his ear. He called a number using the speed-dial menu.

"US Coast Guard Atlantic, Sector Boston. Petty Officer Bud McCall. How may I help you, sir?"

"I need to speak with Command Master Chief Petty Officer Reynolds."

"Yes, sir. Who may I say is calling?"

"It's Chief Warrant Officer Jonathan Swift."

"One moment, Chief."

There was a momentary pause and a click while the call was transferred. "Reynolds here."

"Command Master Chief, I have a long message. Ready to copy?"

"Send."

"I send 4-7-1-0-5-5 November. Break. 5-4-3-0-4-0 Whisky. Break. Break. Tango 0-8-5-0. Zulu. Message ends. Read back."

Breaker held the phone away from his face so Reynolds could be heard by Jupp as he read back the message. Breaker looked over at Franz-Josef to confirm its accuracy. Franz-Josef nodded, and Breaker killed the call.

Franz-Josef raised his eyebrows. "Time to call Herr Oberst?"

"Not yet. I'll make the call, but first I have another call."

"Why? You must call den Oberst."

"Franz-Josef, please be quiet for just one minute." He dialled the number. Hello, I need to speak to Billy."

"Billy's on a run ashore."

"Yeah, I know. Tell him to come home. It's all good."

"I'll tell him right away."

"Who was that man?" said Franz-Josef, when Breaker had ended the call. "I do not know anyone called Billy."

"I'll explain later. Let's finish our supper."

"Und then we go to the casino?"

Breaker let out a loud sigh of irritation. Franz-Josef had been like a child the whole time they had been in the city, unable to let go of his fixation on the casino.

"Listen, Franz-Josef, we aren't going to the casino. We are *never* going to the bloody casino."

His voice was a hoarse whisper. Even so, his exasperation had caught the attention of the people at the next table. Breaker apologized to them. Franz-Josef appeared downcast, and Breaker was immediately sorry that he'd lost his temper.

"I'm sorry. I didn't mean to lose patience with you, Franz-Josef. Honestly, I'm just in a bad mood. It's the ghosts in this city. Please forgive me."

"It is alright, Breaker. No problem. I am sometimes too much the pushy one."

Breaker still felt awful. "Listen," he mumbled as he brushed some crumbs from the tablecloth. "Tomorrow, we need to settle accounts at 10:00. We don't have to be at the airport until late afternoon. We can head over to the casino and play some roulette. What do you say?"

"That would be *sehr gut*, Breaker. Und we can check to see where are the security cameras to tell dem Oberst."

Breaker sighed heavily again, but finally broke into a laugh.

Saint-Pierre-et-Miquelon

Skip and Jules sat at a small table in the café opposite the boulangerie. The sun was setting, and the street was slowly emptying of its foot traffic. Skip's phone buzzed.

"Yes, Breaker."

"Colonel, I called Boston and I also retrieved Billy. Tomorrow Franz-Joseph and I will settle up, and then I promised to take him to the casino. He wants to look at their security system so he can brief you. Honestly Colonel, it's been non-stop talk about the bloody casino."

"Ha, ha. I knew it would be, and sorry to put you through it. I figured it would be good for him."

"No worries, Colonel. I'll check in again tomorrow."

The remainder of Bravo returned on the last ferry. Terry handed Skip Qassem's apartment keys as well as the van keys so he and Jules could drive it off the island.

"Terry, when is everyone leaving for home?"

"Once we loaded Qassem onto the trawler, Harry ordered me to get everyone redeployed home as quick as I could. They're all gone except us, Colonel. Lots of empty flights until about 23:00 for some reason."

Skip felt a sudden chill go up his spine.

"That was a good call, and Harry's right. Jules and I have the van. You take what's left of Bravo and get to the airport. Book whatever flights you need to, and don't worry about cost. We'll sort it all out in Montreal, but right now, I want you off this island."

"Colonel, we're all booked for a 07:15 flight tomorrow —"

"Terry, I want you all off the island tonight, if you can make it happen."

"Yes, Colonel. I'll make that happen." Terry started to walk away.

"Terry?"

"Yes, Colonel?"

"Since neither you nor Harry mentioned anything about using your toys, I assume you recovered them?"

Terry shot a quick glance at Walker, who had the decency to look uncomfortable.

"Something wrong, Terry?"

"No, Colonel, I was about to say something and lost my train of thought. Yes, sir, we retrieved all four devices. I emptied all the fuel, scattered the fertilizer, and disassembled everything. Then we spread all the pieces among various garbage containers on the island and at the two ferry terminals."

"What about the controllers and caps?"

"They're now fully inert. I tossed the parts into the ocean, Colonel. By now the salt water is slowly reclaiming all the base metals in their component parts. No worries."

"Well done, Terry."

"Thanks, Colonel."

"Safe travels."

After Bravo had safely departed, Skip let out a long sigh.

"Colonel, why did you do that?" said Jules.

"I'm not sure, RSM, but Harry's decision just made eminent sense. The fewer of us here now, the better. In fact, you should join them. I'll drive the van to St. John's first thing in the morning."

"Non, mon Colonel. I will keep you company."

The two men waited another hour before entering Qassem's empty flat. The street was deserted as they crossed, and Skip used his key to open the door. He was surprised to see everything so neat and tidy.

"He was a very orderly psychopath," said Skip. "Careful not to touch anything, Jules."

There was not really much to look through. Skip and Jules were there mostly on the off chance that there might be something obvious that would help Bill, but there wasn't.

"Not much of a life, mon Colonel," Jules said, almost wistfully.

"No, not really. His real legacy is hatred and sorrow."

"You are right."

"Let's get out of here. This place is depressing me."

They stepped out into the hallway. Skip locked the door behind them and gave the lock and handle a quick wipe.

"Time for supper, RSM. Let's get our ferry tickets and see what's of interest in the vicinity."

He and Jules made their way to the main ferry terminal at the Quai Mimosa, arriving just as the ticket office was about to close. Jules, once more adopting his half-wit personage, the jolly Acadian, was able to convince the rather dour *fonctionnaire* to sell them tickets for the van and one passenger for the 06:00 ferry to Fortune. The man behind the plexiglass was adamant in warning them.

"*Assurez-vous*," he said. "You must check the Canada Customs *régulations*. Confirm you do not take the contraband into the country. Do not upset *les Canadiens*."

Jules thanked the man profusely and returned to where Skip was standing outside. "All set for 06:00."

"Well done, RSM. I saw a sign up the street for a café. It's called The Guitar-Playing Cat. With a name like that, the food *must* be good. What do you say? My treat."

"Play on, Macduff," said Jules.

"An RCAF chief who quotes Shakespeare? Really?"

"Would you prefer that I quote Molière?"

"Only if you misquote him like you just did Shakespeare."

The two men walked toward the café sharing a laugh. As they passed a bus stop, Skip deposited Qassem's keys in a garbage bin.

The anxiety that had been steadily growing in the centre of Skip's chest since they'd first set foot on this tiny rock was finally starting to dissipate.

They had executed another complex operation, and again, fate had thrown his men a curveball. But everyone had risen to the challenge and once more made him proud. All that remained was the hand-off between Harry and Bill. It was out of his hands now. The QRF in Halifax had some minor cleanups but would return in a couple of days, as would Harry and Alex. He and the RSM would slip away in the morning and fly home from St. John's. Skip was growing confident he could put this mission in the column marked 'success.'

"Colonel, are you alright?" said Jules, breaking into his reverie.

"I'm getting there, RSM. I'm getting there."

The two men were greeted by a young woman as they stepped into the brightly decorated establishment. The hostess was wearing a blouse printed with curled-up cats and a bright orange poodle skirt. She led them to a table by a window.

Thinking aloud, Skip said, "A poodle skirt seems oddly incongruous in a place like this, especially with a kitty-cat blouse."

"Pardon?" asked Jules.

"Never mind," said Skip. "I'm drained, but we've had another successful mission. Call me superstitious. Turn off your phone. Let's not jinx ourselves. We'll have a quiet supper and call it a night."

"Good idée, Colonel."

Jules sensed that Skip was unsettled. But by now he knew enough to leave him with his thoughts. One burning question remained, however.

"Colonel?"

"Yes, Jules?"

"Can you please explain about the poodle skirt and the kitty-cat blouse?"

USAF Base Nellis

Second Lieutenant Jacob Henninger yawned and stretched his arms. When he'd graduated from the US Air Force Academy and been selected to go on the drone pilot course, he was happy. He was getting in on the leading edge of the latest high-tech aspect of air warfare. He had always wanted to fly, but lacking the required eyesight, he knew it was impossible. This wasn't flying, but it was close. When he earned his wings and was posted to Nellis AFB, he was excited, but that didn't last long.

His current mission was not at all what he'd signed up for. He was watching some bay on the south shore of Newfoundland, up in Canada. Not a single vessel had been within ten nautical miles of it, yet here he sat doing a graveyard shift, watching an empty piece of ocean. It was *boring*.

"What's your beef, mister?" said the watch commander sharply.

"Me, sir? I didn't say anything."

"Listen up. Drone warfare is not like playin' cops and robbers. We're the eyes and ears that keep the commanders fully informed, and sometimes that means watching an empty screen for hours, or days, at a time. You feel me, mister?"

Henninger's shift partner, Lieutenant Silvia de Palma, spoke up.

"Major, we get it, but Jake and I got a chunk of empty ocean called Placentia Bay. Sir, we don't even have any ships near Placentia Bay or even Saint-Pierre Michelob. It feels like we aren't doing anything worthwhile, is all."

"*Miquelon*, Lieutenant. It's Miquelon, and whether we have ships in the quadrant or not is not your concern. If I tell you that it's important, then it's important."

"Sir, I ack that, but we aren't going to shoot anything, so what —"

"If we needed to know why we're watching the feed, it would've been part of the mission brief. That's all you two need to know right now."

"Yes, sir," said the lieutenant.

"Yes, sir," the second lieutenant chimed in.

The watch commander strode out of the room to check on some other missions being monitored down the corridor. Silvia made sure he was gone.

"Geez. What crawled up the major's ass?"

"Hey, Silvia. Thanks for running interference."

"No sweat, Jake."

Lord's Cove

The small trawler plied its way through the dark water just south of Newfoundland. It was still several hours before the sun would be fully above the horizon.

"What's this about?" said Harry.

"Who the hell are they?" said Alex.

They stood on the deck staring across the water at the distinctive red hull of the Canadian Coast Guard fisheries patrol vessel heading their way. There was no point in trying to outrun it in their old trawler.

Once he spotted the craft racing toward them, Angus stopped his engine, then turned on every light on his vessel and prepared to be boarded.

"What's up, Captain? What's with all the lights?" asked Harry.

"I know what happens to fishing vessels that try to outrun them Coast Guard cutters, Colonel. I'm not lookin' for no trouble."

The cutter approached and idled its engines. Loudspeakers instructed the trawler to heave to as the cutter came alongside.

"They are playing this for real," said Angus. "Look at all that gear — and weapons to boot. I ain't never seen Canadian Coast Guard with weapons before."

Harry remained silent as they observed the boarding party.

"They don't look like no Coast Guard to me," said Angus quietly, turning to Alex. "Is this here part of your big secret exercise with all of them other organizations?"

Like Harry, Alex did not reply.

The whole process of grabbing Qassem and transferring him across to the cutter took less than two minutes. It then pushed off, the red hull rotating landward, and made for the Newfoundland coast. The fog soon swallowed them.

Harry and Alex stood on the deck in continued silence. Alex looked pensive and far away.

"Did you notice anything odd about those guys?" he said at length.

Harry was fuming. "You're damn right I did. Those bastards robbed us."

"That's not what I meant," said Alex. "That was clearly a Coast Guard vessel, except those guys weren't Coast Guard. They were Mounties, or, more correctly, they wanted us to believe they were Mounties."

"What? Of course they were Mounties," said Harry. "Didn't you see the tac vests?"

"Nope, Mounties are police officers, and if they're making an arrest, they always announce who they are. They warn you to stand fast and not to move. It has to do with protecting your rights, so the case doesn't get tossed for poor procedure. Those guys hit us like we hit the casa. They showed no ID and there was no talking. Those guys behaved like the old SERT, before the RCMP gave that job to us and the JTF-2. Trust me," said Alex. "I trained with them."

Angus had been listening to the conversation, and he now looked completely befuddled. "Sert?" he asked.

Harry finally noticed the Captain standing amidships. He quickly altered his tone, saying, "Special Emergency Reaction Team. That was them. Why? Is something wrong, Angus?"

"I'm confused. You sounded pretty peeved there, Colonel. Wasn't this all part of the plan? Did I do something wrong? Is that why you're so upset?"

"No, no, no. Ha, ha — you have to excuse me, Angus. Andrew and I are army officers, and we like to see things done a certain way, is all. Bristol style, as the navy used to say. The original plan had us meeting a different vessel, with an RCN boarding party. We were going to do a prisoner transfer, which was planned for later this morning. Obviously, somebody changed the exercise master event list, and Andrew and I weren't told. That's why I seemed annoyed. I just hate to be left in the dark, but it doesn't matter, since the prisoner exchange happened. It wasn't exactly as I figured it would be, but you were spot on, Angus. You were a big help to us. Isn't that right, Andy?"

"Exactly," said Alex. "Well done, Angus."

"I'm awful glad to hear it. You had me some worried there for a bit."

"Listen, Angus —" A phone call stopped Harry short. He pressed accept and put the phone to his ear. "Skip. You're not going to believe what happened —" he began, but the caller cut over him.

"Harry, I have Qassem. We will talk in Montreal. Do not forget to feed the fish."

"What did Colonel Skip want?" said Alex.

"That wasn't him," said Harry, relaying the conversation to Alex.

"'Do not forget to feed the fish'? What's that mean?" said Alex.

Harry looked over to see that Angus had moved up to the open bridge and called up to him.

"Take us back to Fortune, please."

"You got 'er, lad."

The marine diesel coughed a small blue cloud of exhaust, and the vessel was soon chugging its way back to the government wharf. Harry motioned to Alex to join him astern, as far from the bridge as possible. When Alex arrived, he found Harry scowling at his boots.

"Harry? What's up with the phone call?"

"No idea." Harry squinted out into the fog, then reached into his pocket and pulled out his phone. He tossed the burner phone into the Atlantic, then sullenly returned to the bench and sat quietly, watching the sun attempting to clear the horizon.

Through the mist, Alex could see the harbour rising to meet them in the far distance off the starboard bow.

"Harry, we're about thirty-five minutes out, I figure."

"Thanks," Harry said, and returned to gazing at the horizon.

Standing alone at the wharf, Jules waved to the fishing boat as it came alongside. He grabbed the painter line that Alex tossed and pulled in the hawser, then secured it to the bollard.

"The lad understands knots," said Angus to no one in particular.

"Thank you for your service, Angus," said Harry. "We appreciate it. Your part of the training went off exactly how we planned it, even if we didn't quite make it to Placentia Bay."

Jules didn't speak as he discreetly pressed an envelope stuffed with hundred-dollar bills to Harry, who passed it into the sailor's leathery hand. He followed Alex up the wharf.

"Do I need to remind you that the RCMP would not be happy to hear you talking down the pub about a secret exercise? Especially since we were surprised by their change?" Harry said quietly to Angus.

The Captain nodded his head in agreement.

"Good man," said Harry as he patted Angus's shoulder. "There's a wee bit extra in there to show the admiral's appreciation."

"Thank you, sir. It was my pleasure. I ain't never done them exercise things before. If you need me again, you know where I am."

"Thanks, Angus. We'll keep you in mind. You just remember our deal."

Wide-eyed, Angus counted out the bills in the envelope, then tapped the side of his nose with his index finger.

Harry walked over to join Jules and Alex on the wharf. He was still visibly agitated, though Alex was strangely calm.

"Where's Colonel Skip?" said Harry.

"Le Colonel is still in Saint-Pierre," said Jules. "He ordered me off the island, and I will explain in the van."

SAINT-PIERRE-ET-MIQUELON

Forcing the RSM to get on the ferry alone had been a trial, but reluctantly, Jules had left Skip as he'd been ordered. Skip watched the ferry pull away as he walked tentatively along the jetty. The sun was just breaking the horizon line as he pulled two cellphones from his pocket. He dropped Jules's onto the pavement, then opened the speed-dial app on his own.

"Yes, Colonel," said Breaker.

"Have you been monitoring attacks against our server?"

"I have, and there was one early this morning, but it was benign. Just some hacker, I suspect."

"Can you tell where it was from?"

"Looks like the DC area."

"Any references to Lopez?"

"Colonel, you mean Qassem?"

"Never mind, Breaker. My mistake. I want you and Franz-Josef to close down and redeploy immediately."

"Are you okay?" said Breaker.

"Just do as I say."

Skip ended the call, then put his phone on the ground alongside Jules's. He looked around for something heavy and spied an errant brick. After he smashed the two phones, he kicked the electronic detritus into the water and ambled back to the café. He knew it would not be long now.

"Another coffee, please," he said to the waiter as he took his seat.

Recognition flashed across the waiter's face. "Yes, sir."

The coffee didn't arrive, but the gendarmes did.

"*Bonjour, monsieur. Votre carte d'identité, s'il vous plaît.*"

Skip looked at him quizzically. "English, please?" he pleaded.

"Good morning, sir. I am Capitaine Moreau of the Judicial Police. Your identity papers, please."

"Good morning, Captain." Skip rose and reached into his inside coat pocket. The policeman flinched and Skip froze.

"I am taking out my passport, Captain." Skip eased it gingerly from his pocket and passed the thin blue booklet to the officer. Capitaine Moreau flipped through the pages.

"*Vous êtes canadien, monsieur.*"

"May we do this in English, please? I do not speak much French."

The first lie.

"*Certainement, monsieur.* But my English is not so strong."

"Is there a problem, Captain?"

"I will ask the questions, monsieur. Why do you come to Saint-Pierre?"

"I am a tourist, and I came to see the museum."

The second lie.

"And your companion — where is he?"

"I have no companion. I am here alone."

The third lie.

"I see. You come to visit *le musée*, but you spend three days drinking coffee with friends in le Centreville and now insist that you are alone?"

"I'm a retired professor and was in no hurry, Captain. I came to your beautiful island to escape the hurry, and yes, I met some fellow tourists in your lovely city. May I please have my passport back?"

"Non, monsieur, you may not. You will accompany me, please." Capitaine Moreau walked toward the door. "This way please, monsieur."

USS Thunder

Shortly before the appointed time, Bill wandered over to the submarine's commander and asked if he could receive messages at this depth. The Captain explained in a slightly condescending tone that yes, he could, but he wasn't at liberty to say how or why. Bill thought for a minute about telling this pouting teenager that his own security clearance dwarfed his, but he let it go. He was trying to be agreeable, though the Captain wasn't making it easy.

The Captain's yeoman arrived with a message, which he read, then passed to Bill.

"That's the lat-long and time for the RV. It's 47 degrees, 07 minutes, 44 seconds north, and 54 degrees, 30 minutes, 40 seconds west. The rendezvous time is 10:50 Zulu."

"Can you make that?" said Bill.

"No problem at all," said the Captain.

Everything seemed to be going smoothly, even if the sub commander was a tight-assed Annapolis grad who was still sore that Bill had diverted him away from a NATO exercise for his clandestine rendezvous.

The Captain announced to Bill that the bay was clear and that he was ready to surface. Bill gave him the thumbs-up.

When Bill had first come aboard from a US Coast Guard cutter off the coast of Massachusetts, the CO was openly hostile. He was only slightly mollified when he read the sealed note from the commander of the Atlantic Submarine Fleet. The two-line hand-written note from COMSUBLANT had been on the admiral's personal stationery. He read it and handed it to the Chief of the Boat. He told the COB to read and then shred it. He then ordered his XO to immediately set a course for Placentia Bay, Newfoundland. Bill had noted an obvious friction between the skipper and his XO but didn't enquire because he didn't care. He needed a getaway car, and the USS *Thunder* was it.

The submarine breached and then levelled on the surface. Bill made his way to the conning tower to go topside. He stepped up through the hatch to stand on the fin's upper deck. The weather was perfect, with a heavy fog bank shrouding the shoreline. The surface was a gently rolling sheet of mercury. Bill checked his watch. They were six minutes early, and he strained to hear the sound of any approaching fishing boats, but all he could hear was waves splashing against the sub's hull. The sooner they stowed their "guest" and headed back to Boston, the better. There were no external sounds except for the reeling gulls screeching for a free meal.

Once outside and above water, his phone came to life, and Bill immediately felt it vibrate in his hand. It was voicemail, and he didn't recognize the voice.

"Hello, Colonel Donovan. I have tried to call a couple of times. Obviously, you have been underwater with work. There has been a hiccup. Your guest will not be joining you. I will explain later. Sincere apologies."

The message ended, so Bill replayed it to be sure he had heard it correctly. The accent was French-Canadian. Bill tossed his phone overboard as the Captain watched.

"Take her down." Bill was obviously upset as he stepped toward the ladder.

Before Bill could get through the hatch, the Captain was raising his voice to him. "What? You've got to be kidding. You took my boat and crew off a NATO LIVEX, and now we're going back without the package. Are you serious?"

He was nearly shouting at Bill, who had his back to him. Bill spun abruptly, and the look on his face stunned the CO into silence. His expression could not have been clearer: "Don't fuck with me right now." Without a word, Bill went below.

"Captain is down," announced the CO once he was below. "Officer of the Deck, prepare to dive."

"Prepare to dive, aye, sir," came the response.

"Submerge the ship," said the Captain.

The XO looked to the CO. "Sir, we've come all this way, and we have nothing to show for it. Are you sure you want to leave now?"

The Captain mirrored the look he had got from Bill, and the XO repeated back the order.

"Diving Officer, submerge the ship," ordered the XO. "Make your depth one five zero feet."

"Aye, sir, make my depth one five zero feet."

"Officer of the Deck, steer two five zero, make turns for two five knots."

"Aye, sir, steer two five zero, make turns for two five knots."

"Captain, I'd like a word in your day cabin, please," said Bill, his voice like an icicle.

The COB watched impassively as the two men left for the CO's cabin. Once they were alone, with the cabin door shut, Bill spoke again.

"I can't tell you what happened because I don't know. The mission is a scrub and we're done here. You and your crew were excellent, and I'll be sure to tell the admiral that when I see him. I'm sorry, Captain. Honestly, I am. If you make speed for Boston, I will arrange to have a Coast Guard vessel RV with us at sea and get out of your hair as quickly as I can. Maybe you can still join the fleet for the remainder of the LIVEX."

The CO, sensing Bill's disappointment, became contrite.

"Aye, sir. I will make that happen. Sir, please accept my apologies for being unprofessional with you. I meant no offence. Sometimes I forget myself, sir. I will signal the Coast Guard."

"No offence taken, sailor. Call it even for the last time me and my buddies at the Point stole Annapolis's goat before the Army–Navy game."

FORTUNE

The three men got into the van parked on the government wharf at Fortune. It was a couple of hours' drive to Come-By-Chance and then another hour on the Trans-Canada Highway to the airport in St. John's. That was lots of time to mull over what happened. Jules drove while Harry and Alex sat lost in their thoughts. After almost forty minutes, Harry broke the silence.

"I think I've figured out *what* happened, but I'm not sure *why*. First, I need you to explain why Colonel Skip stayed behind. I don't get it."

Jules explained what had occurred on the island. The explosion, the fire, Skip's picture on the TV, and then him ordering Jules off the island.

"I think he knew trouble was coming, and that if he was on the ferry, they would turn it around."

"What?" said Harry, exasperated. "Now I really am confused. I'll give Skip a call."

The call went immediately to a nondescript automated voicemail.

"No answer," he said aloud.

"I am not surprised," said Jules. "One moment. I will pull off the road so we can talk."

"Why aren't you surprised?" said Alex.

"Le Colonel turned off the phones last night. This morning, he made me give my phone to him. They are probably in the ocean now. I could see that Colonel Skip did not have a good feeling, but he did not explain why."

"Harry, you said you figured it out. So?"

"I think Bill has double-crossed us. I never trusted him or all that bull about loving Canadians, but who the hell knows why? I guess we'll figure it out back at le Chalet."

"That makes no sense, Harry," said Alex. "Colonel Skip trusted the guy, and he covered our asses in Brazil. Why would he do this?"

"No idea," said Harry. "Jules, we need to get to the airport, so make tracks."

Saint-Pierre-et-Miquelon

At the police station, Skip was photographed, fingerprinted, and made to sit quietly.

"Am I being charged?"

"Monsieur, all will be explained. Patience, please. We have our methods."

"I understand, but may I make a phone call, please?"

"Non, monsieur. You are a foreign national and you have no rights here in France. Do not worry. You will be treated fairly."

"I have no doubt," said Skip, doing his best to remain civil.

Once processed, Skip was guided to a spartan cell and told to undress. His belongings were collected, and he was issued a jumpsuit and a pair of shower slippers. The waiting game began. Skip ran through the conversations he had had to ensure his story would hold up under interrogation. He had lied three times. He needed to keep it simple, and he needed to stay calm.

A uniformed gendarme appeared after an hour. Skip was led to a small room with a table and two chairs. There was a mirror on one wall, undoubtedly a two-way. A man in civilian clothes stepped into the room accompanied by the gendarme. Skip recognized the first man as Moreau, the captain who had questioned him at the ferry café.

"Hello again, Professor Schiaparelli."

"Hello again, Capitaine Moreau."

"*Très bien*. You recognize me. I have a few questions for you, Professor."

"Of course," said Skip. "May I have a lawyer present, please?"

"Non, monsieur, you may not. If you do not wish to answer, then remain silent. You have that right."

"I understand," said Skip. "May I bother you for something to drink, Capitaine?"

The officer motioned to the gendarme, who left the room.

Le Chalet

It had been over twenty-four hours with no word from Skip. Everyone except him was safely back in le Chalet, and Harry had done a quick hot wash while everyone was still fresh. There was no news from or about Saint-Pierre. Evidently CNN didn't much care what happened there. Harry remained sullen, and the men gave him a wide berth.

After a time, Harry went up to Alex, who had retreated to Skip's office. "Why would Bill do that to Skip? Skip said he was a friend."

"That, Harry, is the proverbial sixty-four-thousand-dollar question," said Alex. "Listen to me, Harry. I know that you're feeling like you should've been there to protect Skip. You feel like you let him down."

"It's not like that," said Harry.

"I know you, and you're convinced that your duty was to be there, but you also know, if you're honest, that based on what we know, Colonel Skip would have ordered you off the island."

"And I would have refused."

"Bullshit."

The two men sat in silence in Skip's office, like concerned parents waiting for a teenager to come home. Pappy looked in.

"Lights out," said Harry. "Let's call it a night."

"Aye, Colonel," said Pappy. "By the way, did you taste the baguettes at supper?"

"Don't call me that. There's only one Colonel, and he's not here."

"Aye, Harry. My apologies."

"Wait, baguettes? Yes. Why?"

"Michel made them. He spent his time in Saint-Pierre learning how," said Pappy, obviously trying to lift Harry's mood.

"Well, then I guess the mission wasn't a total goddamn failure," said Harry.

Alex looked up as Pappy was leaving and shook his head gently. Pappy nodded and disappeared.

"Let's have a drink," said Alex. "Where does Skip keep the good stuff?"

Harry rose and walked over to the decanters. He grabbed two glasses, poured a generous portion of scotch into each, then came back to the desk and handed one to Alex. They sat silently for several minutes, sipping their drinks, before Harry spoke again.

"I've been thinking over something Skip said, about his friend the Bishop. I can't help but wonder if he's involved somehow. I don't know. That would make even less sense than suspecting Bill. Until Skip gets back, all we can do is sit it out."

"I know it makes no sense," said Alex. "None of it does."

Pappy reappeared at the office door.

"Now what?" said Harry rather testily.

"Beg pardon. You're not going to believe this, but you have a visitor. I just got a call from Jules. He was outside with Stirling, and a black SUV pulled into the camp. The driver says he's a friend of Colonel Skip's. Jules checked his ID and sent him on. His name is Levesque."

"Thanks, Pappy," said Harry, getting to his feet. "I need to go and greet Mr. Levesque."

"Aye, Harry," said Pappy, and headed off again.

"Do you want me to leave?" said Alex.

"If you don't mind, Alex. This could get unpleasant, and I'd rather speak to this guy alone."

"Are you sure you're going to be okay?"

"To be honest, no, I'm not sure, Alex." Seeing Alex's stricken look, he raised his hands. "Stop, stop. I didn't mean it to come out that way. The Bishop is Skip's oldest friend. It'll be fine. I promise."

"Pappy, Jules, and I will be outside if you need anything."

"I appreciate that, Alex, and I assure you it'll be fine. I'm just being an asshole."

Alex left the office as Pappy materialized at the door with Gaston.

"Thanks, Pappy," said Harry. "Please join Alex and Jules."

"Aye, sir."

Gaston was standing silently in the doorway. "Are you not going to invite me in?" he enquired.

"I'm still thinking about it," said Harry. "I suppose I could ask you how you found this place, but you'd only lie to me, so never mind. Come in and shut the door, please."

Gaston did so but remained standing. Harry extended his hand, and they shook. "I'm Harry Monahan, a friend of Skip's. Please do sit."

"Thank you, Harry. I know exactly who you are, and I know Skip has told you who I am, so allow me to get right away to the reason I am here."

"Good idea," said Harry. "Would you care for a drink?"

"No, merci."

Harry thought Gaston had the anxious look of a young boy who had been caught reading his father's *Playboy* magazines.

"Where to begin? I have Qassem, but I do not have Amadeo. I have a private plane on standby at Mirabel, and I am on my way to Saint-Pierre to speak to him. He is in the custody of la Police Judiciaire of France. This is getting serious, Harry. This afternoon someone called Thierry Breton flew into Saint-Pierre on a French military flight. He is *commissaire général de la Police Fédérale de France*. Initially, Skip was being questioned by the local police regarding the fire. The arrival of monsieur Breton has changed everything, and the charges are now murder and terrorism."

He paused and looked at Harry. "May I change my mind about the drink?"

Harry sat stunned. "What did you say? Terrorism?"

"The drink Harry. Scotch, *s'il te plaît*."

Harry poured a glass of single malt and topped up his own glass. "*Santé*," he said. "I'm listening."

"Harry, let me first say I am sorry, truly I am. I could not warn you of what I was about to do because I could not risk it. I needed you to successfully execute the abduction, which I was sure you would. Your success was the key to everyone's safety. If you had not seized Qassem, there would have been no intervention, no fake RCMP, nothing. You will understand in a minute."

Gaston paused for a small sip of scotch. Harry regarded him wordlessly, looking deeply puzzled.

"For now," Gaston went on, "I cannot tell you everything, but here is what I can say. Some enemies of Bill Donovan quietly arranged for the whole mission to be videoed from an experimental high-tech drone."

"What? Are you serious?"

"Oui, it is so. The critical piece was supposed to be the hand-off between you and Bill on the submarine. The video was going to be used as evidence against Bill. They would argue that he had gone rogue, that he was secretly working with an Algerian terrorist to create a false flag incident on American soil. They wanted to hang Bill out to dry, and all of you would have been the collateral damage. You were all exposed, naked to the world. Canada would have treated you like terrorists and probably handed you over to the US Marshals."

"How the hell?" Harry's face was ashen.

"Harry, I found out only days before you launched. I immediately pulled in every favour I had owing to me. Without the prisoner exchange on the sub, there was no evidence of anything illegal, only several days of HD video of some Canadian tourists visiting Saint-Pierre, walking around the city and visiting the museum. So what? So, they have video of Qassem being abducted. It does not matter because it has nothing to do with Bill, so they cannot use it. You now have it all in a nutshell."

Harry sat in stunned silence. Rather than betray Skip, Gaston had saved him. He'd prevented the entire cohort from finding themselves in an American prison, or worse.

Harry's anger visibly evaporated.

"I hope you believe me, Harry."

"Yes, Gaston, I do, but you could have warned Skip off, and scuppered the whole mission before we even launched."

"No, Harry, I could not. By the time I got all the facts, and confirmed what was happening, you were already launched. Some of you were already on the island and the remainder were arriving. No, I could not risk it. I had to let you succeed. Then I had to rob you."

Gaston could see the inner turmoil on Harry's face.

"I was sure that Bill had betrayed Skip," said Harry. "I never fully trusted him."

"Harry, you were correct to suspect Bill, but believe me, he would not harm Skip. Or any of you for that matter. That is important to understand."

"But none of this explains why Skip is in jail. It's quite a leap from suspecting him of arson to charging him with murder and terrorism."

"C'est ça. You are now with me, Harry. Something is not right here. I do not have all the pieces of the puzzle. At least, not yet, but I will find the missing pieces. I promise you this."

Gaston looked Harry in the eye.

"You do not look convinced."

"Gaston, I believe you. I'm just trying to come to grips with the wheels within wheels. That's not my world. It's never been my world."

"Harry, you are troubled because you were almost put into prison by the intelligence agency of a country that is a best friend. At least it is supposed to be."

"I'm sorry, Gaston. I find this all, I don't know… I'm struggling, lost, and, yes, I saw the American intel community as an ally, not someone to be careful of. At least I tried to see them that way. The word I'm looking for … I don't know," he said again.

"Sordid, disappointing, unfathomable?" offered Gaston.

"Yes, all of those. You work with US intelligence every day. Surely, they're our friends, aren't they?"

"Harry, like our friend Amadeo, you look at the situation as an honourable soldier. That is a bond you and he share, but that is not how intelligence agencies work, I am sorry to tell you. Even the agencies of close allies do not always play well together. We are like cousins, the children of sisters. We love our own mothers, and we love our aunts, but our cousins? Not always. They are tolerated, and if we must, we will be nice, especially if there is a reward of some kind. You must never assume, *never* assume, that we love our cousins like we love our aunts. No, it does not work that way."

"But we have fought together," said Harry, shaking his head. "We've bled together on battlefields around the globe, for generations. Twice I've deployed with them to their wars. That must stand for something."

"It does, yes, especially for soldiers like you and Amadeo — and for Bill. He believes in 'Duty, Honor, Country.' Amadeo believes in 'Truth, Duty, Valour.' You believe in your regiment's motto, 'Pro Patria.' To you, to Skip, and to Bill these are more than mottoes."

"They *are* more than mottoes," said Harry.

"Yes, Harry. They are rules for life. You *trust* each other. You have a bond of brotherhood. But that bond does not exist the same way in my world, Harry. Sometimes between individuals, yes, but between agencies? No. Intelligence agency relationships are like real estate. They are not based on trust. You buy, you sell, you trade, and if you must, you steal. The only loyalty is to your own agency. To behave otherwise is unthinkable. Luckily, I have some personal relationships that are exceptions to what I have just told you, and now I must leverage them to help Amadeo."

"I'm not sure I see how," said Harry.

Gaston finished his drink and put the glass on the desk.

"I am not completely sure right now either, but I will figure this out on my way to Saint-Pierre."

Saint-Pierre-et-Miquelon

The French Air Force Dassault Falcon 50 executive jet sat on the apron. Gaston recognized the markings. The plane must belong to Commissaire Breton, he thought. He told his own pilot to remain ready to leave quickly.

"David, I do not expect to be long. A couple of hours at most. File a flight plan for Ottawa and do not leave the plane."

He walked toward the small airport. Inside there was a man in a well-fitting suit. A *caporal de gendarmes* stood beside him. The civilian extended his hand in welcome.

"Welcome, Monsieur Levesque. I am Captain Theodore Moreau from la Police Judiciaire."

The two men shook hands.

"Follow me please, monsieur." The captain guided him through security to a waiting black Citroen sedan. "Did you have a good voyage, monsieur?"

"Oui, merci."

The sedan drove to the headquarters of the island's police force. Gaston produced his identification as well as his special passport. Once through the scanner, he was guided to the office of the company commandant, a Lieutenant-Colonel Girard Bellevue. The lieutenant-colonel stood when Gaston appeared at his door.

"Welcome sir. It is a pleasure to have you on our island, monsieur."

"Merci, Commandant Bellevue. Thank you for your hospitality."

"Merci, monsieur. You allow my using English, I hope. We have more *Américains* to visit with us these days."

"As you prefer, monsieur. You have been informed, no doubt, that I have come to interview a Canadian that you have in custody, a certain Professor Amadeo Schiaparelli. He has friends in high places, Commandant, and I have been sent to see that he is being well treated."

"I can assure you, monsieur, that your countryman is well. Naturally, our cells are not a hotel, you understand. I do not know what else to tell you."

"Has Professor Schiaparelli been questioned?"

"Oui, by Capitaine Moreau. He insists that he knows nothing of the incident at la boulangerie. He is here only to visit our musée. Because he does not speak French, I have only one officer who can question him."

The commandant suddenly looked stricken.

"Forgive my rude behaviour, monsieur. Un café?"

"Thank you, Commandant, no. I am fine. Do not trouble yourself. May I be taken to the professor, please?"

"But of course, monsieur. You realize that, because of the gravity of the charges, you will not be permitted to speak alone with him. One of my officers must be present."

"Of course," said Gaston.

Skip was returned to the interrogation room and told to sit. After a few minutes, the door opened and in walked Gaston, accompanied by Moreau. Skip kept his face emotionless.

"How do you do, Professor Schiaparelli. I am Assistant Deputy Commissioner Levesque. I am here to check on you, sir."

"Your English is commendable, Commissioner."

"Professor Schiaparelli, you misunderstand, I am not French. I am from Ottawa. A friend asked me to come visit you. You appear well, sir."

"A friend? What friend?"

"That is not important. Are you well, Professor?"

"I would be better if I could have legal counsel. Otherwise, I am well. There is some deep misunderstanding, Commissioner Levesque. I am a retired professor of history. I merely wished to visit the island to see its museum, but these people seem to believe I had something to do with a fire somewhere in the city. I assure you that I did not."

"Professor, I am certain that I can clear this up."

"Thank you, Commissioner. I would appreciate it. They have not allowed me to make any calls. Would you please contact my neighbours? They worry about me. I call them every day — when I travel, that is. They are Mr. Harold Royal and Mr. William Amerigo. I'm sorry, but I don't have my phone and cannot give you their numbers from memory. Tell them I am fine, please."

"Of course, Professor. I will see to it."

The door opened, and the police captain came to attention as another man walked in. Skip and the Bishop glanced at each other.

"This visit is finished," announced the intruder.

The Bishop stood.

"Who, may I ask, are you?"

Capitaine Moreau intervened.

"Commissioner, allow me to introduce Commissaire Général Breton de la Police Fédérale de France. He has arrived only this day from Paris. Commissaire Général, this is Deputy Commissioner Levesque, from le Canada."

The two men shook hands.

"Commissaire Général, I shall continue in English for the benefit of the professor," said Gaston.

Breton eyed Gaston and then looked down at Skip, who had remained seated.

"The professor, if that is really who he is, is a known associate of the terrorist Abu Alaintiqam, who is responsible for multiple bombings in Paris," said Breton. "Alaintiqam came to Saint-Pierre on false identity papers as Omar al-Zawawi. Monsieur al-Zawawi's remains have been positively identified using dental records, and the professor is to be taken by me to a secure location in preparation for trial in Paris."

"On whose authority?" Gaston demanded.

"On my own, monsieur. Now, you will please leave. The capitaine will escort you."

"Commissaire Général. I beg your pardon, monsieur. May I have a short word in private, please? Merely two minutes, nothing more, I can assure you."

The two men stepped into the corridor, and Gaston shut the door behind him.

"I find it interesting, Commissaire Général, that the fire happened only a few hours ago and here you are. You seem to have departed Paris before the fire even began, monsieur."

"That is a coincidence and no concern of yours," said Breton.

Gaston stepped close to Breton. He leaned in and whispered icily in perfect French. "Listen to me well, sir. I will discover why you are lying, and when I do, it will not go well for you. This I can promise you."

Gaston stepped back, and, reverting back to English, raised his voice almost to a shout. "Commissaire Général. Thank you for your time, sir." He poked his head back in through the door. "Professor, I will return soon. Please be patient."

Skip looked up but didn't speak. He merely nodded, and Gaston could see the fear growing on his old roommate's face as he turned and left the room.

Back upstairs in the office, Gaston asked the commandant for a ride back to the airport. He explained that he needed to return to Ottawa immediately.

"I hope to be able to return your hospitality should you ever visit Canada," said Gaston, staring coldly at the commandant.

The visibly trembling Lieutenant-Colonel Bellevue could hardly bring himself to reply.

"Merci, monsieur," he squeaked.

Gaston's plane lifted off smartly, and he waited the five minutes to be in Canadian airspace before engaging his secure telephone. He called his office.

"Sir, there was a call for you while you were away," said his assistant. "He did not wish to have his call forwarded. He said his name was monsieur Henri Dornier, and insisted you knew him. Would you like me to send his number by secure text?"

"Yes, please."

The name rang a bell. Dornier? Why did he know Henri Dornier? The number came through and Gaston called it.

"Oui, allo? Dornier."

"Bonjour, monsieur Dornier. Gaston Levesque. Is this line secure?"

"Une instant." Gaston listened for the telltale beeping. "Salut, Gaston. It is a long time since we do not speak, mon ami."

"Forgive me, please, but I have much on my mind. Remind me where we met."

"Of course, I am from the DGSE. Do you recall the incident in Grenoble, almost two years ago? You have Commissaire Général Breton de la Police Fédérale on your mind, Gaston. This is why I call you. You are still in Saint-Pierre?"

The memory came back. Henri from France's foreign intelligence agency.

"Henri, you must forgive me. How could I forget? Are you still trying to impress German women with your *joli petit accent français*?" He heard Dornier chuckle appreciatively. "No, I am not on the island. I am in the air on my way to Halifax, where I will refuel and go on. Why do you ask?"

"Do not leave Halifax. I am, too, in the air. I can be in Halifax in three hours. We must meet and talk, Gaston. It is extremely important for both of us. I have four men with me. Can you arrange rooms for us? I believe we are the solutions to each other's problems, my friend."

"Text me the tail number of your plane and I will make the arrangements. *A bientôt.*"

"*A bientôt.*"

Gaston ended the secure connection, then dialled his subordinate in Halifax and told her to arrange six rooms near the airport. ETA three hours. Next, he called Harry.

"Hello, Gaston. What news do you have? Is Skip okay?"

"Amadeo is well. He is being held in the Saint-Pierre lockup and I am working on his release. Please call Bill and tell him. Most important right now is that you and Bill do nothing until you hear from me. Nothing. Is that clear?"

"Understood," said Harry. "I'll pass the message right away."

Gaston leaned back and closed his eyes. *Henri? How can Henri help?*

Halifax

"Bienvenu, Henri," said Gaston as he greeted the other man at the bottom of the stairs to the aircraft. The two men shook hands.

A car waited nearby, and next to it was a nondescript van with a driver, presumably containing Henri's team.

"All is ready," Gaston said. "Please follow me."

"Salut, Gaston."

"I have made the arrangements," said Gaston, once they were in the car. "We are going directly to a motel."

Henri could see police vehicles with flashing lights at a security gate that was being held open for them across the apron.

The motel was only five minutes away, and they all assembled in the reception area.

"Maybe your men would like to shower?" Gaston suggested. "Rest a little? You and I can discuss our plans in my room next door."

"Bonne idée," said Henri, who directed his men to relax and told them he would see them at breakfast. That done, he turned back to his host.

"Gaston, we have much to talk about."

WASHINGTON

"Colonel Donovan, I've got Colonel Harry on the line for you, sir."

"Put him through, Gunny."

"Yes, sir."

"Good morning, Harry. How are you?"

"Feeling a bit lost, to be honest."

"I know what you mean. I feel like my daddy gave me a big whoopin' but not sure why he done it."

"Sorry, I don't have any corn-pone expressions to share with you, but I get it. I'm calling with news on Skip."

"Good news, I hope."

"I just spoke with a friend of Skip's, an important player up here in our intel community. He and Skip go back to academy days. Anyway, he clarified some stuff. I'd rather not discuss it right now, but the bottom line is Skip's in jail on the island, and he's charged with arson, homicide, and terrorism."

"What the fuck?"

"You heard right. His friend just visited him. I'm hoping he has enough pull to make this all go away. There's no news other than that."

"What can I do? Do you want me to see if I can leverage my contacts in Congress? I have a good friend in the US embassy in Paris."

"Absolutely not. The last thing Skip's friend said was to do absolutely nothing until we hear from him. He emphasized it, Bill. If we do or say anything, we may get in his way."

"You trust this guy, Harry? Can we count on him?"

"Absolutely, Bill. He's a big player and he's Skip's oldest friend."

"Name?"

"Can't say. Sorry."

"It's okay. Any idea where our Algerian friend is?"

"Not really. All I can be sure of is he's in custody, somewhere."

There was a long silence.

"Bill, are you still there?"

"Sorry, Harry. Yes, I'm still here. Now I'm confused *and* lost. You'll call me when there's more news?"

"Promise."

"Roger that."

Halifax

"Henri, you said we were the solutions to each other's problems. I am not sure I see how this is possible. Café?"

The coffeemaker in Gaston's room was beeping to signal it had finished its cycle.

"Gaston, it is a little bit complicated, and maybe dangerous. Commissaire Général Breton is an important man. He is the number four officer in all of the Paris Sûreté. Two years ago, I was moved from DGSE to the Paris office for contra-terrorism, a part of the DGSI. It is a big job, and an important one for me."

Henri paused to pour himself a mug of coffee. He tasted it and made a face.

"My mission is to hunt for terrorists, but each time I come close, I receive interference from the office of Commissaire Breton. I ask myself, why does he interfere? Maybe he has an agenda, but I do not know, so, I dig, and I dig, and what do I find? Le Commissaire Général Breton is not who he says he is."

Gaston stared at him. "What are you saying? How can the commissaire not be who he says he is?"

"I discover that Commissaire Thierry Francois Breton is not Parisian. He is not even French. He was born Hakim bin Sami al Jezayry, in Algeria. He is an orphan of the civil wars."

Henri attempted another sip of his coffee.

"Wait," replied Gaston, "are you saying that the number four police officer in Paris is somehow related to Qassem? That cannot be, Henri."

"*Absolument*, Gaston. It is true. The *Plénipotentiaire du gouvernement français* in Morocco and his wife had no children, so they adopted a boy and changed his name. After his duty in Morocco, the Plénipotentiaire returns to Paris. He is from an important family, and the new son is sent to the best schools and is raised among la crème de la crème in society. After young Breton graduates from l'École Polytechnique, he joins the federal police."

"There is obviously more to the story," said Gaston.

"Of course. Breton is the cousin of Qassem, but even more, I believe he is also his handler."

"This is madness," said Gaston.

"Oui, I agree, but I have proof. I swear it."

The two men sat in silence for several minutes. Gaston poured fresh coffee into his own mug.

"Henri," he said at last, "I think I see how we can do this. Listen ..."

SAINT-PIERRE-ET-MIQUELON

Skip was shocked awake by a bucket of cold water. The bare concrete had been cold enough, and the water didn't make things better. He began to shiver uncontrollably.

"Hello, Professor. You are rested?" said Breton.

A sudden violent kick to the abdomen followed. Skip vomited involuntarily.

"Poor Professor. You are more accustomed to the faculty lounge, perhaps?"

"What the fuck is your problem?" said Skip, wiping vomit from his face.

That remark elicited another vicious kick, this time to his ribs.

"You have poor manners, monsieur. I know that you are somehow involved with Qassem, but I am not certain of the details. However, I am sure you will tell me. We have time, Professor. We have plenty of time."

Skip forced his aching body up into a sitting position. His head was on fire and every muscle screamed. Breton bent over to him as if to speak, but a powerful backhand slap sent Skip sprawling against the wall of his confinement space. Skip's body went limp, and blood began to pool on the concrete under his face.

The phone on Commandant Bellevue's desk buzzed. He punched the speaker button.

"Oui? Who can be calling so early?"

"Excuse me, Commandant. I have Commissionnaire Levesque on the line."

"Bonjour, monsieur le Commandant."

"Hello, Commissioner."

Girard trembled slightly as he felt a chill go up his spine. This man was dangerous, and he needed to be careful. "How may I help you, Commissioner?"

"I must speak urgently to Commissaire Général Breton, s'il vous plaît."

"*Certainement*, Commissioner. Only, the commissaire général is not in the headquarters at this moment. He has taken Professeur Schiaparelli to a secure location for his own protection."

"You must have some way to contact Breton, no?"

"Of course, Commissioner. One moment, please."

Bellevue recited a private cell number to Gaston.

"Oui, allo?"

"Commissaire Général Breton, it is Gaston Levesque. Bonjour, monsieur."

"How did you get this number?"

"Commandant Bellevue was most accommodating. In any case, I now have proof of your lies. We need to meet, and it needs to be soon, very soon."

"You are an idiot," said Breton.

"Perhaps," said Gaston. "But I am also the idiot who has Qassem in my custody."

Gaston allowed the silence to linger between them.

"Why should I believe you?" said Breton. "Qassem is dead."

"Dead? Shall I send you proof of life? A finger, or an ear, perhaps? I think the easy solution would be to tell you where he has his scars, or that particular birthmark? One moment — I am sending you a text."

Breton's phone pinged. It was a text from a blocked number. When he opened it there was a thirty-second video of a man looking defiantly into the camera and struggling with his manacles. The right side of his face was badly bruised. There was a time stamp on the video displaying this morning. Breton put the phone to his ear.

"Fine, I believe you. What do you want?"

"Not much, only the professor. You know he is an innocent, and I need him returned immediately. That is all I ask."

"An innocent? Do you think I am a fool, Levesque?"

"It does not matter what I think. As I told you, all I want is the professor."

"Why this deep interest in him? What is so special about this history professor?"

"Enough!" snapped Gaston.

The abrupt change of tone caught Breton off guard. Best to let it go for now, he thought. There would be time enough later to discover the connections.

"Agreed," said Breton. "When and where shall we make the exchange?"

It was a few minutes past midnight as the French Air Force Dassault Falcon 50 executive jet touched down in the darkness. The military pilot had landed unannounced and without the aid of lights. He taxied to the end of the runway and throttled back the engines to idle while five men quickly descended and melted onto the airfield. The plane's engine quickly came back to full throttle as the jet turned and raced down the runway. The pilot lifted off to the sound of an air traffic controller shouting in his headset. Darkness ruled the airfield once more.

Twenty minutes later, the controller was re-awakened by a call.

"Saint-Pierre tower, this is French Air Force 573 requesting permission for an immediate landing."

The French military aircraft was unscheduled, and the plane's transponder was not emitting a signal.

"French Air Force 573, this is Saint-Pierre tower. Do you have an in-flight emergency?"

"Tower, French Air Force 573. No, but I have a high-level diplomat on board. For security reasons, he needs privacy. Please check your incoming traffic notices."

There was a momentary pause.

"French Air Force 573, tower. I confirm special arrangements by DGSI. Permission granted to land and to taxi to the end of the runway. I will turn on runway lights."

The engines slowed to idle but did not shut down. Gaston opened the door to his aircraft and scanned the airfield. He saw nothing. He turned and looked at the small control tower and hoped that at this distance the controller would mistake his plane for the French military jet.

He lifted his shirt cuff to check his watch and saw that he was almost ten minutes early. Something caught his eye. There were headlights on the airfield and a vehicle was driving toward the plane. Gaston lowered the stairs and carefully positioned his charge at the top of them. He adjusted the detainee's hood and placed the handcuffed hands where they were clearly visible. The awkwardly slumped body was now side-lit by the plane's interior. Gaston descended to the tarmac and walked away from the plane.

"Stop!" shouted Gaston as he raised his arms, waving at the approaching black sedan. "That is close enough," he called.

The car's headlights illuminated him, and from behind the wheel, Breton could now clearly see the shoulder holster under Gaston's left arm. He brought the car to a stop and exited with his hands raised.

"I want no trouble, Levesque. I have your professor in the back. Where is my prisoner?"

"Your cousin is sitting drugged at the top of the stairs. Do you see him?"

"My cousin? Are you mad?" Breton began to gesticulate wildly. "Have you forgotten who I am?"

As he shouted and made exaggerated motions, a pistol appeared in his hand. Before Gaston could react, a shot rang out and Breton fell onto his back. Gaston trotted the short distance to the fallen man. Breton was still breathing, and blood flowed freely from his right shoulder. Gaston relieved him of the pistol and stepped over him. He then moved quickly to the car and saw Amadeo lying on the back seat, handcuffed, badly bruised, and apparently unconscious. Gaston reached in and tried to move him, and Skip screamed.

"No, no! Don't touch me, please."

"Amadeo, I am sorry. We will get you out. One moment, my brother." He watched with relief as recognition dawned in Skip's eyes.

Gaston returned to the wounded commissaire and bent over him. Breton was muttering.

"*Aidez-moi, je suis blessé.* Help me, I am wounded," he groaned, and he began to whimper loudly.

"Yes, Breton. I can see that you are wounded," said Gaston. "There are some men here who will assist you in a moment."

Gaston nudged the stricken man's shoulder with his foot, and Breton screamed in agony.

"I see you spent some time interrogating the professor. Maybe I should interrogate you?"

Breton was now whimpering as the pool of blood expanded under his shoulder.

"That was lucky, no?" said a voice close by. "I did not expect the fool to have a pistol."

Gaston looked up to see Henri nearing him.

"Neither did I," said Gaston. "Thank you. That was quite a shot."

"Me? *Mais non*, not me. That was Erich. I did not bring these men because they are good company. I bring them because they have skills."

Henri leaned over Breton.

"*Tu es un traître de merde.* Do you hear me, Breton? You are a piece of shit, and a traitor to France." Henri spat in Breton's face and signalled for two of his men to go to the sedan. "These men are *paramédicals*. They will look at your friend."

"Careful," said Gaston. "His condition is grave, and I am sure he has broken bones."

Henri nodded and shouted to his men to take extra care with Skip.

"Merci," said Gaston. "Can they place him on the plane, please?"

"Of course," said Henri. The two men with Skip called for a third to ease him out of the sedan and onto the plane. Gaston saw one of the men pull out a syringe.

"Stop!" he shouted. "What are you doing?"

The man called back to Henri and said something unintelligible.

"It is alright, mon ami. He is giving your friend a sedative so he will not suffer too much when he is moved."

Gaston frowned but nodded his approval, and the medic administered the dose.

In the distance, there was the sound of a jet engine. Henri and Gaston turned and saw a plane descend to the runway and approach.

"My ride," said Henri.

"What will happen to Breton? How will you explain shooting him?"

"Explain? It will not be difficult, Gaston."

Henri motioned to Erich, who had been standing to one side. The sniper dropped to one knee, pulled an étui from his trouser pocket, and removed a syringe from it. Deftly, he found Breton's left carotid artery and injected him in the neck. In seconds the commissaire was quiet and lifeless. Gaston looked at Henri in shock.

"What have you done?"

"*Chlorure de potassium*. By the time we are in Paris it will be gone from his system, untraceable."

Gaston was suddenly disoriented. He stood staring blankly at Henri.

"You murdered him," said Gaston, "in cold blood."

"Gaston, you know my world. This *espèce de merde* was a traitor. He killed many dozens of innocents. He is from a wealthy family, and money buys judges, even in France. This is his justice. His family will be allowed to bury him as a hero who died on duty. I will explain the wound …"

Gaston stood speechless.

"You should take your friend home, mon vieux," said Henri. "I hope he is okay. Do not worry about your friend's associates. I will make the arrangements as we discussed."

With that, Henri and his squad dragged the commissaire's lifeless body to their waiting aircraft. Two men quickly returned to search Breton's vehicle.

Gaston returned to his own plane. At the top of the stairs, he picked up the hooded mannequin and tossed it back into the aircraft.

"We must go, David."

He pulled up the stairs as the plane began to power up and went aft to check on his friend. The paramedics had made a makeshift bed room blankets, and Skip was nestled among some pillows. He had a temporary splint on his right arm and another on his right leg. Even in the dimmed light of the cabin, Gaston could see extensive bruising and swelling on Amadeo's face.

"Salut, Gaston," Skip slurred weakly.

"Amadeo, how are you, my brother?"

"Don't know what those guys gave me, but I feel pretty numb. Where are we?"

"Relax, Amadeo. We will be home soon."

Gaston touched his friend's leg gently. He steadied himself on an armrest as the plane began lifting off.

"I will return in a moment."

Gaston slipped into the co-pilot's seat and put on the headphones. He could hear the air traffic controller shrieking that permission had not been given to depart. David smiled at him.

"Bad connection. Must be a weather anomaly. Sir, I don't have enough fuel remaining for Halifax. St. John's is half the distance, so we will have to land there."

"Fine. Request an ambulance at the apron. Use our special priority code. Colonel Schiaparelli needs to get to a proper hospital quickly."

"Yes, sir."

Gaston went aft to check on Amadeo and found him in a deep sleep. His breathing was even. Gaston checked his pulse. It was strong and regular. Must be all that scotch, thought Gaston. He went to the desk with the secure comms and put on a headset. "Are we back in Canadian airspace, David?"

"Yes, sir. We entered shortly after takeoff. St. John's International acknowledged our special clearance request. An ambulance will meet us at the ramp. ETA forty-two minutes."

"Thank you, David."

Gaston dialled a Washington number.

"Hello?"

"Good morning, Colonel Donovan. We have not met. My name is Gaston, and I am a friend of Amadeo."

"What time is it?"

"Forgive me, I know it is early. I am in the air with Amadeo, and I thought you would like to know."

"May I speak to him?"

"I am afraid not. He is in bad shape and heavily sedated. I am less than one hour from hospital, but most important, he is now safe and under my protection."

"Thank you, Gaston. I appreciate your call. What can I do?"

"For the moment, nothing. I will be in touch soon. There are issues we need to discuss."

"Really?"

"Indeed yes," said Gaston. "Again, I am sorry to wake you."

The ringing phone woke him.

"Aye, hello."

"Bonjour, who is this?"

"Who wants to know?"

"This is the Bishop."

"Sir, excuse me. This is Pappy. I didn't recognize the voice. Only Colonel Skip and Harry have this number. How may I help you, sir? Is there news about the Colonel? Do you need me to go shake Harry?"

"No, let him sleep. Tell Harry I have Amadeo, and that I am en route to St. John's Hospital in Newfoundland. He will need treatment, but he is now safe. All is well. All is finally well."

All at once, Gaston could feel the emotional strain taking its toll on him and ended the call.

Pappy hung up the phone and went immediately to Harry's room, knocked, and entered.

"Harry, wake up."

Harry was instantly awake.

"The Bishop just called, and he has Colonel Skip. He's taking him to a hospital in St. John's, Newfoundland. He told me not to wake you and said all was okay now."

"Wake the O Group and put on coffee," Harry said, sitting up and swinging his legs over the edge of the bed. "Get Jamie to ready one of the SUVs and tell Franz-Josef to get his ass to a computer and look at direct flights from Montreal to St. John's. Cost is irrelevant."

Harry was on his feet and dressing.

"What the hell are you waiting for, Colour Sergeant? Move!"

RECOVERY AND RETRIBUTION

MAY 2013 – JULY 2013

St. John's General Hospital

At St. John's, Skip was taken directly into the ER. CAT scans showed a broken arm, a broken leg, and three badly broken ribs. He had a mild concussion and a hairline fracture of the left cheekbone. Concerns about a cranial hemorrhage and internal bleeding proved ill-founded, though both his kidneys were bruised. His arm and leg were set properly, and he was medicated and placed on an IV drip.

"Where are we taking him, Doctor?" asked the orderly, who had just pulled him out of the emergency operating room.

"Take him up to the secure ward on four. There's an RCMP officer already there."

The two orderlies stepped out of the elevator to find a uniformed RCMP outside the destination room. Later that day, the corporal was relieved by another uniformed officer, who was accompanied by two men in civilian clothes.

"Who are they, Rick?" asked the new RCMP corporal.

"You're not going to believe me," replied his fellow officer, "but one is an RCAF chief warrant officer, and the second guy is a cranky master sergeant from the German Army. They have clearance to be here."

"So, who's the guy in this room?"

"Beats me," said Rick as he grabbed his cap in preparation to depart.

🍁 🍁 🍁

Skip awoke almost twenty hours after being admitted. He could hear voices talking over him.

"He's awake, Doctor."

"Thanks, Fionna. Colonel Schiaparelli, can you hear me? Colonel?"

"Yes, I can hear you. You're a bit blurry, though."

"I'm Doctor Tobin. I'm chief of surgery here. You're a fortunate man, Colonel. Everything looks good, relatively speaking. We should be able to move you to Montreal in a few days. By the way, lay off the booze. Your liver is begging for mercy."

"Booze, check. Not feeling quite so fortunate, to be honest. Where am I?"

Tobin explained how he'd arrived and what had been done to him. "By the way, whoever worked on your pelvis was very good. That's a beautiful job."

"Thanks," said Skip. "Nice to know."

"I'm sure you're feeling a bit groggy, but there shouldn't be any pain. I've seen to that. You have some interesting friends, Colonel. It's not often the provincial minister of health wakes me in the middle of the night and tells me to get my butt in to work."

The doctor made a grunting sound.

"Just an old soldier down on his luck," offered Skip. "Nobody special, and no, no pain, thank you."

"Nothing special? Then why are there two intimidating-looking men keeping an RCMP officer company outside your door?" Skip said nothing. "Want to know the scary part? The cop is the least threatening of the bunch — and he's the one who's armed. By the way, who's Lopez? You were muttering his name as you woke. Anyone I should contact?"

"No," said Skip. "A boyhood friend of mine, that's all."

The door opened, and Harry walked in.

"I'll give you gentlemen some privacy," said the doctor.

Skip looked up at his friend. "You look like hell," he said.

"I've had a rough week," said Harry. "Not like some people who just lie in bed all day."

"Listen, did anybody get the plate number of the truck that ran me over?"

"Skip, you haven't looked this rough since I dragged you through the Brigade Ironman Challenge when we were captains in Petawawa."

"Wait a minute, smartass. I dragged *you*."

"I always get that wrong," said Harry. "How's the pain?"

"I feel surprisingly well. Either it's because of strong drugs, or I'm not as broken as I look."

"Drugs," said Harry. "The doc says you need to stabilize, but he wants you out. He's worried about his nurses. You have a reputation, buddy."

Skip began to laugh, but the sudden pain stopped him short.

"Sorry, Skip. I forgot about your ribs. Apologies."

There was a rap at the door, and Gaston stepped in. "Hello, Harry. How is our boy?"

"Being his usual annoying self," said Harry. "I would suggest we exile him, but without a passport, he's stuck here."

"I have already taken care of that. It is on its way by diplomatic pouch. So yes, we can ship him out."

"Hey, you two, I'm right here."

"Harry, may I have a moment with my old roommate?" asked Gaston. "I need to get his credit card number to pay the hospital."

"I'll go down to the administrative office to review the sexual harassment complaints from the nurses," Harry said, and left the room.

Gaston took the visitor's chair next to the bed and looked at Skip appraisingly. "It is a relief to see you so animated, mon vieux. I am sorry that I was not here when you woke up. I had pressing matters. In fact, I have business in Ottawa later today, but I will return to fly you home to Montreal when you are well enough."

"Gaston. That's not necessary."

"I know. That is why I do it."

"Gaston, we need to talk about this. About what happened here."

Gaston was quiet for a moment. "What are you asking me?"

"I was starting to put together what went wrong. Then that sadist from Paris grabbed me. I honestly don't remember much after that. Drugs? Brain trauma? I'm not sure. You need to explain what happened. Who burned down the boulangerie? None of it makes any sense."

Gaston could see that his friend was becoming swamped by confused thoughts. *How much to tell him?*

"Skip, it is quite complicated, and I have explained most of it to Harry. When you are better, he will share it with you. For now, you must rest — and stay away from the nurses, mon cher."

"Gaston, I haven't thanked you for saving my life. I owe you a debt I can't repay."

"Non, Amadeo. It is I who owe you."

"Owe me? No, you don't owe me anything, Gaston."

"You are wrong, mon ami. I would never have survived Rook Year without you as my roommate — never. Going home to see my RSM father in disgrace would have destroyed me. It is as simple as that. I will always owe you for that, always. I do not think you know how deep my debt is to you." Gaston was beginning to choke up. He stood and cleared his throat. "Anyway, as I said, I must go, but I will return."

"Wait," blurted Skip.

"Oui, mon frère?"

"I have …" He stopped. "Sorry."

Gaston could see the effects of the sedative in Skip's IV drip sending him back to sleep.

"Gaston. Do you have Lopez in custody?"

"Lopez? You mean Qassem."

"Sorry, but they're connected, aren't they? I suspected, but I can't …"

Skip was fading out. Gaston reached over and stopped the IV drip. He waited a few moments for Skip to open his eyes.

"Amadeo, are you alright?"

"The pain is coming back."

"I apologize, mon frère, but I must be sure of something."

"Did you just break my leg again?"

"Amadeo, I will turn on the drugs again in a moment. I promise. First, you must tell me who you have shared your suspicions with."

"Suspicions? What suspicions?"

"You suspect a connection between Lopez and Qassem?"

"Are you sure you didn't break my damn leg again? Yes, I have suspected for some time, but I can't say why. Software sub-routines, the lack of a passport, setting the fire … Ow, ow, turn on the damn drugs!"

"Yes, in just one second. Who did you share your suspicions with? Harry? Bill? Anybody?"

"No, nobody. Ow, ow, that hurts. No, Gaston, nobody. I swear it."

Gaston turned on the IV drip and punched the dose up two notches. Skip groaned and sighed as relief came, and then quickly slipped away into unconsciousness. Gaston lowered the dose again to pre-questioning levels.

WASHINGTON

"Eagle Investments. How may I direct your call?"

"Hello, Gunny. It is Gaston Levesque."

"Hello, sir. Would you like to speak to Colonel Donovan?"

"Yes, please."

"One moment, sir."

"Colonel Donovan, I've got Mr. Levesque on the line for you, sir."

"Put him through, Gunny."

Bill heard the handset go into the cradle and picked up his own phone.

"Good morning, Gaston. How is everything? Harry brought me up to speed on Skip, but I haven't called him yet. I figure he needs rest more than talk."

"You are correct."

"How can I help you, Gaston?"

"When I called you last week, I told you I would explain. I would like to do it face to face. Obviously, there are leaks in my system. What I have is too sensitive."

"You have my attention. Do you want me you come up there?"

"No. If there are leaks, they will be here in Ottawa."

"Where, then?"

"How easy is it for you to get to northern New York?"

"Easy. The commander at Fort Drum is a classmate. You want to meet me there?"

"No, I will send RV coordinates to Gunny by secure means. We've been on this open line too long."

Before Bill could answer, the line was dead. He now knew that whatever it was that had Gaston's back up was serious. He punched a button on the phone.

"Gunny, can you step in here, please?"

"What's up, Colonel?"

"Levesque will send you a secure message in a few minutes. Don't write it down. I want no record. Tell only me what the message is."

"Aye, sir."

Blackpool

Two days after Bill and Gaston spoke on the phone, a nondescript black sedan with US government plates approached the parking lot of the Café Voyages, just north of the Canada Border Services Agency station at the Quebec–Vermont border. The sedan pulled up to the front door, and Bill got out and entered the café. The car then crossed back over the border.

One hundred metres away, Gaston put his own car in gear. "Time to go," he said to no one.

Thirty seconds later, he pulled into the café parking lot. Stepping inside, he saw Bill seated at a booth in the furthest corner from the door. A tired-looking older waitress was pouring coffee.

"Another, please, madame," said Gaston as he walked past her.

The startled waitress looked up. She grabbed a mug from the stack next to the condiments and poured another cup, then shuffled to the table where Gaston had joined Bill and the two men now sat in silence.

"Two poutines and two slices of cherry pie, please," said Gaston.

"Oui, monsieur."

The waitress deposited the mugs, then lumbered away.

Gaston reached across to shake Bill's hand, then took a tentative sip of the coffee. He looked back at Bill, who continued to sit silently.

"Sorry about all this cloak-and-dagger," said Gaston. "There are too many coincidences lately, and I do not like coincidences. Did you have any trouble getting here?"

Bill took a cautious sip of his own black coffee and, shaking his head, said, "Geez, pass me about twelve of those little creamers. No trouble, no."

"Bill, I will put my cards on the table. Amadeo trusts you and feels he owes you. That means I must trust you, but I will be blunt. That feeling is not shared among everyone. However, we are loyal to Amadeo, and Amadeo is loyal to you."

Bill stared at Gaston, then into the cream that he was swirling into his coffee, as if he might find some insight there.

"So long as there's trust between Skip and me," said Bill quietly.

The waitress returned to the table and deposited four plates heavily between them.

"Would you like more coffee, messieurs?"

The two men shook their heads no, and she went back to her station behind the counter.

"Why are we here?" asked Bill, smiling weakly. "If I didn't know better, I'd be worried that this was a mob hit."

"Bill, initially I had you in my sights as the one who betrayed Amadeo. I was wrong, and I am sorry for that."

Bill didn't reply.

"Now it gets complicated," said Gaston, inspecting his two plates and sampling his poutine. "I need to explain in detail why your handover on the USS *Thunder* went sideways, but I am certain you will not like what you hear, Bill."

Gaston took a second forkful of poutine.

"I have not yet told Amadeo because he does not need more shocks for the moment, but I told Harry everything. Here is the bottom line, as you say. I intervened. I was the one who sabotaged the prisoner transfer."

"I beg your pardon?" whispered Bill, incredulous.

"I did it to save Amadeo because people in your organization put a price on your head. You were the target, Bill. Amadeo was only collateral damage."

Bill looked shattered. Wordlessly, he made to pick up his coffee, but changed his mind. Then he picked up a fork and played with the poutine.

"I'm not sure how to respond. Do you have details?"

"Yes, Bill. I will lay it out for you." Gaston did not like the look on Bill's face and thought he should lighten the moment. "First, you need to taste this poutine. It only works as a heart attack trigger if it is eaten warm.

You eat and I will talk."

Bill took a few exploratory bites of the hot, gooey fries soaked in gravy and melted cheese curds.

"What did you call this?" said Bill, making eating noises. "This is delicious."

"Poutine," said Gaston. "Should I go on explaining how you almost ended up in Leavenworth?"

"I'm sorry, Gaston. Please continue."

"I have friends in your intel community, and, by chance, one of them learned about Senator Fredericks' vendetta mission —"

"Vendetta? What vendetta?" Bill set down his fork.

"Bill, the Senator has a senior officer from US Air Force Intelligence in his pocket. Through him, he discovered that you were about to use a USN submarine for an unauthorized task. Fredericks arranged for the whole mission to be videoed from an experimental high-tech drone, from start to finish."

"What? A drone? Are you serious?"

"Like I said to Harry, every step, every minute."

"Andy Anderson," murmured Bill to himself.

"Pardon?" said Gaston.

"Nothing. Sorry to interrupt." He picked up his fork again and speared another fry.

"The key to the entrapment was the hand-off between you and Harry on the submarine. The video was to be evidence against you and proof that you had gone rogue, that you were secretly working with Algerian terrorists. Bill, *you* were the target."

Gaston paused to gather his thoughts, but he could clearly see that Bill was reeling, struggling to assimilate the news.

"Why not warn Skip?" said Bill.

"It was too late," said Gaston. "I found out only days before mission launch."

"That son of a bitch." Bill stopped sopping up gravy with the last of the fries and took a forkful of the pie. "Does this friend of yours who warned you have a name?"

"No," said Gaston.

Bill was simultaneously relieved and furious. Relieved to understand that his trust of and friendship with Skip had bought him a last-minute stay of execution, even if it was accidental, and furious at the duplicity. The utter venality of Robert E. Lee Fredericks was breathtaking. Bill's mind was filling with dark thoughts.

"Bill, are you still with me?"

"Sorry, Gaston. My mind sort of wandered into a couple of dark corners. I'm not sure what to say right now, except that this is tasty pie," said Bill, looking a little like a lost child.

"I am pleased you have enjoyed your food," said Gaston. "Bill, you must be careful. You are still in some danger. I do not think this matter is over for you. I cannot share my thoughts with you, but I suspect other forces may be at work here."

Bill stared blankly at the large French-Canadian opposite him for a moment.

"Probably right," said Bill. "I appreciate this, Gaston, and I owe you in a big way. Have you shared your suspicions with anyone else?"

"No. No one needs to know what I think, at least not for the moment."

Bill rose without warning, startling Gaston. "Sorry to dine and dash, but I have a lot to think about. I also have some housecleaning to do, something I probably should have done sooner."

"Nothing drastic, I hope," said Gaston, still startled at Bill's sudden change of demeanour.

"Not sure," said Bill. "That depends on how you define drastic. Ask me no questions and —"

Gaston raised his hand. "I know how it ends."

Bill pulled out his phone. "Come get me."

He stuffed the phone back into his jeans and reached for his West Point baseball cap, then he dug into another pocket and pulled out some bills. Gaston stopped him.

"This heart attack is on me," he said.

"Thanks, Gaston. For the bad coffee and the artery cement. If it kills me, promise you'll visit me in Arlington."

With that, Bill turned and walked to the door. On cue, the waitress appeared with the check. Gaston put an overly large American bill on top of it and told the delighted waitress to keep the change.

WASHINGTON

Gunny walked into the office at the usual hour to find his boss already sitting at his desk.

"Morning, Colonel. Is everything okay? You're in extra early this morning, sir."

"Yes, Gunny," said Bill. "I'm fine. I just have some business to take care of today, so I thought I'd beat the traffic into the city."

"Can I get you a coffee sir, or a donut maybe?"

"Thanks. I've already had one of each, but there's still some coffee in the pot for you."

"Are you sure you're okay, Colonel? Anything at all I can do for you?"

"I'm fine, Gunny. Please call for a driver. I need to go see the boss."

"Maybe a walk to the Hill would help, sir."

"Not that boss, Gunny. The real boss."

"Yes, sir." Gunny walked to his desk and picked up the phone.

"What's up, Gunny?" said the voice on the other end. "Does the colonel need a driver?"

"Yes, Chief. Right away."

"Where to?"

"NSA HQ." Gunny put down the receiver. "It's on its way, sir," he told Bill.

"Thanks, Gunny. I'll wait outside."

A few minutes later, the car pulled up to the curb and a uniformed lance corporal jumped out. She opened the door and saluted.

"Good morning, Colonel Donovan."

"Morning, Marine," said Bill, getting into the back of the sedan. "Did the chief tell you where I'm headed?"

"Aye, sir. He said to take you to NSA HQ up at Fort Meade. Do you have a route preference, sir?"

"Take the US 295, please. It's probably the quickest at this hour."

"Aye, aye, sir."

The drive took almost an hour. Choosing to come in off the Patuxent Freeway, the lance corporal avoided the army base and dropped Bill at NSA HQ main security.

"Colonel, I'm going over to the army side to get fuel. I'll be waiting for your call in the VIP parking section, sir."

"Thanks," said Bill absently as he walked away.

He was already focusing on the upcoming office call with General Paul Wilson, Commander of US Cyber Command and Director of the NSA. He'd known Wilson a long time, but they had never served together, and they were not close, although the general had always treated Bill with respect. The one thing they shared in common was their dislike of Senator Fredericks.

Once inside, he placed his phone in the Faraday cage lockup and proceeded through the various security checks and detectors. He then took the elevator to the command suite.

"Good morning, Colonel Donovan. I haven't seen you here in donkey's years."

"Hey, Command Sergeant Major, I heard you got fired. Bad intel, I guess."

"I didn't see your name on the commander's daily agenda."

Bill cleared his throat. "No, Top, I was summoned rather abruptly."

"It's been nice knowin' ya, sir. Maybe you shoulda stayed in the infantry." The Sergeant Major smiled broadly and offered his hand. "You're in luck. I just passed the general's office, and I didn't see no plastic on the floor in front of his desk."

He chuckled at his own joke and walked down the corridor.

"Colonel Donovan is here, General."

"Send him in."

Bill entered the office as Wilson came around his desk to greet him.

"Welcome, Bill. It's been a while since we met face to face. Please sit."

Taking his seat, Bill made a crack about the lack of plastic sheeting on the rug and the general guffawed softly.

"No Bill, no executions today. You're not in any kind of hot water. I just needed to assure myself of several things that I've been concerned about."

"Yes, sir. How can I help you?"

"First, how are you and that prick of a senator getting along? That man is a giant pain in my ass, but I guess you know that already."

"Well, General, I think the Senator is going to cease to be a problem very soon."

"Anything I should know?"

"My sources indicate that the Senator is contemplating retirement."

"Really? That's not what I heard."

"I could be wrong, sir. But I doubt it."

"I'll let that drop. The real reason for my call is I wanted assurances regarding this Algerian terrorist incident. I've been briefed, and I know he's in Canadian custody for now. Gaston Levesque called me."

The general paused and stared at Bill without speaking. "I'm not entirely sure of why Qassem ended up with CSIS," he said after a moment. "I thought you were going to take possession somewhere off the coast of Newfoundland."

"Yes, sir. That was the plan. I can fill in any gaps you may have if you like, sir."

"No need. I've known Levesque for years and he assured me that all was well. My pressing concern is whether the Canadians have any inkling of the connection between grabbing Qassem and that operation in Brazil. Gaston didn't hint at it, but that doesn't mean he doesn't suspect there's more."

"I'm not entirely sure, sir. I had a meeting with Mr. Levesque yesterday. We had a long discussion, and he didn't mention that issue, but I know he has suspicions of some kind. General, I have kept that connection very close hold. No one on my team has any knowledge of it, and I didn't share any of it with Colonel Schiaparelli. I am the only person at Eagle who knows. Other than you, I have no idea who in the wider community knows. So, General, the answer to your question is no."

"We need to monitor that closely, Bill."

"Yes, sir. I will."

Bill could see the general relaxing a bit.

"Bill, I don't tell you often enough, but you're doing great work."

"Thank you, General."

Wilson stood. It was Bill's cue to leave.

"Thank you, Bill."

Back in the lobby, Bill retrieved his phone from the lockup and saw the driver waiting outside. As he stepped out, he called his office.

"Gunny, I'm on my way back. Anything important while I was away?"

"No, Colonel. All quiet, sir."

He climbed into the car and the driver closed the door behind him. "Back to the office, Lance Corporal," he told her when she had resumed her seat behind the wheel.

"Aye, aye, sir."

Gunny stood as Bill came through the door.

"Everything okay, sir?"

"Yes, Gunny. Thanks. I'll be in my office, and please hold all calls."

Bill composed himself, then hit the speed dial.

"Hello, Miss Loretta. It's Bill Donovan. How are you this fine day, ma'am?"

"Well, good mornin' to you, Colonel Donovan. I am very well, thank you, sir," said the Senator's secretary, sounding like she'd come off the set of *Gone with the Wind.* "The Senator is in a meeting with some members of his committee, I am afraid."

"I understand. Thank you, ma'am. Please look at the Senator's calendar. I'd like to know if he is available to join me for a drink this evening." Donovan was positively purring.

"Well, yes, he is, Colonel Donovan. But the Senator normally does not allow me to book his evenings without checking with him first. May I get back to you in an hour or so?"

"No, Miss Loretta. You may not," said Bill, whose voice had turned instantly cold and acerbic. He had never spoken to the woman in this caustic tone. "You tell your Senator that I will be waiting for him *tonight* at the bar in the Louisiana Steak House at eight o'clock. He knows the place well. Tell him to come alone and not to be late. Am I being clear?"

"Yes, Colonel. I will pass along to the Senator that he needs to meet you *tonight*."

The line went dead, and for reasons she could not explain, Loretta began to tremble uncontrollably.

Bill sat at a secluded table in the dimly lit bar and let the cold fury he felt fill him. The trip from Quebec back to DC had been like a nightmare. His mind had been filled with dark thoughts and images. He had coolly gone through options before retiring to bed for a restless sleep and had spent the next morning deciding how he would deal with Fredericks. He had chosen the simplest solution — and the most devastating.

He saw the waiter weaving his way through the crowded bar with Fredericks in tow. The Senator had a look of suppressed anger on his face.

"Gentlemen, may I bring you a drink?"

"Two Maker's with water and ice on the side," said Bill. "Bring some snacks please. Whatever is handy."

As he was ordering, he rose to greet his guest, extending his hand. The Senator ignored both him and the waiter and dropped his considerable bulk onto the chair that had been pulled back. Bill thought he more properly resembled a surly, overweight teenager, summoned to his father's den, than a senior US senator. The instant they were alone, the Senator was raging at Bill.

"I don't know what you are playing at, Donovan, but this time you have gone too far. Miss Loretta was in tears. She told me that you frightened her. So, here I am. What the hell is your problem?"

"It surely is unfortunate that Miss Loretta was upset. However, I suspect that had she not been, you wouldn't be here. I'm sure she'll be fine. She can recover during her well-earned retirement, after you announce your departure from politics tomorrow, due to personal reasons."

Bill let the words settle on his companion. He watched with pleasure while the blood rose in the Senator's face.

"You are out of your bloody mind," barked Fredericks. "I am not going anywhere. I am running for re-election this year, and you are in one heap o' shit, boy."

"Listen to me, you pervert," snarled Bill, who was now leaning forward across the table, his whispered voice dripping with venom. "First off. I am *not* your boy. You can save all of that homespun bullshit for your constituents down at the church picnics, you fat fuck."

Fredericks was shaken by the sudden vulgarity, and his eyes grew wide as Bill continued his assault.

"I warned you the last time we spoke, but obviously you thought it was a bluff. I reminded you that I keep my promises. Did you really believe that sabotaging one of my ops was going to be that easy? If you did, then you are even dumber than I thought you were. This is the major leagues, Senator. We play for keeps here."

The waiter appeared and deposited the drinks and the snacks. Bill was instantly all smiles.

"Thank you. That's all for now. I'll call you if I need you."

The young man bowed slightly and departed.

"No," said Fredericks, "you listen to me, you foul-mouthed son of a bitch. I am a senior US senator, and you are way outta line. How do you think it made me look to find out you were running an operation off the books with the help of your Canadian friends? I had to work fast to change the story. I was —"

The Senator didn't get to finish his sentence.

"Shut the hell up."

Bill was leaning in and whispering again, and he was beginning to build a head of steam. He could discern bits of his own spittle hitting the Senator's chin, and the look on the old man's face told Bill that Fredericks finally understood that he was headed for a terminal encounter. Excellent, thought Bill.

"You will resign," he said evenly, "and you will do it *tomorrow*. If you don't, then I will release all the material I have. The only thing that will save your family from complete and utter humiliation is if you all enter the witness protection program."

Bill's voice trailed off. He wiped his lips with his napkin and took a sip of his Maker's Mark.

"What if I call your bluff? What if I take you down with me?"

"Excellent idea," said Bill. "Bring it on. Let's play Russian roulette, old man. I have nothing to lose compared to you. Not to mention that there are a lot of people in my world who would not be upset if you vanished without a trace. I wonder if the director of the NSA would be willing to sacrifice his career on the altar of your ambition?"

Bill took another sip of his bourbon and let the words sink in as he rolled the smooth liquor on the back of his tongue.

"Are you threatening me?" said the Senator.

"In a word, yes," said Bill. "My daddy raised me to be a God-fearing man, but maybe life with you on the dark side has eaten into my soul. I'm afraid I have done things for my country that my reverend father would be shocked to learn. Not to mention how I might contemplate even darker options. For instance, I might convince myself that your disappearance was necessary for national security."

Bill eyed the Senator icily.

"We are done, old man. It's time for you to go and write your retirement speech. These two boys," Bill looked to a spot slightly behind Fredericks, "are here to ensure that you get home safely. Don't be surprised if they strip search you to be sure you didn't have any electronic insurance policies hidden on your person. I'm sure they'll be gentle."

For the first time, Fredericks realized there was a tall muscular man at each elbow. The two men began slowly easing him up and out of his chair.

"Be agreeable and go along with these here fellas, Senator. I say that because they don't have to worry about *their* reverends, because, well, they have no souls."

The Senator's knees buckled, but four strong arms steadied him. The men guided him away from the table. The waiter saw the Senator leaving with his two associates and rushed over.

"Is something wrong? Your guest didn't look well. Should I call someone?"

"No, nothing to worry about. My friend the Senator was feeling poorly, so he had to leave. At his age it's best not to take unnecessary risks. Those two gentlemen are his security detail, and they'll see him safely home. He'll be fine. I, on the other hand, am famished. Can I order a meal here, or do I need to go into the dining room?"

"Whatever you prefer, sir."

"I'll have the twelve-ounce striploin, please, medium, with the baked potato. All the trimmings, and please bring the wine list. Thanks."

"I'll be right back, sir."

The next morning, Bill walked by the HQ of the Veterans of Foreign Wars and thought how lovely the weather was going to be today. There was a slight spring in his step, and he practically skipped up the steps of the brownstone where Eagle had its offices. Inside, he found Gunny waiting.

"Morning, Colonel. You're looking cheerful, if I may say. Have you seen CNN this morning?"

"No, Gunny. Why do you ask?"

"Senator Fredericks just held a press conference and made a brief statement. He didn't take any questions. He looked like crap, if you'll pardon my French. Believe it or not, he announced he's retiring, effective immediately. He said he'd had a minor health scare and decided that he wants to spend his remaining years taking more time with his family."

"I'm sorry I missed it," said Bill.

"The Senate Majority Leader put a brave face on it," said Gunny, "but he was obviously blindsided. Honestly, sir, I thought the Leader was going to have a stroke."

"Well, what do ya know about that? There *is* a God. Is the coffee fresh?"

Gunny was mildly surprised at how offhand Donovan seemed at the news. "Is that all you have to say, sir?"

"Nothing else to say," said Bill. He walked away and into his office, leaving Gunny standing there with a puzzled look on his face.

Gunny could faintly hear him humming a showtune again, and was fully expecting Dorothy, Toto, and the Tin Man to appear at any moment.

MONTREAL

It was early Sunday morning and Skip was sitting on his condo balcony, watching the sun rise over the cityscape of Old Montreal. He was lost in thought as he cradled a cup of dark-roast Colombian coffee, a parting gift from Augusto. Joni Mitchel, his favourite Canadian poet-musician, softly crooned a mournful, lilting tune that somehow matched his mood.

Even after he had put all of the pieces of the puzzle together, he still struggled to understand how it had all come to pass, not to mention the depth of Gaston's friendship. His friend was right about him not understanding that world. Skip was glad that he, Harry, and Bill did not have to live by Gaston's rules. He couldn't imagine how lonely it would be to live in such a faithless world, where there were no men of honour, and no trust. The last mission had been a succession of double-crosses and redemptions. How did Gaston live in that world, he wondered? The ringing phone jarred him back to reality. He switched off the music and picked up his phone.

"Oui, bonjour."

"Herr Oberst. I know that it is early, but I know also that you like mornings. Sorry if am disturbing you already."

"Jupp. What's wrong? Your voice is strange. Are you okay? Is something wrong?"

Skip was sitting straight up in his chair now, preparing for the expected bad news. Franz-Josef, an inveterate night owl, had never called him so early in the morning.

"Nein, Herr Oberst, nein. Nothing bad. I am sorry to concern you, only I think that you would like to know how are the finances, because we lose the Algerian. For that, I have been looking at the bank accounts since last night."

Franz-Josef cleared his throat. "Herr Oberst, how do I say it? We have in our bank too many monies."

"I beg your pardon? Did I hear you correctly?"

"Yes, you did hear me correctly. Late in the night, more than two million dollars is deposited, but when I check the SWIFT code for the banking, it is not from Eagle. I am suspicious, and so I check it two times. When I make more research, the SWIFT code does not exist at all. I do not understand, and so I am worried, Herr Oberst."

Skip pondered the news but didn't speak.

"Are you still there?"

"Yes, Jupp. Sorry, I'm still here. Out of curiosity, can you please convert the deposit into euros? Does it amount to about one point six million?"

"One moment, please."

Skip could hear his friend tapping on a keyboard.

"Herr Oberst. It is not about one point six million; it is *exactly* one point six million euros. How did you know this?"

"All is well, Jupp. Please get some sleep, my friend. I can explain the money, and it is not a mistake, I assure you, but I thank you for your concern. I appreciate your diligence, Jupp."

"Danke, Herr Oberst. I wish you a good day."

As was usual on Sunday mornings, Skip and Harry met in the lobby of the condo. The two men walked in silence along the Boulevard René Lévesque toward the Café Olimpico for their ritual coffee. Skip was staring into the distance.

Harry was getting worried about his friend. He didn't seem right, somehow. "You good, Skip?"

"What? Sorry, Harry. Did you ask me something?"

"I was wondering why you were muttering about the JFK shooting. Do you really think it was Rudolf Hess? I thought that we weren't supposed to talk about it."

Skip stopped and gawked at Harry. "What the hell are you babbling about? Rudolf Hess? JFK?"

Harry was grinning. "You were off in Neverland, mate. I was trying to get your attention is all."

Skip began walking again. "Sorry, Harry. My mind was wandering again." He pursed his lips. "It wasn't supposed to be like this, Harry. Somehow it all got complicated so fast. I didn't agree to put together the Cohort for it to end up like this. It was supposed to be some challenging missions to let us use some of the skills we had. Obviously, I was naïve. I was remembering an elevator ride that you, me, and Alex took years ago in Ottawa ..."

The elevator doors began closing on the three men. Skip smiled as he watched the doors slide shut, and a thought came to him.

"Harry, it strikes me that we have the skills and the experience in this little moving box to knock off the casino across the river at Lac Leamy in Hull. What do you say?"

Harry made a face. "I'm in if Alex is in."

Alex burst out laughing. "Sure. Why not?" he said.

The three men stepped out into the lobby and headed for the steak house.

Harry nodded his head gently and chuckled, recalling the elevator ride.

"I remember that, but hey, all's well that ends well, Skip."

They walked into the café. Skip held the door for a woman who had followed them in, then walked over to his favourite table. Harry went to the counter to get their usual Sunday treats. When Harry turned toward the table, he saw Gaston standing with Skip.

"Good morning, Gaston," said Harry.

"Bonjour, Harry. Excuse me for intruding on you and Skip during your Sunday *rituel de la caféine*. It is a pleasure to see you again. Better circumstances, yes?"

"Much better," he said.

Skip still seemed a bit off-balance. "I didn't know you were in town, Gaston. What brings you back to Montreal, mon vieux? Visiting your father?"

"No," said Gaston, "some minor issues."

"Is there a bench warrant out for your arrest in Ottawa? Please sit, join us." Skip took a seat, and Harry took the one opposite him. Gaston remained standing.

"Merci, non, Amadeo. I apologize for surprising you, but I only wanted to ask you if I have been forgiven yet. I could have handled that situation better, perhaps. Am I forgiven, old friend?"

Skip looked over at Harry, then back to Gaston.

"What a question. I cannot be angry with you. How could I be?"

"Merci, mon frère. I remind you that Papa is expecting you next weekend. Do not forget, or we will both pay penance. We must kiss the ring, mon vieux."

With a quick pat on the shoulder and a nod to Harry, Gaston turned for the door. Skip noticed that the woman who'd entered at the same time as him quickly stood, and a man rose from a different table, poised to follow. He'd seen enough personal protection teams to know what was happening.

"Just a minute," called Skip, interrupting his friend's departure.

"Does Revenue Canada know that you throw government money around the way you do, into untraceable bank accounts?"

Gaston furrowed his brow. "*Cher* Amadeo, I really have no idea what you are saying. However, I will make inquiries with my cousin the banker."

"You have a cousin who's a banker?"

"Oui. She is the daughter of my Tante Louisa. Her name is Marie-Claire. Marie-Claire Lagasse." Gaston winked. "See you next weekend. Adieu."

With that, the enigmatic Bishop walked out of the café as Harry and Skip stared at each other in awed silence. Harry passed Skip a cannolo.

"Thanks," said Skip, frowning.

"Should we —"

"No. Not now, Harry."

Harry loved working with Skip, and he loved working for him. The look on his friend's face this morning had initially worried him. That look was potentially telling Harry that retirement might be coming to beckon him once more. That thought had scared him more than anything he had ever been through while in Her Majesty's service. His mind flashed back to that awful time before Skip had offered to save him from a future he had dreaded, but discussing it with Skip was the last thing he wanted right now.

"What was that crack about Revenue Canada?" said Harry.

Skip didn't answer.

"Skip? Hello?"

"Sorry. Early this morning I got a panic call from Franz-Josef. He was going over the books last night, and, as he so quaintly put it, 'We have in our bank too many monies.'"

Harry almost spurted coffee across the table. "What?"

"There was more than two million dollars deposited late last night. When Franz-Josef checked, it wasn't from Eagle. Further investigation revealed that the SWIFT code attached to the transaction doesn't exist. Franz-Josef was worried, so he called me."

Harry investigated his cannolo without speaking. "Wait," he said after a moment. "Isn't two million dollars roughly one point six million euros? That was our cut of the French bounty."

"Indeed," said Skip. "And it isn't roughly one point six million. The deposit is *exactly* one point six million euros."

Harry was still contemplating the news about the cash. "Are you telling me that your RMC roommate stole our prisoner, then gave us the reward?" Skip nodded. "But how can that be, and how did he know how much we were in for? Now I really am confused."

"That makes two of us, buddy."

Harry was beginning to fret when Skip's face brightened.

"Harry, this is all too complicated to dissect on such a beautiful Sunday in Canada's greatest city. Whatever else is true, one thing is certain. If I weren't already deeply indebted to Gaston Levesque, I am now. What the hell, Harry. Let's seize the day, my friend. *Carpe diem.* Life is short, and we'll be dead for a long time."

Epilogue

August 2013

ROME

The summer heat was punishing, but that was exactly what Skip wanted. He had returned to Rome to recapture a sense of equilibrium. His physical wounds had healed, but the events in Saint-Pierre had left him feeling dislocated. Skip couldn't seem to shake his malaise. He wasn't exactly depressed; he simply wasn't feeling like himself, and so he had decided not to sit in Montreal to recuperate. He'd handed over the Cohort to Harry and returned to Italy to regain some of his strength and to seek some inner calm.

Skip was enjoying the sun warming his face, half dozing in a chaise lounge by the hotel pool. It was a perfect Mediterranean day, with a slight breeze filtering through the pines that surrounded the pool area. The city and the hotel were nearly empty except for the occasional tourist like him. The Italians were either indoors or, if they could afford it, had escaped the heat into the Tuscan hills. Mad dogs and Englishmen, thought Skip.

He could hear someone talking a few feet away. A man was ordering a light lunch for two. Skip didn't bother to open his eyes or look over to see who was intruding upon his calm.

"*Scusi, è occupato qui?*"

The voice was closer now. Skip opened his eyes and looked up to see who was asking if the space were occupied. He discovered a large man casting a shadow over him. Skip removed his sunglasses.

"Gaston? What are you doing here? Is everything alright?"

"I happened to be in the neighbourhood and thought I would look in on you."

"You happened to be passing a hotel on the southern edge of Rome? That is quite a coincidence, my friend. Please sit."

Gaston pulled out a chair, and Skip moved to the table, took the other chair, and adjusted the large patio umbrella to put them both in the shade.

"It's always a pleasure to see you, old friend, but seriously, why are you in Rome?"

"I had some business with a colleague in London and decided I needed to come and visit you, Amadeo."

"Needed to visit? What are you saying, Gaston?"

The waiter appeared with two salads, some bread, and two bottles of sparkling water. Gaston told the waiter to wait ten minutes and then bring the remainder of the order. Skip sat with his mouth agape.

"You bastard," said Skip. "You speak better Italian than I do!"

"I also spend more time in Rome than you do, but that is another story. How is your recovery coming along?"

"I feel better every day, but you could have phoned me or even Harry to know that."

"You know that Harry lives in fear that you will not return to Montreal?"

"I tell him every time we talk to stop worrying. This is a holiday. I'm not escaping like I did when I quit the army. Anyway, we talk routinely, so he should know that."

"It is one of those talks that has brought me to you, my friend."

"Pardon me?" said Skip.

"Harry keeps me informed of your talks, and last week he asked me why you might be thinking of visiting Malta. I told him it was your abiding interest in the Knights Templar, but we both know that is not the reason, do we not?"

Skip tilted his head slightly and stared at Gaston with an inquisitive look.

"My friend," said Gaston, "you have put the pieces of the puzzle together, have you not?"

"Puzzle? What puzzle?"

"Do not play the fool with me, Amadeo. You know what I am talking about. How did Harry put it? 'Accumulate and assimilate'? As Agatha Christie might say, 'The 'little grey cells' you used to joke about have worked it out, n'est-ce pas, Monsieur Poirot?'"

"Fine. Yes, I've made the connection between Lopez and Qassem, between Brazil and Saint-Pierre," admitted Skip.

"Do you recall me interrogating you in hospital?"

"I remember the pain."

"I am sorry for that, but I must ask you now, as I did then, if you shared your conclusion with anyone. Bill or Harry, perhaps?"

"No, Gaston, I have not told anyone. I swear it, my friend."

"Good," said Gaston. "You would be in grave danger if you did, and you must keep this to yourself. Do you understand me, Amadeo?"

"I understand you, Gaston, but with both Qassem and Lopez in custody and Breton dead …" He let his words trail off.

"Amadeo, they were important, but there remain many pieces on the board, and the game is not yet finished." He picked up his fork. "But enough of such talk. Let us enjoy our lunch before I must return to London."

"Amen," said Skip.

About the Author

Colonel (Retired) Chuck Oliviero, CD, PhD is an internationally recognized expert in simulation supported training and has twice been the Keynote Speaker at international training conferences and fora. He has over four decades' experience as an educator and trainer. For two decades, he was responsible for designing, developing and delivering some of the most complex collective training events ever conducted in synthetic environments for military, government and corporate entities. Colonel Oliviero served more than 30 years in the Canadian Forces, retiring as a Colonel. His career included command of Canada's then only tank regiment, The 8th Canadian Hussars (Princess Louise's), establishing Canada's Arms Control Verification Unit and being both an instructor and the Chief of Staff of the Canadian Army Command and Staff College. He is a graduate of the Royal Military College of Canada, holds a BA (Hon) in History, an MA and a PhD in War Studies. He is also a graduate of the two-year German War College (Führungsakademie der Bundeswehr) course. His last military duty was as Special Advisor to the Commander Canadian Army. In 2011 the Minister of National Defence appointed him as Honorary Lieutenant Colonel of the Queen's York Rangers (1st Americans). For more than a decade, he was an Adjunct Professor of history and strategy at both the Royal Military College and Norwich University in Vermont, USA. He is married and has two sons, both of whom are serving officers in the Canadian Armed Forces.

DOUBLE‡DAGGER

— www.doubledagger.ca —

DOUBLE DAGGER BOOKS is Canada's only military-focused publisher. Conflict and warfare have shaped human history since before we began to record it. The earliest stories that we know of, passed on as oral tradition, speak of war, and more importantly, the essential elements of the human condition that are revealed under its pressure.

We are dedicated to publishing material that, while rooted in conflict, transcend the idea of "war" as merely a genre. Fiction, non-fiction, and stuff that defies categorization, we want to read it all.

Because if you want peace, study war.

www.ingramcontent.com/pod-product-compliance
Lightning Source LLC
Chambersburg PA
CBHW020352010826
48973CB00005B/1368